CINNABAR

CINNABAR

A NOVEL OF CHINA

ROBERT B. OXNAM

ST. MARTIN'S PRESS

NEW YORK

Design by Robert Bull Design
Illustrations by Judy Stagnitto
Maps by Vantage Art Inc.
Calligraphy by Fred Fang-yu Wang

Library of Congress Cataloging-in-Publication Data
Oxnam, Robert B.
Cinnabar / Robert B. Oxnam.
p.   cm.
"A Thomas Dunne book."
ISBN 0-312-03801-1
I.   Title.
PS3565.X36C55   1990
813'.54—dc20   89-27066
CIP

First Edition

10 9 8 7 6 5 4 3 2 1

To Daisy Kwoh
Master teacher and incomparable friend

FOREWORD

Cinnabar was written with two distinct, though interwoven, purposes. It is a mystery, pure fiction, shuttling the reader between two cultures, China and America. It is also reality, as best I could convey it, exploring another fascinating mystery—Chinese history and contemporary life.

The tragic Tiananmen Massacre of 1989 casts a chilling shadow over this novel. In its original version, written in the early 1980s, I set the ultimate clash between China's moderates and hardliners in Tiananmen Square and the Forbidden City on May 4, 1989 (the seventieth anniversary of the famous May 4th Movement of 1919). It was an ironically accurate guess about timing, though not about the outcome—I had the moderates emerging victorious through adroit statesmanship and tough politics. Now I have altered the dates so that the finale occurs in the early 1990s. I can only hope that China will have adopted a more pragmatic, humane, and open style of governance by that time.

Readers will note that *Cinnabar* is written on the optimistic assumption that the forces of moderation are back in command in the early 1990s. Whether the assumption is accurate or not, I hope we shall not soon forget the Tiananmen martyrs who inspired the world with their courage and conviction. They have changed the spirit of China. Let's pray they change the politics as well.

Two aspects of *Cinnabar* require some explanation. Romanization systems, ways of rendering Chinese language in Western tongues, are the constant bane of sinologists. I have chosen *pinyin*, now used in the People's Republic of China, for most proper names. The only exceptions are given names in Taiwan, where I have used the older Wade-Giles system that remains in vogue in that island republic. Presuming the reader is not really interested in perfecting romanization, I have not included a conversion chart (i.e., Chang is the same as Zhang, which is actually pronounced "Jahng").

Translations of Chinese philosophy and poetry are all my own. While several fine anthologies exist, none caught the spirit of all of the original works in classical Chinese. Like *Cinnabar*'s hero, Roger Walden, I have also struggled with the Chinese language, eventually finding the results rewarding. I hope the reader senses that.

While I take credit or blame for *Cinnabar*, I would like to express deep appreciation to many who have offered assistance. This book would not have been possible without support from the J. Aron Charitable Foundation, Inc. and the Aspen Institute. Among those who have read drafts and offered great help are Jonathan Spence, Ross Terrill, Harry Harding, Jr., John Major, Daisy Kwoh, Porter McKeever, Charlotte Brenneis, Richard Barickman, Jan Arnet, Patricia Lloyd, Carol Rinzler, Osborn and Inger Elliott, Anthony Kane, Judith Sloan, and my brother, Phil Oxnam. I am deeply grateful to Fred Fang-yu Wang who did the superb calligraphy in this volume. It has also been a great pleasure working with a fine agent, James Stein of the William Morris Agency, and an excellent editor, Tom Dunne of St. Martin's Press. My enduring gratitude is extended to my wife, Barbara, who spent countless hours reviewing and revising.

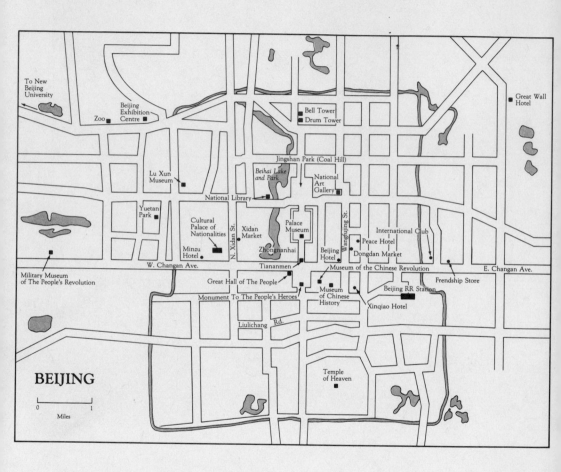

To New
Beijing
University

Beijing
Exhibition
Centre

Zoo

Great Wall
Hotel

Bell Tower
Drum Tower

Jingshan Park (Coal Hill)

Lu Xun
Museum

Beihai Lake
and Park

National
Art
Gallery

National Library

Yuetan
Park

Cultural
Palace of
Nationalities

N. Xidan St.

Xidan
Market

Palace
Museum

Wangfujing St.

International Club

Peace Hotel

Dongdan Market

Minzu
Hotel

Zhongnanhai

Beijing
Hotel

W. Changan Ave.

Tiananmen

Museum of the Chinese Revolution

E. Changan Ave.

Military Museum
of The People's Revolution

Great Hall of The People

Monument To The People's Heroes

Museum
of Chinese
History

Beijing RR Station

Xinqiao Hotel

Frendship Store

Liulichang   Rd.

Temple
of Heaven

BEIJING

0   1

Miles

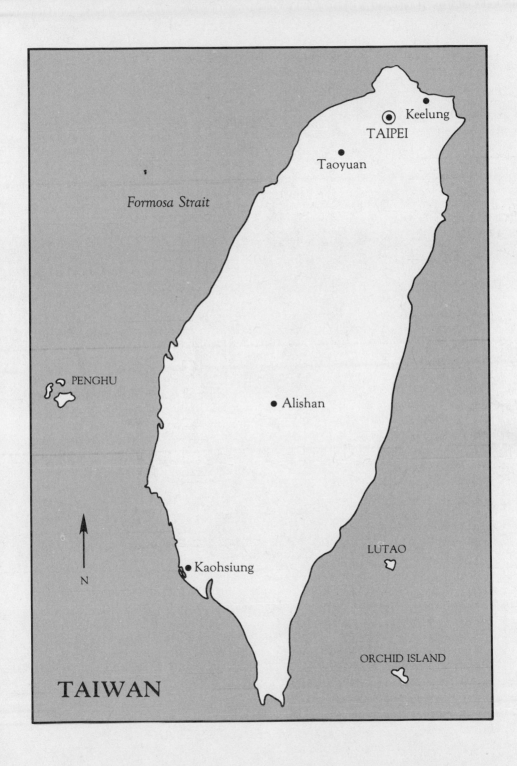

Keelung

TAIPEI

Taoyuan

Formosa Strait

PENGHU

Alishan

N

LUTAO

Kaohsiung

ORCHID ISLAND

TAIWAN

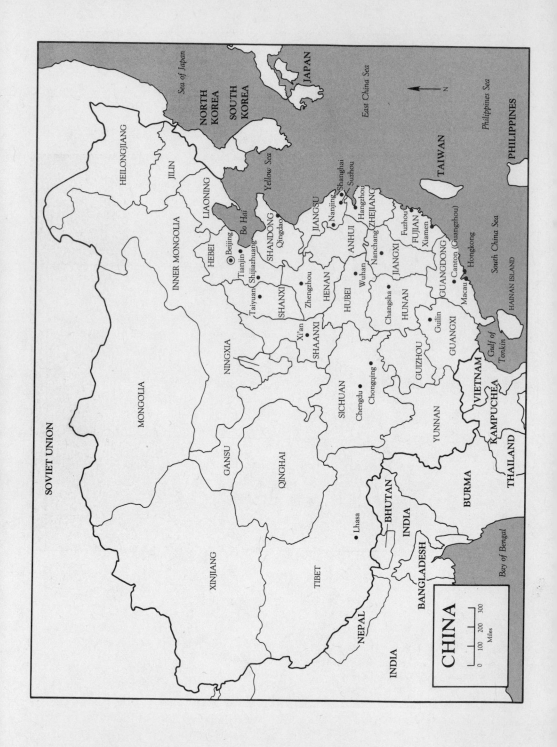

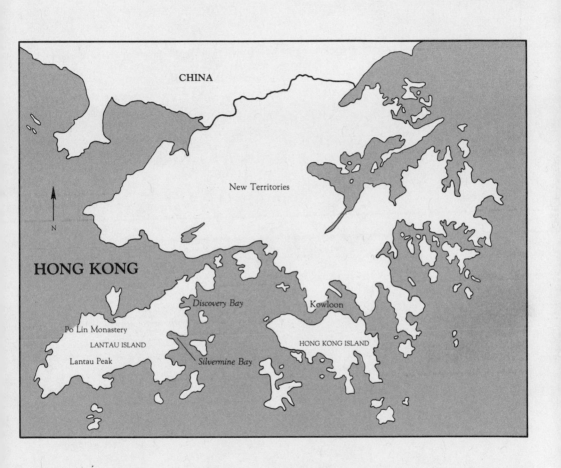

CHINA

New Territories

HONG KONG

Discovery Bay

Kowloon

Po Lin Monastery

LANTAU ISLAND

HONG KONG ISLAND

Lantau Peak

Silvermine Bay

N

CHAPTER ONE

LEGACY

BEIJING, JUNE 1900

EVEN WITHOUT THE REBELLION,

the early summer of 1900 would have been almost unbearable in Beijing. Spring rains had been light, leaving a veneer of yellow dust across the north China plain. Then in early June, the heat wave started. Beijing's great walls turned the city into a cross between a steam room and a dust bowl.

Among the few inhabitants who weren't thoroughly miserable was a group of Manchu bannermen, the elite soldiers who protected the Forbidden City and the Imperial Family. They patrolled the Tiananmen, the Gate of Heavenly Peace, strolling in the elevated walkway under its yellow-tiled roof and above its great red wall, sucking on chunks of ice wrapped in towels. Only the very rich could get ice during the summer; it was absurdly expensive to transport huge slabs of Manchurian ice by sled and wagon several hundred miles south. But you could get ice if you had connections; luckily the watch sergeant's sister was a concubine to a lesser Manchu prince.

"We should have to pay for these seats," shouted a soldier. "Look down there!" He pointed a jagged icicle at the congested late-afternoon traffic on Changanjie, the great east-west boulevard bisecting Beijing.

A band of red-turbaned youths forced through the crowds waving spears and swords, sending a pulse of panic before them. The bare-chested leader, a hefty peasant who could not have been more than twenty, halted directly in front of the Tiananmen. He raised two long-handled swords, clanged them together, and began a weaving dance. The others joined him, clearing a space with thrusts of their weapons. The speed of the central figure increased until he was spinning frantically. His eyeballs turned upward as he went into a trance, spitting blood and sputum. Suddenly he stopped and brandished his two swords again. "Long live the Harmonious and Righteous Fists Society!" he chanted shrilly. "Kill the Hairy People! Kill the barbarians!"

The bannermen watched silently from their perch, restrained by their strict orders not to interfere. "Sergeant," a smooth-faced young soldier raised his voice. "Do you believe what they say about the Boxers? Is it true that the foreigners' bullets can't hit them? That they have invisible shields?"

"Private Dorbo, you'd believe anything. Remember last week? You wanted to know if it's true what they say about the private parts of Western women."

His soldiers' laughter took the sergeant's mind off his fury at his new orders—vermilion seal, the highest authority—not to interfere with the thousands of Boxers who had swarmed into Beijing in the last few days—looting, raping, killing. Most of the rebels were xenophobic peasants who thought one massive uprising could revive a failing economy and restore China's pride. The Boxers despised foreigners—missionaries, businessmen, diplomats—who had carved out enclaves in China's eastern coastal cities and in the Yellow and Yangtze River valleys in the late-nineteenth century. "Hairy Persons," the Boxers' term for non-Chinese, was sometimes applied to influential Chinese who befriended barbarians. In the late 1890s, the frenzy spread rapidly across north China, eventually reaching inside the Forbidden City itself; the superstitious Empress Dowager, the most powerful member of the Imperial Family, threw her support to the Boxers. Now backed by the infamous woman who controlled the Son of Heaven, the rebels' rampage had no limits. The Empress Dowager hoped Boxer violence would purify the ancient Celestial Kingdom.

The sergeant leaned over the broad red wall again. "If you really want to see something funny, take a look. Old man Gao is about to get the ride of his life!"

The soldiers watched as Gao Zhenggai's white-draped palanquin, a small carriage on poles supported by four servants, moved out from under Tiananmen's portals into the chaos of Changanjie. Gao was President of the Board of Rites, one of the most powerful men in the empire, and one of its most practical—the draperies of his palanquin were white because he knew that light colors reflected the hot rays of the sun. He had shrugged when his carriage master reminded him that white was also the color of death.

The four palanquin bearers, wearing sweat-drenched blue uniforms with the Gao family crest, waited patiently at the edge of the boulevard. The carriage master hit a wooden clacker sharply with a stick, signaling pedestrians to make way. For some reason, no one was moving today. The carriage master shouted in exasperation, "DON'T YOU KNOW WHO THIS IS? IT'S PRESIDENT GAO. MAKE WAY. NOW!"

The red-turbaned heads, scarcely a hundred yards down the boulevard, snapped toward the shout. *Board President Gao! A founder of the Imperial College and a friend of foreign diplomats and missionaries! Obviously a Hairy Person of the first order! What luck!* The red turbans surged toward the commotion.

"Boxers! Here they come again!" someone shrieked.

Realizing his terrible mistake, the carriage master grabbed a thick iron rod from under the palanquin and began to swing it wildly in front of him. As two beggars and an old woman fell before his blows, a sliver of escape opened. The tiny vehicle bounced up and down as the four bearers tried unsuccessfully to run in unison; just behind were the Boxers, using their weapons like scythes.

The carriage master sighed audibly with relief as he made a sharp turn and brought the procession into Wangfujing, where he hoped his palanquin would melt into the hundreds of others carrying rich passengers to expensive shops that lined Beijing's most prestigious shopping area. Too late he remembered the white draperies that would mark them. Shoppers and servants stood mesmerized by the chase. Rivers of sweat were pouring down the bearers, with the Boxers just out of sight, their screams splitting the air. A massacre was only seconds away.

The Boxers suddenly halted and whirled around in confusion. They scattered along the street, peering into shops and alleyways, but the white palanquin had vanished. As the rebels retreated in frustration, they slashed viciously at pedestrians to vent their fury. They had just missed their first good chance at a really high official.

4

* * *

Two hours later, Lao Wu hobbled out to the road shaking his cane at a nondescript blue-draperied palanquin stopped in front of the Gao mansion. "How dare you?" yelled the Gaos' senior servant. "Merchants and artisans are never allowed after two o'clock! *Who do you think you are?* This is the house of a scholar-official." Although he was in his seventies, Lao Wu's voice was surprisingly vigorous.

The bearers set down the palanquin and opened the draperies. Lao Wu instantly realized the occupant was no mere merchant. This was a mandarin. The man's short black coat carried an embroidered flying white crane, symbol of the very highest rank in the civil service.

Lao Wu bowed his head. "Oh, Master Gao. I couldn't know. What happened? Are you all right?"

Gao Zhenggai held out his arms as usual, letting the servant brush the dust from his robes. Then he took off his cap, shaped like a flat cone with a pale white jade stone on top, and handed it to Lao Wu for brushing. Replacing the cap on his silver hair, Gao answered calmly. "Just a little breakdown in the palanquin. The only thing we lost was some time."

Lao Wu knew that Master Gao was lying, and Gao knew that he knew, but both of them also understood that it was important for the Master to appear completely in control. Gao made a mental note to send a handsome reward to the Wangfujing palanquin shop that had immediately provided a different carriage and fresh uniforms. Thank goodness the Boxers were still ignorant about the big city, particularly about underground service entrances concealed by metal plates flush with the road.

Gao Zhenggai stared at the two stone lions guarding the gate to his home—the male with the globe underfoot, the female with the baby lion cub—and at the intricately carved spirit wall that stood between them. For once, he wasn't bemused by the superstitions. Today he needed all the help he could get.

Zhenggai pulled his heavy court robes around him as he stepped into the reception court and faced the familiar receiving line. He felt more than his usual disappointment as he looked at Gao Zhonglu, his pallid eldest son, wearing the deep-blue silk robe of a successful scholar. Zhonglu was a master of the Classics, but at thirty he still showed little ability at doing anything practical with his learning.

Zhenggai scanned the rest of the group—his two younger sons, his wife, his two principal concubines, and finally his three daughters. At least they all knew the right order. Rectifying names—knowing your place in life—was crucial to making the whole system work; assuming there would still be a system ten years from now, he thought sourly. Zhenggai, outspoken advocate of Westernized education and industry, felt rising frustration as rebels and reactionaries crushed his hopes for progressive change within the dynastic order. The whole imperial system, four thousand years in the making, seemed destined to fall into the hands of warlords, imperialists, revolutionaries. If the Court wants to destroy itself—Zhenggai's jaw clenched with the thought—then we must preserve the core values within the family.

Try to look confident, Zhenggai counseled himself, forcing his usual tight smile as he nodded formally to the group and then turned to his youngest daughter, a four-year-old wearing a tunic gaily embroidered with flowers and butterflies. He softened his voice as much as he could. "My little cricket," he said, stroking her black hair. "What's that? What are you holding in your hands?"

The little girl gave a nervous little giggle, wondering as always whether her father's interest meant love or reprimand. Slowly she pulled her hands from behind her back and held up a small hoop and stick. "It's a gift from the big-nosed people. You see, you hit it like this and—"

Zhenggai's face darkened as he drew himself erect. The little girl scampered to the sheltering skirts of her nursemaid.

"You must not call them big-nosed people," Gao commanded. "It's true they look strange, and some even act like barbarians. But these are our friends. Look at people's hearts, not at their features." He nodded his head sharply, the signal for the line to disband.

Zhonglu remained behind after the others had bowed and departed. His voice was high-pitched and tentative, eyes cast downward like a child unsure how to broach a difficult issue. "Father, er . . . we've got a problem. I wonder, could we talk now?"

"Not here. Let's walk together." Why couldn't Zhonglu speak without whining?

The two men strolled through richly furnished reception rooms and meeting chambers. Passing a small courtyard with tiny cypress trees, they entered a large central complex of buildings capped with gracefully curved roofs—Gao's private quarters, buildings for his wife and concubines, bedrooms for his children, and a large study. Farther to the back and off to the sides were the servants' quarters and the kitchen. The first smells of the evening meal were heavy in the still, hot air—oil, garlic, onions, ginger.

They were drawn to a large green-roofed building. In symbol and reality, the Ancestral Hall was the center of the Gao mansion. Zhenggai opened the massive doors and walked in reverently. Long carved beams supported by heavy red circular pillars created a formal warmth echoed by rosewood furniture. The inlaid lacquer shrine against the far wall, burning incense rising from a bronze bowl in the center, was bracketed by giant calligraphy scrolls.

Zhenggai prayed longer than usual, as if he needed extra help tonight from the deceased generations of the Gao family.

"Father, please."

Zhenggai twisted his still-bowed head and glowered at his son. "Never interrupt my prayers. Our ancestors are more important than your trivial concerns." Finally he rose, checking his anger. "Now what is it, my son, that causes you such concern?"

Zhonglu's eyes darted about, trying to avoid his father's hawk-like stare. "Father. It's the Ma couple, the missionaries. They came here today with all their belongings. They said you'd understand. Lao Wu was about to shoo them away like beggars, but I prevailed. They're in the guest quarters now."

Zhenggai put his hands firmly on his son's quivering shoulders. "You acted properly. They gave us English-language books for the new Imperial College. I told them that I must repay the favor. Mr. Ma said he and his wife might need a place to hide if the Boxers came closer—"

"Father, how could you?" Zhonglu blurted. "How could you endanger your family for these foul-smelling strangers?"

"So now you're the master of the house?" Zhenggai snapped back. "Yes, they're barbarians, but they're barbarians to whom we owe a debt. Gaos always pay their debts, no matter what the cost."

It was hopeless, even hazardous, to argue with the Patriarch. Zhonglu followed his father's tall, elegant figure into the garden, the elaborate Meandering Mind Garden built with artificial mountains of Soochow limestone a half century before. After a demanding day in the Imperial Court, Zhenggai usually found himself comforted, almost seduced, by the mysterious crevices in the gray-white rocks.

Zhenggai stopped abruptly and pulled a large gold pocket watch from his robe. He snapped open the cover, stared at its face, and

7

then beckoned to his son. "This could be the most expensive gift I ever received. Mr. Ma gave it to me. See, it tells everything—six thirty-five in the evening, June eighteenth, the year nineteen hundred, with the full moon approaching. How wonderfully Western! As if by achieving total knowledge of time, one has total control of one's environment."

Zhonglu smiled respectfully, relaxing a little; his father was putting their argument behind him. The two men moved carefully over moist black stones toward a lily pond. Yellow, red, and silver carp swam gracefully under the murky green water. A breeze whispered through the intense heat; Zhenggai and Zhonglu sighed audibly as they rocked their necks back to let the air circulate into their heavy gowns. As their eyes drifted skyward, they could see a man-made mountain of stone towering almost a hundred feet above them. Along its side a path wound through clusters of miniature pine trees, skirted a waterfall, and finally led to a small wooden scholar's studio at the top. "The Pinnacle," a miniature of the needlelike mountains of Guilin, had been built by Zhenggai's father during the happier years of the Tongzhi Restoration, back when the Emperor smiled on reformers and before the Empress Dowager had become omnipotent.

Zhenggai remembered his now-deceased father's words on the summer day when the Pinnacle was completed in 1872. "Old men need symbols. This is mine. When you look at it, think of the Gao dream. Massive reform of our country, making use of Western science and technology, but always honoring and protecting Chinese roots. Never forget, my son: Without a dream, a Gao cannot exist."

A jagged scream pierced the air. Zhonglu sprinted through the archway toward the sound. Zhenggai moved after him as fast as he could, tripping over his gown.

More screams, mixed with animal-like whimpers, pulled Zhenggai toward the reception court. Zhonglu, ashen-faced with shock, seized his father by the shoulders, trying to restrain him. "By the name of our sacred ancestors," he pleaded, "don't go into the court-yard!"

Zhenggai shoved his son aside and forced his way through the frenzied servants. On the floor lay the lifeless body of his youngest daughter. Blood spurted from the two stumps that had been her wrists and from a deep gash in her tiny throat. Her severed hands still clutched a hoop and a stick. Above her stood a Boxer, waving his bloodied long knife, his face contorted in a snarling grin. Alongside him, four laughing companions snapped their spears in Zhenggai's direction. Zhenggai tried to leap at the grotesque figures, but Zhonglu and Lao Wu held him back.

The squat, sweating Boxer leader pointed his long knife at the child. "There lies the daughter of a true Hairy Person. You serve the villainous Manchus. You have friends among the Christians who smell like butter. Christ was the son of a pig. You were sired with the sperm of a pig."

Zhenggai exploded in rage. "You scum! You're the lowest form of humanity. Kill us all now or leave this house immediately!"

"Don't tempt us." The Boxer swung his knife in a big circle. "We want only you. But not now. We're going to give you a choice. Isn't that what you clever little Confucians really like—choices? We'll be back later tonight, then you can choose. Either all of these Hairy People die and we'll spare the master. Or we'll just kill the master of the Hairy People."

"Don't bother to try to escape," the Boxer sneered as he beckoned his reeking companions to follow him through the door. "The pig-sperm Gao mansion is surrounded. You may have twenty servants. But we have hundreds with us. You're not going to get away again."

Zhenggai fell to his knees and embraced his daughter. Picking her up gently, he placed her corpse on the hall table, her blood staining his clothing. Removing his robe, he covered the still-warm child.

He straightened up and glared at the terrified gathering, shocking them by shouting at Lao Wu, whom he had always treated with the utmost gentility. "Your job is to keep order in this house. Are you too feeble? Take my daughter and prepare her for burial. When it is done, come to see me in the study." He had to shock them all into orderly behavior; there was no time for a lecture.

Grabbing Zhonglu by his sleeve, Zhenggai led his son to the study. Sweeping aside the brushes, rice paper, inkstones, and engraved paperweights from the top of his massive desk, Zhenggai fell into his chair and motioned his son to sit across from him. "Tonight we must talk as never before. We must talk as equals. Tonight we must face the transformation of the Five Relationships. The Classics demand filiality. You have usually been obedient to me. Now others

9

must be obedient to you." Zhonglu listened with astonishment—how could he ever acquire the steely composure that permitted Zhenggai to move instantaneously from bereaved father to imperious Patriarch?

Lao Wu hobbled into the room, carrying a red velvet bag. "The Gaos have always trusted you," Zhenggai said, knowing the servant understood why he had been sharply scolded earlier. "Don't try to hide anyone from the rebels, except for that foreign couple. Put them in the secret vault beneath the Pinnacle. Keep everyone quiet. I'll be out soon."

Zhenggai turned back to his son. "I've been taking some precautions over the past few years. You may have noticed that the household art on display is all inferior, mostly pieces from the last fifty years. The Gao treasures—scrolls, statues, ceramics, jades, and bronzes—have all been removed. I was amazed to find we've accumulated over ten thousand objects in all. Lao Wu has put them all in safe storage." Zhenggai leaned back in his chair and mused for a moment. "It's not as large as the Palace Collection, but it's superb art with many objects the imperial family would covet. Ah, the Gao Collection—true Confucian connoisseurship and the perfect slap in the faces of our boorish Manchu monarchs."

Slowly opening the velvet bag, Zhenggai continued. "I've taken one further precaution. This is the only key to finding the Gao family treasures."

Zhonglu gasped at the magnificent lacquer box, delicately incised at various layers to let the cinnabar red, yellow, and black take on swirling three-dimensional forms. On each of the box's four sides were scenes of Chinese life, vividly glowing in polychrome carving. On its top, one word of the family motto had been executed in Zhenggai's distinctive calligraphy—*wang*, meaning "dream." Although the object looked like a jewelry box, there was no apparent way to open it.

Zhenggai ran his hands over the box, touching its beauty and enjoying its secret. He looked up at Zhonglu. "Lao Wu had this box constructed to my specifications. On the outside is my dream for China. All Gaos, all Chinese reformers, must seek to understand it. Inside, for those stupid enough to seek a shortcut, is death. On one level, my son, that's the message."

"Is there more?"

"Only a true Gao will seek the dream first. And, in the process, he will find the art collection. It can't work the other way around. The box has the power to kill, as well as the power to save."

"But where's the art?"

"It's south of here, near Shijiazhuang. Lao Wu knows exactly. If the treasure ever must be moved, give Lao Wu or his heirs a place name. They'll have the box changed; the new location will be written in a hidden place on the box. Only the master of the Gao household, or his chief servant, will know."

"But what if both should die, Father?"

"Then it will require the best research in the classic Gao tradition. There's a code, in a book, that will provide the key to finding the art. One must become a historian, cutting into the past as if it were layers of lacquer."

"I don't understand."

"Just understand this. The box is a key to more than just a treasure. He who finds its secret will have touched something much more precious. He will know himself. And he will be able to lead others to transform themselves. And that's why I've let a few others into this secret—"

Zhonglu was shocked. "Others know about this box?"

Zhenggai allowed himself a smile. "Don't worry so much. They don't know anything more than that there's a box and that it holds a clue to a great treasure. Someone outside the family must know. Even if all Gaos were to die, the search must continue."

Zhenggai folded his hands within the sleeves of his gown and walked deliberately into the Ancestral Hall. He circled the room slowly, looking into the eyes of his family. He placed his hand on the bowed head of his second daughter. "You're my new little cricket," he said. The girl willed herself not to tremble. Then he nodded in the direction of Lao Wu, showing appreciation to all the servants.

Standing under the portal, Zhenggai crossed his arms, keeping his voice firm and controlled. "The Boxer villains give me no choice at all. You're trained to see my life as more valuable than your own. That's right and proper. But more important is the life of the lineage. After this night, should I live to old age, how could I face my ancestors?"

Zhenggai looked around the hall. "When the thugs return, you will all keep perfect order. There will be no noise, no display of emotion. This is a great house. It is a Confucian house. It will, it must, survive."

No one moved. The oil lamps spluttered in the stillness, shifting their silhouettes against the paper walls.

With a thunderous crash, the doors to the reception court were forced open. "Where are you, pig sperm?" Heavy footsteps pounded up the central passageway.

Zhenggai turned to face the invaders, who stopped short as they saw him. The Boxer leader, sweat drenching his filthy jacket, walked up to Zhenggai and stood an arm's length away. Holding his knife to Zhenggai's throat, he spit out his words. "Well, have we consulted our books and made our choice?"

"Only you vermin, who stand beneath actors and prostitutes, would see it as a choice. If you illiterates had the brains to read, you'd understand that the family as a whole is always more important than any master of the family. What's the use of talking? You idiots can't understand big words. All you have is smelly bodies and bloody knives. I stand ready."

The Boxer used the blade of his knife to slit open Zhenggai's robes. He motioned his excited colleagues to strip off the mandarin's undergarments. Naked except for his white loincloth, Zhenggai was shoved to the central pillar in the Hall, his hands and feet roughly bound with hempcord.

The Boxer checked his knife's sharpness with his finger. "So the learned pig sperm wants to give us a lesson." Zhenggai flinched as the Boxer's knife cut into his cheek. "Looks like the Hairy Person has cut himself with a razor." The other Boxers laughed. "We spit on your family. But we don't need to be taught the law. The worst criminals require the worst punishments. Isn't that the law? And isn't this the worst of criminals?" His comrades all shouted their agreement. "Then it's the lingering death."

Zhenggai shut his eyes and bit down on his tongue as the slicing began. Deep cuts, drawn slowly across his chest, exposed his ribs and oozed rivulets of blood. Horrible gagging screams came from his mouth as his eyes rolled back under the lids.

More cuts, now on his thighs, formed neat ribbons of skin through which the muscles protruded. Each long cut was followed by a pause so that the pain could shoot to the brain before the next began. The knife turned to his head, the same rhythmic slicing now was applied to his ears and nose. Zhenggai bit through his tongue and torrents of blood flowed from his mouth as he gave a last guttural scream.

As Zhenggai collapsed, the Boxers cheered and closed on him like hounds. Each in turn hacked off a hand, a foot, a limb. Pushing the others aside, the Boxer leader snarled. "We must prepare him properly to meet his ancestors." Pulling off Zhenggai's loincloth, the Boxer sliced off the genitals and shoved them brutally into the dead man's gaping mouth.

The Boxer turned to the Gao family, who were trembling with shock but still silent. "What's the matter? Have you lost your tongues as well? Do you all want to be finely sliced pork?"

Teasing Zhenggai's five-year-old son with the bloody point of his knife, the Boxer finally forced the child to jump and hide behind a servant. "At least this one has some feelings left," the Boxer snickered. "The rest of you wouldn't be worth our time." He swung around and cut off Zhenggai's head.

Still the family made no sound. With a harsh laugh, the Boxer signaled his companions to leave. "And they call us stupid. These Gaos may have brains, but they have no emotions. And old pig sperm—now he has neither."

When they had gone, the great Ancestral Hall remained silent. On the floor in a pool of blood lay a gold watch, its crystal cracked, its face forever set at eight-seventeen at night, June eighteenth, nineteen hundred, with the full moon approaching.

CHAPTER TWO

MARATHON

NEW YORK CITY, LATE 1980s

"THIRTY MINUTES. THIRTY MINUTES.

This is your first warning."

The loudspeakers blared near the Staten Island end of the Verrazano-Narrows Bridge. A tremor passed through sixteen thousand runners, momentarily quieting anxious chatter, athletic shoes bouncing in place.

A young blonde in a fuzzy pink warm-up suit jumped up from the pavement and started a high-stepping jog, pumping her arms and legs energetically.

"Linda, there's no need to do that." Roger Walden sat on the pavement, his long, muscular legs stretched out. "I used to do that too, but then I figured out I was running an extra three or four miles."

"I'm sorry, Mr. Walden." She sat down very close to the lean man whose rumpled jet-black hair set off a coolly handsome face. "It's just that I'm so jumpy. Weren't you nervous before your first marathon?"

The other five students listened intently. "Sure. I almost dug a trench running back and forth from the starting line to the john. It never changes. I'm just as nervous now." It was a characteristic Walden comment—candid, tinged with self-deprecating humor, teaching without preaching.

"You're nervous?" she asked in disbelief. "It doesn't show at all. You look like you could go to sleep."

"It's just a trick I play on myself. You pretend you're totally relaxed, very tired. If you really fake it well, your body sort of believes it." Although "relaxed and youthful" was the usual description for Roger Walden, he knew the truth was much more complicated— he was a thirty-three-year-old man with the body of a twenty-five-year-old and the anxieties of a fifty-year-old. Those who knew him well, as Diane had known him, saw his deepening worry lines, tiny porcelainlike cracks at the edges of his eyes. "Compulsive crow's feet" was what Diane had called them.

"Mr. Walden," an earnest-looking young man said, "I've tried to consider everything. It's kind of hot today, so I was thinking of starting slow, but then I've been doing a lot of miles, sometimes fifty a week." His voice sped up. "I'm feeling strong, maybe like I peaked at just the right time, so perhaps I should go out fast and then—"

"Wait a minute, Billy." Roger used his seminar voice, friendly but authoritative, avoiding condescension. "You've got to remember one thing above all. For each one of you, this is your first marathon. Go out slow, stay slow, and finish." Roger tapped his knuckles on the pavement to punctuate his practical advice. "Dammit, Roger," Diane used to scold him, particularly on their winter holidays in Garmisch when he insisted on getting up at six so he could ride the first chair lift. "Why don't you act like you look? Aren't professors supposed to be laid back and absentminded?" Though he'd accused her of henpecking, Roger inwardly acknowledged his contradictions—thin, trimmed beard contrasting with unkempt black hair, easygoing demeanor belying inner compulsiveness. "Body by Michelangelo, face by Warhol, and soul by Freud" was Diane's verdict on Roger.

"Okay," Roger said, standing up, "let's do the stretching exercises now." He led the six younger runners in what seemed slow-motion aerobic dancing—heads rocking back and forth, arms sliding up and down the body, weight shifting from leg to leg, limbering bodies without startling hearts or lungs.

"TWENTY MINUTES. TWENTY MINUTES. TWENTY MINUTES UNTIL THE START."

Roger grinned at the group. "I know you'll all make it. You've trained right. You've got the right attitude—"

The sharp double honk of a horn cut short his pep talk. Turning

17

around, they saw a silent caravan of exhaustless electric cars that would lead the race. In the first car, a slight, dark-haired figure waved at the cheering throng. Roger recognized Frank Shorter, high priest of the Marathon Movement, his current media prominence symbolized by the bright-yellow blazer of an ABC Television sports commentator.

"Walden. Roger Walden. Right?" Roger nodded as Shorter beckoned him over.

Shorter cleared his throat and smiled for the camera. "Most people don't associate the name Roger Walden with marathon running. Actually he's better known for something else. Right, *Professor* Walden?"

"Actually the rank is assistant professor," Roger replied flatly. "I'm just a teacher." Roger hated self-promotion. Besides, it was true: he had a great following among the students, but not among all the professors; the system had not yet granted tenure, the gold ring of the academic merry-go-round.

"Hardly just a teacher," Shorter replied, shuffling through some papers. "Here it is. Assistant professor of American intellectual history at Columbia University. Voted Teacher of the Year in 1987 by the undergraduate student body. Author of several important articles and—"

"Thanks for the curriculum vitae, but that doesn't count for much today," Roger interrupted. "It hasn't even amounted to much at Columbia." I don't care if the department chairman is listening, Roger thought bitterly. He would never forget the chairman's comment: "It's nice to win a popularity contest; now how about something serious, like finishing a book?"

"What's remarkable is that a Columbia professor is also a world-class runner," Frank Shorter continued, enjoying his job of providing color. "Professor Walden was ninety-fourth in the Boston Marathon last spring. Time of two twenty-nine. That's remarkably good. How can you combine running and scholarship?"

"Believe it or not, running helps me think. When I'm out training, I put my mind to work on lectures and articles." The honest truth was that running cleared his mind for teaching, but it also consumed dozens of hours every week, leaving little time for serious research. Tenure was looking very remote.

"And what are you hoping to do today?"

"I'd like to shoot for a two twenty-five. But who knows?" Actually, he had set his sights on a 2:20, aiming for the top forty finishers, but he thought it would be better not to announce that on national television.

"That's a tough target. You'd better get moving up to the front. You don't have to start back here."

"Thanks, Mr. Shorter. We all have to start back here some-time." He waved at the camera as the caravan pulled away. Then he winked to his students as he headed toward the bridge.

"FIFTEEN MINUTES. FIFTEEN MINUTES. PLEASE BEGIN TO MOVE TOWARD YOUR STARTING STATIONS."

Roger weaved carefully around runners, edging to the front. Now, before the race itself, was the time for self-control. Champions required reason as much as emotion. He began his "running monologue"—he had invented the technique of lecturing himself during his first marathon five years earlier.

Remember what you told the students. Lots of time left, take it easy, just stretch a little. Walk easily, make those funny yawning expressions, it'll keep you relaxed. Shake your arms and legs just like a swimmer, that'll free up the muscles. Maybe the shoelaces are a little tight, better loosen them a bit. That feels better. Now roll the neck. I wonder why it's always tighter on the left side from the shoulder to the ear.

Less consciously, Roger initiated his second ritual, a rapid phys-ical exam. His fingers kneaded out the tension in his sharply featured oval face—dark eyebrows, high cheekbones, strong chin under the black beard, slightly small nose. He gently rubbed around his black-flecked eyes. Diane had called them puppy eyes—playful and sad, the kind that prompted mothering.

Tugging off his warm-up suit, Roger massaged his six-foot frame. His height gave him stature, but his smallish bone structure made him seem approachable. After thousands of miles of running, every hint of fat had melted into an efficient machine of muscle, sinew, and bone. Reaching into a red sports bag, he dipped his fingers into vaseline and smeared a thin coat over his upper torso to help ward off the sticky sweat that would soon try to fuse nylon to skin. After adjusting his dark-blue nylon shorts and bib top, he stroked his long, powerful thighs and calves.

Roger sat down on the grassy traffic island and finished the warm-up ceremony, forcing his legs wide apart and touching his head to his knees in a fluid rhythmic motion. He pulled a clipboard from his bag and checked his desired split times. Glancing down at his wrist, he confirmed that his Seiko Marathoner was set at "00:00" for total elapsed time and for each of the split times. The watch and the clipboard were reassuring props. Long ago Roger had acquired the long-distance runner's instinct for sensing minute variations in time with remarkable precision. Scrupulous race-day preparations were really designed to fend off creeping anxieties.

"TEN MINUTES. TEN MINUTES. STARTING POSITIONS, PLEASE."

Roger stood up slowly, trying to stay calm; he zipped his bag and tossed it into a truck that would transport it to the finish line. *It's just another long race*, Roger told himself, trying to quiet stabs of fright that knifed at his chest and danced through his limbs.

Looking behind him, he knew it was more than another long race. Roger could see the endless river of bright nylon-clad runners shimmering in the sunlight as tiny heads bobbed up and down. The river, dammed in place by a broad white line in the pavement a few yards ahead, surged and ebbed with the weight of bodies pressing and bumping. The Goodyear blimp, symbol of the world's most marketable athletic events, glided smoothly overhead.

Roger glanced at an oversized TV monitor at the roadside, briefly tempering his jitters as he saw the same events from a more detached perspective. The scene switched abruptly from the starting line to a studio where a balding, self-impressed commentator was delivering his pre-race rap. "I've got to tell it like it is. You're about to witness one of the greatest sporting events of our times. Other than the Olympics, it is indeed the greatest competition of the late-twentieth century. It spans the streets of New York, the Big Apple, the center of finance and culture, the home of all ethnic groups. Like the Statue of Liberty, the New York City Marathon is a symbol of America's openness, its energy, its quest for greatness."

The commentator droned on. "Pheidippides wouldn't believe it. You all know Pheidippides, the famous ancient Greek runner who started all this in 490 B.C. He died taking the message of a military victory to Athens. But what a noble death! An inspiration to all athletes! An inspiration today!"

Roger's voice added to the chorus of boos from the top runners close enough to hear the grating words. The legend was really an insult to the great *hemerodromoi* of ancient Greece, the "all-day runners" who were capable of carrying their messages a hundred miles in a day. The marathon—with its strange distance of 26 miles, 385 yards—would have been a light romp. One running expert offered the theory that new marathoners were motivated by the "Pheidip-pides Complex": the belief that by completing the race, they were somehow overcoming their own signs of aging. Elite runners like Roger were of a different cut, worrying more about achieving fleeting immortality than staving off inevitable mortality.

"FIVE MINUTES. FIVE MINUTES UNTIL THE START. PLEASE STAY IN YOUR POSITIONS. DON'T TRY TO MOVE FORWARD."

Roger was buffeted by growing pressure from behind. He tried to hold his place, shaking his arms to stay loose. The force of bodies surging toward the bridge made it difficult to breathe.

For the first time, Roger Walden was in the front ranks of a major marathon. He could see the elite ahead of him: Antonio Sandano, the human machine whose ability and arrogance matched each other; Ichiro Ito, the phenomenal Japanese who seemed to feel no pain. *You're almost one of them.* The thought shot a charge of electricity through him. He shut his eyes, looking inward as he continued to shake his muscles, trying to loosen them from their tight grip on his bones.

Use your experience. It's more important than youth in a marathon. Channel the anxiety. Don't let it overcome you. Remember self-confidence. It's your strongest suit. Stay in control.

"TWO MINUTES. TWO MINUTES. HOLD POSITIONS. ANYONE START-ING BEFORE THE GUN WILL BE DISQUALIFIED. PLEASE DON'T PUSH."

Bodies tensed for the moment when the starter's gun would release tightly coiled springs in their limbs. Stretching and yawning didn't help anymore. The anxious jumping of other runners around Roger irritated him.

Wiping sweat from his forehead, Roger looked with dismay at the water covering his hands and arms. Who would have thought that the mid-morning temperature in late October would already be above seventy degrees? The sun shone intensely in the cloudless sky, a grim reaper for marathoners.

"ONE MINUTE. ONE MINUTE. DON'T JUMP THE GUN. YOU'VE WORKED TOO HARD TO LOSE AT THE START."

Roger felt a sudden fear deeper than his fear of the race. He tried to suppress it.

"THIRTY SECONDS. THIRTY SECONDS."

He would never be able to block out that Saturday four months ago when two police officers had told him to sit down. They had tried to make it easier on him, but he knew.

"Diane?" He had held his breath.

"Yes, Professor. A junkie stole a car. He was driving like crazy when he hit your wife at an intersection. She was killed instantly. There was no pain, none at all. We're so sorry."

"BANG!"

Until this race, Roger had started farther back in the pack, waiting several minutes for the throng to begin moving. Now he felt the relief of starting almost at once. Touching the button on his watch, he followed the lead runners across the two-mile bridge. Almost immediately, he was bumped by a couple of teenagers sprinting to the front, trying for a moment of glory before the TV cameras.

Let them go. You've seen it before. Just find a pace. Make it fast, but not too fast. Oh, I feel stiff. The legs are tired already. Don't worry, that'll go away. It's like starting up an old sports car. She'll cough and sputter a little. Then she'll purr almost like new.

He could glimpse the leaders a couple of hundred yards ahead. Just beyond them was the TV truck with Shorter and an electric car with a huge digital clock flashing elapsed time for the race.

10:30—two miles. Roger could see the lead pack of ten runners begin to make the sweeping curve that led off the bridge into the Bay Ridge section of Brooklyn. Behind them, perhaps fifteen yards off the pace, was a cluster of fifty or more runners. Another eighty yards behind, Roger was sharing the lead of a group of more than a hundred.

His time was very good—5:15 average for the first two miles —just ten seconds a mile off the superstars. Even better, the pains were gone. Now he was running easily, flowing across the pavement with his whole foot, trying to keep the pressure off either the ball or the heel. The upper part of his body remained almost motionless; his spine stayed supple and straight. He liked the first part of a marathon. He could turn to automatic pilot and run by instinct, too early for the inevitable physical agony and mental anguish. Cheers from the crowds added fuel and buffered pain.

He had run so much this year, this sabbatical year, which had begun with Diane's death. Long-slow-distance in the morning was followed by faster intervals in the afternoon and often by more distance running in the early evening. Food and sleep, closely monitored by the caloric scale and the alarm clock, served only to revive energy for running. The distances became staggering, sometimes well over a hundred and fifty miles a week. He was race-fit by Labor Day and knew he should have begun tapering off in preparation for the marathon. But he couldn't. A fifteen-mile day left him angry and restless. After a few hours of fretful reading, he was back on the streets, trying to pound out the memories.

31:00—six miles. His shorts and jersey were now drenched with sweat that poured off his body and limbs; the dark-blue band restraining his hair was sopping. A young boy on a bicycle suddenly swerved in front of him, forcing Roger to dodge aside and awakening him to his surroundings.

Several runners around him had begun to fade in the heat and punishing pace. Most were younger men who had overstressed to feel the joy of the lead and now slipped back to struggle against the ignominy of quitting. Roger could see the second pack, now down to about twenty. Three hundred yards away were the five or six champions whose race was being telecast around the country. He remembered watching the race at home a few years back—a party for their friends, three televisions, one in each bedroom. All empty now.

For a decade, ever since their marriage right after graduation from Swarthmore, Diane had tried with limited success to release Roger's evident talent and to ease his concealed torment. He loved teaching; he even enjoyed research, particularly on short, provocative articles. But he loathed bigger projects that chained him to the library. Roger's doctoral dissertation had taken him five agonizing years. Now, six years into teaching at Columbia, his projected book had a promising title—*Philosophers and Politicians: Origins of Manifest Destiny*—but only three chapters were finished.

"Maybe tenure isn't all that important," Diane had said gently, just a couple of weeks before she was killed. "After all, we don't need the money."

"It's not the money!" Roger had shouted. "Who makes money in teaching? It's pride. It's overcoming the goddamm system."

Pride and stubbornness were big factors in their relationship. Roger had inherited nothing when his father died; the limited estate was allocated to caring for his mother, a permanent invalid residing in an Arizona rest home. Diane MacDonald Walden, by contrast, was the beneficiary of a $3 million trust fund, part of her grandfather's fortune from an oil-refinery business he had established after returning from China at the turn of the century. The MacDonalds resided in a Greenwich, Connecticut estate, surrounded by art objects and cherishing a reputation as "old wealth," supporting local philanthropic causes while sneering at most other Americans who lacked "MacDonald values." In spite of her father's disapproval, Diane had married Roger, living in what her father called "genial academic poverty"—a seven-room apartment on Riverside Drive near Columbia. Diane, with a B.A. from Wellesley and an M.A. from Yale in French literature, occupied herself as a part-time adjunct professor in Romance Languages at Columbia. After her father's death, Diane avoided her family, particularly her stepmother, Dorothy Mac-Donald, who frequently remarked at Roger's resemblance to a Chinese gardener they had once employed.

It was Diane who had suggested jogging to Roger. "Maybe it would relax you to get some regular exercise." She secretly hoped something would get his mind off tenure. She couldn't have known that jogging would turn into serious distance racing. Later, as running became Roger's new obsession, she asked cynically, "Are you after a record? Or perhaps a requiem?"

A water station was just ahead. Weaving through runners, Roger reached out and grabbed a paper cup from the last table, managing a quick sip. Looking ahead, he felt a sudden electricity, the first surge. Both leading groups suddenly increased their pace, taking advantage of the slowdown that always occurred at water stations. He threw down the cup and began running faster.

God, it hurts. Agony in lungs. The left thigh. Feels like an ice pick. Must keep running. See the guy in green. Just look at his back. Catch up. Can't be too long. Everybody hurts. Just a test. Darwin tactics. Must survive. Christ, please stop. Don't quit. Don't quit. Don't quit.

He had been through surges before, but never so intense. The marathon wasn't a single race but dozens of races within one, no winner until the last race, often the sprint to the finish. All the other races were designed to produce losers, the weak of body or mind who crumpled before the pain; the better runners called it "throwing out the garbage." The fundamental law of animal life was the fundamental tactic of the marathon.

When the pain subsided slightly, Roger looked around in amazement. He had survived the surge and joined the second pack, now only about ten runners. Ahead a couple of blocks, sweeping through the streets of Queens, he could see four leaders. Easy to spot in their midst was Sandano, with his striped shorts, running close to the ground; he could make out Ito, who ran like a robot.

1:06:27—thirteen miles. The halfway point flashed past as Roger turned onto the Queensboro Bridge, covered with carpet to protect the runners from the torture of the metal grates; the bridge was the end of the long sprint through Brooklyn and Queens and the gateway to Manhattan's upper East Side. More than a million people waited ahead, lining the streets that led north to the Bronx and then south to the finish in Central Park. Six years earlier he and Diane had stood together on First Avenue; it was where he made up his mind to prepare for this grueling race.

I can't believe it. I don't hurt. I'm averaging almost 5:05 miles. Where's the pain? Even the heat isn't too bad. Leaders are still in sight. Nice breeze off the river. Guy ahead of me looks like hell. Feel like singing. Not sportmanslike. Just hum a little.

He came off the bridge in fifteenth place and began to follow the long blue line up the avenue. He knew he was enjoying a lovely case of the marathoner's high. Not all marathoners had the experience, but for those who did, it was an additional incentive for running. Roger felt himself flying above the pavement, almost watching himself and the crowd from above. He laughed appreciatively as he saw the Columbia University banner with an added slogan, "We Love Roger The Lionhearted," next to a caricature of the lion mascot in jogging shorts.

Then it happened, with no transition at all, like running into a cold shower. Agonizing tremors shot through his body and mind; the ecstasy turned into raw pain. His surroundings disappeared and he could see only within himself. He stared into a world of pain, a world of death, Diane's death.

Shock had been his first reaction to her death, then guilt. "Perfectly natural," the psychiatrist had said comfortingly during Roger's one visit to his office. Roger didn't dare tell the truth. More than anything else, he was angry. How could she leave him? He needed her. He wasn't sure if he'd loved her, not in the classic romantic sense, but they had established a circle of comfort and confidence. Maybe, he'd often hoped, greater excitement, including more varied and stimulating sex, would come with time. But now, there was nothing. How dare she leave him alone?

He was also angry about something else. There was no question Diane and Roger shared a deep affection, but money had become an important factor. Roger had become accustomed to affluence, although he tried to hide the fact from his academic colleagues. An extensive personal library, superb stereo system, season tickets to the opera—all had added considerably to the life of an assistant professor. Being well-to-do wasn't a sin, Roger explained to himself, as long as you're devoted to causes beyond a simple quest for wealth.

"I'm sorry," the lawyer had explained over the phone. "Diane's will was drawn up by her father. He would have disinherited her if she didn't sign it. You knew his feelings about you. Now everything—the income of the trust and the principal—reverts to her stepmother. Diane probably hoped her trustees would change the will later on. But no one expected her to—"

"Are you telling me I don't get anything?"

"Nothing at all. Except for the ten thousand dollars in her savings account. And also one art object, something from China."

"You're kidding."

1:31:30—eighteen miles. He'd finished the stretch up First Avenue and the quick loop into the Bronx. Now he was on the long final run toward Central Park, still holding his position, pounding along with the small band of almost-greats. The leaders were out of sight, hidden by the sharp turns in the northern section of the race.

The youthful Roger who had been running north just ten minutes before was now a gaunt, hollow-eyed man, body jerking like a bony scarecrow, hair matted in sticky clumps to his forehead and cheeks. His left arm hung limply at his side while the fingers of his right hand tried to press out the needles of pain in his thigh.

Roger knew it was the "wall." Somewhere around the twenty-mile mark, the race really began, the race against one's self. For some runners, the wall was an occasional problem, a mounting exhaustion in the last stages. For others, like Roger, it always occurred, with excruciating pain and an overwhelming desire to stop. The doctors differed. Some said it was dehydration and high body temperature; others argued that it was a loss of blood volume and depletion of glycogen in the muscle fibers. Whatever the physiological explanation, it terrified him. With the heat and high speed, it was intolerable.

Macabre thoughts began to wander through Roger's mind. *I'm damn near a living corpse. Overtrained. Failed to take water. Almost fatal in this heat. Pace is ridiculous—a little over five-minute miles from the start. This is suicide.* A curious grin flickered across his contorted face. *Who cares? Why not pull out all the stops? Who gives a damn? Go for* it. *The modern Pheidippides. Maybe it's better to die an almost-hero. Better than living almost-dead.*

1:42:20—twenty miles. Roger forced himself to look up; the crowd was growing larger, screaming encouragement to the top marathoners as they began to run through northern Manhattan. He had slipped back to a trailing position in what used to be the second pack. Now it was a broken string of aching bodies, five or six in sight, none of the superstars visible.

You're weakening. Last two miles slower. Average dropping toward 5:10. Push through the pain. Drive yourself. Faster. Faster.

The television cameras were too far ahead. Only those in the crowd at the top of Fifth Avenue caught a glimpse of a remarkable transformation. They were used to seeing exhaustion. Now in twentieth place came a determined runner in dark blue, number 341. His body was drenched as the nylon merged into the vaseline on his torso; his muscles were stretched to the limit, throbbing along his arms and legs. But this runner seemed to be on the verge of smiling; his face was almost relaxed, eyes half-closed in concentration, lips fixed in a disciplined tight grin.

1:52:20—twenty-two miles. Roger's pace picked up dramatically. Precisely ten minutes for the past two miles. For the first time since First Avenue, a half hour back, he was aware of his surroundings. He was running through an urban canyon formed by the apartment buildings to his left and the massive brown forest of Central Park to his right. Thousands of spectators lined the wall of the canyon, straining at the barricades, yelling and waving. The swelling cacophony propelled him.

His feet barely touched the endless blue line that traced the entire course of the marathon. He hadn't passed runners since the first surge in Brooklyn: instead he had hung on while others wilted. Now it was different. Roger's body was a high-powered weapon, setting its sights on a runner, focusing on the color of his scanty uniform, rushing to the kill, then swiftly targeting the next victim.

2:01:55—twenty-four miles. An incredible pace—a 4:47 mile down the avenue—faster than anyone in the marathon. Rounding the corner of Central Park South, he saw three runners less than a quarter mile ahead: Sandano and Ito, pin-striped and white, stride for stride, and another figure in red he didn't recognize.

No pain at all. Legs numb. Push faster. Spit it out. Spit out the blood. Faster. Faster. No wall. No limits.

2:06:35—twenty-five miles. Roger stared in disbelief at the

27

figures on his watch. His eyes grasped what his brain couldn't comprehend. The last mile was 4:40; he was running scarcely a hundred yards behind the leaders. The red shirt had burned out as Roger exploded past him. Just two now, bolting ahead through the undulating roads of Central Park.

Thousands were screaming. The television crew focused their lenses as much on Walden as on Sandano and Ito. Shorter was barely able to control his voice. "It's unbelievable. Sandano and Ito are both surging, first one, then the other. What they don't see is another runner. He's gaining with every stride. He's number 341 . . ." Shorter checked his clipboard. "My God, it's the professor! Walden. I knew he was good. But this good? Twenty minutes faster than his best time?"

Roger came up on the heels of the two leaders. Ito, sensing another presence, looked back and was visibly startled. Sandano responded to Ito's quick burst. Roger followed the surge, sprinting around the long bend and up the final hill. He reached inside for even more. He knew he had them. They were running as fast as mortals could, running for the joy of victory, running to avoid the pain of defeat. He could run faster.

2:11:12—twenty-six miles. Shorter's screams were barely audible over the roar of the crowd. "He's done it. He's done the impossible. His last mile was 4:38. Sandano and Ho are falling back. Walden has them by ten yards. Only 385 yards, less than a quarter mile, to the tape."

Roger's blurred vision was suddenly obliterated by a cold darkness. The fog seeped into his eyes and through his body. His legs, still without pain, now wobbled like the spindly shanks of a newborn fawn. His arms flopped about as he stooped forward. The run became a drunken walk, then a blind man's stumbling. He pitched forward, crashing into the pavement. His arms and legs made a feeble effort at a crawl. Then his body heaved in a contorted shudder as he sprawled on his back and his breathing stopped.

CHAPTER THREE

RESURRECTION

A DISTANT, DISEMBODIED VOICE SPOKE

softly. "Professor Walden. Can you hear me?"

The weak, almost inaudible reply. "Yes . . . yes, I can."

"How do you feel?"

"Tired . . . very weak."

"Do you know where you are?"

All he saw through the haze was whiteness. "I don't know . . . Is it a hospital?"

"Yes, Professor Walden. You're in the ICU of Lenox Hill. I'm Dr. Abrams. You—"

Turning his head slightly toward the voice, Roger broke in with fatigued surprise. "But . . . you're a . . . woman."

The physician responded briskly. "I'm not supposed to reprimand critically ill patients, but I must inform you that the medical profession has kindly admitted women. Maybe not as smart, but a hell of a lot cuter than men—"

Roger closed his eyes. "I'm really sorry . . . Just wasn't thinking . . ."

"Forget it" came the softer reply. "It just takes you down a peg on my hero list. We can work on your prejudices later. Now I'm here to make sure you stay with us. By the way, I'm a runner too. Proudly finished in the top three thousand women last Sunday."

"The marathon," Roger said, more awake now. "When was it?"

"Today's Thursday. You've been in a coma for five days. We almost lost you. You hemorrhaged, lost a lot of blood, both from the gash on your head and internal bleeding. You were totally dehydrated, like a week on the desert without water. Worse yet, you weren't breathing. If the medics hadn't used CPR, your brain would have died in a few minutes for lack of blood. You're damned lucky."

The slim, red-haired doctor pulled out a small penlight and examined Roger's pupils. "You know, you're the most famous case I've ever had. I guess they picked me because I'm a fellow runner. I spend half my time with you and the other half with the press. The papers say you're the modern Pheidippides. Except you're still alive."

Roger turned his head away.

"What's the matter? You're a national hero. Nobody remembers who won. Once you're off critical, the press will eat you alive."

Roger struggled up onto his elbows and looked earnestly at her. "Please . . . please . . . I really don't want any publicity. I mean it. Tell them anything. But please keep them, keep everyone, away from me."

"I understand," she said sympathetically, "you're not strong enough yet."

"No," Roger answered emphatically, "you *don't* understand. No interviews. Not now. Not anytime. You can arrange that, can't you?"

She smiled back conspiratorially. "So the chauvinist is really a humble intellectual? Of course I can arrange it. Costs more, but we'll charge it to Columbia's medical insurance."

"Thanks. You're a real doll . . . I mean a real professional."

"Shut up, before I change my mind." She pulled down the sheet and jabbed Roger's left hip with a syringe. "That'll give you another eight hours of sleep. It's the best thing for you." Dr. Abrams looked gently at Roger as he faded into unconsciousness, pushing his tangled hair out of his eyes and patting him on the forehead.

Within ten days Roger was back on his feet, walking with some difficulty, undergoing therapy to restore his muscle tissue. A few days later, he was moving with almost normal ease and had resumed a standard hospital diet. But unlike most patients returning to health, he showed little interest in leaving the hospital. Dr. Abrams also found it strange that an extraordinary athlete had no curiosity about

31

a race he had almost won. Walden asked only about six obscure runners, beaming when he heard thay all had finished the race. Overlooking his curious behavior, she concluded after three weeks that there was no reason to keep him.

"Professor?" she asked as he was leaving. "Could you do me a favor? Would you mind autographing this book? I've actually read it. A little dry, but not bad." Damn, he's cute, she thought, wishing she had the nerve to suggest some outpatient care.

Roger picked up the familiar blue volume—*Old Thoughts, New Ideas: Reconsiderations of American Political Philosophy*—and flipped to the chapter he had authored. Smiling as he noticed that it had indeed been read, he wrote in the top margin: "To Dr. Abrams. A fine physician and a great press agent. You brought a body back from the dead. The rest is in my hands. With appreciation and affection. Pheidippides, alias Roger Walden."

Gazing down the expanse of Park Avenue, Walden felt cold and alone. No one was there to greet him—no students, no marathon crowds, no family. He hailed a cab and felt briefly secure in the warm backseat until the cabdriver recognized him.

"Aren't cha the guy who almost killed himself in the marathon? Sure ya are! I'll bet ya know better now. I told the wife, I said, 'Look at that guy, he's famous, but so what? Runs his balls off. What's it get him? Flat on his back, maybe a slab of marble. Who knows?' She gives me crap about these weeds. So I says to her, 'I'd rather cough myself to death, it's better than blowing out my guts on live TV. At least I can kick in my own bed.' I'm not tryin to put ya down. But ya know what I mean?"

"You've got a point," Roger said as he overtipped the driver. His smile faded as he looked at his apartment building, almost a tenement in the twilight zone between Columbia University and Harlem. Piles of rubbish, rusty wrought-iron railings, white spray-paint graffiti on sooty brick walls—it was all he could afford now; he had just begun to move in the week before the marathon.

Roger wasn't ready for what he saw in the cracked hallway mirror. His overcoat hung on a skeleton; his sunken eyes, hollow cheeks, and grey lips made him look like a corpse. Weaving around packing boxes in the cramped two-room apartment, Roger slumped onto the couch and began leafing through the stack of mail, anything to keep his mind occupied. He was mildly amused to discover that his athletic mail outweighed his academic mail.

. . . I'm a graduate student working on a thesis entitled "Religious Experiences in Contemporary Western Athletics." From my observations of your marathon on television, I am convinced that you experienced what we call the exhaustion-induced heaven/hell crisis. If only you will allow me to interview you, I can explain this phenomenon which is at the forefront of psycho-religious studies. It would only require three days of study in a controlled laboratory environment. Although my research grant from the federal government does not allow for honoraria, I can promise you great psychic rewards.

. . . You had it coming. The Lord said, Remember the Sabbath. Keep it holy. The Lord brought His Vengeance upon you. Should you die, the fires of Hell await you. Should you live, we shall take pity on you. He who confesses shall be made whole again. We await your confession at the Church of the Holy Pentecostal.

. . . Have you ever heard of Doctors Against Masochism (DAM)? Well, we're against all kinds of things that are bad for you—including long-distance running. What better proof than your New York Marathon fiasco? Now we'd like to invite you to be our Annual Dinner Speaker and to receive our prestigious "GIVE A DAM" trophy. . .

By the time Roger was halfway through the pile of letters, he had kicked up his feet on the coffee table and was relishing each new one. For a moment, he thought about calling someone to share the enjoyment. But no one was really close enough to trust. Roger brewed himself a cup of tea—Dr. Abrams' suggestion, "much healthier than coffee"—and sat back on the sofa. All that remained on the coffee table was a manila envelope marked CONFIDENTIAL and bearing the return address of Baldwin, Tipplefield, & Marsh. Slitting open the envelope, he read the letter typed on heavy bond paper:

Dear Professor Walden:
I realize that this is a doubly difficult time for you. I hope that this letter finds you returned to good health.
As I told you earlier on the telephone, our firm is handling the estate of your late wife, Diane MacDonald Walden, whose life came to such a tragic and untimely end.
I have already described to you the basic disposition of her estate. Some of her family's art collection, including the Chinese object which she has bequeathed to you, is housed in the Manhattan Art

33

Storage Warehouse. We would like to arrange a date, at your convenience, to visit the warehouse with your late wife's only other surviving relative, her stepmother, Mrs. Dorothy MacDonald.

Please call me to arrange a suitable time. Meanwhile, our deepest condolences. And also, again, our hopes for your rapid recovery.

Sincerely yours,

J. Richardson Marsh

Roger reread the letter and drummed his bony fingers on the coffee table. He suppressed another surge of anger. His paltry inheritance wasn't really Diane's fault, although she might have tried harder to change her will. She might have even had the decency to tell him about the problem in the first place. But then again, he thought, you don't usually see death coming in your early thirties. He shuddered and drew in his breath. Maybe the time had come to confront Diane's death. Maybe he could find a balance, something between elation and despair, without her around to show him how. Maybe, he allowed himself a fantasy, the art object might be worth something.

Five days later, a uniformed security guard admitted him to a windowless brick building that occupied an entire block on Second Avenue in the East Nineties. Inside, the reception area exuded comfort and confidence with mahogany paneling, exquisite oriental rugs, and Winslow Homers on the walls. It didn't surprise Roger that rich people like the MacDonalds put their excess art here—it was a fortress outside and a palace within.

"Oh, Roger." He turned quickly, drawn by the familiar strident singsong voice. "Oh, Roger, my dearest, you've been through so much. I haven't seen you since poor Diane's funeral. Then that awful marathon business. You look so awful, like a corpse."

"Thanks, Mother." He had always found Diane's stepmother a bit hard to take. Privately he and Diane called Mrs. Dorothy MacDonald "Snotty Dotty." She looked the part in her frosted blond chignon and expensive blue suit, cut well enough to hide most of her excess thirty pounds. "Thanks for your concern. I'm really okay."

"Roger, dear. You shouldn't have run so hard."

"It wasn't the running part that hurt. It was the part when I decided to fall down. Anyway, thanks for the card."

J. Richardson Marsh, portly and in his sixties, entered the room and embraced Mrs. MacDonald. "So good to see you, Dotty dear, looking lovely as always."

"And Professor Walden, a pleasure to meet you." He spoke with practiced professional warmth, shaking Roger's hand in both of his. "Again my condolences about Diane. And what a terrible accident you suffered."

Marsh escorted them to a high-ceilinged conference room and introduced them to a grey-haired older woman. "Ethel Sickelman, my secretary." He began efficiently: "You each have copies of the will in front of you. We usually do this in our offices, but it seemed more efficient to read it here. It won't take that long. Shall we begin?"

Marsh cleared his voice and read the familiar litany. "I, Diane MacDonald Walden, being of sound mind and body . . ." The only relevant passages for Roger, sandwiched into the fifteen minutes of boilerplate, were three short paragraphs:

". . . give, devise, and bequeath the house and land at 6 Boulder Road in Greenwich, Connecticut, and all the possessions therein, to my stepmother, Dorothy MacDonald.

". . . acknowledge my father's instructions that, should I predecease my stepmother, my trust fund shall be transferred to her for disposition as she sees fit, and the family art collection, much of which is in storage, shall also pass to her.

". . . request that my husband, Roger Walden, take possession of a Chinese art object that was given to me by my late father in accordance with instructions held by our family attorneys, the firm of Baldwin, Tipplefield, & Marsh."

Roger listened, his fists clenched but his expression opaque, occasionally glancing at Mrs. MacDonald, who barely suppressed her smug smile. Her inheritance of the Greenwich house did not really bother him. The place held unhappy memories and cost a fortune to maintain. The last time Roger had been there was for Diane's burial in the MacDonald mausoleum. He winced as he remembered her coffin being wheeled through the iron doors of the white marble structure, her body encased forever behind a black slab with bronze bolts, next to dozens of identical tombs waiting for future generations of MacDonalds.

What infuriated him was the more than $10 million Mrs. MacDonald had already inherited in securities. Diane's $3 million was added to that amount, as were the art objects in storage. Mrs. MacDonald hardly needed or deserved it; she would surely spend it on lavish redecorating. Diane would not have wanted it this way at all, but it was too late to change things now. Roger nastily hoped Mrs. MacDonald's art inheritances would be second-rate.

A self-impressed manager and an armed security guard led the procession—Roger and Mrs. MacDonald, Mr. Marsh and Miss Sickelman—through bare corridors into a stainless-steel elevator. They stopped at the fifth floor, marked "High Humidity Vaults," then passed through two barred and locked doors, the air growing cooler and moister as they walked on. Finally, the procession halted at a room marked "Vault No. 18." The manager unlocked a small door covered by a heavy metal screen, and the guard carried about two dozen objects, wrapped in brown paper, into an adjacent viewing room. The manager pulled on a pair of white rubber surgical gloves. As he opened each object, placing it on a heavy easel or the wooden table, he described it as if announcing guests at a royal reception.

"Monet," the manager said pompously. "Quite extraordinary. An early example. Still experimenting with the control of light, but the mature Monet is already evident. Magnificent."

"Ooh, magnificent indeed!" Mrs. MacDonald replied, trying to sound knowledgeable. "Is it worth a lot?"

"We don't appraise art here," the manager said. Noticing Mrs. MacDonald's disappointment, he spoke softly in her ear. "At least a million." She kissed him.

Roger watched stonily for half an hour until the sides of the room looked like illustrations in a textbook on French impressionism, including two Monets, a Manet, four Renoirs, a Degas. Two small bronze sculptures, both by Rodin, sat on the table. Roger couldn't help overhearing the manager's stage whisper to Mrs. MacDonald: "Altogether, at least twenty-five million." Roger gritted his teeth as she clapped her hands and accepted a warm hug from Mr. Marsh. "Give a few to the Metropolitan Museum and five million in endowment," the manager stage-whispered to Mrs. MacDonald. "Then they'll surely put you on the Board."

"Now it's Roger's turn," Mr. Marsh said, inviting Roger to sit at the wooden table. "Before doing anything, you're supposed to look at this." Roger opened a large manila envelope and pulled out two letters and a key. The first letter was written in Diane's precise Miss Porter's penmanship:

February 4, 1978

Dearest Roger,

One hates to be morbid. But if you're reading this, I'm already dead.

I'm hoping to change my entire will. That will require convincing my trustees to alter the trust fund. But there's one thing over which I have total control. I frankly don't know what all the secrecy is about, but my father talked to me vaguely about this matter before his death last year. He said that his mother had received a package she was holding in trust from a friend she knew back in her China days as a missionary. Grandma MacDonald, whom you never met, was quite a lady, always telling great China stories.

She passed along the attached letter to my father shortly before her own death in 1956 at the age of eighty-eight. My father gave me strict instructions not to read the letter, nor to use the key, unless I was approached by a Chinese who was able to write the Chinese character that matched something on the art object inside the package. Only then was I supposed to use the key, which opens a vault. If the match was exact, then I was supposed to give the object to him.

On the chance that I died before anyone claimed the object, my father asked me to select the person I trusted most to take possession of it. You have always had my total trust—and my total love.

I know it sounds a little spooky. But I want to adhere to my family's instructions. I adore you.

Diane

Roger held the letter gently. He almost heard Diane's voice speaking the words.

He turned to the second letter, on yellowed paper, from Diane's grandmother to Diane's father:

August 12, 1956

Dear George,

I am passing along to you something that comes from China, from a friendship that dates back over sixty years. In those days, some terrible things happened that Sterling and I have never fully told you about. But wonderful things happened as well, including a definition of friendship and loyalty that I have never seen in our part of the world.

What I am transferring is something that must be handled with

37

the utmost confidentiality. The key opens a vault at the Manhattan Art Storage Warehouse that contains a package from China. Inside, so I am told, is an art object. I do not begin to understand its full significance. I do know that it means a great deal to the gentleman and his family who passed it to me. He gave me strict instructions not to reveal it to anyone except my own heir, and then only as I approach my own death. You are to hold the object in trust. Don't reveal it to anyone unless the Chinese family wants it back. Then they will write the Chinese character that matches the one on the art object. Don't give it to anyone else.

If no one claims the box for two full generations, then it should be placed in the hands of the closest relative of our family who can most be trusted. That person should seek to find its rightful owner or, failing that, keep it in his or her possession. We do not own it. We are keeping it in trust.

As if to add to the drama, my Chinese friend also said something else. He told me never to tamper with the art object. He said, "It has the power to save and the power to kill."

Yes, my dear, China was mysterious at times. But in that mystery lies a remarkable and rich civilization. Personal ties in China are extraordinarily powerful, sometimes even wrapping up foreigners. This work of art is but one special example. Please take my word: this is something dear to my heart. It represents a debt I cannot repay. I must, you must, and our descendants must respect these wishes.

My love, affection, and respect as always,

Mums

The manager took Roger's key and walked back into the vault. He returned shortly with a hemp-covered bag sealed with wire strips, which he placed on the table. He cut the wires; each one twanged slightly and its echo reverberated around the small room. The man stepped back and joined the circle watching Roger.

Roger peeled back the hemp cautiously, exposing a worn red velvet sack. Gingerly opening the gold drawstrings, his fingers touched a sharply incised cool surface, and he drew out a lacquer box. He placed it carefully in the middle of the table and looked at it for a moment. It was perhaps eight inches long, four inches wide, and three inches high. Its rich red exterior glowed luminously in the soft light; the delicate incisions revealed a counterpoint of yellow and black. When his eyes became accustomed to the colors, he began to make out a profusion of tiny scenes on the sides of the box— landscapes, houses, and people. The top was decorated with a large Chinese character; on the bottom he saw flowing strings of Chinese writing moving up and down like tiny streams.

Holding the box with the tips of his fingers, Roger brought it closer to his eyes. He turned it over several times, trying without success to figure out where it opened. Then he shook it a little. Nothing. Bringing it close to his ear, he shook it again. Still nothing.

Roger looked at the manager for an explanation. The manager shrugged. "Sorry. I don't know oriental art. Looks like a pretty piece of cinnabar lacquer. Wish I could tell you more." The manager nodded to the guard to rewrap the box so Roger could take it with him.

"What do the letters say?" Ethel Sickelman asked casually.

"Ethel," Mr. Marsh scolded. "I'm surprised at you. We don't pry into our clients' private affairs."

"Oh, I don't mind," Roger said. "It's an inheritance from Diane's grandparents. Originally from China itself. I guess I'm supposed to hang on to it. I wish I could figure out how to open it."

"Be careful," Mr. Marsh counseled. "Fine art can be wrecked through tampering. If you're interested, you should go to an expert. Actually, there's a talented young woman at our firm, Rebecca Aspen, one of our youngest partners. She collects Chinese art. You might want to give her a ring." An attractive widower might be just the thing for Becky Aspen, Marsh reflected; she's got to settle down after her divorce. She likes guys with brains, and Lord knows I pay her enough for both of them.

"Oh, Roger," Mrs. MacDonald chimed in. "I think it's a nice little box. Wasn't it sweet of Diane to give you such a special object? It's probably very valuable."

Roger glanced around the room, enough for a small museum exhibit, and scowled at Mrs. MacDonald. "Yes, Mother, very valuable, I'm sure."

CHAPTER FOUR

RED DUST

BEIJING, MAY 1949

THE ELDERLY SCHOLAR STOOD SHAKILY

on a raised lectern, one gnarled hand grasping the worn wood, the other holding down yellowed lecture notes. He peered through heavy glass spectacles, trying to remember where he was in the passage. Not many professors still wore dark silk Qing dynasty gowns, but Gao Zhonglu did. The students saw him as hopelessly out of date, but most hid their feelings from old Gao. After all, the man was nearly eighty, and his father had helped found this place when it was called the Imperial College. Now it was Beijing University, Beida for short.

"Ah yes." Gao Zhonglu spoke with a sense of discovery, not because he had thought of anything new but because he had found his place in the notes. "Philosophy. East or West. It's all like a forest. Every tree has the same roots. Only the branches, the leaves, and the flowers are different. So it may be said that all men ask the same questions, even that all men get similar answers. But it is always expressed in their own cultural context."

Once, perhaps thirty years before, those words had seemed important to Professor Gao. Now they were just something to fill up the few remaining minutes. The students, sitting on hard wooden benches in the dimly lit classroom, pretended to take notes.

"The cross of Christianity," continued the professor, "is like the word 'king' in our own tradition. Both have horizontal elements. In the character for 'king' there are three lines meaning heaven, earth, and man, all linked by a vertical line symbolizing sovereign. In Christianity, the linking force is faith. So it's all a matter of linking. Of connecting . . . maybe of intersecting . . . of . . ."

Professor Gao's voice stopped. His glasses had fogged up. He removed them and wiped the lenses with a handkerchief, but they remained clouded as his trembling hands replaced them on his nose. Lifting the pages a few inches from his eyes, he squinted at the fading characters. Nothing came through. Sadly he replaced the notes on the lectern and folded his hands inside his gown. Luckily, his glasses were still foggy; otherwise the students would have seen tears falling from the deeply lined eyes of a once proud mandarin scholar. Even more luckily, the corridor bell rang, ending the period.

Professor Gao pretended that the lengthy pause had been the planned conclusion of the lecture. "Class dismissed," he said firmly as he prepared for the ride home, just as he had every school day since he began teaching at Beida forty-three years before. He placed his notes into a ragged file folder and then into an ancient brown leather briefcase. He put a black fedora on his head and hobbled with his cane into the courtyard of Beida.

Pausing in the courtyard, Gao Zhonglu set down his briefcase and looked around him. It was exactly thirty years since the May Fourth Movement—May 4, 1919—when a Beida campus uprising prompted a tidal wave of Nationalist revolution across China. He remembered the chanting: "Down with Imperialism" and "Long Live a Unified China." He had sympathized with the students, but kept his distance as warlord policemen beat them with sticks.

Since the fall of the Qing dynasty in 1912, Gao Zhonglu had witnessed the Chinese revolution from the safe haven of his office window. Beida was the intellectual crucible of the Nationalist and Communist leadership; Sun Yatsen had lectured there and Mao Zedong had been an assistant in the library. The architecturally uninspiring buildings provided a stage for China's modern historical drama. Countless warlord generals had tried to lure new college-educated recruits into their armies. After their invasion in 1937, Japanese officers lectured Beida faculty and students on the Greater East Asian Co-Prosperity Sphere. While other faculty joined the resistance movement centered in Chungking in the south, Gao stayed behind, weaving anti-Japanese comments into his lectures so subtly that all but his brightest students missed them. When the Japanese were defeated in 1945, Chiang Kaishek's Nationalists took over the city and the campus, proclaiming purity as they fostered corruption. Gao accurately observed that, while the Communist guerrilla mobilization won the civil war in the countryside, it was the Nationalist bungling of the economy that guaranteed Chiang's loss of the cities. And now, in the spring of 1949, Beida was under Marxist sway as Mao's Communists moved toward final victory. This tumble of events occasionally interrupted the teaching schedule; he always turned off his office light so he could watch without being seen.

Professor Gao nodded formally to his chauffeur and entered the gleaming 1939 Ford convertible; the top was down because the weather was pleasant and also because Professor Gao wanted the people to see a real scholar. He sat proudly, hands folded on his cane, bowing in acknowledgment of passers-by as if they really were paying attention to him.

"Did the lecture go well today, Professor?" the chauffeur asked politely.

"Why yes, Lao Wu. Yes, of course" was the familiar response. "I wish you might join my class someday."

"Perhaps. But the Wu family does not have much scholarly ability. We're servants. My job, like my father's, is to serve your family. We're proud of what we are."

Professor Gao smiled warmly; it was the right answer. He asked Lao Wu the same question at least once a week and always received the same answer. It was important to check; you never could be careful enough. The old traditions might slip away when you weren't watching. Gao favored democracy, but he had real doubts about the notion of equality. Now that the dynasties were gone, Gao felt old mandarin families had a special obligation to serve as role models. Maybe the elites didn't have as much money, but at least they still had style. Twenty years ago, he would have written a lecture or an article on the subject. For now, it was sufficient to realize that at least one servant knew his place.

Lao Wu checked the rearview mirror and smiled to himself as he noticed a black limousine a few yards behind. They were always tailed by limousines, ever since he had begun driving the Gao automobile twenty years ago. Before that, it had been rickshaws following rickshaws, and before that, palanquins chasing palanquins. Who was in the limousine? The Nationalists, the Communists, some warlord? It didn't make any difference. They would always be there, ready to pounce. All they needed was a hint about where the treasure was hidden, a small clue about where to find the lacquer box. Everybody seemed to know about it.

Fortunately everybody also believed the Gaos would not respond to bribery or torture; it was widely rumored that anyone who tried force would die. Gao Zhenggai, rationalist that he was, must have smiled in his ancestral tomb at the help his family was receiving from the enduring power of Chinese superstition.

Lao Wu slammed on the brakes, barely missing a runaway donkey chased by giggling children. The following limousine skidded alongside. Sitting in the backseat was an undersized Westerner muttering obscenities at his driver while haughtily straightening out his black silk jacket and pink cravat. Ah, thought Lao Wu, it's the Frenchman, the latest pursuer. Lamarche, that's his name—Lao Wu recalled his research—adventurer and small-scale art dealer, living the high life in Beijing, trying to supplement a limited inheritance from his father, who had once imported silks from China. Lamarche, his fluent Chinese learned in Beijing's shops and brothels, bought collections of art from impoverished gentry and merchant families, his modest investments reaping substantial profits from collectors in Europe and America. Lao Wu laughed as Lamarche busied himself lighting a cigarette so he wouldn't be seen staring at the Gao automobile. So now we get the imperialists, Lao Wu thought, chuckling at the affected Frenchman, whom he guessed to be in his twenties. Lao Wu snapped the steering wheel quickly, leaving Lamarche's limousine moving into a hopeless cul de sac clogged with rickshaws, flour sacks, wine barrels, and coal bricks.

Lao Wu, son of the original Lao Wu who had served Gao Zhenggai, realized there was no danger unless they did something unusual. Today nothing special was planned. Tonight was a different story. Lao Wu shuddered when he considered the job ahead.

"Professor Gao," asked Lao Wu, "do you mind if we stop at the Western Market? The cook wants a fresh carp."

"Oh, if we must." Zhonglu affected exasperation. "I just don't know why you can't do all the shopping earlier." Zhonglu did know why, of course. He could not afford all the servants his father had employed, and gasoline was outrageously expensive. Two round trips to Beida per day was all that the Gao budget would permit.

For five centuries the Western Market had been the same; you could smell the pungent aromas of fish, oil, and spices a half mile away. At a quarter mile, you could hear the hawkers haggling with the shoppers. The limousine stopped at the edge of the market— you could not drive inside because of the crowds. Lao Wu wriggled into an alleyway and let his body float on the current of people.

Everything was tougher these days because of the inflation— prices had increased more than two hundred percent in the past month alone. Shopping was tougher, physically as well as financially; those who shopped for the wealthy had to carry large boxes filled with paper currency that was losing its value by the minute. Lao Wu bumped through walkways between small food stalls, each with its specialty: melons and pumpkins, live chickens stacked in crates, mushrooms and dried herbs. At the fish stall, he pointed to a fat red carp swimming in one of the crowded tanks. "Eight hundred dollars!" Wu exclaimed with shock. "Just last week it was six hundred and fifty. When does it stop?" The shopkeeper shrugged and placed the currency in a large trunk that had iron weights on top to keep the overflowing cash from blowing out.

"Esteemed elderly gentleman." Professor Gao had been waiting patiently in the limousine. Pretending not to hear the woman's voice, he sat impassively with his hands still folded on his cane.

"Clearly, sir, you're a man of great taste. High breeding." Still Gao Zhonglu did not respond. He had lived in Beijing all his life and knew that the first lesson of the city was that you could not respond to beggars. You could not give them money or food because they would only want more. You could not give them sympathy. Above all, you could not give them an opening. At best, they would take your money; at worst, it would be your life.

"Please, sir. Please listen to me." A stooped, emaciated woman pulled herself up to the running board of the car. Her clothes were rags sewn together; her eye sockets had no flesh around them.

Gao Zhonglu raised his cane and swung it at the beggar woman, but she lifted her hands for protection and backed off the running board. Jonglu shook his head and uttered a sigh of relief that the episode was over. He leaned back and tapped his cane impatiently on the floor. Where was Lao Wu? This really was becoming tiresome.

"Kind sir. Please don't hit me. Perhaps this will interest you." Zhonglu turned his head slowly. The woman was standing just out of range of his cane. She struggled to hold up a young girl, ten or eleven years old. Hunger had not yet destroyed the beauty of the child—her face was round and smooth and her pigtails gave her a little bounce. The mother shook the girl, who did her best to smile and show that her teeth were intact and white.

"You're a scholar. You know how to read." The woman shook the girl again. The girl held up the sign that was strung around her neck. Written by a calligrapher for an all-too-imaginable favor was a short four-character message: MY NAME IS GU. I'M FOR SALE.

"She's got just what you need. Hard worker. Trustworthy. And a virgin." Still in her mother's arms, the girl lifted her skirt and spread her legs. "See? Your spear will be the first through her shield."

Neither mother nor child heard Lao Wu behind them. He grabbed the two beggars and pulled them around the corner into an alleyway. "Never do that to a scholar again!" he shouted loud enough for Professor Gao to hear. "If I ever see you again, I'll beat you first and then I'll turn you over to the authorities."

"I'm really sorry, sir," Lao Wu apologized. He placed the carp in the footwell of the front seat. "I try my best to keep those damned beggars away from people of quality, but it's so hard."

As they drove away, Lao Wu glanced into his rearview mirror. The black limousine was still there, and so were the woman and the girl, smiling and waving the box of cash Lao Wu had left with them. Perhaps it might save the girl from prostitution for another week or two.

The streets of Beijing were deserted at midnight. It was dangerous to be out alone after the sun was down. Since revolution had brought down the Manchu Qing dynasty in 1912, no Chinese government had been strong enough to protect its citizens. Instead Beijing, like all Chinese cities, had regressed to feudalism: powerful warlords employed mercenaries who controlled large sections of the city, and little warlords—"thugs" was the more appropriate word—terrorized smaller neighborhoods. Everyone paid for protection, usually in kind or services rather than in unstable currency.

The moon cast eerie shadows over a crooked street known as Liulichang, near the Qianmen, the Front Gate of Beijing. Liulichang, Beijing's famed center for arts and crafts since the Qing dynasty, had become a prime target for marauders. Warlords loved jades and ivories; foreign businessmen and diplomats favored wooden sculptures and lavish screens; Chinese merchants and old mandarin families preferred landscapes and calligraphy. Everyone wanted the lacquerware—bowls, boxes, chests, screens—especially those of the Liulichang Lacquer Shop.

Two private guards stood in the shadows outside the front door of the shop. Their eyes, accustomed to the almost total blackness, could pick out other watchmen posted in front of each shop on the street. One guard pulled out a pack of Camels, offered one to his friend, and lit them both. It was all the time Lao Wu needed. The guards had been briefly distracted and their night vision momentarily destroyed. Lao Wu slipped by them into the alley, moving soundlessly in black cotton shoes, deftly picking the lock to the basement back door of the lacquer shop.

No one had heard him. No one could have seen him, dressed as he was completely in black from hood to shirt, pants, and gloves. At fifty, Lao Wu was still supple. He crept across the basement, eyes fixed on the shaded green electric light at the other end. He weaved through a labyrinth of tables, sawhorses, chests, and screens in various stages of lacquering, then gingerly put down his hemp-covered package on a bench. A hunched old man was seated on a small stool in front of him, totally absorbed in his work. In one hand he held a cinnabar-and-black lacquer bowl. Half of the bowl had been delicately incised in a pattern of birds and flowers; the other half remained uncut, but its patterns had been outlined in ink. In the man's other hand was a knife he manipulated like a calligraphy brush. The two hands worked together in almost musical rhythm. Birds and flowers, each one different, each with its own personality, emerged from the bowl's surface. The carver stopped for a moment and tapped the bowl against his wrist to let cinnabar shavings fall to the floor. Then, seized by a sudden racking cough, he put down the bowl and knife. He suffered from tuberculosis, the chronic disease of all lacquer masters. Lacquer had to be worked in a damp environment; eventually all of them succumbed.

Lao Wu waited patiently. It would not have been right to destroy a masterpiece. As the lacquer master wiped the phlegm from his mouth, Lao Wu made his move swiftly. One arm locked around the man's neck and shoulders; the other hand clamped firmly over his mouth.

Lao Wu spoke quietly. "Don't scream. Don't speak. One move and your neck is snapped. Just nod if you understand."

The lacquer master, eyes bulging in panic, nodded several times.

Slowly Lao Wu released his grasp. The little man struggled for air and began coughing heavily. Lao Wu waited for the spasm to pass. "Don't turn around," he ordered. "Just open this package carefully."

Lao Wu reached over the man's head and placed a package gently on his lap. The lacquer master peeled back the hemp and removed the velvet sack. His body trembled, but his practiced hands remained steady as they slowly turned over the polychrome lacquer box. His fingers moved over the carvings with reverence.

"It was carved by your father, wasn't it?"

The lacquer master nodded.

"You know what it is, don't you? You know it's the Gao box?"

The man hesitated. Then he nodded again.

"Then do you know why I've come tonight?"

The lacquer master shook his head.

"Surely your father told you about the bargain. The Gaos will always support your family, but the master of the family has an obligation. You know what that is, don't you?"

The reaction came slowly this time, a series of little nods indicating resignation.

"All right. Now you may talk. But don't turn around."

The lacquer master looked at the box and caressed it for a moment. Then he spoke softly. "I've dreamed of seeing this box. Yet I dreaded the day it would come. It's the best we've ever produced. I've come close, but never this good. What is it you want? To change the name?"

"Yes. You know where to do it? How to do it?"

"Of course. My father told me everything."

"But won't the repair be obvious?"

"Not at all. We're the best. I kept small samples of the original lacquer for just this purpose. Even a professional wouldn't notice it."

"How long will it take?"

"Probably two weeks. The actual name change can be done tonight. But I want five or six coats to dry on top of it. Then just a touch of antiquing. Give me two weeks."

"You know what must happen then?"

"Yes, I know. But these are terrible times. My family will need the income, and I'm an old man. I must tell my oldest son, of course. And what's the new name?"

Lao Wu whispered in the lacquer master's ear. "*Zhengtian*. As in 'keep the fields level.' Can you remember that? I must not write it down."

"I've got it. But . . ."

"But what?"

"But I don't know of any *Zhengtian*. I don't know where it is. Truly I don't. Does the obligation still hold? Even if I'm totally ignorant?"

Lao Wu winced. "Yes. I'm afraid it does."

"Then do it quietly. Don't destroy anything. The lacquer box will be ready, on the table here. Two weeks from now, when I work late at night."

Lao Wu crept back up the stairs. He waited, his anger building in the darkness, for the guards' next cigarette break. Why did he have to do this terrible thing? Professor Gao Zhonglu was a senile old babbler. But Lao Wu knew it was for nobler spirits than Jonglu. It was partly for Gao Zhenggai, and, even more, for Lao Wu's own father. He knew the lacquer master would also play his part without question. The obligation was deeper than giving your own word; you were acting on your father's word. It must be obeyed.

Gao Jinru had not set foot in his father's house for two years, since he had been graduated from Beida with a degree in Chinese history. It's only when you've been away for a period of time that you really see the changes, he thought. The Gao mansion looked tired, almost shabby. Half the rooms were closed off, dust sheets on the furniture. The smells he remembered were still there, but the noises were subdued. At the entrance, a beggar child sat between the guardian lions, and it took almost two minutes for Lao Wu to answer the door. In the old days the chief servant would never have doubled as both carriage master and doorkeeper.

"Where's the Master?" asked Gao Jinru. "Where's my father?"

Lao Wu smiled to himself. He remembered the screaming match when Jinru and Zhonglu had parted. "Where's the Master?" meant that Jinru was going to give it another try.

"I think it will surprise you, Young Master," Lao Wu replied, using the form of address that had died out with the end of the Qing dynasty.

Jinru laughed. He knew that Lao Wu shared many of his own feelings about the old terminology. Lao Wu was like his older brother. They had gotten drunk together, even gone whoring together. Their friendship had convinced them that one could preserve crucial core values without retaining archaic patterns of speech or behavior.

"Thank you, First Servant of the Gao clan. May your children become scholars. May they have the intelligence that escaped your generation. And now, before I do you the favor of whipping your hide, could you inform me of the whereabouts of the Esteemed One?"

"It may cause your heart to stop, My Lord."

"The heart is young. But your aged bottom may soon be red. Speak words of truth, slave of the Gao family."

"He stands in the foothills of Heaven, Son of Exalted Master."

"And where the fuck is that? Thou who art but one of the Hundred Names."

"On the Pinnacle, Superior Intelligence."

Jinru could not believe his ears. The charade stopped. "All the way up the Pinnacle! How did he get there?"

Lao Wu also stopped playacting. "Your father is not well," he answered soberly. "He said he wanted to see you up there. He was a bit dramatic, said it would be his last time. It took over an hour to help him up the path. Luckily, I had help. Let me introduce someone."

Gao Jinru followed Lao Wu to the library. Jinru's compact body was hardened from many months as a political adviser in the border regions of Shanxi and Hebei, where his movements were coordinated with those of the Communist Eighth Route Army. As the army made its final moves toward Beijing, Gao Jinru stayed with the villagers, providing basic education and organization. By 1946, when Jinru joined the Party, Mao Zedong had over fifteen years of experience with mass mobilization and the people's war. Mao's strategy depended on Gao Jinru and thousands like him—"cadres," urban educated elites, leading peasants toward victory. "The countryside will surround the cities" was Mao's slogan, but in fact a lot depended on skilled men and women from China's congested east-coast cities. Heroism was part of Gao Jinru's motivation—the Long March of 1934–35 was already a glorious legend to young Chinese Communists, six thousand miles of trial and terror, escaping from Chiang Kaishek's troops to new base areas in the caves of Yan'an in the northwest. Hatred was also a factor—Jinru detested both the Japanese, "rapacious invaders," and the Nationalists, "corrupt compromisers." He envisioned an independent China, without imperialism and without tyranny.

"Dr. Ren, this is Gao Jinru." Lao Wu spoke quietly so as not

51

to startle the lean young doctor, nattily dressed in brown corduroy sports jacket and beige wool slacks, who was leaning against the desk absorbed in a book.

"Oh, Mr. Gao, I hope you don't mind." Dr. Ren stood up, placed the book gently on the desk, and thrust out his hand. "One of the joys of coming to your mansion is this incredible library. Where else could I find a Song dynasty *Classic of Internal Medicine*? Are these vermilion ink notations really what I think they are?"

"Yes, indeed, Doctor, from the imperial brush of Song Taizong himself. My great-grandfather acquired it when he bought the Weng Tonghe Collection. But, I would assume, you're not here to discuss books?"

"No, Mr. Gao, sadly you're right. Lao Wu has retained me these past several months to look after your father. I'm pleased to do whatever I can . . ."

"Dr. Ren is too modest," Lao Wu interrupted. "He's one of the few fine physicians in Beijing today. Johns Hopkins, first in class, restricts his practice to the great families. I even convinced him to postpone leaving for Taiwan to care for your father. He's taking considerable risks."

"Oh yes, big risks," Gao Jinru intervened sharply, looking askance at the doctor. "But not so big as to prevent some last-minute income before the revolution. Making money off other people's pain."

Dr. Ren scrutinized the fiery-eyed young Gao, suppressing a surge of anger. "Mr. Gao, I make money by alleviating other people's pain. I serve people, not politics. I didn't enter medicine in quest of revolution. I don't think it's wrong to earn a good income by offering quality medical care. As to your father, I'm sorry to tell you he has a terminal lung disease. I'd guess he only has a few months. I'm doing what I can—drugs for pain, menthol vaporizer, even some herbal medicines. You can't believe the trouble we had hauling him up that rock mountain in your garden. Your father is very sick, but he's proud and stubborn."

"I didn't mean to insult you, Doctor." Jinru's voice had softened. "Your help is appreciated. Maybe I've become a little too ideological."

"Perhaps a little rest would help."

"Revolutions are not for rest." Gao Jinru nodded good-bye and walked swiftly out of the library.

"Sorry, Doctor." Lao Wu shook his head. "Proud and stubborn is a Gao family disease."

"Lamentably, it's a disease I can't cure."

Jinru reached the base of the Pinnacle and straightened his cadre suit, buttoning the blue cotton jacket and pulling it down neatly over the matching slacks. Although foreigners would later call it a "Mao jacket," the form of dress had actually been invented by some junior political officers from the cities. It was a sensible garment—cheap fabric, a comfortable cut, and a style derived from the Communist military uniform. By the late 1940s, cadre suits were becoming popular among Beijing intellectuals, as much out of practicality as political inclination. Although he had never worn one in his father's presence, Jinru was certain Gao Zhonglu would find cadre suits deplorable. Jinru certainly wasn't going to exchange it for a gown, but at least he could make it look as neat as possible.

Jinru climbed easily up the craggy path, musing about how clever his great-grandfather had been. The mountain was a daunting climb only for the very young and the very old, the times when people most needed myths. Jinru paused to appreciate a tiny pine tree reaching out into space from roots that barely grasped the sharp edges of a gray boulder. It seemed impossible that the tree could hang on, but it had for almost a century. Jinru looked more closely at the tree—two of its miniature branches had white tips, signs of a recent pruning. It was crazy, but there was enough pride left in the Gao legacy to motivate a gardener to dangerous acts. Was there enough pride to motivate an heir to hold on as well—finding a compromise between political ideals and family traditions?

"Welcome, my son." The feeble voice came from a rough scholar's hut, its front open so that the occupant could look out over the mansion and the city. Inside the hut his father sat on a heavy wooden bench, hands resting on an open book. "Welcome. I'm glad you have come back."

Jinru ducked his head as he entered the hut. He took the bench opposite his father. "Thank you. It's good to see you, Father. How's your health?"

"It's been better. But what can one expect? Seventy-nine years. A long life. Not much more now. That's why I wanted to see you."

For most of his life, Zhonglu had complained about his health.

Usually the filial son was expected to humor the father, but Jinru would not play that game now. For one thing, he no longer believed in the old Confucian notion of strict filiality. For another, it was clear that his father was dying.

Zhonglu waited, hoping for the appropriate gesture, but Jinru kept his silence. Zhonglu fought back irritation. "Well, my son. It is time to address your inheritance. The last time we discussed this matter, you refused to consider any inheritance at all. You said to give it all to the poor. Is that still your view?"

"No, Father, it is not," Jinru replied carefully.

"It's not?" Zhonglu smiled. "Do you really mean it?"

"Yes, Father. I've changed my mind. But let me explain—"

"Not so soon. Let me enjoy this moment. Look out there." Jinru followed his father's trembling hand. Beijing's red walls and yellow roofs sparkled in the radiance of the setting sun, the spectacular creation of the Ming dynasty, the ultimate statement of order. The city was built to impress everyone—the barbarian foreigner, the humble commoner, even the exalted emperor.

"See, my son? We must never forget the essence of China. Remember the statement of your grandfather. *Jong xue wei ti.* 'Chinese learning as the essence.' *Xi xue wei yong.* 'Western learning for practical purposes.' "

Jinru was not so disrespectful to interrupt the old man's train of thought. Instead he looked down into the walls, gates, and palaces of Beijing. The gigantic stone walls were shaped into interlocking rectangles, representing the square symbol of Earth. From south to north, each rectangle was smaller—the Chinese City, the Manchu City, the Imperial City, finally the Forbidden City. In the center of the Forbidden City were the Three Great Halls. The largest hall, where the imperial audiences once had been held, was surmounted by a brilliantly decorated dome, the circular symbol of Heaven.

"What does it mean to you, my son?"

Jinru had hoped to avoid this kind of dialogue, which was certain to end in an argument, but he could not refuse to answer. "What does *what* mean, Father?"

Zhonglu's watery eyes sharpened. "What does the city of Beijing mean to you?"

Jinru thought carefully. "Two things. First, it does represent a certain essence of tradition—order, discipline, scholarship, connoisseurship. I can respect those things. There were great scholar-officials in the past, like grandfather. You see, I've mellowed a bit, Father . . ."

Zhonglu beamed as his son spoke.

"But second, it also represents oppression and tyranny. It's a city built on hierarchy. It's a feudal city, one that demands revolution."

Zhonglu pursed his lips. "You know, my son, I don't totally disagree with you. I don't want us to stay with the old order. We must change. Perhaps a little revolution is a good thing. Maybe it will pave the way for reform. A mixture of old and new is what China needs."

Jinru tried to restrain himself but failed. "Father! Don't be so muddle-headed. Take a stand! The essence of China isn't found in some ridiculous traditions. The essence is the people. We must fight for the people. Even more, we must fight with the people—"

"Hold your tongue! You *will* show some respect. You may be a Communist outside these walls, but here you're a Gao, and you will act like one."

Jinru glowered at his father. He stood up, his hands grabbing the edges of the table. "You . . . you try to tell *me* about the family . . . You're the only failure in four generations—"

Jinru stopped himself in mid-sentence. Now he'd done it— totally lost control—just what he promised himself to avoid. He had to make amends. "I'm sorry," he said softly. Dammit, there was a higher cause; he couldn't let his own feelings stand in the way. "Please forgive me, Father"—speaking more loudly now. "I wanted to bring us back together. Not farther apart."

Gao Zhonglu's eyes, flashing with hurt, moved from Jinru to the bench. Jinru obeyed his father's silent instructions and sat down. "You say you want to bring us back together, but you insult me. You say ugly and terrible things. How can I believe you?"

"I—"

"Be still. Now you listen to me. You think I don't know what my students say about me?" Tears streamed down his face. "I know that I've failed my own father. In my prime, I was brighter than he ever hoped to be, but it's been all thought, no action."

"That's not entirely true—"

"Don't humor me. I've tried to fulfill the Gao legacy. At least I managed to keep the mansion." Zhonglu moved unsteadily around the table. "You want to make amends. Why? Tell me why!"

"Father, I didn't mean to insult you. I've had time to think in the past two years. Yes, I'm a Communist, but I'm also a Gao. I think I can bring the two together. To realize the dream, the dream that you told me about when I was a child."

"Oh, I see," replied Zhonglu dryly. "You'd like the inheritance to give to the Communists. Gao treasure for the People's Revolution. Isn't that right?"

"That's not exactly how it is." It's precisely the issue, Jinru thought to himself, lowering his eyes to avoid his father's stare.

"How, exactly, is it?"

"I promised the Communists I would devote my life to the revolution. And I did tell some leaders I might be willing to provide some financial support for educational modernization. That's in the Gao tradition, isn't it?"

Gao Zhonglu placed his hands in the sleeves of his gown. "Educational modernization? Yes, that's in the Gao tradition. But giving away your inheritance before you've received it? That's *not* in our tradition."

"I thought you wanted me to inherit."

Zhonglu shook his head sadly. "I did, before you went away, before you decided that my ways were totally wrong. Before you came back only because you wanted the family's fortune for your own purposes."

Jinru's handsome young face was creased with worry. "What are you saying, Father? Have you decided to disinherit me?"

Zhonglu turned slowly and walked to a large pine tree outside the hut. Under its largest branch was a brass gong. He lifted the stick with the padded end and, his body shaking with age and anger, hit it firmly. The deep sound carried across the Gao mansion, echoing through its courtyards and reverberating into the streets beyond. Moments later Lao Wu arrived at the summit bearing a tray with warm wine and sweetcakes. He poured wine into two small white cups and lit a kerosene lantern.

Gao Zhonglu spoke gently to his chief servant. "Thank you, Lao Wu. We can manage for ourselves. Now you have a duty to perform. I'll expect you back here at midnight."

The two Gaos watched Lao Wu disappear over the edge of the mountain. Zhonglu turned back to his son. "Now we will find out *if* you are serious about receiving your inheritance."

"Father." Jinru spoke as earnestly as he could. "I am serious. I

don't want it for frivolous or selfish reasons. I want to help the
Chinese people, to help realize the Gao dream."

"If you want the inheritance, you'll have to prove yourself."

"How?"

"First, you must promise that you'll always live in this house.
You will protect it to the best of your ability. This property is a
precious inheritance."

"But—" Jinru had hoped to sell the mansion and move into
more modest quarters.

"Do you promise?"

"Yes. I do." Dammit, Jinru thought; well, the art collection is
worth a lot more than the estate.

"Now sit down." Zhonglu gestured toward the bench. He picked
up the book he had been reading earlier, a modern edition of the
Four Books, the classics of the Confucian tradition. "I want you to
refresh your memory. I've marked two passages from the *Analects* of
Confucius. Read them."

"But Father, I already *know* them."

"Read them!" Zhonglu commanded. "I know you *know* them.
But I want you to take the lines to heart, to think about them. We
will discuss them again at midnight."

The scholar's hut was lit up from the inside like a lantern. Its
reddish-yellow glow remained steady as the sun spent its last rays in
arcs of blue and purple. Inside the hut, China's oldest tradition was
being preserved. A son was studying according to his father's instructions.

The lacquer master worked with fixed concentration. He was
making a gift, a three-color polychrome dish—cinnabar, yellow, and
black—in the style of the late-Ming dynasty. The model sat on the
table in front of him, a lacquer box glimmering under the bulb. The
gift was for his eldest son, to show him how a truly fine work still
could be carved, the way his own father had done it, just in case his
son never saw the Gao lacquer box, which he prayed he never would.
The dish was about two-thirds finished: a magnificent mountain
landscape with waterfalls, forests of baby trees, houses, bridges, even
a small caravan of people and horses.

Lao Wu did his duty in the same way his father had almost
fifty years earlier. Once again he waited until the lacquer master had

tapped out the shavings and put down the dish and the knife. Then a cord of white silk flew around the lacquer master's neck. One twist, a loud crack, no more sounds. Lao Wu placed the man's head gently against the workbench, as if he had fallen asleep.

Wu shifted the light so that it illuminated the Gao box. It looked untouched, just as the lacquer master had promised. Lao Wu put his black knapsack on the bench and pulled out two red velvet bags, two pieces of hemp, some long wire, and a pair of wire crimps. Then he removed a copy of the Four Books. Wrapped in the traditional tao binder, the volumes were almost identical in size and weight to the lacquer box. He looked at his watch. Only ten o'clock. Still plenty of time. Methodically, he placed the lacquer box in the velvet sack, wrapped it tightly in hemp, and tightened the wire around the package, making several loops of wire and clipping each one neatly at the end. He did the same to the *Four Books*. In a half hour, Lao Wu had two identical packages. The only difference was that the package containing the lacquer box had an extra turn on the wires that held the hemp—two turns for the lacquer box, one turn for the Four Books. He put both packages into his knapsack.

Now he removed a small bag. It was filled with gold, not inflated paper currency. Depositing the bag in the center of the master's almost finished polychrome lacquer dish, he turned and left.

At the stroke of twelve, Lao Wu walked into a scene that was like a painting—the father stood unmoving behind the seated son whose eyes were focused intently on a book. Zhonglu gestured to Lao Wu to put his knapsack on the cupboard and then be seated on a stool next to it.

Zhonglu turned to his son. "Now. The time for reading is over. The time for proving yourself has arrived. What is the first text?"

Jinru closed the book and stood before his father. He spoke with confidence. "The first text is *Analects*, Volume Four, Chapter Five:

When a son follows his father's instructions during his lifetime, one can say that he has a strong sense of duty. But when a son follows his father's way after his father's death, for the full three years of mourning, only then can one say that he is truly filial.

Zhonglu stood as erect as he could and spoke sharply. "And what does that mean to you?"

Jinru always found it awkward to interpret the obvious. "I think it means what it says. Filiality is measured by adherence to a father's will after his death. Not before."

"Is that to be taken literally or figuratively?"

Jinru pondered for a moment. "Figuratively, I think. Otherwise it would be difficult to fulfill Confucius' other admonitions."

"What other admonitions?"

"About changing your costume to suit the seasons. Changing your approaches as circumstances alter."

"Are there no permanent truths in the tradition?"

"Of course there are. One is expected to be filial, to work within the context of family tradition. To shape that tradition to meet new needs."

Zhonglu met his son's eyes. "And you, Jinru. Have you been filial?"

"Yes. I think I have. Within my own sense of that tradition. Can you possibly understand?"

"Of course I understand."

"Would you agree? Have I been filial?"

"I'm not prepared to answer that question at this moment."

Zhonglu looked out over the lights of Beijing. "And now, my son, the other passage. Not all of it, just the part about 'when one is forty . . .' "

Jinru responded without hesitation: "When one is forty, he shall have no doubts."

Zhonglu turned to Lao Wu. "Bring me the package. The one with the single-twisted wire."

Lao Wu tried to conceal his dismay. "Single-twisted wire?" he asked as calmly as he could.

"That's what I said. Bring it now!"

Lao Wu gave the package to Zhonglu, who cradled it as if making an offering to his ancestors. "My son, I would like to give this to you now. But I do not yet think that you are ready. I want to make sure that you fulfill your obligation to live in this house, to protect the Gao mansion. Lao Wu will put the package into hiding until then."

"Until when, Father? Until the end of the three years of mourning?"

"No, my son. Until you have no doubts."

Jinru's mouth fell open. "Father, do you realize!? I'm now twenty-three. That's seventeen years! Almost twice my lifetime. It will be 1966."

"So it will be, my son. So it will be."

Zhonglu died six months later, and Dr. Ren emigrated to Taiwan. Gao Jinru moved back into the Gao mansion and tried to fulfill his bargain, seeking an uneasy balance between Confucianism and communism. After paying homage at the Gao Ancestral Temple, he attended daily Communist Party meetings and assisted the intelligence network paving the way for Mao's takeover. Jinru closed most of the mansion and lived with his wife, the studious daughter of a merchant family, in modest quarters near the Ancestral Temple, a couple of servants providing all their needs. He was the fourth generation of Gao masters to work at the big desk in the library. Now a typewriter shared space with calligraphy brushes; the works of Marx sat alongside those of Mencius.

Shortly after Jinru became master, he gave Lao Wu permission to go to New York to settle the estate of his deceased uncle. What Gao Jinru did not know was that Lao Wu took with him a hemp bag, bound with circles of wire, each circle ending in two twists.

Jinru had thought Lao Wu and he could finally establish the right relationship now that Zhonglu was gone. But Lao Wu remained distant, and soon after his return from New York, he introduced his oldest son to Jinru. "Master," Lao Wu said, "the time has come for my retirement. This is my son. If he pleases you, I can train him fully. I can tell him everything that he must know. Everything."

"But why can't you remain? Why can't you tell me everything?"

"You know why, Master. I gave my word to your father. And my father gave his word to your father's father. Please know that it causes me great pain to hold back anything from you."

Lao Wu's son became the new senior servant. In the summer of 1950, he asked for a day off, an unusual request because new servants never had a day off. But his excuse was genuine. He had to attend a funeral. Lao Wu had hanged himself by the silken cord.

CHAPTER FIVE

HISTORY

NEW YORK CITY, DECEMBER LATE 1980s

"BE RIGHT WITH YOU, MR. WALDEN,"

she shouted down the hallway, "just putting some rocks in the Scotch."

Rebecca Aspen was a surprise. He had expected a severe woman in a Brooks Brothers suit. Instead, Rebecca ("call me Becky") was a green-eyed blonde whose burgundy slacks and white angora sweater covered a well-proportioned, slightly overweight body. A striking woman, thought Roger, but also calculating and a bit cold. He could imagine her aloofly giving commands at the office and determinedly jogging at some Manhattan health club.

Becky's residence was also something of an anomaly. The building itself had the "right" address—Eighty-sixth Street and Madison Avenue—but the apartment was hardly typical. Actually, it looked as if two different interior decorators were still wrestling with each other for the contract. One of them favored glass, chrome, bright fabrics, and a lot of mirrors. The other seemed to have unloaded his wares from a China clipper. Long scrolls hung between the mirrors; muted green-and-blue landscapes and black-and-white calligraphy decorated the other walls. A dozen cases of Chinese sculpture and ceramics made the room resemble a small museum; a large brown-and-white-glazed horse pranced on the buffet.

"Why do you run marathons?" Becky asked, handing Roger his

drink and sitting down across from him. Becky's gambit startled Roger, her eyes sharply scrutinizing like a cross-examiner scoring initial points. Roger paused. He'd just met her. He'd never told anyone, not even Diane, the real truth. Marathoning was a quest for inner power deeper than anything else in life. Maybe, he mused, sex at its best might be the same—power beyond organization and intellect, power not from controlling, but from releasing. He wasn't sure about sex, but he knew competitive running unleashed some potent *it* in his being, letting his soul conquer his body. Why couldn't marathoning, he often fretted, infuse other aspects of his life?

"Why marathoning? Masochism, of course," Roger lied, not pleased that her slight smile caught his perjury. "Now, I need a little advice." He sipped his Scotch. "Mr. Marsh says you're a China expert."

Becky noted the casually professional way he deflected her question, a style reinforced by Roger's open-collared shirt, V-necked rust-colored sweater, rumpled brown tweed sports jacket. "Old JRM tends to exaggerate if he can impress a client," she countered his compliment. "I'd rather describe myself as a China-lover. I've been at it for almost fifteen years now." She explained about taking courses in Chinese language and history—"just to keep my sanity during law school at Stanford." She'd been surprised that her skills became useful when Nixon's famous trip reopened the China trade in 1972. "American businessmen couldn't live without lawyers, and the Chinese needed outside help. So now I'm part of an old tradition—matchmaker between barbarians and the Middle Kingdom."

"Of course, the right-wing idiots almost destroyed everything when they massacred their own people at Tiananmen Square. Thank God, the moderates seem to be on their way back. But when it comes to predicting China's future, you never know—" Becky paused, smiled a little, and continued. "Sort of like predicting my own future. 1989 was a lousy year for me as well as China. Not a pretty divorce. Sort of boiled down to the fact that while I'm a one-man woman, he wasn't a one-woman man."

Why's she going into this? Roger squirmed, never liking the modern penchant for telling-it-all to new acquaintances. He surmised Becky herself had been a big cause for the divorce, sensing her bossy self-confidence would drive most men crazy. Roger cleared his throat and spoke crisply. "Before we get into it, let me assure you I want your advice on a professional basis. I'm happy to pay whatever you think is fair. To save both of us some time, I've put together a short list of questions."

Becky wrinkled her nose. "Don't be silly. In the evening I turn off the clock. Besides, your story—at least what you told me over the phone—intrigues me." Not just the story, she thought to herself—why do I always fall for professors?

He unwrapped the package on the coffee table. "I frankly don't know a thing about it," he explained. "I don't even know if it's valuable. But my late wife's family felt strongly about it, so I wanted to have an expert look at it."

Roger opened the velvet bag and placed the cinnabar box on the table. Becky stared in silence. Carefully lifting it, she inspected its top, sides, and bottom, her fingers probing the flowing shapes in the box and tracing the patterns on the sides. Finally, she put it back on the table and spoke reverently. "I'm no expert on Chinese lacquers, but I'll tell you this. That's one of the most beautiful pieces of lacquer I've ever seen. Exquisite carving."

Roger patted the box like a pet dog that had learned a new trick. "That's very helpful, Becky. Now how about my list?" He glanced at a piece of yellow paper taken from his pocket. "Could you take a guess at how old it is?"

"I guess you're not big on aesthetics," she said tartly, sensing he was being aloof to fend off any semblance of intimacy. "If it's genuine—and that's always a big 'if' with Chinese art—then it's Ming dynasty, late-sixteenth or early-seventeenth century." Gently picking up the box and tipping it sideways to catch the light, she continued. "You can tell that from the small label here on the bottom—it says, Made in the Ming Wan-li reign.' "

"That old?" Roger raised his eyebrows, then glanced back at the yellow sheet. "Now how much is it worth? Is it really valuable?"

"How much?" She remembered what Mr. Marsh had said about Diane's will and Roger's financial straits. "Well, it's tough to say. If the box is genuine, it's quite valuable. The exact price depends on a rapidly changing market. You'd have to work through a reputable dealer, or you could put it up for auction at Christie's or Sotheby's."

"But can't you take a stab at it? A rough estimate?"

"It's not quite that easy. Art's like real estate. You don't know its actual worth until you sell it. But it's not likely to decline in value—Asian art has been a blue-chip investment for over a decade now."

"So we're talking a few thousand?"

Becky shook her head and raised her thumb.

"More?" Roger tried to sound nonchalant, his hopes rising.

"I'd say at least thirty thousand, perhaps forty, maybe even more." She walked to an illuminated display case, withdrew a small round red box, returned to the couch and placed it next to Roger's box. "This doesn't deserve to sit on the same table with your beauty, but it'll show you why I'm so excited. It's dated much later—eighteenth century, Qing dynasty, Qianlong reign. All one color—traditional red cinnabar—unlike the mixture of red, yellow, and black on your box. Look more closely. See how the lacquer is less consistent? How the carving is less skilled? It's a nice effort, but not museum quality. Cost me fifteen hundred in Hong Kong in the early seventies. Probably ten grand today."

"So mine is worth?"

"God, you never give up!" Becky laughed, more from sympathy at Roger's predicament than anything else. "Well, if I were a rich bitch at an auction, I would probably continue bidding until it reached fifty or sixty thousand dollars."

"Terrific," Roger smiled victoriously. "Finally. A straight answer from a lawyer. Now my other questions. How do you use it? Where does it open? Is there something valuable inside?"

Becky threw up her arms in exasperation. "I can see why you didn't go into law—you move too fast to make any money. Well, you've got me there. I've never seen a Chinese lacquer box that didn't open."

"Never?"

"Nope. This is the first time. You see, in old China, lacquer was appreciated as a fine craft, but it was never seen as one of the highest arts. It was the work of artisans. Scholars wouldn't have considered dabbling in it. It's pretty messy stuff. When it came to art, scholars saved themselves for painting and calligraphy. The elite saw lacquer as having a functional purpose. So a lacquer box like this was used for documents or jewelry, maybe a fine mah-jongg set, something like that."

"So maybe there's something inside?" Roger asked hopefully.

Becky held the box to her ear and shook it gently. "It doesn't sound like it. I know it's heavy, but many layers of lacquer make any object heavy. Only two possibilities I can see. One is that it's the rare exception—designed solely for aesthetics and symbolism.

The other is that it might be something like a Chinese puzzle. There could be a way of opening it if we could figure out the trick. But I sure as hell wouldn't try it unless I knew what I was doing. You might be wrecking a masterpiece."

Roger glanced at his watch and then back at his list. "Last question, okay? Can you take a quick look at these two letters? They were both part of my wife's estate. My real question is, do I own the box? Or am I holding it in trust for someone else?"

Becky read the two letters, wondering whether her physical attraction to Roger would survive her aversion to his obsessive style. Try to understand him, she told herself, the poor guy has been through hell. "Roger, there's no question about the law," she said, putting down the letters and leaning back in the couch. "In this state, indeed I think in any state, you are unquestionably the owner of this lacquer box. You're free, in legal terms, to do anything you like with it."

Roger heard something in her voice. "It sounds like you're about to say, 'But there's a catch . . .' "

"No catch at all so far as the law is concerned. The problem isn't legal but moral. Clearly your late wife's grandmother felt very strongly about this box. It represents her deep personal obligation to a Chinese who seems to have done a great favor for her and her husband. She's right. You do have to know China to understand the extent of some of these obligations. It's all caught up in a word— *guanxi.*"

"*Guanxi?*" Roger repeated.

Becky wove her fingers together. "It's the network of connections among people. Diane's grandmother assumed the Chinese owner would return someday to claim his possession. She wanted it kept in trust. I can't advise you on what to do—"

Roger began wrapping up the box. "Thanks, Becky, I learned a lot; I'm not sure what I'm going to do with it." He was genuinely perplexed: he didn't want to violate Diane's trust, but he sure could use fifty thousand dollars.

Becky suddenly grabbed Roger's wrists, her face reddening in anger. "Don't put that away so soon. I've got to say I'm annoyed. I know you need money, but you're forgetting you've got a thing of exceptional beauty. All you care about is—how old? how much? what's it good for? whose is it?"

Roger looked baffled. She pointed at the box. "Maybe you don't want to know any more, but I do. Your lacquer box raises all kinds of other questions—about art, history, symbolism, calligraphy, allegory—who knows what." Becky spoke more softly as she saw shock on Roger's face. "I'd like to answer these other questions. Could I take a few pictures of it before you take it back to the vault?"

"I'm really sorry," he said contritely, chastising himself with a loud sigh. "I was just trying to save you some time. I didn't mean to insult you with my questions. Of course, you can photograph it, with my apologies."

She shot him a forgiving nod and squeezed his hand. A reformed Roger might be more attractive.

He followed Becky into the study, carrying the box in both hands. Hundreds of books lined the walls, many in Oriental languages. Two oversized desks dominated the room. The first, illuminated by a draftsman's lamp, was covered with stacks of books; the other, a plywood table on sawhorses, held two cameras with tripods and several small photographic lamps. Taking the box from Roger and gently positioning it on a piece of white cloth in the center of the plywood table, Becky adjusted the lamps and selected a closeup lens for her Hasselblad. She snapped two rolls, then turned off the lights and handed the box back to Roger.

"If I find out anything, I'll give you a call in case you're interested. Make sure that the box is kept in a moist environment, maybe put a humidifier near it. I'd hate to have it split open."

Becky looked out the window and watched Roger hail a taxi. She wished she hadn't scolded him, but she couldn't stand insensitivity. Maybe, if he returned, he might be a little different. After all, he was good-looking, smart, and famous in a curious way. Just what her mother always wanted—no, she corrected herself, just what Becky had always wanted. She bet he would be great to spend a weekend with—the whole weekend. She'd stick to her principles, but couldn't she find a way to see him again?

At home, Roger became depressed. Maybe she wasn't his type, but Becky's life seemed so ordered, so balanced. What a nice combination, interesting work and fascinating hobbies, not marathon teaching and marathon running. He hit his fist angrily into his palm. He hadn't meant to insult Becky. Why did he act like that? He often resented being an only child. When he was young, his parents spoiled him rotten. An only child also learns to entertain himself; maybe that was why he had few close friends. And since parents expect wonders from an only child, it was inevitable to feel driven all his life.

He sunk in his desk chair and inspected the package. Fifty thousand? But what if there was something inside that was worth a lot more? Besides, he didn't really need the money immediately, not now that he had moved into real junior-professor accommodations. Maybe hanging on to the box would permit him to see Becky again, and . . .

He didn't allow himself to finish the thought. Instead he removed the wrappings from the box and placed it on his desk. Pushing aside books, papers, and typewriter, he set the box dead center in front of him. Spotlighting the box with the desk lamp, he sat down and examined his inheritance. It wasn't all that big, but it was striking at a distance and extremely complicated up close. A large Chinese character dominated the top, with a dragon and a bird cavorting around the border. Putting on his glasses and pulling out a large magnifying glass, he studied the intricate scenes carved in red, yellow, and black. The front looked like a Brueghel painting, a crosscut of busy everyday life. He scrutinized the other sides of the box: figures sitting on rocks, gazing at a stream, chatting with each other, kneeling in palaces. Roger wondered if old China had really been like that. Probably an idealization, he decided. He looked at the calligraphy—one character on top, the date on the side, many lines on the bottom. The writing styles were quite different.

After a while, his fingers touched the carving. He slowly traced the large character on top. Then his eyes and fingers moved to the front panel following the figures and landscape clockwise around the box. An odd rhythm punctuated his moves—slow, fast, slow—as if sensing a musical composition in the lacquer. Turning the box over, he looked at the vertical strings of characters, running his fingers over them at a rapid tempo. The bottom, he thought, was allegro, the top was andante. He stopped at the small, clearly incised characters on the side, remembering Becky's translation, "Made in the Ming Wanli reign."

The box grabbed his eyes for days. Becky was right, he thought remorsefully. The box had a power he'd missed altogether. Without any knowledge of the Chinese language, he could nevertheless hear it speak, even sing. A grin flashed over his face. Why not learn the secrets of the box? Surely it must be worth a few hours, perhaps a few days, to figure out its significance. Besides, maybe he could find a way to get inside. At least he would know more about its value.

But how to get started? It had taken Becky more than a decade to acquire her knowledge. There must be a way to speed up the process. Of course. Why couldn't one just apply the standard techniques of historical research? Ask the right questions, go to the proper sources, take careful notes. After all, it's not such a big deal—just some pretty carvings on a small red box, a nice diversion on a sabbatical, a new hobby. Besides, he was finding it difficult to sustain interest in the article he had agreed to write—"Survival of the Sickest," a revisionist look at Social Darwinism.

Opening his desk, Roger pulled out the tools of his trade: a fresh package of five-by-eight note cards, a new pad of legal-sized yellow lined paper, file folders, and research-card boxes. He measured the box with a ruler—8.5 inches long, 5.5 inches wide, and just over 3 inches high. Now, first off, we need to know about lacquer making. How was this made? Who made it? For whom was it made? And then we need to know about the uses of lacquer. Why construct a box like this? Isn't there a better explanation for the absence of hinges and a fastener? What else? Of course, we need to know about when it was made. What was its historical setting?

His worn, lumpy briefcase in hand, Roger walked out of his apartment, bracing himself against the early-winter winds. Walking north on Broadway, his step had a sense of purpose. He was looking forward to the research; the first steps in a new project were always exciting. After a few blocks, Roger slowed a bit. He had an eerie feeling that he was being followed. Looking back, he saw a few students and an old woman wheeling a baby carriage. Roger, old boy, he counseled himself, don't get carried away with your mystery. It's not so strange if people notice you. After all, do you know anyone else who practically killed himself on live TV?

At the reception desk in Kent Hall, Roger discovered that he was indeed something of a celebrity. "Professor Walden," the librarian gushed in a loud stage whisper. "Oh, it's good to see you. We thought we'd lost you. Look everyone, Professor Walden's back." A small crowd of welcomers gathered at the desk, shaking his hand, and agreeing that under the circumstances, he looked "almost himself."

Getting off the elevator, Roger walked for the first time into the East Asian Collection, astounding the librarian by asking for books on lacquer and the Ming dynasty. "But why?" wondered the owlish man. "It's a far cry from American history. Well, no matter. Can you read Chinese?"

Roger shook his head.

"I thought not. Too bad. Most of what we have will be in Chinese. Indeed some of the best sources are in Japanese. No Japanese either? Well, let's see what we can find in English."

Four hours later, Roger's table in the library was piled with books, many of them oversized and with covers faded with age. "I threw in a few Chinese-language books," said the librarian with a faint smile, "but don't worry. They're art catalogs and maybe the plates will prove useful. If you're serious about this field, you really ought to take classical Chinese, you know."

Roger sifted swiftly through the books, marking passages for future study. He worked for several hours, until he had winnowed down the books to the few he would take home and the few that yielded passages for the Xerox machine. Back home, after a fast supper of noodle soup and a ham sandwich, Roger began taking notes about lacquer. He felt a growing satisfaction that the research process, part cerebral and part mechanical, seemed to work so easily on a subject so foreign. Roger wrote in his clean vertical style, enjoying the fact that he still used a fountain pen, stacking the completed cards in logical order:

<table>
<tr><td>Lacquer</td><td>Origins and Process</td></tr>
</table>

Evidence of lacquer dates back two to three thousand years. Used first as preservative for wood in the Shang dynasty, back at least to the 12th century B.C. Substance is taken from the lacquer tree—Rhus verniciflua—much as we take sap from the maple. Very sticky stuff in its raw form. Also poisonous, causing skin disorders, ruining hands of lacquer workers at an early age. After extraction, lacquer is strained and stored in airtight containers until ready for use. Best lacquer trees in China and other parts of East Asia. Western lacquer very crude by comparison.

Lacquer is laid up in several coats, usually on a wooden object. When exposed to air, it produces a remarkable hardening process, like the polymerization that makes modern plastics. Solid lacquer, after drying, extraordinarily hard and resists both heat and moisture. A century ago, lacquer dishes were used for chemical experiments because impervious to most acids and to high temperatures.

Lacquer   Historical Evolution

In the first millennium B.C. lacquer used most often to preserve and protect wood. Frequently employed to cover armor and to coat wooden parts of chariots. By the Han dynasty—roughly 200 B.C.–200 A.D. — it was used to paint objects. Most famous architectural find was the Mawangdui tomb, which housed the noble lady who was preserved for over 2000 years. Swirling lacquer decoration on the coffin produced by mixing lac with tung oil. Fantasy land of dragons, tigers, and clouds.

In the first 1500 years A.D., Chinese experimented with all forms of lacquer. Painted lacquer, inlaid lacquer (often silver, gold, or mother of pearl), incised lacquer, and eventually carved lacquer. A rich family in the Tang dynasty, 7th–9th century A.D., might have hundreds of pieces of lacquer—plates and bowls, chopsticks, boxes, chests, chairs, even pillows (tough on the neck, but nice protection for ladies' coiffeurs).

Lacquer became a central aspect of life. Marvelous combination of functionality, durability, and creativity. It symbolized elite life and accompanied them in death.

Lacquer   Factory Production

Song dynasty woodblock print (see Xerox) shows lacquer factory dating from the 11th century A.D. Dozens, sometimes hundreds, of workers. Lacquer requires a moist environment to prevent cracking and blistering. Thus the apprentices, often young children, faced constant colds, skin diseases, and tuberculosis.

Top-quality lacquers usually made under patronage for those in the wealthy merchant classes or for the scholar-officials. Often required as many as two hundred—repeat, 200—coats to make a single object. Each coat required four to five days to dry. Then it had to be polished. Thus as much as two, three, sometimes four years to complete the first stage in a work of lacquer!

Polychrome lacquer, i.e., several colors, required a special process. The base wood was covered with a fabric impregnated in lacquer. Then came several layers of raw black lacquer mixed with ash to provide a strong base. Then followed the various layers of colored lacquer—black with no ash, yellow, and red. The famous cinnabar red lacquer was the result of adding mercuric sulfide to the lac. In between each layer was a black band, consisting of a few coats, to warn the carver that he was entering another layer.

Master carvers were the top of the factory pyramid. Used wide array of knives and picks. Carver might require a year or two for a fine piece of lacquer, like a top-quality letter box. Master carver not unlike the painter, just a lower social class. He was really painting and writing with his knives. His greatest hope was to make his craft into art. His greatest *fear was to slip, thus ruining in a split second what had taken four years to make. Any fine-art expert can detect the mistakes, thus isolating those failures, or "seconds," as we would call them.*

As Roger's head began to nod from fatigue, he neatly stacked his note cards, slipped them into a plastic box, and marked the section "Lacquer/General." He stared for a moment at his lacquer box with new appreciation at the craft it represented. He smiled a bit, as a doctor might smile at a sleeping patient. Historical method, like the scientific, would yield the truth.

The next morning Roger walked across Central Park to the Metropolitan Museum. On the second floor, he discovered a display case of Chinese lacquers. He spent two hours looking at the more splendid examples from the Ming and Qing periods: a large bowl with silver figures and calligraphy, a square box with glossy painted birds and trees, a stem cup covered in gold patterns, a vase with mother-of-pearl inlaid flowers. There was even a small round container with a lid, dated late Ming, perfectly carved in cinnabar and black. But nothing remotely resembled Roger's box. He guessed the Metropolitan must be on the prowl for additional gifts of Asian lacquer to augment a good, but not yet encyclopedic, collection.

For the next several days, Roger moved back and forth between his apartment and the Columbia Library. He tried lunch one day at the Faculty Club, but soon regretted his decision. Everyone asked two questions: Are you *really* okay? And what are you *really* working on? Henceforth, he found solitary sandwich lunches in his office more tolerable.

His collection of note cards and file folders of Xeroxes now required several plastic boxes and a drawer of his file cabinet. Clearly it was important to learn something about the late Ming dynasty, the date on the box:

Ming Dynasty   Wan-Li Reign, 1573–1620

The Wan-li Emperor was the 14th of the Ming dynasty. Longest reign in the dynasty. A period of decay as the court faced growing threats of corruption, eunuch dictators, domestic rebellions, and foreign invasions. Traditionally, Chinese historians saw this period as the death knell of the last ethnically Chinese dynasty, the Ming (1368–1644), and the harbinger of the Manchu invasion and the Qing dynasty (1644–1912)
. . .

Ming Dynasty   *Wan-Li Cultural Trends*

Recent Western scholarship on the late Ming has produced a fresh appreciation of its importance as a seminal period in art, philosophy, and education. The general deterioration of life, not dissimilar to the period of Confucius (roughly 500 years B.C.), made intellectuals question the roots of society. Among the outstanding revisionists studying this period is Theodore DeBary of Columbia University (where else?!).

Several schools of philosophy emerged, ranging from strict efforts to recapture the essence of traditional Confucianism to those which stressed Zen-like (Chinese: "Chan") meditation to capture one's inner spirit. New forms of landscape painting flowered as well, perhaps best represented by the vigorous philosopher-artist Dong Qichang. Some leading scholars were influenced by Western scientific thought, transmitted by outstanding Jesuits like Matteo Ricci.

Communist historians have argued that the late Ming and early Qing periods (16th–17th centuries) showed the "buds of capitalism" because of the flourishing merchant class in major towns. Without the stultification of imperial rule and the emergence of neo-colonialism, so the argument goes, China might have naturally experienced the collapse of feudalism and the advent of a bourgeois-democratic revolution.

Other nationalist historians have looked back to the late Ming as the last stand of Han Chinese (that is, native Chinese) brilliance. They have laid much of the blame for China's collapse on the Manchu invasion of the mid-17th century. Thus in the early-20th century revolution, many nationalists opposed the Manchus as much as they did the foreign imperialists.

From time to time, Roger leaned back and surveyed the growing piles of cards and files, looking like walls around the little lacquer box. Surrounded by wisps of steam seeping upward from the humidifier, the box took on a peculiar air of mystery, floating in tiny clouds that hovered over the desk. Occasionally, Roger pushed aside some of the papers and let his fingers flow along the texture of the carvings. He hoped that the research and the lacquer box, both lying on the same table, would begin to speak to each other. Granted, he had answered his initial questions about lacquer-making and the Ming dynasty, but he still knew next to nothing about his own lacquer box.

The excitement of the hunt was fading into frustrated boredom. Maybe if he read more broadly? For the next few days, he plowed through a standard two-volume textbook on Chinese history, taking copious notes—dynasties, emperors, rebellions, artists, poets, philosophers. Then he labored his way into an anthology of great Chinese thinkers—Confucians, Taoists, Legalists. Comparisons to

Western philosophers came readily to mind. But none of the reading provided any keys to the object perched in front of him.

Maybe I'm making more of it than there really is, Roger thought, moving across the living room to the window and trying to regain some perspective. Maybe the box is just a lovely work of art. Maybe that's why old Mrs. MacDonald's Chinese friend wanted it kept in a safe place. After all, modern China hasn't been a very good place to keep valuables. Perhaps there's no further meaning. No message, after all . . .

Roger's train of thought stopped short as he noticed an old woman in a shawl standing across the street. Her hands were on a baby carriage, but she was staring at Roger's apartment. Catching sight of him at the window, she suddenly spun the carriage around and wheeled it swiftly down the street.

Roger ran down the flight of stairs to the street. It was empty except for three teenagers playing stickball. "Did you see an old lady with a carriage?"

"Sure," one boy shouted back, "she stands there all day long. We were going to use her for third base."

Roger smiled tensely and went back upstairs, triple-bolting his door with special care.

CHAPTER SIX
CULTURAL REVOLUTION

BEIJING, OCTOBER 1966

THE NEW BEIJING UNIVERSITY WAS A

far more attractive place for China's premier educational institution than the old Beida. Shortly after the Communist takeover in 1949, the authorities had appropriated the Yanjing campus in the north-western suburbs. American money had created buildings combining Yankee functionalism with the horizontal architecture of China, green tile roofs swept up at the ends.

On most days Gao Jenggai would have been proud of the new Beida—it was an appropriate setting for molding the fine minds who would lead China to modernization. But on October 18, 1966, he would have been appalled.

An outdoor courtroom had been set up on a sloping field. Thousands of young people milled around a raised platform, as if waiting for a concert or play to begin. All wore blue cotton jackets and blue or green slacks. Behind a long table on the platform sat the six "democratically" chosen prosecutors: two radical instructors, two students, and two university staff, all with "proper class back-grounds," meaning they claimed proletarian or peasant families.

"THE NEXT CASE"—the words bellowed over the loudspeakers suspended above the prosecutors' platform—"IS THAT OF PROFESSOR GAO JINRU. DEPARTMENT OF HISTORY. CHARGE IS CONSPIRACY. AGAINST THE UNIVERSITY. AGAINST THE PEOPLE. TEACHING FEUDAL AND BOURGEOIS IDEALS. CAPITALIST ROADER."

The crowd hushed as Gao Jinru was led from the top of the hill. The students surrounding him all wore red armbands announcing "Red Guard" in white characters. A month earlier, Chairman Mao Zedong had addressed the multitudes, donning a red arm band as he stood in the guards' walkway on the Gate of Heavenly Peace, thereby legitimizing the movement.

Professor Gao, exhausted after three days of interrogation, struggled to appear composed. His face was haggard and unshaven, his silver-and-black hair uncombed. Unwashed clothing hung limply on his frame as he stumbled forward. The inquisitors had tied his hands with rope—not because there was any chance of escape but rather to emphasize his guilt. As he was pushed up onto the rickety platform in front of the table, Jinru turned toward the prosecutors, but two Red Guards spun him around. He would not face his accusers; he would face the people.

Jinru surveyed the throng, picking out a few faces, some students from the History Department, even one or two younger faculty members. But most of the crowd had nothing to do with the university. They were just spending a Sunday afternoon watching a public trial. Kangaroo courts were already a popular feature of the Cultural Revolution, generally targeting those like Gao Jinru who had "bad class backgrounds"—mandarins, landowners, merchants, intellectuals. Mao had unleashed a reign of terror—those judged guilty were usually dismissed from their posts and sentenced to public humiliation, hard labor in the countryside, or capital punishment. Suicides, especially among intellectuals, became commonplace.

Hearing a familiar voice calling his name, Jinru looked up and saw his wife standing toward the rear of the crowd, tears streaming down her face. He mustered a smile and shook his head slightly, trying to tell her to keep silent; there was no point in involving the rest of the family in this awful moment.

"PROFESSOR GAO. HOW DO YOU PLEAD?"

"Not guilty." Jinru spoke as forcefully as he could, but his microphone was set at half volume; he could match them only by screaming, and he knew that would accomplish nothing.

"NOT GUILTY? WHAT EVIDENCE DO YOU HAVE TO SUPPORT YOUR CASE?"

"I am the accused, not the accuser. What is the case you are bringing against me?"

"DO YOU HAVE THE AUDACITY TO QUESTION THE REVOLUTIONARY TRIBUNAL? THAT IS DISRESPECTFUL OF THE PEOPLE!"

"The entire history of jurisprudence and our own constitution demand that the case be fully explained to the accused—"

"BOURGEOIS HISTORY. EVEN OUR OWN CONSTITUTION WAS DE-SIGNED BY CAPITALIST ROADERS. FRIENDS OF YOURS NO DOUBT. NOW PROVE YOUR INNOCENCE!"

"I protest! On what authority do you try me?"

"ON THE AUTHORITY OF THE PEOPLE. WHAT DO THE PEOPLE SAY?"

After a moment of silence, a high-pitched voice shouted: "He looks guilty. Let him prove he's not guilty. Looks like a rich professor to me." Murmurs of agreement rippled through the crowd. Then a chant started. "Prove it. Prove it! PROVE IT!"

"PROFESSOR GAO, YOU HAVE THE PEOPLES' JUDGEMENT. PROVE YOUR INNOCENCE!"

Gao Jinru drew in his breath. Standing as straight as he could, he spoke in measured tones. "Someday all of you will regret this moment. You feel so powerful in a crowd, but I can see your faces. I will remember what you did, and you will remember it, too. You are denying every principle of law, every principle of humanity. Every principle that we have tried to teach in this great university."

"PROFESSOR GAO. WE DO NOT NEED ONE OF YOUR DECADENT LECTURES. PROVE YOUR INNOCENCE!" A cheer swelled up from the crowd, but as Jinru scanned the amphitheater, focusing on people whom he recognized, he saw each one drop his eyes and stop cheering.

"I will say this. I have been a member of the Chinese Communist Party for two decades. I was a political officer during the Civil War against the Nationalists. I graduated from Beida in 1946. It is an institution founded in part by my own family. I have taught here since 1951. I have taught Chinese history. My goal is to help bright minds to understand our past so that we can have a clearer view of our goals in the future. I am committed to China's independence, to China's modernization, to China's communism."

"DO YOU TEACH ABOUT THE FOUR OLDS? DO YOUR STUDENTS LEARN ABOUT OLD CUSTOMS, OLD SYSTEMS, OLD BELIEFS, AND OLD METHODS?"

Jinru allowed himself a small chuckle, but no one appeared to appreciate the irony. "Of course, I teach about many old things. That's the nature of history. A lot of the past is old—sort of by definition, one would think. I teach about the past so we won't make the same mistakes again. I also teach about it because we Chinese have much to be proud about in our five thousand years of civilization—"

"PROFESSOR GAO. YOU'VE ANSWERED THE QUESTION. YOU TEACH ABOUT THE FOUR OLDS. YOU'RE EVEN PROUD OF CHINA'S PAST. IS IT TRUE THAT YOU ALSO TEACH ABOUT WESTERN GOVERNMENTS, WESTERN PHILOSOPHY, AND WESTERN TECHNOLOGY?"

"Yes, of course. I must teach about them so that we fully understand what happened to China over the past three centuries. And because we need to take what's best from the West in order to enhance our own modernization—"

"SO YOU ADMIT IT ALL. YOU ADVOCATE FOLLOWING THE WAY OF THE BOURGEOIS AND CAPITALIST WEST. THAT MAKES YOU A CAPITALIST ROADER. YOU ADVOCATE STUDYING ABOUT THE FOUR OLDS. THAT CERTAINLY MAKES YOU A SUPPORTER OF FEUDALISM."

"I have been a Communist all of my adult life, longer than almost anyone in this crowd. I seek to shape fine minds to a life of reason and a life of commitment. This whole proceeding makes a mockery of intellectual life."

"SO, PROFESSOR GAO, YOU LAUGH AT US?"

"No, I pity you."

"WE DO NOT NEED YOUR PITY. HOWEVER, YOU MAY NEED OURS. YOU DO BELIEVE IN DEMOCRACY, DONT YOU?"

"Yes. Not in the Western bourgeois-capitalist sense, but in the communist sense—a democracy of the proletariat, a true democracy of the people."

"AND THAT IS PRECISELY WHAT WE HAVE HERE TODAY."

"No, it isn't. You've assembled a mob with no rules and no procedures. You're out for the fun of humiliating people in authority, which is a lot easier than achieving authority yourselves. This whole Cultural Revolution is an excuse for the losers in China to band together, losers trying to pretend they're winners. You wait, a few months, maybe a few years, you'll all be losers again." Jinru had said what he had to say—his deepest belief was that intellectuals had to stick to their principles. That was what he had inherited from his ancestors.

"MAYBE SO, PROFESSOR GAO. BUT TODAY, WE'LL HAVE TO SEE WHO THE LOSER WILL BE. IT'S TIME FOR THE VERDICT. CRIME OF CONSPIRACY. IS PROFESSOR GAO INNOCENT OR GUILTY?"

The shouts began in the front row, carefully orchestrated as they had been all day. Soon a chorus screamed in unison. "GUILTY! GUILTY! GUILTY!"

"THEN THE SENTENCE IS CLEAR. PROFESSOR GAO WILL BE SEN-TENCED TO . . . ER, JUST A MOMENT." There was a buzz at the pros-ecutors' table. Jinru, unable to make out the garbled words over hand-muffled microphones, stood stiffly throughout the deliberation.

"NEW EVIDENCE HAS COME TO OUR ATTENTION. PROFESSOR GAO'S FULL SENTENCE WILL NOT BE DELIVERED NOW. INSTEAD WE MUST ESCORT HIM HOME. RED GUARDS ALWAYS TAKE SPECIAL CARE OF PRIS-ONERS. DON'T THEY?" The initial groan of disappointment—no im-mediate sentence—gave way to a laughing cheer about Red Guard hospitality. It was always fun to humiliate someone in public.

Jinru was shoved off the platform and pushed through a gauntlet of shouting bystanders who hit and kicked him. By the time he reached the road, his clothes were ripped and blood ran from gashes in his face. He was forced into a mule-drawn cart where a guard put a white dunce cap on his head and hung a crudely penned sign around his neck: GAO JINRU. SO-CALLED PROFESSOR. TEACHER OF CAPITALISM AND FEUDALISM. Hundreds of people paraded alongside as they drove him through the streets of northwestern Beijing on the two-mile ride to the Gao mansion. The two Red Guards managed to stay clear of the barrage of rotten vegetables, pieces of dung, and chunks of coal.

A scant hour earlier, the chief prosecutor, a nineteen-year-old Red Guard, had been on top of the world, thousands listening as he interrogated Professor Gao. Now he was just another sniveling adolescent, his pimpled face hanging in disgrace. Now he was the accused.

"You stupid little twerp," screamed Cai Dongshi, a powerful man in his mid-fifties who frightened most people even at a distance. He held the arms of the boy's chair so that his face was just inches away. "Do you realize what you've done?"

"I thought he was just another professor" came back the weeping reply. "I didn't know he was *somebody*. Chairman Mao said—"

"Don't you tell me what Chairman Mao said. The Cultural Revolution Group controls China with the Chairman's blessing. We control everyone. Don't you understand, you idiot?" As Deputy Di-rector of the Party's Propaganda Department, China's ideological braintrust, Cai brandished his growing power.

The boy began to sob. "I don't understand. I don't understand anything."

"Well, understand this. You have just committed an inexcusable act. You have held a public trial without permission. And you have rendered a guilty verdict on someone of extraordinary importance to our country. And now the masses will demand punishment. We have a problem—"

The boy suddenly sat up in his chair and tried to smile confidently. "Don't worry," he said energetically, pushing his red armband back to its proper position. "I can fix it. We'll have another trial. And I'll find him innocent. It's easy. You watch. I'll just—"

The metal edge of a ruler caught the boy across his nose and cut through one eyelid, causing him to scream in pain and terror. Two guards held the boy pinned to the chair and stuck a rag in his mouth so that he couldn't scream anymore. He tried to look at Deputy Director Cai, blood streaming down his face.

"You won't do anything at all. The guards will make sure of that." Cai's neck was red with fury. "Take him away. He will have a life sentence without any chance for release. But just in case he tries to escape, I want him a cripple. Not the legs. Break the backbone."

The boy struggled with the guards for a moment. Then one held him firmly. The other put a knee in his back and snapped the shoulders back. It sounded like popcorn exploding.

Cai turned around sharply and walked to an adjacent room, pleased that the two waiting guests had heard the screams. "Welcome, my friend." Cai smiled pleasantly at Zhou Rong, Assistant Minister of Public Security, no stranger to violent methods of interrogation. "Sorry about the messy business. Little fools shouldn't get involved in politics. It's like fire and fingers. Yes?"

Zhou Rong laughed. "I thought it sounded more like a loser at mah-jongg." Youngsters often lost badly at mah-jongg, and the sound of the tiles clacking was not unlike that of a back breaking.

Zhou gestured toward the door where a foreigner stood, looking confused and uncomfortable. "It's my pleasure to present Daniel Lamarche."

Cai stared at the small man, who he already knew spoke fluent Chinese. The stranger was dressed in a striped black continental suit with a large red silk tie and matching breast-pocket handkerchief. Curly black hair wreathed his roundish face; his eyes darted around the room. It was difficult to place the ages of foreigners, Cai thought, but he guessed that Daniel Lamarche was in his forties. Cai enjoyed the fact that the fidgety Frenchman seemed uncertain whether to run from the violence or to stay in hope of a profitable deal.

"Welcome, Mr. Lamarche." Cai made Lamarche's decision for him, gesturing both men to seat themselves in blue upholstered chairs on either side of him. Cai began without preliminaries. "Assistant Minister Zhou has told me you might be helpful to us. That we might work out a certain deal?"

Lamarche's hands shook as he lit a cigarette, sucking in the smoke and trying to maintain composure. "I don't want to become involved in anything dangerous." Lamarche tilted his head toward the interrogation room. "You see, I'm a legitimate businessman."

"Of course," Cai laughed. "A legitimate businessman. You mean you're a capitalist hoping to suck a little blood from China. Forget pretending to be a sweet art dealer. We know the real truth about capitalists. Only the ruthless ones make a lot of money."

Lamarche tapped the ash off his cigarette and shot a nervous smile at Cai, acknowledging his point. Cai knew that the Frenchman, while trying to preserve his honest broker image, had occasionally relied on threats and blackmail to get his hands on important art collections. Lamarche preferred Hong Kong enforcers—experienced, tough, and inexpensive—to do his dirty work. "Okay, Mr. Cai," he said flatly, "I do want a deal. A deal with big potential for both of us. Mr. Zhou says you're looking for foreign capital."

"Quite true," Cai replied. "There's no harm in your knowing about it. We're sick of selling out China to the West. We want to preserve our uniqueness, our own roots. Of course, we must have certain elements of modernization. The problem is we can't afford foreign technology, particularly in military fields where we need it most. And we don't want to become wedded to foreign trade. We did that once with the Russians. The bastards left us standing in shit and took away the shovel."

Lamarche laughed, beginning to enjoy his assigned role of greedy capitalist conversing with needy communists. "The Russians are the biggest pricks in the world. If you can find art, fine Chinese traditional art, any genre, I'll give you the best price. I sell to the biggest collectors in the Western world. They covet Asian art these days. Then, as they get older, they all want the ultimate prize: to give their collections to New York's Metropolitan Museum. It's aesthetic immortality. Everyone involved makes a fortune to permit a few to achieve cultural sainthood. Yes, Mr. Cai, I'm the Pope of Asian art."

Cai pondered for a moment. "We have wondered whether art might be a source of foreign capital—without foreign trade."

"Think about it, Dongshi," Zhou Rong said quietly, putting his hand on Cai's arm. "It *is* the answer. The bastards in Taiwan stole the Palace Museum. Someday we're going to take that back, so we don't have to keep other treasures. We can sell them and make a fortune. Modernization without contamination. Screw the sell-outs like Zhou Enlai."

Deputy Director Cai squeezed his hands together and blew air through his palms. Zhou smiled. It was a good sign: Cai's signal that he was thinking carefully about a proposition. Cai knew about Lamarche's soaring success story as a dealer in Asian art; he had made a fortune by staying in China during late 1949 and early 1950, roaming from Shanghai to Guangzhou, buying collections from once-rich refugees willing to sell anything to escape the Communists. A total outlay of less than fifty thousand dollars, borrowed from bankers in New York and Paris, had yielded hundreds of times that amount when the art was marketed in Western auction houses during the 1950s and early 1960s. The Cultural Revolution was bound to be another bonanza—"decadent art" from private collections was already piling up in warehouses outside Beijing. The Gao Collection, ever since he'd heard of its possible existence on his first trip to China after World War II, was Lamarche's Holy Grail, the Eldorado of Chinese culture. "A pompous little fellow, but he'll deliver" was Zhou's verdict on Lamarche.

"Tell me, Mr. Lamarche," Cai asked. "What does good Chinese art bring on the market these days?"

"It depends on the quality of the object. But it's safe to say that Chinese art is beginning to soar in value. Major landscape paintings are already fetching over a hundred thousand in American currency."

Cai looked at Zhou Rong. "It would take a lot of landscape paintings to make much money that way. Besides, where do we find such treasures?"

Zhou lit another cigarette. "We've already begun scouring old homes for good antiques and artwork. And, of course, we can sell what's left of the Palace Museum."

"And what will all that add up to?" Cai asked.

Zhou Rung gestured to the Frenchman. "Mr. Cai," Lamarche replied earnestly, "all of that may be worth a few hundred million. I would have to see it in person."

"A few hundred million is not exactly what I had in mind. We need to be talking about billions."

"That's where the little episode with Professor Gao might be useful," Zhou intervened with a thin smile. "Tell him, Mr. Lamarche, what you told me."

Lamarche cleared his throat. "Gentlemen, I've been researching the Gao family art collection for the past several years. In my opinion it was China's greatest private collection. Not the Palace Museum, it's true, but perhaps forty percent of the Palace Museum. And all first-rate quality. What arrogance! The Gaos were clearly doing the unthinkable. Rivaling the Qing dynasty emperors as collectors."

"And how much would that be worth?" Cai asked.

"Between half a billion and a billion dollars at *today's* market prices, which are going up about twenty percent a year. Of course, it might take a series of auctions and a year or two for the market to absorb such riches."

Cai beckoned to Zhou and whispered in his ear so Lamarche couldn't hear. "Can we get our hands on the Gao Collection? Can you make up for what that idiot Red Guard did today?"

"Maybe the kid wasn't as stupid as we thought," Zhou whispered back confidently. "I think all we need is another interrogator, perhaps a Red Guard who just happens to be with the Ministry of Public Security. Then maybe we can get the Gao lacquer box. That is crucial. It holds the clue to the art collection."

"But is there really a box?" Cai wondered. "Does Gao really know? Why not just torture him?"

"It's not so simple," Zhou answered. "He comes from a tough family. They don't succumb to torture. But maybe we can prompt him to consider a deal—his life, his family, his property in return for the box."

"And then we can get the art?" Cai asked.

Zhou shrugged his shoulders, turned back toward Lamarche, speaking out loud again. "Who knows if the Gao Collection is still intact? It's a long shot, but I think it's worth a try. Right, Mr. Lamarche?"

"All I know is that the box is supposed to unlock the art. You find the art and I'll sell it. Fifteen percent commission. A fantastic deal for all of us."

Cai looked carefully at both men. He blew air through his hands once again. Zhou Rong watched carefully for his next move. Cai picked up a clear glass ashtray, held it in his hands for a moment, and then slammed it down on the table. Lamarche looked startled, but Zhou smiled confidently. It was Cai Dongshi's signal that a deal had been struck.

The crowds milled outside the Gao mansion all afternoon, waiting for the news. Two Red Guards stationed themselves high on the spirit wall so that they could lead cheers with a megaphone. "RICH CAPITALIST ROADER." "FEUDAL OVERLORD." "WESTERN COMPRADOR." "LOVER OF THE FOUR OLDS." "GUILTY! GUILTY! GUILTY!"

Other guards, undercover policemen from Internal Security, screened every entrance to the mansion and surrounded the Ancestral Hall. Seated behind the altar table was a slender man in his early thirties wearing a trim gray suit, expensive eyeglasses, and two silver pens in his pocket; his Red Guard armband fooled no one.

Gao Jinru sat opposite the prosecutor. His beaten body had been cleaned and bandaged; his wife had brushed his hair and dressed him in fresh clothing. To Jinru's left sat a beefy guard; to his right his wife, stoically holding back her tears. The Gaos' five-year-old daughter sat between her mother and the third Lao Wu, now in his mid-forties; the little girl seemed mesmerized by the yellow duck appliqued on her overalls.

"Professor Gao," the interrogator opened the proceedings quietly. "As you know, you have been judged guilty of conspiracy. Our duty here is to pass a sentence. Is there anything you would like to say before we do so?"

"I can only repeat that the so-called trial was conducted illegally and without any semblance of procedure. I haven't heard the charges. I haven't faced my accusers. I haven't had the benefit of counsel. I haven't been able to call witnesses. This whole thing is a farce."

The gray-suited man remained placid. "You have a point, Professor, but we have a problem. Hundreds of people outside think you're guilty. They want to know how we will punish you."

"How the people feel is not the question. What's fair *is* the question."

"I'm afraid you're wrong, Professor. It's too late for questions of fairness. Now, wouldn't you like to find a way out of your dilemma? You have something we want. You hand it over and we will strike an appropriate deal with you."

Jinru was genuinely perplexed. "What is it?" he asked.

"Surely you know."

"Frankly I don't."

"It's the art. The Gao Collection. You give us that and we'll strike a deal. Where's it hidden?"

Jinru thought for a moment. He was forty now and "without doubts." He could take his inheritance and hand it over. "Frankly, I have no idea about where the collection might be hidden."

"What about the lacquer box?"

Jinru thought again. He could give it to them, but only for the right deal, a Gao deal. "First, tell me your terms."

"You give us the box and we'll provide freedom. For you, your family, and your retinue."

"That's not good enough. You know that box is worth a lot more than freedom for an academic." Gao stared at his interrogator and made a quick calculation. The professor finally had some leverage. It was his only chance. Professor Gao's voice grew stronger. "I'll tell you exactly what it's worth. First, I want total immunity for me and my family." He ticked off his terms on his fingers. "Second, the Gao mansion will remain untouched and in my family's possession. Third, I will have the right to select a hundred works of art which will be exhibited here at the mansion for the people of China to see. Fourth, I will continue to teach at Beijing University. Fifth, Beida itself will remain protected from the Cultural Revolution. I will serve as Vice-Chancellor of Beida with the total right to develop its curriculum, its faculty, and its student body. And there's one final condition . . ."

The prosecutor finally lost patience. "Stop! What do you think you're doing? You're the accused. I've got to make a telephone call."

He walked to the corner, dialed a number, and spoke quietly into the receiver. After a moment he returned to his chair, leaving the phone off the hook. "Your five conditions are accepted. Without qualification. And what is the final condition?"

"There will be a press conference with all the foreign journalists present to announce officially my new roles. There will be another such press conference every month for a progress report. If the conference does not take place, a press release will be issued outside of China. It will explain that your people have sold Chinese cultural treasures for personal gain. The whole world will know what your bosses are doing."

The man returned to the phone. The screaming voice on the other end carried across the Ancestral Hall. "The fucking bastard. We've got to accept."

Gao turned slowly toward Lao Wu and nodded. The time had come to receive his inheritance. But Lao Wu sat motionless. Gao Jinru's voice became sharp. "Lao Wu, come on. Get the package." The servant still didn't move. "I mean it! It's an order! It's my due! Now!"

Lao Wu stood up unsteadily. "But, Professor Gao, it's not what—"

Jinru was no longer a man speaking to a friend; he was a mandarin screaming at a servant. "Get it now!"

After leading the procession to the base of the Pinnacle, Lao Wu climbed a short way up the path to a ledge just under a small pine tree. Removing a small black stone from the face of the mountain, he twisted a lever beneath; a stone door opened below him, revealing a cave. Wu guided the group inside, lighting two kerosene lamps on the walls. They watched as he felt his way down a damp wall, touched an area with his fingertips, gently dislodged a stone, and pulled out a burlap-covered package.

Gao Jinru grabbed the package and walked swiftly into the sunlight. Left in the damp for seventeen years, the wire had almost rusted away; it was easy to pull off the remainder by hand.

His hands shook as he removed the burlap and opened the drawstrings. His eyes opened wide in horror. It wasn't lacquer. It was a tao binder. His head dropped over the package, concealing it for a moment longer. Then he started to shake with hysterical laughter. The unfilial son had received the ultimate punishment.

"Where's the box?" the prosecutor asked sternly.

"I don't know," Jinru said quietly. He looked in desperation at Lao Wu; the servant shook his head, bound by the same oath as his father. Jinru turned to the prosecutor. "I really don't know."

The prosecutor picked up the books and walked to the front gate of the Gao Mansion. The guards pushed Gao Jinru and his wife out into the street where onlookers drew closer in anticipation.

The prosecutor shouted. "HERE IS PROFESSOR GAO'S CONFESSION.

HE CHERISHES THE FOUR OLDS. WHAT BETTER PROOF THAN HIS MOST PRECIOUS TREASURE—THE FOUR BOOKS. DO YOU WANT TO KNOW HIS SENTENCE?" The crowd hushed to hear the prosecutor's voice. "THE SENTENCE IS XIAFANG FOR BOTH PROFESSOR GAO AND HIS WIFE. DOWN TO THE COUNTRYSIDE. THE MANDARIN AND HIS CONCUBINE WILL SIT IN SHIT."

There were loud cheers as Gao and his wife were shoved back to the mule cart where dunce hats were placed on their heads and signs hung around their necks. The crowd threw curses and dung at the couple as the cart rumbled down the road.

People started to drift away. "DON'T LEAVE SO SOON. IT'S NOT OVER YET." Was there more? They ran back. "THERE'S ONE MORE CASE HERE."

The guards pushed Lao Wu out into the street. "HE'S PART OF THE CONSPIRACY TOO. BUT WE'LL GIVE HIM A CHANCE." Turning to Lao Wu, the prosecutor continued, "RENOUNCE YOUR TIES TO THE GAO FAMILY. RENOUNCE THEM AND YOU'RE FREE. FAIL TO DO SO AND WE MUST ADMINISTER PUNISHMENT."

Lao Wu gathered all of his courage and that of his ancestors. "I will not renounce the Gaos," he said proudly. "Your verdict was wrong. They are loyal Communists."

"JUST AS WE THOUGHT. YOU'RE GUILTY TOO. THE PEOPLE WILL DECIDE HIS FATE."

"Death," screamed a voice. Others joined in. "Death! Death! Death!" It had been a frustrating day—many trials, several convictions, but not a single execution.

"DEATH IT IS! LET THE PEOPLE CARRY OUT THE SENTENCE!"

Lao Wu realized his mistake just before the crowd closed over him. "Don't kill me. Don't kill me. I'm the only one who really knows where—"

The crowd surged. He tried to crawl, but then the kicks began and the shouts drowned out his screams. Lao Wu writhed on the ground, searching in vain for a gap in the wall of kicking legs. Finally broken bones cut through his organs and drained away his life.

As the sun set on the Gao Mansion and the remains of Lao Wu lay in the street, a small figure huddled next to the female guardian lion. She sucked her thumb and stared at the yellow duck on her blue overalls.

CHAPTER SEVEN

ALLEGORY

NEW YORK CITY, LATE 1980s.

ROGER HAD JUST DECIDED IT WAS
crazy to be jumpy about an old lady with a baby carriage when he was startled by the sudden loud ring of the telephone.

"Roger. It's Becky here. I don't know if you've really got any interest in your lacquer box, but I think I'm on to something." Of course, the ploy was shameless, but Becky rationalized that she really had acquired some unusual insights.

"Give me your number, Becky; I'll get back to you if I can switch an appointment," Roger replied. Although Roger hadn't had an appointment in weeks, he didn't want to make it sound as if he were eager for a personal relationship. He whiled away half an hour drawing doodles around Becky's telephone number.

"Oh, Becky," he said casually. "I was able to shift things around. Okay, I'll bring it." With renewed excitement, he wrapped the box and locked his apartment carefully. Closing his eyes in the cab in anticipation of a promising encounter, Roger was oblivious to the blue stretch limousine that followed his taxi, waited for him to enter Becky's building, and then quickly pulled away.

The bookcases in Becky's study were covered with blown-up color photographs of the box. The object itself, on Becky's desk,

90

looked as if it were being prepped for major surgery, surrounded by X-rays for the surgeons.

Roger laughed at the photographs. "Becky, you're incredible! Did you take a sabbatical from that stuffy law firm?"

She grinned back, putting her hands to her cheeks in feigned shock, well aware that the gesture drew Roger's eyes to the gentle bounce of her breasts under her cashmere sweater. "Don't tell Marsh. That box of yours is a demon. I even called in sick two days. But I'm afraid I've raised more questions than answers. Remember how I told you the inscribed date is late Ming—"

Roger couldn't resist. "Yes. Ming Wan-li reign, if I remember correctly. Wasn't he the fourteenth emperor, 1573–1620? Now some scholars have focused only on the chaos at court. But Professor DeBary of Columbia has a different view—"

"Roger. What the hell have you been doing?" Oh, this is going to be fun, Becky told herself, hoping that Roger might have done what she had—a lot of research, but with an ulterior motive.

Becky listened attentively as Roger repeated the whole story, except for the part about the old woman. Excusing herself for a moment, she returned with a pot of almond tea. As they sipped from small Japanese cups, her face took on a motherly look. "I don't want to insult you, but Roger, you're a classic Western scholar. You want everything in neat little boxes, and you want it too fast. Slow down a bit.

"Let me tell you a Chinese story," Becky continued, hoping Roger wouldn't mind the mothering too much. "Many years ago I had a Chinese-American art history professor, an unusual guy, I thought he was a bit wacky at first. He said, 'There are three things you must learn. First, you must pick the thousand most important works of Asian art, and you've got only a semester to do it. Second,' he said, 'never read texts, only read footnotes. Third,' he said, 'know that all knowledge is a pyramid standing on its head.' "

"Isn't the professional term inscrutable?"

"Maybe so," Becky replied. "But just think about his three points for a second. A thousand objects—just a metaphor, a way to make us organize a lot of information in a short period of time. Footnotes—you've got to understand where someone gets his ideas before judging his arguments. And the pyramid—that's the most important one of all. You've got to get excited about something specific, something that turns you on, before you can see the bigger picture. And he said one more thing: 'Never read textbooks, instead seek to write your own.' "

Roger folded his hands in mandarin fashion and bowed to Becky. "Okay. Not so inscrutable after all. I can see your old professor now." Standing up, still with hands folded, he played the role of the Chinese professor lecturing the chair he had just vacated. "My son. If you're interested in a lacquer box, don't begin by trying to scan all of Chinese history. Instead let the box guide you. If it sings, study music. If it lights your eyes, study calligraphy. If it stimulates emotions, study poetry. That, my son, is the wisdom of the East."

Becky smiled, then became serious. "He was right, you know. People aren't robots. Somehow that's a lesson that the Chinese missed. Memorization was the tradition of the old civil-service exams. Today as well—in both Taiwan and Mainland China—it's still rote learning."

Becky walked to the photographs thumbtacked to the bookcases. "Okay, Roger, ready for some serious detective work? Let me share a bit of my ignorance with you."

"Ignorance?"

"Ignorance *is* the right term. I've assembled the wisdom of the world on Chinese lacquer. Everything sheds new light on your box, but it's like trying to see details in a landscape painting. The closer you get, the more you see individual brush strokes, and the less you see the total picture."

"Now here"—Becky flipped through an art catalog—" is something that might interest you." Roger leaned over the table and looked at a photograph of a magnificent lacquer dish. The three colors—predominantly red, but with details in black and yellow— matched his lacquer box perfectly. The border consisted of red flowers and birds against a black background. In the center a dragon and a phoenix circled each other as if preparing for battle.

"That's it exactly!" Roger said excitedly. "Same style. Same colors. Where did you find it?"

"It's a recently published book on Chinese lacquers. Probably not in the Columbia Library yet, otherwise you would have come across it yourself. The dish is in the British Museum. It's dated 1593, right smack in the middle of the Wan-li reign."

"Fantastic!" Roger beamed. "Now we know it's genuine."

"Not so fast. All we know is that the *style* is genuine. But we don't know anything more."

"Oh, come on, Becky. You're letting the lawyer in you take too much control."

"I've got my reasons to be skeptical," Becky replied, tapping the box gently with her finger. "Now let's turn to the box. You talked about its music? Okay," she coaxed him, "try it again, don't be bashful, where did you start?" She took his right hand, opening his index finger, gently moving it to the box.

Roger, feeling more than a little self-conscious, put his finger on the large character on top.

"Right," Becky said emphatically, "it's the first message. That's *wang*. It means hope or dream in the Western sense. Could be a noun or verb, even an adjective or adverb. It can also mean expect, or gaze, or to face. Classical Chinese had a lot of meanings, great for poetry, but it drives beginning students up the wall."

Roger looked up, his finger still riveted to the character. "But what does it mean?"

"We can't tell till we probe further." Becky finally lifted her hand from his, but not until she had squeezed the tip of his finger, pretending she was emphasizing a point.

"What about this dragon?" Roger asked, ignoring her gesture while running his fingers along the borders on the top.

"Good question. Beautiful, isn't it? Look closely. See how it once probably had five claws? That's the symbol of the emperor. Note that now there are only four—one claw is missing from each foot. It might be an effort to conceal a theft from the Imperial Collection. Or maybe, just a guess, a criticism of the court intentionally made by the artist or his patron. Weak court symbolized by weak dragon."

"It's such a small detail," Roger said. "Are you sure it means anything? Who'd care how many claws on a dragon's foot?"

"You'd care if you were emperor. The artist might be saying that your predecessors were tough cookies and now your dragon is losing its power. Remember, everything around the emperor was prescribed—gestures, language, clothing, protocol, foods, colors, the works. One thing out of place and everyone knew about it. The way you might if someone jumbled the furniture in your apartment."

"Now Roger," Becky said, taking the box in her hands. "Before we go any further, I've got to ask you a question. This is going to take some time. We can only begin today. Do you really want to get into it? I mean, really get into understanding this box?"

"Yes, I do," he replied softly, staring at the box. "I'll be honest. I hope it's worth a lot—I sure need the money. But it's also fascinating, an interesting project for both of us." As soon as he looked at her face, sparkling with eagerness, Roger knew he had given the wrong signal. He coughed to break the mood and shot his eyes back to the box.

Becky raised her eyebrows, then let it pass. "Okay, let's get started. We're going to have to look for incredibly small details." She took the box and rotated it slowly to cast light on the various scenes.

"That's just the way I turned it," Roger said, feeling a twinge of guilt as he noted her fingers were slender and expressive, just like Diane's.

"Just what you're supposed to do. You see, the four sides of this box are like a handscroll. It's an early version of the motion picture. It begins on the front right and moves clockwise around the box. Narrative, art, allegory, and music—all wrapped into one."

"So we're supposed to figure out the symbols like in a Bergman film?"

"Exactly, but easier said than done." Becky walked over to the photographs. "I'm still baffled, but let's give it a try. These blown-up photos give you pretty good detail. I've arranged them in the same order as the box."

Roger fitted his reading glasses and joined Becky, perusing photos of the front panel. The first vignette featured a mountain towering above a garden in which an older man stood talking to a younger one, perhaps a father lecturing to a son. The father was holding a box. Farther along was a set of interlocking boxes, one inside the other, with a ball in the smallest one. The last scene on the panel showed an old man lying on a bed with a younger man kneeling at its foot.

"I'll give you my hunch what it's about," Becky said. "I think the first figures, father and son with the box, is a message. Maybe he's telling him, and telling us, to study this with care. But the rest?"

"You're sure this isn't just a nice bunch of scenes about old China?"

Becky shook her head, inching toward Roger, enjoying the closeness of their bodies. "Chinese usually don't create this kind of detail without a purpose. Ideology and art are close bedfellows in China."

"Okay, so we can't figure out the specifics. But doesn't it look like there's a single theme for the first panel?"

"Which is?"

"Family," Roger said with rising confidence. "Most of the scenes deal with parents and children. Maybe an idealized version of the Confucian family?"

"Exactly. In fact, every side of the box seems to have a theme. Now look here at this next section." She pointed with the long red-lacquered nail of her little finger.

The setting changed on the second panel to small clusters of people against the background of a rocky meadow. A stream rushed across the lacquer, little waterfalls seeming to separate the panel into three scenes. A solitary scholar stood at the far right, looking confident in regal robes; one hand held a writing brush, the other pointed back toward the first panel. An ancient teacher with a thin beard lectured to a few students; he held a book open in one hand while pointing to his stomach with the other. The panel ended with another teacher standing on a rock; the carver's knife had brought out the sharp details in his face, leaving his mouth slightly open as if admonishing the students who were seated before him. The figure was holding up one hand, thumb and finger at right angles.

"Education?" Roger wondered.

"Right again. You're getting the themes."

"But what about the specifics?"

"Forget the details," Becky replied with a graceful wave of her hand. "What's the overall impression? It's rigorous, all-consuming education. Another side of Confucianism. It all seems linked by the stream and by that little fellow pointing back to panel one. Now could you let me have the box? The third panel is really interesting."

Roger picked up the box and started to hand it to Becky. His hand suddenly slipped. The box crashed to the hard wood floor. Roger and Becky froze. It bounced on one corner, flipped over and settled upside down. The sound of the box striking the floor was sickening enough, but it also made another strange noise as it hit, something between a crack and a click.

"God, I hope it's not broken," Roger exclaimed, kneeling on the floor and grabbing the box tightly between sweating palms.

Becky took the box gingerly and examined it carefully. "You're really lucky. Just a tiny nick here on the edge. I could have sworn I heard it splitting apart. Probably just the sound of my heart."

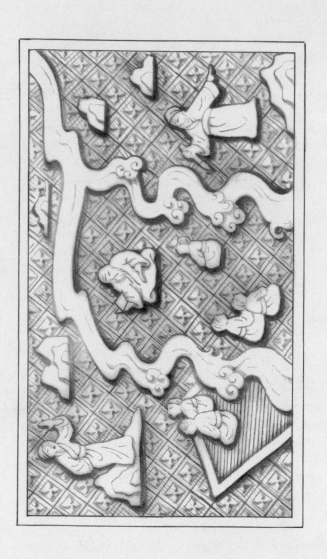
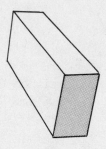

Something on the floor caught Becky's eye. "Roger, look. See the tiny hole in the varnish? And this white powder? What's that?"

"I don't have the slightest idea. Maybe the box nicked the varnish. Couldn't the powder be some kind of filler used in the corners of the box?"

"Maybe, but it's odd that the box would make a clean little hole, almost like a needle instead of a dent."

Roger took the box from Becky and examined it for himself. "It shows how tough lacquer really is."

"We clearly need a break," Becky said firmly; "besides, it's time for lunch."

Roger browsed through her library, wondering why Western bookbinders had spent so much time on leather covers with bindings of stitchwork and glue. Taking down a set of books, he marveled at the simple ivory pins; then he opened one of the paperbound booklets inside. He gulped as he saw the pictures—pornographic woodcuts, frequently involving threesomes in improbable sexual contortions. One woman was having sex in a tree-suspended swing, being rocked by another nude woman, while the man remained motionless in front of her, his organ inside her, his hands fondling her stocking-covered bound feet. Roger was so absorbed he didn't hear Becky's footsteps.

"I'll bet you're not reading that for its subtle allegories."

"Caught in the act." Roger smiled sheepishly, returning the book to its binder and putting it back on the shelf.

"It's the *Roupu tuan*, the Prayer Mat of Flesh, a classic of pornography. It's the other side of the Confucian prudish tradition."

Roger tried not to show his embarrassment, but Becky was enjoying it. "I'll bet you thought all of those positions were impossible. Didn't you?"

Roger colored. "I guess so. Unless it was Houdini's sex life."

"Hardly," she giggled, "some are just difficult. Practice makes perfect—as we lawyers say."

Roger needed to regroup. He picked up the box, turning it to expose the back panel, rocking it slightly so that the light would catch the carving. "This side is so different from the rest. A lot of it is empty, just flat layers of red and yellow lacquer. Four small scenes out in empty space."

"Back to school?" Becky smiled archly. "Okay, think about what you just said, and about what you've read in Chinese philosophy. What's the box trying to say?"

"Maybe it's Taoism?" Roger wondered, grateful that Becky was not pushing things too quickly.

"Good for you!" she exclaimed. "It's almost entirely Taoism. A neat contrast to the Confucianism we saw earlier. This panel deals with the self and the eternal, the others with the self in society."

"I like that a lot," Roger said, looking at the photographs and then at Becky. "And Taoism—finding power by not trying to be powerful—I like that, too."

Becky tapped a pencil on a blow-up. "These are fascinating details. I can even figure out a couple of them. And one is going to tell you something you don't want to hear."

Roger was puzzled. "What don't I want to hear?"

"In good time. First, look at this one."

Becky pointed to a simply dressed man reclining at the side of the swirling river; a large turtle was swimming in the current, its head stretched above the water almost as if it were communicating with the man. "That's Zhuangzi, one of the earliest Taoists," Becky said. "One day Zhuangzi was sitting by a river when he was approached by an emissary who asked him to serve as a high official in the court of a famous king. But Zhuangzi, good Taoist that he was, refused on the grounds that he'd prefer to stay with nature. He said, 'Wouldn't that turtle rather play in the river, rather than be a dead turtle in a pretty box?' Actually there was a tradition in those days of using dried turtle bones to divine the future."

"I know how Zhuangzi felt," Roger mused, "and sometimes how the dead turtles felt." Then he looked at the other photographs of the third panel: a strong man swinging an ax against some object on a table, and an elderly man admiring his cinnabar-colored bird in a cage.

Becky shook her head. "I don't get either of those." Then she tapped the next photograph with her pencil. "But this one I *do* understand." Roger focused on a young child, clothed in red, sitting on his mother's lap. The mother, dressed in soft yellow robes, caressed her child's head; the child had a tiny yellow object in his slightly open mouth.

"Roger, this is a real gem. The child is Baoyu, hero of China's greatest novel, *Dream of the Red Chamber*, written in the eighteenth century. Baoyu was born with special powers, signified by the jade stone on his tongue. Baoyu lived in a world of women—that's what the red chamber means—a world of pressures, conflicts, temptations.

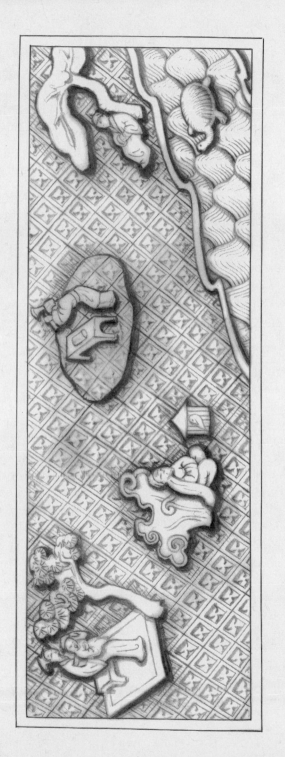

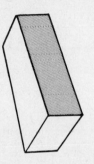

He had to decide between being alive and in constant torment—or escaping to another world, literally becoming stone."

"So the Taoist side of the box focuses on the self. The other two sides on family and learning. And now we have the dream theme again. Isn't that right, Becky?" Roger smiled at his summation.

"You're missing something," she said coolly. "You're the historian. *When* did I say that the *Dream of the Red Chamber* was written?"

"In the eighteenth century."

"Think about it."

Roger's eyes opened wide. He looked at the photograph again and then back at the box. "Oh, my God. If it uses an eighteenth-century theme, then how could it be . . . ? It can't be a sixteenth-century box. Are you telling me the box is a forgery?"

Becky's lips tightened. "I'm afraid so. A complete forgery, a blatant forgery. I can't figure out why it's so obvious. Most forgeries are designed to make money. This little discovery will cost you thousands if you ever want to sell the box."

Roger picked up the box, somewhat more casually than before. "Worthless?"

"Not worthless, but not a Ming masterpiece either. Whoever commissioned the box apparently didn't care about its intrinsic value. Instead he seems to want to push us to think about the late Ming period—a time of corruption and of creativity. I don't know—"

Roger put the box back on the desk, looking betrayed. "Well, it's been fun, Becky. Sorry you had to waste so much time on this. Damn, it's the ultimate disinheritance—teasing someone with money." Roger tried to hide his anger, but his teeth were clenched.

"I know you're disappointed, Roger," Becky said, hoping the revelation wouldn't end their relationship. "But I don't think you should give up so soon. What's fascinating is the quality of the forgery. It's a *perfect* fake. To a knowledgeable Chinese, it would be a *perfectly obvious* fake. Sometime, probably in the very late Qing, a skilled craftsman produced this work of genius, and the person who commissioned it was trying to tell us something. And that's—"

The phone on the desk rang.

"Dammit," exclaimed Becky, "we were just getting to the good part." She picked up the receiver. "Yes, Roger Walden's here. How did you get this number?" Becky looked startled. "It's the police. From your apartment. They found my number on your desk."

Roger took the phone. He listened for a moment. Then his face paled. "When? Did they take anything? I'll be there as fast as I can." Replacing the receiver, he turned to Becky. "Someone's broken into my apartment. I don't believe it. I've got to go."

"I'll go with you," Becky said firmly, wrapping up the box.

CHAPTER EIGHT

GUANXI

ROGER'S APARTMENT WAS A SHAMBLES,

books scattered everywhere, every packing box dumped on the floor, mattresses and cushions slit apart. The police lieutenant shrugged his shoulders. "Professor, this is the strangest break-in I've seen in a long time. Your locks are good, but they were picked. The burglars were obviously looking for something in particular. What did they get? What's missing?"

Roger looked around. "I don't think they took anything except the portable TV. I don't have any jewelry or money. They didn't even take my camera or the stereo. What the hell were they after? Who could have done this?"

The lieutenant shook his head. "The only stranger anyone saw in the building was an elderly lady. The people downstairs said they figured she was somebody's grandmother. She isn't in the building now."

"Are you telling me some old lady did this, ripped the place apart and ran off with a TV? Without being seen? Come on, that's fantasyland."

The lieutenant stiffened. "Professor Walden, I'm not saying anything except it certainly doesn't look like your usual petty thieves." The lieutenant gestured around the room. "But this isn't exactly a high-rent district. You can never tell who might have done it."

* * *

"Don't you have any idea at all?" Becky asked when they were alone.

"I do, but it's too farfetched to tell the cops. You're going to think I'm crazy." He told her about the old woman with the carriage.

"I don't think it's that crazy," Becky said. "Maybe she spies on apartments, setting up others for the job. You ought to tell the police." Glancing around the apartment, Becky decided it had probably been a mess even before the burglary. His running trophies looked like silver corpses floating in a sea of books. Diane, Becky guessed, had been Roger's source of emotional balance and organization. What a pathetic existence, she thought; no security, no style, no nothing.

"But even if you're right, why risk yourself for a cheap television set?" he asked. "Why not take something else?" He followed Becky's eyes around his apartment, embarrassed at how he lived, nervous that he'd allowed someone else inside.

He walked to the desk to check his insurance policy. Suddenly he tore open the desk drawers. "I don't believe it!" he shouted. "You know what else they took? My notes! All the cards, the Xeroxes, the library books—all my research on the box."

"Are you sure? It doesn't make any sense."

"Of course I'm sure. And that's insane."

"Call the lieutenant."

"What for? I can't claim any insurance on my notes. Besides, what would the lieutenant do? Look for a criminal who's an expert on the Ming dynasty?"

Becky didn't laugh. "You know, Roger, there's a legal maxim: Always consider the obvious. One obvious possibility is that someone wants your box."

"Of course it's a possibility, but it's not enough to call the police about. They'd think I'm bonkers."

"At least let me help clean up," Becky said, shaking her head at his stubbornness, but recognizing the futility of arguing. "And then, if you still have enough energy, we'll finish looking at the box. How about a pizza?"

* * *

They huddled together over the desk, Becky standing behind Roger as she moved the magnifying glass back and forth. It wasn't the most comfortable position, but she didn't want to alter it.

"I was about to tell you something back at my apartment," Becky said, "before your robbery. Your box might be more valuable than you think. I've got a hunch that it has a code on it."

"A code? What do you mean?"

"Bear with me. Take a look."

They stared through the magnifying glass at the fourth panel; filled with buildings and figures, it was totally unlike the previous Taoist section. It began with two officials standing in front of the emperor on his throne. One official wore a robe with flowing sleeves and full skirts, his head covered with a cylindrical cap; the other wore a hip-length coat with hoof-shaped sleeves and a hat shaped like a cone. Kneeling below them was a single figure dressed in simpler scholarly robes. In one hand he held a large calligraphy brush, in the other a microscope.

Roger looked at Becky. "Can you figure it out?"

She shook her head; her blond hair fell behind her shoulder, exposing her graceful neck. "The imperial-audience scene is beyond me. But maybe the microscope tells us something, maybe that we should look hard at the calligraphy, use a microscopic approach to the brush. Anyway, the microscope wasn't common in China until the nineteenth century, which is further proof of the forgery. But what does it really—"

They both started at the sound of the doorbell. Roger peered through the peephole. "We're both spooked," he laughed. It was the pizza delivery boy.

"I can't begin to understand this one," said Becky, pointing to another palace scene on the last panel. This time the official stood on the edge of the throne, pointing to the emperor with one hand and gesturing above his head with the other.

Roger shrugged. He wiped his hands with a napkin and pointed at a corner of the box. "How about this poor little fellow? Seems all alone." The figure's arms were outstretched; he wore a cinnabar robe and an odd black hat. Putting his hand over Becky's, Roger tilted the magnifying glass. "Looks like in one hand he's holding a box. And in the other a yellow jewel, like the one Baoyu had earlier."

Becky took a big bite of her pizza and pinched off the thread of mozzarella that hung between her lip and the slice. "Thazimpordand."

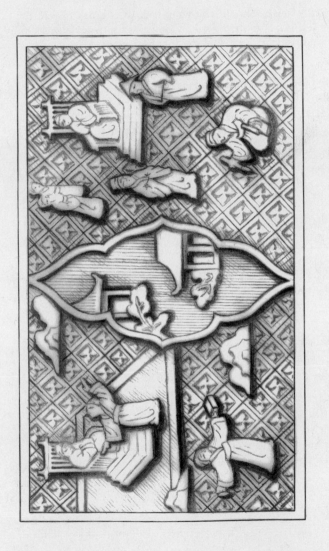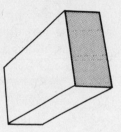

"What?"

"That's important," she laughed, swallowing her mouthful. "It's Confucius again. Terrific passage. I've even memorized it:

If you had a lovely jewel, should you wrap it up in a box to keep it? Or should you sell it for the best price? Confucius replied: Sell it! Of course, you should sell it! I am looking for the best price!

"Do you get it?" she asked Roger, a devilish smile on her face.

"Not really," he replied, shaking his head. "But then again, I haven't had two weeks to think about it."

"Don't be so damned proud," she said tartly, softening it with a smile. "Maybe we lawyer types might just be faster at this kind of thing. It's a Confucian admonition to fine scholars. One should serve in public office—sell one's jewels—rather than stay out of politics. Just the opposite of our Taoist friend, Zhuangzi. But poor Confucius was a frustrated office-seeker. That explains his last comment. He was always looking for a job. A classic case of 'those who can't, teach.' "

Roger stuck out his tongue at the insult to the teaching profession. "Okay, so you figured out the passage. But what's the message?"

"I just wouldn't know," she said, smiling wide-eyed at Roger, trying to create a playful atmosphere. "You tell me, Teach. It's so exciting to watch a fine mind at work."

Sensing things were becoming too personal, Roger turned his chair back to the desk and slowly rotated the box. "Okay, we shall see how superior intellect responds to superior income." He was having a hard time concentrating with Becky's face so near to his. "We know that the jewel in the passage is not the box itself."

"And how do we know that?" replied Becky. "Do tell us."

"Because the story says that," he said, putting the box back on the desk. His palms were beginning to sweat. "It says don't put a jewel in a box. So maybe there's a jewel—literal or figurative—outside the box."

"Now we're on the same wavelength." Becky nodded. "That's what I meant. I think the box is a clue to something else. A code."

"Maybe we're pushing too hard. Maybe it's all just philosophy and metaphors. Maybe we're just getting an exaggerated view of its importance. Maybe . . ."

"Maybe what?" Becky shook her blond hair flirtatiously.

Roger looked into her soft green eyes, her mouth moist with a ready-to-be-kissed look. "Becky," he said quietly, "you are a very attractive woman. Part of me wants to take you in my arms . . ."

"Who's stopping you?" she interrupted.

"I'm stopping me," he continued, grasping her hands with firm gentleness. "No," he hesitated, "Diane's stopping me. It's only been a few months. I can't consider another relationship. Not for a while at least." Inwardly Roger knew it was a half-truth at best. As he looked into Becky's eyes, what he'd guessed earlier now became a certainty. Underneath the eager veneer, he saw a restrained, calculating woman. He sensed that Becky's inner self would remain forever locked, encased in cold stainless steel, never giving the key to anyone else. Without being able to articulate it, and having only partially experienced it with Diane, Roger envisioned much-deeper depths of romantic and emotional experience. Becky was not the partner he sought.

"I respect your feelings," Becky said, inhaling softly to restrain frustration. "You're passing up what would have been a great evening. Well, what about sometime later? Perhaps?"

"Perhaps."

"Oh well," Becky said, pulling herself erect. "I hope you're not giving up on the lacquer box. We were really getting someplace. I think the beautiful calligraphy on the bottom may be the key."

"Can you read it?" Roger asked hopefully, relieved at the return to a businesslike mood.

"No. Sorry. It's grass script. Only an expert could tell us. I know someone. Christina Chang. She lives in Chinatown. I take a course with her every week." Roger heard the tentativeness in her voice.

"What's the matter? Do you doubt her honesty?"

"No. Certainly not that. I think she's very trustworthy."

"What then?"

"It's her looks."

"What?"

"She's very attractive. And very talented." Becky stopped herself. "God, I'm sounding awfully possessive. And a little paranoid, aren't I?"

"A little," Roger replied with a tentative smile. "The feelings are appreciated. Anyone would be paranoid after the day we've had." He gave her a quick peck on the cheek as she left his apartment, repressing a surge of desire as he watched her cab draw away. Roger nodded to himself—he'd made the right decision.

CHAPTER NINE

CALLIGRAPHY

ROGER AND BECKY PAUSED OUTSIDE the Canal Street subway station. Pulling up his topcoat collar and clasping his arms tightly around the white plastic shopping bag containing the lacquer box, Roger exclaimed, "I'll bet it's been twenty-five years since I was here." The density of the experience was overwhelming—thousands of people clogging streets and shops, vertical neon lights pulsating with Chinese characters, strange smells softening the icy air. The sidewalk crowds were predominantly Chinese—black-clad old women with net bags holding vegetables, fish, and poultry; men standing in the shadows, chatting and smoking; teenagers sporting jeans and parkas.

Roger and Becky moved briskly down Canal Street, crossing Baxter and Mulberry, turning right into Mott Street, the center of old Chinatown. They wriggled through a large tourist group gaping at the window of a Chinese drugstore. A florid-faced man swept the scene with his videotape camera while his wife held the microphone toward a shouting Caucasian guide. "Gotta backache? How about some nice little acupuncture needles in the spine? Headache? Nice little potion of fungus and cinnamon! Constipated? Try some wolf's milk and burdock roots! Drowning? Burn some wormwood on your navel! And for you old guys having trouble in bed, don't miss a nice ginseng root cocktail, it'll work wonders on your cocktail! Okay, folks, stay with me. Haven't ya heard about tong wars and cleavers?"

Becky, murmuring about where she'd like to put an acupuncture needle, tugged Roger away. They walked down a darker, almost empty side street and up the steps of an apartment house. "You'll find this more interesting than tourist Chinatown."

At the top of a dimly lit staircase, Becky and Roger entered a hallway unfurnished except for a Chinese scroll hanging over a table. The hallway opened onto a small living room where a woman was speaking quietly to a dozen or so Caucasians, each seated in front of a small folding table, holding a calligraphy brush and writing Chinese characters.

Standing outside the living room, Roger could hear but not see the teacher. "Remember now, clean, controlled, and balanced. Every stroke must have the four qualities. Bone—it must have strength. Flesh—it must have the right thickness. Muscle—give it some life. Blood—be sure your ink is right."

Roger glimpsed Christina Chang as she helped a young woman manipulate her brush. The teacher, wearing a blue smock over her slacks, was a small Chinese woman, just over five feet tall, with delicate features and strikingly smooth skin. Her black hair flowed down her neck and a few wisps fell across her forehead. Roger stood still and stared, little charges of electricity running through him as if seeing an inspired sculpture the first time, entranced by her form and sensing a depth of spirit.

"I told you so," Becky whispered, already regretting her suggestion to bring Roger to Chinatown. Roger slapped her hand as if to say "Come now, she's pretty, but you're overreacting." Becky tossed her head and gave a little you-know-that's-bullshit look.

Miss Chang moved to the other side of the room and smiled as she glimpsed Becky. Then she addressed her class. "I know it's only been a few months, but it's not too early to think about composition. We'll continue to work on *yong* until you get a better sense of its overall form. It has six basic strokes, it demands a sense of balance. Maybe we keep working on *yong* because it means 'eternity.' If some of you don't practice more at home, that's how long it'll take to perfect it."

Gathering her laughing students around her, Miss Chang spoke with the lilt of a devoted teacher. "Let me leave you with a little four-character phrase. You can work on it this week." She sat at one of the small tables and took the brush of the student who had been working there. Straightening out the brush hairs, she dipped the tip in the ink and rolled it slightly. Then, holding the brush perfectly

115

perpendicular to the paper, she gave them a gentle reminder. "Let's not forget good posture in our bodies and the proper positions of our hands. When it becomes second nature, the characters can flow through you." With a dancer's grace, she moved the brush rhythmically, keeping her body almost still. Four characters emerged on the paper, each with a balanced liveliness, each seeming to respond to the presence of the others. Her students watched reverently.

Miss Chang put down the brush next to the inkstand and held up the paper. "It says eternal studying produced eternal knowledge. Gives you a chance for two *yongs* in one phrase. That's enough for today. Now clean up and I'll see you next week."

Miss Chang stood up and crumpled the paper. The students gave a collective sigh of anguish. "Miss Chang, why do you always wreck your calligraphy?" an older woman asked. "I'd love to take it home."

"I didn't wreck it," she said, shaking her head. "The joy of calligraphy is in the doing, not in the saving."

Walking to the doorway, Miss Chang greeted Becky. "Ah, my prize student. How are you, Miss An?"

"You embarrass me, Miss Chang," Becky said with a smile. "I think it's your flattery that keeps me trying. Let me introduce a new friend of mine, Professor Roger Walden."

Christina smiled politely as she shook Roger's hand, surprising him with the strength in her long, delicate fingers. "It's a pleasure, Miss Chang. And thanks for letting me watch your class."

"Not at all. Always glad to have more potential converts. Are you a China expert like Miss An?"

Becky touched Roger slightly on the sleeve, a subtle but intentional signal that she sought a more than professional relationship. "No, he's just beginning to learn about China. He's a professor of American History at Columbia, a specialist on barbarian minds."

"I had no idea anything could be so beautiful," Roger said, staring at Miss Chang's face and causing Becky to snap her head in surprise. "Your calligraphy, I mean," Roger blurted. "It's exquisite."

"Why not try it?" Miss Chang replied, waving good-bye to the last students. "Here," she said, placing Roger in a chair, positioning a brush in his hand, standing next to him, one hand on his fingers, the other on his wrist. "We'll make a dot. Looks simple. But it's not."

Roger struggled with the brush, arm rigid and shaking, awkward blotches marring the paper. "You're trying too hard," Miss Chang said quietly. "Let go. Think of it this way. The brush is a key. The paper is a lock. The ink is the lubricant. Open the lock. Open it gently. Inside is a great treasure. Your own creativity." As Roger relaxed his forearm, letting Miss Chang guide his wrist and fingers, shapely black teardrops flowed down the paper. "Now, Professor Walden, why not do it yourself?"

"No." Roger shook his head, placed down the brush, and stood up. "Thanks for the lesson. It's fantastic. But I'm not here to show you how bad I am at this. I'm here to learn. By watching you . . . And Becky, of course."

Christina and Becky knelt on the floor, pulling a large piece of thin paper taut. Becky was of average American height, but she appeared much larger next to her tutor. Christina's compact body seemed at home in what would have been a painfully awkward position for most Western women. Her spine stayed erect while her thighs and calves came together, forming a platform under which she tucked her small shoeless feet. She opened a mother-of-pearl inlaid box and pulled out a giant calligraphy brush with an ebony handle and a radish-shaped cluster of bristles.

"Today, Miss An, we use this brush. White wolf hair, made by a Hangchow brush master, over a hundred years old, bought by my father's grandfather. My father took it with him to Taiwan in the late nineteen forties, and then gave it to my mother when she brought me and my brothers and sisters to New York in the fifties." Roger remembered fragments of Becky's description of Miss Chang —"powerful family . . . traditionalist father, won't leave Taiwan . . . mother's dead . . . influential and rich brother in New York . . . went to Wellesley . . . sort of a knock-out old maid . . . I'd guess she's in her mid-thirties . . . devoted to teaching . . . actually I think she's very lonely . . ."

Carefully rolling the tip of the huge brush in a black pool of ink, Miss Chang handed the brush to Becky. "Now just relax. Stand firmly above the paper. Bend at the waist. Keep your knees loose. Empty your mind. Focus on one character, your name—peace—*an*. Then let it flow. No breaks. Just mind, hand, brush all in one."

Becky drew in her breath, holding the brush over the paper, and then moved smoothly—making a sharp elongated dot at the top, a long line with two hooks underneath, and three clean strokes below that, forming a sort of extended triangle.

117

"Good start, Miss An. Nice shape and balance, but a little on the small side. Let the brush do the work for you. Like a Stradivarius, the instrument should speak for itself. Think about your name—peace—roof above and woman underneath."

Becky made several more attempts, each one a little larger and more fluid. Roger watched with admiration.

"Better and better, Miss An. Remember the story from Zhuangzi about the butcher? When the butcher first started, he only saw whole cows. Later he stopped trying to *see* the animal with his eyes and instead began to *feel* its form with his mind. At that point his cleaver would move fluidly, cutting the meat cleanly without any waste. It's the same with a brush."

"That's it!" shouted Roger, prompting Becky and Christina to whirl around and stare at him.

"Please, Roger, don't interrupt," Becky scolded. "I know you like Taoism, but this isn't the time."

"But, don't you understand? That's one of the stories on the box. Remember? Panel three—the man with the cleaver, striking the meat on the table? It's from Zhuangzi."

Christina Chang rocked back on her feet and stood up, looking incredulously at both of them. "I don't have the slightest idea what you're talking about, but I do have one rule." Her voice hardened. "No interruptions during a lesson. Now, Miss An, back to work. And Professor Walden, would you be good enough to fetch our supper?"

The purple neon lights flashed PLUM BLOSSOM RESTAURANT directly above Roger's head. He worked his way past a crowd waiting for tables. The middle-aged matron, her sagging body challenging the seams of her tight cheongsam, gave him a friendly smile when he asked for Christina Chang's order and quickly brought a white plastic shopping bag. As Roger jostled his way back into the street, a knifelike wind tore at him; he hugged the bag to his chest for warmth.

Turning down the dark side street, Roger felt a presence behind him and looked back. Ten yards away, he saw a powerfully built Chinese in a dark leather ski jacket moving rapidly toward him. Tightening his grip on the bag, Roger began a fast-walk, then broke into a quick jog when he saw the man was keeping pace, heavy shoes hammering the pavement. Roger accelerated to a full sprint. Glancing back, he was relieved to see a growing distance between himself and the man. Suddenly another figure jumped from an alley, throwing himself at Roger's knees. Roger fell to the pavement, hitting his head and shoulder but still clutching the plastic bag.

Roger saw the two men above him through the blood flowing from his forehead. One pinned his arms while the other snapped open a long switchblade knife. He held the knife to Roger's neck and spoke gruffly. "You make one move and you'll look like me." Roger squinted up at the man's face. An ugly scar stretched from his ear to his chin, reddened tissue standing out a half-inch above the skin.

"What do you want? I'll give you anything." Roger tried to free an arm so he could hand over his wallet.

The scar-faced man grabbed Roger's arm with one hand and pushed the knife into his cheek. A trickle of blood flowed from the wound. "You stupid bastard. Don't tell us what we want. One more move like that and you're dead."

A siren sounded nearby. The two men flinched. The one pinning Roger's arms pushed him hard against the pavement, the other kicked Roger's side and grabbed the bag. Roger lay sprawled on the sidewalk as he heard their footsteps disappear. Pulling himself to his feet, he stumbled the few remaining steps to Christina Chang's apartment.

Christina opened the door and screamed as she saw Roger slumped against the wall, blood streaming down his face. Becky pushed past Christina and shuddered; she draped Roger's arm over her shoulder and helped him to the sofa.

"What happened?" Becky asked.

"Two men . . . they mugged me."

"Miss Chang, can you get something to clean him up?"

Christina returned quickly with water and towels. Becky began to clean the wounds. "You're really lucky. Just some scratches and one cut on your cheek—"

Roger interrupted her. "The cut is from a knife. Better use some Merthiolate. Big Chinese guy with a switchblade."

"Could you recognize them, Roger?" asked Becky. "Would you know them if you saw them again?"

"It was pretty hard to see anything, but one had an awful scar down his face. Thank God they were scared off."

"What did they get?"

"They didn't get anything. Didn't even want my money. All they took was the Chinese food."

"The Chinese dinner? You're kidding! That doesn't make any sense."

Roger looked at Becky. "I'm not so sure," he said, pointing to the hall table. "The box is also in a white plastic bag. I think that's what they were after. Someone wants it very badly."

Becky's eyes widened as she looked over at the hall table and back at Roger. "Oh my God! You're right. Now we've got to call the police."

"You want me to tell them I was mugged for chicken chop suey? I'm already on their wacky list after the marathon."

"As a lawyer, I must urge you to—"

"You're not my lawyer. And I'm not going to call the police," Roger retorted. "It's my body. And my box. I can make up my own mind."

Christina Chang looked curiously at both of them. "Would you mind explaining what's going on? I'm glad Professor Walden's not hurt, and I'm happy to provide advice about calligraphy, as you asked. But I don't want to get involved in something illegal."

Becky told Christina the story while Roger went to the bathroom to bandage his cuts. When he returned, Christina addressed both of them. "I'll try to give you a little help. But I must insist on three points. First, I reserve the right to stop if it seems too dangerous. Second, when we're chatting like this on a friendly basis, please call me Christina. 'Miss Chang' is only for classroom situations. And third, Professor Walden, please never accuse me of ordering chicken chop suey. Chop suey is an awful Western invention. Now I'm going to phone in another order, only this time I'll request home delivery!"

Even smarting as he was, Roger couldn't help admiring how Christina took command. Becky had said it earlier—"teaching's her style of life and we barbarians are all her pupils."

When the dishes were cleared, Roger unveiled the box, gleaming against the black lacquer dining table. Christina gasped as her long fingers ran across its surface and gently turned it around and over. Her eyes sparkled as she recognized symbols and calligraphy, but Roger caught a trace of fear in her face.

"I don't know if either of you has the slightest idea what you have here," Christina said quietly, staring into their faces. "You're right. It's superb craftsmanship and it's also a forgery of a sort. It's full of symbolism about Chinese philosophy and literature. Your initial guesses weren't far off. But you're missing so much . . ."

Roger sat on the edge of his chair. "I know we're missing a lot. That's why we came to you."

Christina leaned forward, the light above the table caught a slight tremor in her cheek. "I can provide a little help with the symbols and calligraphy. But it's a lot more than that."

"What do you mean?" Becky asked.

"My father once told us a strange story about a family named Gao. At one time they had close connections with my own family, back in China. Their patriarch was executed by the Boxer rebels almost a century ago, and it was rumored that he had managed to hide an incredibly valuable art collection before he died. A lacquer box was supposed to be the clue to discovering its hiding place. People have been after it ever since. The box was rumored to have great powers—it could kill evil people, only the noble-minded could find its inner secret."

Becky stared at Christina and then at the box. "You really think this could be that box? The Gao box? How come I've never heard anything about it?"

"I'm only saying that it reminds me of that story. A lot of Chinese legends never get written down and are never discussed with strangers."

Roger, eyes afire with fascination, picked up the box by its edges. "Even if it's only remotely possible, it suddenly makes everything else seem tolerable. Please, Christina, help us understand it."

Christina shook her head. "I really can't. Maybe it's just Chinese superstition, but until I know more, about the box and about you, it would be wrong for me. If my guess is right, then the box is both precious and dangerous. I would have to ask my father for his advice before proceeding."

Roger sighed in frustration. "I really don't understand. You seem so rational." The word "inscrutable" had come to mind, but he restrained himself.

Becky grabbed his arm and squeezed it sharply. "Roger, you're forgetting yourself. You're Miss Chang's guest. She's given you dinner and taken care of you. Maybe you're the one who got hurt, but try to understand that she must be baffled by this whole business. She's got every right to refuse to help."

Accepting Becky's apology on Roger's behalf, Christina continued. "Well, maybe I can help a little. I don't think I should attempt the symbolism, but there's no reason I can't help you with the calligraphy. Anyone familiar with classical Chinese could do that. Besides, you might benefit from the messages." Becky forced herself to smile in spite Roger's appreciative glances at her teacher.

Inverting the box, Christina examined the strings of characters on the bottom. "That's fabulous calligraphy! It's in the style of Wang Xizhi, the fourth-century master of grass script."

"Why in the *style* of Wang Xizhi?" Roger asked. "Why not just a direct copy so that the message would be clearer?"

"Good point," Christina replied, taking a book off her shelf. "Here's an example of Wang Xizhi's calligraphy from a stone rubbing. Look here at his character *dao*, "the way." The *dao* on your box has a little more flair. It's not a mistake. The calligrapher is revering tradition and demonstrating his individuality at the same time, suggesting that we must adapt the past to serve new needs."

"I can't believe you can extract that much just from some handwriting," Roger said admiringly. "You haven't even begun to translate the calligraphy." She's like her apartment, Roger thought, alluring in an unpretentious way. Becky had said that Christina could afford to live anywhere, but that Chinatown made her feel closer to her roots. She had refused to follow the migration of affluent Chinese-Americans to Queens, New Jersey, and uptown Manhattan.

"That's the easy part. It's all from the *Dao De Jing*—the classic work of Taoism."

Christina picked up her brush and touched it to the ink. "It's easier for me to translate this first into regular-style calligraphy, and then into English. Looking at the box, Christina swiftly wrote the first verse in characters. "Now let's see"—she hesitated, then spoke slowly:

> Knowledge comes from understanding others,
> True insight comes from understanding one's self.
> You need strength to conquer others,
> But even more strength to conquer yourself.
> You are rich if you are satisfied with what you have.
> If you are violent, you can sometimes get results.

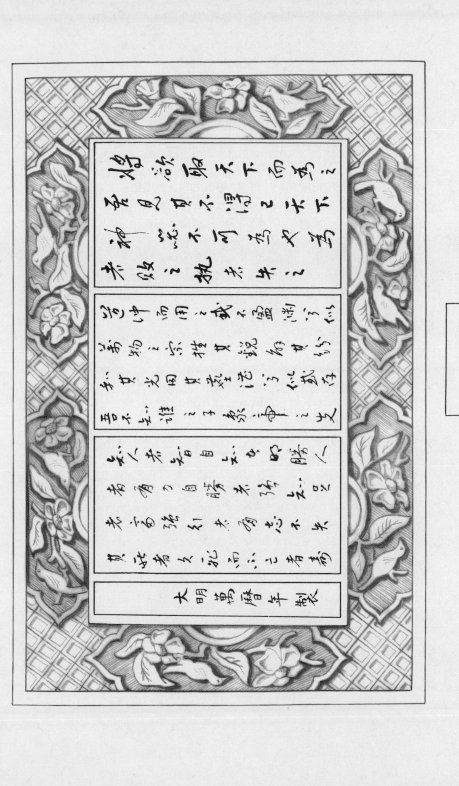

But only by not moving can you last forever.
Even death does not bring the end,
It's the only way to live beyond yourself.

"Sounds like a hippie version of Christianity," Roger said.

"Probably because of my poor translation."

"More likely because Roger took a blow to the head," Becky offered. "It goes very well with the general themes on the side panels. Knowledge for self-understanding. A purpose in life that goes beyond death. Sort of like a Taoist benediction to a Confucian sermon."

"Hey, that's pretty good," Roger said admiringly.

"Not bad for a lawyer, eh?"

"You might even become a scholar someday."

Christina glanced at her guests suspiciously, wondering whether their word games implied other, more intimate games. "The next one is a little hard to understand in Chinese, to say nothing of English."

The Way is something that is empty, but it can be used.
You can use it forever without having to fill it.
It is very deep, the origin of all things.
It dulls all sharpness,
Unties all knots,
Softens all glares,
Quiets all dust.
It remains forever profound and pure.
We cannot know if it is the offspring of something else,
Since it appeared before all ancestors.

Roger, visibly excited, put his hand on the box. "I think I understand it. It describes the box itself. We think it's empty, but it may have considerable uses, perhaps a didactic tool, possibly a clue for a jewel someplace."

Becky broke in. "Maybe it tells us how to use the box. It 'unties all knots'—implying a solution to a puzzle. At the same time—'you can use it forever without having to fill it'—sounds like a valuable treasure."

"Just one last verse," Christina said. "A lot easier than the last."

124

Those who try to control the mortal world by manipulating,
They do not succeed.
The mortal world is like a holy container,
It is very dangerous to tamper with it.
If you try to manipulate it,
You will destroy it.
If you try to grab it,
You will lose it.

"What a warning sign!" Becky exclaimed. "Don't trespass. Guard dogs and barbed-wire fences!"

"Right!" Roger agreed emphatically. "But it's more than just a 'private property, keep off' sign. It's sort of like the Greek Sirens: we want to listen, but we know we're running a great risk."

"That's good, Roger, very good," Becky replied, "but where does it leave us?"

Christina rose, placing her hands on the box. Her face and body were almost invisible in the dark shadows, but Roger saw her fingers tremble as she touched the red lacquer. "If I were you, I'd stop this search right now before it's too late. Understand what you understand, don't try to understand what can't be understood."

"I think that's a bit overdone," Roger said. "You're turning this into a Chinese ghost story. We've already agreed not to try opening the box, but nowhere does it say that we should give up the hunt."

"Oh yes, it does," Christina replied. "Not in so many words, but how can you miss the warning? Don't tamper, don't grab. The power to kill. And for heaven's sake, how do you interpret a robbery and a mugging two nights in a row? Someone's going to be killed in this process. Please give it up."

"I hear you, Christina," Becky said as dispassionately as possible. "But try to understand. We've devoted weeks trying to crack this crazy code. You've saved us many more weeks in one night. We can't thank you enough, but we don't want to give up. Can you understand that?"

Christina paused. "It might be safer for you if I made some very private inquiries through my family."

"Isn't that dangerous?" Roger asked. "Won't involving more people increase the risk of exposure?"

Christina stiffened. "I'm talking about extremely private conversations with my own family. Eventually I'll be talking with my father. If I can't trust my family, whom can I trust? Now hide that box. Don't let anyone else know about it."

"How long will it take before we know anything?" Roger asked impatiently.

"Weeks, maybe months. Maybe never."

"But what do I do in the meantime? I can't just sit still and leave the mystery in a vault."

"Sitting still might be best of all. But if you really want to do something, learn more about China and its art. Reading is one way. Another is immersing yourself in a different world."

"Immersing myself?"

"Yes. If you're interested, my brother is giving a dinner on Saturday at the Golden Pavilion Restaurant. A real Chinese banquet. I'd be pleased to have you come as my guest."

"I'd be delighted," Roger replied without hesitation.

"You'll have to be careful not to mention the box," Christina said. "One of the guests is Daniel Lamarche, an art dealer. He's there because he once helped my brother sell some of our ceramics when we badly needed the money. He's a real expert on Chinese art. But I've never trusted him very much. You might learn something if you keep your ears open, but please be careful."

"Brother, did she put a move on you," Becky exclaimed to Roger in the taxi.

Roger looked at her quizically. "Becky, that's just plain ridiculous. If that was a move, it's got to be an Oriental understatement of the highest degree."

"Understatement, my ass. Oh, Roger, if you *really* want to learn more about China, then *immerse* yourself. *Come* to dinner with me. What she didn't say was who *wasn't* invited to dinner."

"Maybe there aren't any extra places, or maybe they want an equal number of men and women."

"That's a crock of cow poo. Chinese banquet tables are always expandable, and I'll bet you five to one there'll be more men than women."

They rode silently until Roger broke in. "Becky, how the hell am I going to stay safe?"

"Put the box in the vault and move into my building," Becky said briskly. "The security is superb—always a doorman and an elevator operator."

"Becky," Roger said sharply. "We've been through this before. I'm not ready for a relationship . . ."

"Roger, give me a chance to explain! I'm talking about another apartment, on another floor. It belongs to a friend of mine who's off for a month in Europe."

"Sorry," Roger said sheepishly. "Then I accept your hospitality. Besides it would make it easier to work on the box together from time to time."

"And you might change your mind, about us, I mean."

"You never know."

CHAPTER TEN

CUISINE

CHRISTMAS IN NEW YORK, ESPECIALLY

in a blizzard, tends to exaggerate everyone's mood. For the light of heart, it's a time of joy when the soul dances to bells and the eyes sparkle in the collage of lights. For the ill or the angry, it's a terrible time when other people's happiness and the biting cold make loneliness unbearable.

Roger Walden, brushing the snow from his black topcoat in front of the Golden Pavilion Restaurant, wasn't sure which side of the line he fell on. He appreciated the protection of Becky Aspen's apartment building but felt relieved to escape the self-imposed house arrest for an evening. Although Roger continued to resist a closer relationship, Becky's possessiveness prompted her to spend the entire day fretting about his date with Christina. Catching his reflection in the restaurant window, Roger brightened; there was color in his face, his body no longer looked cadaverous. Besides, he reminded himself, he'd never gone out with a woman of a different race. No, it was more than that: Christina seemed deeper and more promising than Becky. Christina, like Becky, kept locks on many facets of her personality; but unlike Becky, Christina's locks were of enchanting Chinese craftsmanship and, so Roger hoped, they might be opened if he earned her confidence. After spending the day reassuring Becky, now he found himself worrying that maybe Becky was wrong about Christina's ulterior motives.

Christina Chang watched Roger from a darkened corner, pausing to quiet her nerves. She hadn't had a date in in a long time. Instead she was reconciled to living alone, convincing herself that teaching offered sufficient emotional satisfaction. Christina's implicit decision to remain single perplexed the Chang family in Taipei and New York who, after fifteen years of abortive matchmaking, had reluctantly given up. "He's too absorbed in business," or "no sense of culture," or "too much of a playboy"—those were her favorite excuses when eligible bachelors were suggested. The real reason was more complicated: she didn't seek perfection in a mate, but she had an incorrigible romantic notion that marriage should be a joint quest for new experiences and insights. It was admittedly a Western notion, but after all, she was at least half Western. Roger, she sensed, was the first man she'd met in years who had the potential.

Christina stood in the snowfall, trying to empty her mind as though preparing for calligraphy, but it wasn't working. The riddle of this man was more enticing than that of his lacquer box. Maybe finally, this was a relationship that . . . The thought was cut short as she saw him check his watch; she couldn't delay any longer.

"Roger," Christina said softly, "it looks like you've recovered from the mugging."

Opening the door for her, he saw how the powdery snow highlighted her silky black hair. When she removed her coat for the checkroom attendant, he couldn't help staring. Her light-blue silk dress, embroidered with yellow flowers and birds, had a high collar with tiny yellow frog fastenings and was slit slightly along the legs. The dress accented her soft skin and the outlines of her small, firm body.

"Do you like it?"

"You look absolutely beautiful," he breathed, wishing he could have said something more subtle.

They walked through the main dining room, decorated in Manhattan mandarin style with bronze framed mirrors, gray felt wallpaper, and hanging lanterns. Entering a smaller side room, Roger felt swept back to the Ming dynasty. Deep-brown rosewood chairs were incised with recurrent interlocking-square patterns. Two lacquer landscape screens, featuring gaily costumed figures and lavish palaces, set off the large round table in the center of the room. The banquet tablecloth and chair cushions were embroidered yellow silk; a large platter held a perfect imitation of a peacock, eggs and cold meats forming its plumage. Each place setting included a pair of ivory chopsticks

131

in a ceramic holder, three glasses of different sizes, and a green-and-yellow porcelain soup bowl and spoon.

Christina warmly greeted the five people in the room, introducing Roger first to her brother and sister-in-law. "George is—how should I put it—in many ways, he is Mr. China of New York. He owns the oldest bank in Chinatown. He's central to politics and social life in the Chinese community. Together, George and Angela—"

"Stop it, Christina, before you perjure yourself." George Chang chuckled. He was a short, stocky man, but his well-cut three-piece suit gave him presence. Angela, wearing a clinging red dress and heavy gold jewelry, was much younger than her husband.

"Don't listen to Christina," George said. "I'm just a humble merchant. The Chinese have always looked down on merchants—we're incapable of working either with our minds or with our hands."

"Now," George continued, "here's a *really* important man. He controls a billion people. I'd like you to meet Minister Chen. He's China's Minister of Finance—Mainland China, that is. He's just come from some International Monetary Fund meetings in Washington, and is here for some relaxation—and a little business on the side." Minister Chen, a tall man in a trim cadre suit and wire-rimmed glasses, smiled and shook hands. "Incredibly powerful," Christina whispered to Roger, "my brother says he's got a great future."

"Given your political views, George, I must assume that your compliment is a case of *yan bu yu jung*—words that do not come from the heart." The Minister ran his hands over his closely cropped gray hair, politely anticipating his host's rebuttal, much the way a chess master waits for the response to his opening move.

"Quite the contrary," George countered deftly, "*cheng wang bai kou*—the conquerers become kings; the vanquished become outlaws. No compliment at all. Just stating a fact, Mr. Minister. You're kind to dine with an outlaw."

The Minister smiled. The banquet jousting had begun. A few months earlier the Minister had confronted more deadly combat. Labelled a "counter-revolutionary" during the wave of 1989 demonstrations, the Minister was dismissed from office and subjected to house arrest. Had it not been for two timely deaths of Politburo hardliners and the quick mobilization of the Beijing Garrison troops loyal to the moderates, Chen might well still be under arrest or perhaps even executed. George Chang knew Minister Chen was embarked on China's most dangerous mission—seeking support for modernization abroad while his enemies conspired behind the walls of the Forbidden City.

"Now let me introduce a man of different fame," George continued. "This is one of the world's most successful dealers in Oriental art, Mr. Daniel Lamarche."

Roger observed the diminutive figure in his sixties whose face was outlined by a pudgy chin, over-large ears, and curly graying hair. He wore a maroon continental tuxedo, and an oversized signet ring glistened on his right hand like that of a papal emissary waiting for a genuflection and a kiss. His small black eyes flickered about suspiciously. Roger's first impression of Lamarche was of an unattractive figure trying to impress like a bit-part clown in a traveling circus. Why had Christina been so fearful? Roger felt only bemusement and a touch of pity.

As Roger shook Lamarche's hand, he saw that the fellow had already consumed a lot of liquor. Lamarche reached out and touched Christina's hair. "*Ma cherie.* My little China doll. What a work of art! She'd make Yang Guifei jealous. Too bad I'm so ugly, otherwise I'd have a chance. Don't you think so, Professor Walden?"

Ignoring the question but trying to appeal to Lamarche's desire for recognition, Roger replied carefully. "Christina has told me about your skills in Asian art. It's a pleasure to meet you, Mr. Lamarche."

"Oh, don't say that. I'm Danny Boy to all my friends, and you, dear Professor, must be my friend."

"Forgive me, uh, Danny Boy. And please call me Roger. 'Professor' reminds me that I should be working harder during my sabbatical."

"Ah, to rephrase Veblen—the leisure of the theory class. Those of us who have to work for a living salute you. I just came from work, an awful auction. Sixty thousand for a Ming red lacquer miniature temple. Outrageous—a fortune for a chunk of carved cinnabar. You don't have any interest in Chinese lacquers, do you, Roger old boy?"

Roger was startled. "No, I don't know anything about Chinese art. Why do you ask?"

"Oh, no reason in particular. You just looked like a man of taste, and fine lacquer goes with fine tastes."

Roger glanced toward Christina, wondering whether she had told Lamarche about the box. Christina, eyes open in wonderment, shook her head slightly, implying her surprise at Lamarche's curious question.

George Chang gestured toward the table, placing Minister Chen in the seat of honor facing the door; by ancient Chinese tradition, the chief guest was the best-protected from intruders. Roger noted Becky had won her bet—four men and two women.

Two Chinese waiters, dressed in tuxedos, poured wine. Roger reached for his glass and was about to take a sip when Christina touched his arm and shook her head. "Wait until the first toast," she whispered, "we Chinese don't believe in drinking alone." She was enjoying her role of cultural instructor; he was obviously relishing being her student. They shared a shy smile, just a fleeting glance, fanning a spark in both of them.

George Chang, alertly catching the unspoken communication, shot a concerned look at Angela, who shared his alarm. No Chang had ever developed amorous ties to a *waiguoren*, a foreigner, "an outside-the-country person." To break the mood George stood up and separated the peacock-shaped cold appetizers, giving small portions of each delicacy to Minister Chen and Lamarche.

Christina began to serve Roger, but he stopped her. "I really do know how to use chopsticks."

"I hope so," she laughed. "Otherwise you're going to starve. It's our custom to begin each new dish by serving the guests. When someone says *ziji lai*, that means 'serve yourself.' But go easy. There could be as many as twenty courses and you're expected to eat a little of each."

Roger took a few bites. "What are these marvelous things?"

"Just the standard appetizers. Shrimp, beef, abalone, pigeon eggs, thousand-year-old eggs."

Roger blanched.

"Don't worry. Really the eggs are only about a hundred days old."

"Let me offer a humble toast," George Chang said. "*Yu peng zi yuan fang lai, bu yi le hu?* 'When friends come from afar, isn't this a pleasant occasion?' "

Everyone raised his glass and sipped a bit of the wine. Christian explained the toast was the first verse in the Confucian Analects. "Roger, it's like a standard Christian blessing. Now you can drink when you like, but always gesture with the glass toward someone else as if making a private little toast."

Minister Chen stood and responded. "I'd like to express our thanks to our host and his lovely wife. I've seldom experienced such fine hospitality. I only hope that someday we can invite you to Beijing so that we may try to repay your kindness. Now with the Cultural Revolution behind us, we can give proper respect to two of your loves, Confucius and Chinese cooking. A toast to the health and long lives of our host and hostess. *Ganbei.*" The Minister drained his glass of yellow rice wine, turning it over to show that it was empty. The others around the table followed suit. *Ganbei*, Christina explained, means 'drain your glass dry.'

Lamarche stood up unsteadily, tapping his signet ring on his wineglass. "A toast," he said, "a toast to Chinese tradition."

The group started to clink glasses, but Lamarche stopped them. "To Chinese tradition. Mr. Minister, what a pity you've wrecked it on the mainland. It's George here who preserves true Chinese tradition, which is to make lots of money, so you can buy anything— big houses, great art, beautiful women, even foreign governments. Now that's a tradition I can understand and—"

George Chang broke in with a shout to the waiters. "Bring in the chef!" His outburst quieted everyone, including Lamarche. When the chef arrived, George yelled at him. "This meal is not up to the standards of our guests. We have insulted them. The service is terrible. I'm humiliated." The chef nodded three times, mumbled some words of sorrow, and then walked out backward.

Roger was shocked, even more so when he saw that he and Lamarche were the only ones not laughing. "Brilliant," said the Minister sotto voce. Scolding the chef, Christina quickly explained to Roger, was an ancient ritual designed to show that one's guests were always better than one's food. What was brilliant was that George had used the ploy at the perfect moment—responding to Lamarche's comment about tradition and cutting off Lamarche's offensiveness. Lamarche was momentarily quiet, sullenly rolling his wineglass in his fingers, leaving Roger feeling more compassion than contempt for the little man who so desperately sought the spotlight.

At a nod from George, the waiters removed the peacock, still only half plucked, and placed two large bowls on the table, each holding what looked to Roger like a pile of thin transluscent noodles garnished with black mushrooms and broccoli leaves. The Minister clapped to show his approval.

"Come now," said George, "it's just a little shark's-fin soup."

Roger tasted a few strands of the needlelike cartilage, finding it bland, rather like gelatinous chicken soup. Roger glanced at Christina, almost imperceptibly raising his hands and opening his palms as if to say, "so what's the big deal?"

Minister Chen caught Roger's gesture and smiled. "It's an acquired taste." He held up a few strands between his chopsticks. "You see, we're a little like the French. All art forms are connected—food is linked to music, and music to philosophy. You know about yin and yang? Chinese courses must complement one another, just like movements in a symphony. Each dish must have its yin and yang. We have five basic tastes—sweet, sour, salty, bitter, and pungent. They play on one another, like . . . what do you call it?—the counterpoint in baroque music. Take the shark's fin. See the touch of green and black against the white and yellow? You must try to taste the subtle duck and chicken stock in the midst of what is a fish dish."

Roger sensed a perfect opening for his first Chinese toast. "Let me raise my glass. Food is more than art. It brings together people of different outlooks. To our hosts and our new friends. *Ganbei.*"

Everyone applauded and watched as Roger gulped a small glass of clear alcohol. He gagged and covered his mouth with a napkin. "What the hell is that?" he asked Christina.

"It's *maotai*," she said, grinning as the others laughed. "Sorghum liqueur, about 130 proof. The Chinese version of white lightning. Tastes like hell until the third or fourth glass."

The waiters brought in the next course, asparagus spears aligned in long rows interspersed with little dumplings shaped like ducks. "What?" exclaimed George, "I didn't order this. Who called for Beautiful Lady Marries Gifted Scholar?"

"I did," said Minister Chen with a grin. "Please everyone join me in a toast to the Changs. Today is their anniversary. You must *ganbei.*" The second round, Roger found, was much easier than the first.

"My goodness, a Confucian gesture from a Communist official?" George chuckled as he explained to Roger that the dish had been invented by the first Ming emperor to symbolize his eternal love for his empress.

Roger's head spun from the *maotai*; the conversation flowed around him, often more in Chinese than English, rendering him a spectator rather than an actor.

Minister Chen turned to Christina. "What about calligraphy

and cuisine?" he asked, priding himself on good staff work, including such details as knowing about his host's sister.

Roger didn't really listen to Christina's answer, particularly since it was half in Chinese. Instead he watched her answer. She picked up a chopstick, thoughtfully running her fingers over its graceful shape as she spoke; her eyes sparkled with a teacher's excitement. Roger watched her body speak a more subtle language, shoulders and hips moving slightly to reinforce a point. Her silk dress restrained small firm breasts; her wrists rocked in small circles, little calligraphic gestures to punctuate her speech.

Christina felt Roger's stare as she finished her explanation, her eyes touching his again and lingering for a moment. Lamarche smirked slightly; even in his inebriated state, he had not missed the look. Angela, her lips tightening, gave a "you've got to talk to your sister" glance to George.

The waiters proudly carried in two large carp with crispy crusts of sesame, garlic, and pepper. "Hunan carp! How did you know my favorite dish?" asked the Minister with genuine gratitude.

"So my sources were correct." George smiled. "Actually it was simple. Our family chef in Taipei has a brother who is an assistant chef in Beijing's Great Hall of the People. Just some basic espionage. If only I'd been given responsibility for Nationalist Intelligence in the forties, we might have won the Civil War."

The Minister's eyes twinkled. "Are you sure this isn't King Wu's fish?"

Everyone but Roger laughed. George explained that King Wu, in the sixth century B.C., had been killed by an assassin who put a knife in a fish whose belly was facing away from the monarch. Since then, it was customary to serve fish with the belly facing the guest.

"I told the chef to serve this the other way around," George said, trying to shift the position of the platter.

"Too late now," parried the Minister, holding the platter tightly, "about forty years too late." Both men laughed again.

Roger broke in. "I wish we could find a way in the West to overcome politics with a nice supper." The laughter evaporated. Everyone stared at the stranger.

"Professor," Minister Chen said after an embarrassed silence. "You don't understand. Mr. Chang and I both lost family in the Civil War. We stand for very different things. There's bitterness beneath our laughter."

George Chang took a deep breath. "The Minister's right. We

have an old expression. *Zuo jing guan tian.* Sitting in the well and looking at the sky. It suggests that we should keep our silence if we don't see the whole picture."

"But I really didn't mean any harm—" A sharp nudge from Christina abruptly stopped Roger's apology.

"How about another toast?" Christina suggested to the silent table. "To the health, happiness, and continued education of all of us. New friends and old friends."

A subdued *ganbei* followed; the guests tasted a few bits of carp. Roger looked sullenly at Christina, who replied with a forgiving smile and a wave of her hand to indicate that all was forgiven and forgotten.

Angela Chang urged Roger to sample the next dish, *Mapo doufu,* Mrs. Pockmark's Bean curd, named after an old Sichuan woman. "The peppers make it hot, the bean curd cools it down. I think maybe the timing is right. Now, Professor Walden, what's intellectual history anyway? What's your work all about?"

There was a curious tone to her question—respect for professors mingled with scrutiny of this particular professor—and Roger didn't miss it. "It's the history of how ideas influence action," Roger explained, relieved at the change of subject. "I'm most interested in liberal reformers like Franklin Roosevelt, Jack Kennedy, Jimmy Carter. They always seem caught between extremists on either side of them, often spending more time fighting enemies than pursuing policies."

Minister Chen nodded strongly. "It's the same in China. I've always been a reformer. My hero was Zhou Enlai, who wanted to strengthen China—especially our educational system—while developing new ties abroad." The Minister spoke fervently. "But in China, just like here, reformers must always contend with extremists. Right-wing Nationalists almost destroyed China forty years ago, left-wing radicals almost did it again in the Cultural Revolution. Then the cycle starts again—right-wing hardliners giving orders to kill our own people in Tiananmen. And each time I'm sent off to the countryside to become an expert in shoveling manure."

"Reformers often have to shovel manure." Roger smiled sympathetically. "My job is to pull them out of manure posthumously. If we understand dead reformers better, then maybe live ones will have a better chance."

"China doesn't have the luxury of rescuing the reputations of dead liberals," the Minister replied. "We've got to implement our reforms now. We're on the right track. We only need three things:

political stability, better education, and foreign technology. Pragmatism and patriotism—"

Daniel Lamarche tapped his chopsticks together. "I beg to differ. It's Beijing Opera—idealists, pragmatists, radicals, conservatives. Most people don't care about such values. They care about money."

"Please, Mr. Lamarche," George Chang cajoled. "You're an expert on Chinese art. What about aesthetics?"

Lamarche laughed as he waved his chopsticks in the air. "I don't sell art because of some romantic love of beauty. I sell it because it's valuable. People don't love art, just money."

"Don't be shocked," Lamarche admonished the silent table. "You're upset only because you're the most hopeless moralists in the world, the Chinese and the Americans. I expect less from people, so I end up getting more from life, *n'est-ce pas?*"

"That's the crudest philosophy I've ever heard," Roger exclaimed, his anger overcoming previous pity for Lamarche. "It's pure hedonism. Around this table, we may not agree about politics, but we all agree about the value of human life." Struggling for words, Roger raised his glass. "To human dignity. To human decency." A murmur of assent joined his *ganbei.*

"You're trying too hard," Lamarche laughed, his face flushed with alcohol. "You want dreams. You can't see the basic truth. It's not so bad once you accept it."

"Yes, I want dreams," Roger almost shouted. "Civilizations have all been made of dreams, like the dream of democracy. And not just in the West. What about China? Weren't the great men all moved by dreams? What about Confucius? Mencius? Zhu Xi? The nineteenth-century reformers?"

Christina kicked Roger under the table to make him stop speaking. Lamarche's eyes danced in triumph. "Methinks the professor knows more about China than he lets on. One wonders where you learned such wisdom. Not the sort of thing you pick up from a box top—as you Americans say."

Roger and Christina froze; the others looked puzzled. George Chang tried to retrieve the evening by telling engaging stories about the final dishes, but the life was gone.

"You must let me make amends," Lamarche pleaded as he held open the rear door of his blue stretch limousine parked in front

139

of the restaurant. Minister Chen had already left, transporting George and Angela Chang in his own limousine.

"No, thanks," Roger said sharply, "we'd rather take a cab."

"A cab? In a blizzard? Don't push me to give another speech about idealism!" Lamarche gestured into the limousine and smiled. "Besides, I'm sure you'd enjoy a ride with some friends of yours."

Roger could make out two forms in the spacious passenger compartment, a man and a woman, but the light was too dim to see their features. Lamarche's invitation was obviously an order. A heavy automatic with a silencer gleamed in the streetlight, held by the man inside the limousine, the barrel pointed directly at Roger's chest.

"I knew you'd accept my hospitality." Lamarche ushered Roger and Christina into the limousine, placing them in the jumpseats, while he joined his two companions on the rear seat.

"What the hell do you want from us?" Roger demanded as the limousine glided silently down the snowy avenue.

"Oh, so impatient. You'll soon see." Lamarche flipped open a panel next to the armrest and turned a knob, slowly illuminating the woman. Her face, still shrouded by shadows, was outlined by gray hair drawn up in a bun.

Roger felt a glimmer of recognition and a stab of fear. "Miss Sickelman? It *was* you."

"Yes, Professor." She smiled warmly. "You've given me something to occupy my spare moments since Mr. Lamarche induced me to leave my job with Mr. Marsh." Roger sat in frozen shock.

Lamarche turned down the light and smiled at his prisoners in the darkness. "Now I'm truly upset. You two don't seem to enjoy my hospitality. You must have a drink." He flipped a switch on the panel, opening a highly polished wooden bar between the jumpseats.

Lamarche took the automatic from the man sitting at his side, gesturing for him to pour drinks. "Champagne, of course," Lamarche said.

The burly figure knelt in front of the bar, pulling out a silver bucket, ice, and glasses. As the man poured champagne, Lamarche slowly turned up the overhead light, revealing the thick red scar that ran from the man's ear to his chin. Christina stifled a gasp and Roger shuddered.

Lamarche shouted at him. "You idiot. You're so ugly you frightened her." He turned to Christina. "Don't let him scare you. It's just Lucky Liu. We call him Lucky because you should have seen the other man."

"Stop the car," Roger demanded. "Let us out."

Lamarche handed the automatic back to Liu, who held it to Christina's head. "Why do you Americans always want to jump over formalities to the central issue? Okay, my friend, you can go. But first we have some business. I know all about your lacquer box. I'm not out to steal it. I just want to make an offer. I'll give you a million dollars."

Roger discarded the idea of feigning ignorance; it was useless with Marsh's secretary here. He had always prided himself on remaining calm in a crisis, finding alternatives when others were paralyzed. He had to think fast. "You want a deal, Danny Boy?" he said, trying to sound confident. "Okay, you can have the box, but your price is way off. Let's try again." What a scam, Roger thought, Sickelman alerting Lamarche to estates so he could pick off the art. Roger cursed himself for being incorrigibly naive—how could he have missed Sickleman's chicanery? How could he have felt sympathy for Lamarche's buffoon-like demeanor? Dammit, maybe he *was* just a gullible liberal academic.

"You're in no position to bargain, Professor." Lamarche nodded and Lucky Liu pushed the barrel firmly against Christina's ear. "Now we're going to drive together. You will give us the key to the vault. Any tricky business and you're both dead. Now let's—"

A muffled horn sounded behind them, Lamarche's limousine skidded and came to an abrupt stop. Lucky Liu was distracted for a second. Christina pressed her hands together, raised them high in the air, and brought them sharply against the back of Liu's skull. His body snapped backward and he slumped down unconscious.

Roger grabbed the automatic and pointed it at Lamarche and Sickelman. "Quick, Christina, get out of the car," he shouted. Christina reached inside the car, tore out the cellular telephone, and threw it across the road into a snow drift.

They started to run together, but Christina's dress and heels kept her back. Roger tossed the gun into a drift, picked up Christina, and struggled through the snow. He glanced back. Lamarche stood outside his car, slamming a door and kicking a tire that was deeply stuck in the icy snow.

Roger hailed what must have been the last cab in Manhattan and gave Becky's address.

"Where did you learn that?" he asked in astonishment and fright.

"Wushu, martial arts," she said, her body shaking. "I studied

141

it once. Actually, I wanted to make a move with my feet, but it's pretty tough dressed like this."

"Thank God," Roger said, wrapping his arms around her for warmth. "If you hadn't done that, we'd probably be dead by now. But we've got to warn Becky; she's in as much danger as we are."

The cab skidded to a stop in front of Becky's building, and Roger told the driver to keep the meter running. He ran in with Christina and asked the doorman to buzz Becky on the intercom. Roger would tell her to come right down; he wanted to keep an eye on the taxi, their only means of escape.

The doorman pushed a button and waited a moment. "That's strange. I know she's been there all evening."

Roger and Christina ran to the elevator; there was no response to their ring, so they rushed up the service stairs. The elevator operator was sprawled unconscious on the first landing.

The door to Becky's apartment was wide open. Inside, art objects lay on the floor, most of them torn or broken; the furniture was slashed. Roger ran into the study; books and papers were littered around the room. There was blood on the carpet.

He followed the trail of blood into the bedroom. Becky lay on the bed. Her face had been sliced with a knife and blood seeped from deep cuts in her abdomen. Her eyes were still open. Roger put his arms around her lifeless shoulders.

"My God," he whispered in shock. "They tortured her for nothing. She never had the key to the vault. She didn't know any more than we do." He looked into Becky's face and pushed back her hair. "Why? What did she ever do?"

"We've got to run, Roger," Christina said, shaking him by the shoulders. "The police can't save us. Lamarche will get us if we wait. Becky would want us to leave. We're going to be killed next. Let's go. *Now!*"

CHAPTER ELEVEN

ESCAPE

IN THE SUMMERTIME, PADANARUM

on Buzzards Bay is a magnet that attracts thousands of tourists. In the winter, its rocky harbors and sloping shores sleep in stillness. The night before, a blanket of snow had transformed Padanarum's chiseled features into soft sculptures. Graceful yachts, cradled and canvas-covered, looked like white-shrouded corpses. Above on the hills, great estates and green forests offered touches of color to the drifts enveloping them.

No one but a passing sea gull was likely to see the wisps of smoke escaping from a chimney on the hill. Even the footprints marking a path to the mansion's white clapboard guest house had been obscured by the blizzard. The large carved sign in front of the estate, so noticeable in the summer, was almost invisible in the ice and snow. Only someone who knew Chinese calligraphy very well might have detected the character—*piao* or "fluttering in the wind"—hiding in the holes of the cedar slab. It was an apt description of the woman who sat huddled under a comforter on a couch absorbing waves of warmth from the granite fireplace. Christina Chang had often stayed here, at her older brother's summer home, a perfect escape from July and August in New York.

Roger Walden, sitting across from Christina, stared at the fire. He held a steaming mug of coffee tightly with both hands, trying to make the shivering stop.

144

Christina spoke hesitantly. "Roger . . ." He moved his head slightly and looked at Christina through the reddened shadows of the room. "Roger. I'm so sorry. I wish could do something."

Roger stared vacantly.

Christina drew the comforter around her and moved to the fire. Her face, partly obscured by her long black hair, took on the soft light of the burning logs. "Roger," she spoke with a tremor in her voice, "it was my fault. I shouldn't have asked you to dinner. I knew that Lamarche was untrustworthy. But I couldn't have guessed he was already involved in this."

Roger looked up at Christina's silhouette. "It wasn't your fault," he said flatly. "Lamarche would have gotten to us anyway."

"I'm so sorry about Becky," she said mournfully. "You loved her, didn't you?"

"No, I didn't love her, nor did I live with her," he replied quietly. "But I admired her talents. And I'm going to miss her."

"So am I. She *was* my best student."

"Oh, Christina, I feel like I killed her. That stupid box. If only I hadn't taken it to her. If only I hadn't . . ."

"Hush. Stop it," Christina said, dropping the comforter and walking in her bathrobe to Roger's couch. "I know it won't help, but we Chinese see such things as fate. None of us, least of all you, knew what we were getting into." She raised her hands slowly and placed them gently on Roger's back. Her firm wrists and delicate fingers began to knead out the pain that filled his body. He leaned into her massaging hands.

"Just relax a bit," she breathed. "It's Chinese massage. Acupressure."

"God, that feels good. I only wish things were different. That I could turn back the clock. That I hadn't dragged you into all this."

"I wasn't dragged. I was intrigued. It was my own curiosity."

"I know. The box did it. To all of us."

"Only partly the box."

"I don't understand."

Christina slid around Roger and sat next to him on the couch, her fingers still kneading his forehead and temples. She pressed open his eyelids and held her hands still; their eyes met cautiously at first, then they looked more and more deeply into one another, both hesitating to blink lest the moment be lost. Their faces mirrored each other—first a gentle smile, then a look of wonderment, then teardrops down their cheeks. Roger wanted to kiss her, but held back; to kiss Christina, to look in her eyes at the same time, seemed somehow too intimate, a premature penetration of her soul. Christina watched Roger talk with his eyes; she nodded ever so slightly, partly to say to him she understood, even more to say to herself that it had finally happened; this was the man.

Right now they needed each other desperately for protection; tears obscured their loving stare. They fell into each other's arms and comforted deep-welling sobs. Christina broke their embrace and held Roger's face in both hands, stroking away his tears, reassuring herself that this was actually happening. She hadn't intended it, but her bathrobe parted slightly, exposing her right breast; she knew Roger saw it, but she made no move to cover herself. Instead she smiled at the situation, and even more at Roger, who kept his eyes on her face. Intimacy would come at the right time.

The lights suddenly flashed on and George Chang stood at the doorway. When Christina jumped up in surprise, the top of her bathrobe opened fully; she spun around, closed the robe, and turned back meekly. George, shocked and angry, spoke sternly in Chinese.

"But Elder Brother," Christina replied tearfully, "you don't understand. It's not what you think. We *are* aware of the terrible situation."

Roger stood up next to Christina. "George, there's no need to scold Christina. Nothing happened. At least not what you're thinking. And even if it did . . ."

"Professor Walden, I'm not making moral judgments. Christina has every right to choose her own company. You're both adults. It's just that you might have a better sense of timing. We've got a crisis on our hands, and we need a plan."

"George," Roger intervened, "I've been thinking about it all night. With the right lawyers and police protection, we'll be able to stay safe and put Lamarche behind bars. You see, first we—"

"Professor Walden, don't always try to control everything. You have involved my sister in a perilous situation. I know you didn't mean to, but the fact remains that it's terrible. More than that, you've involved our family. We Chinese always take care of our own. And we don't like to turn to the authorities. It hurts the family image and, in this case, it could make things worse."

"So what do we do?"

"There already is a plan, and it will work: the family has approved it."

* * *

Roger awakened with a start. An attractive young Chinese woman in a blue uniform was touching his arm.

"Sorry, sir. I didn't mean to scare you. We'll be landing in Honolulu soon. Would you like something to drink? Coffee or orange juice perhaps?"

Roger shook his head and tried to focus. Slowly he remembered that he was fleeing for his life. He looked around the first-class cabin of the China Air Lines Boeing 747. Most of the passengers justified the higher fare on the grounds of service, silence, and space. Roger had an even better reason: the smaller number of people in first class improved his odds of leaving the plane alive.

His seat, 13F, had been chosen carefully. Nestled by the window and protected by a bulkhead at the rear of the cabin, it gave him the best view of the other passengers. 13E was occupied by an intense American businessman who balanced a constant intake of cocktails and cigarettes with a constant output of little taps on a Japanese hand-held calculator. The frenzy of his seatmate gave Roger an un-threatening barrier protecting his flank.

Unbuckling his seat belt, Roger stepped around the man and walked shakily to the lavatory. Locking the door behind him, he was startled once again by what he saw in the mirror. His beard had been shaved off; instead, he sported a newly dyed gray moustache, neatly trimmed gray hair, and wire-rimmed glasses. The total effect was not a drastic change in features but rather the addition of thirty years to his age.

Roger returned to his seat. It had been only three days since Becky's murder. As the plane began its descent, he breathed deeply, trying to steady himself. *What would Becky have wanted me to do? What about Diane? What would she have said?* Neither thought helped at all. The trembling became more pronounced. Then another voice flashed through his head. *Give up trying to control. There is a plan. The family has approved it.* His shaking stopped as the plane touched the runway in Honolulu.

The Chang plan had been devised and implemented shortly after Christina called her brother with the frightening news. As the Changs made all the arrangements and sent him on this bizarre flight, Roger recognized the enormous power of a Chinese extended family to cope with crisis. Roger signed papers subleasing his apartment and placing his belongings in storage. His modest savings account was transferred into cash. His disguise was fashioned by a Chang relative who worked in a hairdressing salon. The forged passport, photograph matching the disguise, was in the name of sixty-year-old Albert Simpson from Silver Pass, North Dakota—all the work of a China-town printing and engraving shop. More papers gave both George and Christina access to the vault that contained the lacquer box.

Responding to Roger's questions before his departure, George systematically dismissed other options. Why not call the police? "There's absolutely no conclusive evidence against Lamarche," George said. "And besides, as soon as you call the cops, Lamarche's men will close in. The police can't protect you forever."

Why not just give Lamarche the box? "That won't work," George objected, "he would still kill you. You know too much— about the box, about who killed Becky, about Lamarche's whole game. Since you've got to escape, you might as well escape with a purpose. The fact Lamarche wants the box so badly should make you more stubborn. It's obviously worth a lot to them. Make it worth the same amount to you."

Roger gave Christina the key to the vault, which he had kept in his eyeglass case ever since the robbery. "We know it has the power to kill," he said solemnly. "Maybe someday we can find out its power to save."

"I hope so," Christina said, staring at the key. "But for now, you're going on a long voyage. There's a pretty good chance you'll be safe. At times like this, Chinese families draw closer, relying on very few trusted servants. It's kind of like the inner court of the old dynasties—we only trust the eunuchs, those whose power depends totally on us. We're relying on our best eunuchs."

"If I make it, will you join me in Taiwan?"

"Maybe. But your voyage is longer than merely to Taiwan. It's a journey to a completely different culture. You're going to have to lose yourself in order to find yourself. You don't understand, do you, Roger?"

"Maybe . . . a little," he replied, shaking his head.

"No, you don't understand at all. It's only when you begin to understand that we'll see each other again. And it's only when you understand fully that we can even consider . . ."

"Consider what?"

Christina kissed Roger gently on the cheek and ran back inside the Padanarum house.

148

* * *

Less than a day later, Albert Simpson was sitting in a corner of the first-class lounge at Honolulu International Airport, resting his hands on a black cane, watching warily for anything unusual. "China Air Lines Flight 016 is now ready for passenger boarding on the continuation of its flight to Taipei." Limping slightly to match his passport persona, Roger moved slowly through the corridor to the airplane.

Danger! Roger sensed it as soon as he reentered the cabin. Something was different, but what was it? *Oh my God*, he gulped silently. The compulsive chain-smoker was gone; 13E was now occupied by a well-built Chinese man in his early fifties, wearing a sport coat and holding an ominous-looking black leather bag in his lap.

When the elderly man stopped short, the stewardess took his arm. "Mr. Simpson, are you all right? Here, let me help you. We've got to get ready for takeoff."

The Chinese man stood up and looked hard at Roger. Strength draining from his legs, Roger had no problem appearing feeble as he fell into his seat. His heart beat rapidly as the big jet took off over the Pacific. Dinner was served and the man in 13E ate quietly, speaking to the flight attendants in Chinese about menu preferences. Occasionally he smiled in Roger's direction. Roger watched the first movie, a James Bond rerun, keeping his reading light on for greater security. When the movie was over, with its usual heroic and sensual conclusion, Roger and the man exchanged knowing smiles. But something was still wrong. The man kept examining Roger out of the corner of his eye.

Roger's seatmate slept for an hour or two; then he stirred, stood up, and walked to the lavatory, leaving his black bag behind. After making sure no one was looking, Roger grabbed the bag and opened it. His hands froze as he saw a file folder with a typed tab: "Walden, Roger." He leafed frantically through the file, looking in disbelief at photographs, newspaper clippings, medical records, even a dental chart. Barely able to make his fingers move, Roger opened a small leather pouch. It contained hypodermic needles and injection vials. Hearing the lavatory door opening, Roger desperately tossed everything into the bag, zipping it up and throwing it under the seat just before the man returned.

Roger looked fixedly out the window. Sitting down, the

Chinese man reached forward, retrieved the bag, and slowly started to open it. Roger reached up and rang the call button.

"Yes, Mr. Simpson," said the stewardess gently, deferring to his age, "how can we help you?"

"Uh . . . it's the smoking section. I'm allergic. Can't I get another seat?"

"I'm sorry, Mr. Simpson, the plane is absolutely full. Didn't you request 13F?"

"No. I'm worried about my heart. Too much smoke could cause palpitations."

The stewardess turned to the man next to him and spoke a few phrases in Chinese. The man looked with concern at Roger and then responded quickly to the stewardess. The exchange in Chinese increased Roger's anxiety; maybe the stewardess was also part of Lamarche's plot?

The woman smiled. "Don't worry, Mr. Simpson. This man doesn't smoke either. I think you'll be all right." She patted Roger on the arm and started to leave.

Roger thought quickly. He grabbed his chest and uttered a sharp grunt of pain. The stewardess pushed the other man out of the way and shouted for help. Roger writhed and threw his body into contortions. Within seconds the first flight officer and several attendants responded. Together they gently helped Roger out of his seat into the aisle, where they put his head on a pillow and covered him with blankets.

Roger grimaced and held his chest. "Oh God, my heart. It's an attack."

The first flight officer held back the crowd. "Is there a doctor here?" he asked loudly.

From behind him Roger heard a voice. "Yes, I'm a doctor. Let me through."

Roger closed his eyes in relief; he was safe, it had worked. Then he opened his eyes and shuddered as he saw the Chinese man hovering over him. The Chinese man opened his black bag, removed the small leather kit, assembled a syringe, and inserted the long needle into a vial.

Roger screamed. "No, not him! He's trying to kill me! Please don't let him touch me."

The man held Roger down by his shoulders and gestured for the others to assist him. He spoke fluent English. "It often happens with heart-attack victims. They tend to hallucinate." The attendants held Roger immobile. "Don't worry," the man said, "this is just a sedative." He injected the needle into Roger's arm and depressed the syringe. "And this," he said, holding up another syringe, "will stop the palpitations." Roger struggled to free himself, abandoning any pretense of looking like an old man.

"For God's sake," Roger shouted, "I was just faking. No heart attack. Just trying to escape this man. I'm really a professor. And a marathon runner. Doesn't anyone recognize me? Remember the New York Marathon? I . . ."

The needle bit into Roger's arm. He struggled weakly and then, with a quiver, his body relaxed. He was carried to a bunk in the flight attendants' quarters on the upper deck. The Chinese man rode next to the motionless body for the remaining five hours to Taipei.

Christina Chang threw herself into her eldest sister's arms and wept. They were sitting on the veranda of her sister's home on Lantau Island in the British Colony of Hong Kong. Ahead of them was Hong Kong Island itself, with Victoria Peak jutting through a bank of clouds. High-rise apartment buildings were draped like tinsel down the sides of the mountain. Below was the harbor, choked as always with tiny junks and ferries that somehow missed one another in the late-afternoon rush-hour maritime traffic. Lantau, with its monastery and fishing villages, was an island of peace and meditation, a perfect place from which to view Hong Kong and, beyond, the People's Republic of China. It was also a perfect place to reflect on the uncertain futures of nations and families.

"Dajie," Christina whimpered as her elder sister wiped the salty streaks from her face. "Oh, Dajie, I need you so much. Never so much as now."

"Quiet now," her sister said gently. "Tell me what's the matter."

Christina surprised herself by starting where she meant to end. "I've fallen in love. With a wonderful man. He's smart. He's handsome. He might even become rich someday."

Her sister's face brightened. "That's wonderful."

"No. No, it's terrible."

"Terrible to be in love? Why?"

Christina had meant to say it differently. "Because he's not Chinese."

Her sister frowned. "You know *I* have nothing against marrying a foreigner. But you know your father. You'll have to convince him."

"Dajie?" Christina spoke with a little pout on her lips. "I was wondering . . ."

"Wondering what?"

"If maybe you would talk to Father. You're the oldest. He'll respect your opinions."

"Xiaojie," her big sister replied a little sharply. "Did you come all the way to Lantau Island just to ask me that favor? You'd better tell me the whole story. Then I'll decide."

Christina began to tell her sister everything—the loneliness, mystery, horror, and unrealized passion. Her sister listened attentively, occasionally asking a question. "But Xiaojie, you've just met this professor. How do you know you love him?"

"I just do," Christina said firmly. "I've been around long enough in life to know."

"I wasn't doubting you," her sister said gently, "but I had to ask. Is there more?"

It was early evening before Christina finished her story. Her older sister looked into Christina's eyes and spoke gently. "You've come back to the *jia*, the family. You'll be safe here. The household has bodyguards. We'll take care of you. Everything will be all right."

"I can't thank you enough. But . . ."

"But what?"

"I need more than just safety. I need—"

"I know what you need." Her sister stroked Christina's hair. "You need a go-between to talk to Father, to make him understand that your professor might have the makings of a good Chinese. That will take some convincing."

"Will you do it?"

"Yes, of course. First over the phone. And then I'll go to Taipei and talk to him in person."

Christina hugged her sister. "You've always been there when I needed you."

"But will your professor friend really abide by Chinese customs? Will he prove himself fully to Father? Are you sure he loves you that much?"

Christina took a deep breath as she transformed herself from a pleading little sister into a composed and calculating adult. "I'm not sure he loves me. Certainly he has a lot of feelings about me, maybe a mixture of respect, intrigue, and need. Maybe a lot more than that. I just don't know. And I doubt he does."

"Is that enough to make him follow Chinese customs?"

"No, Elder Sister." Christina paused and smiled. "But that's not what will motivate him. He will have no choice. Learning to be Chinese will be essential to his survival."

"But what about your relationship with him? How will that develop?"

"In the Chinese way." Christina smiled a little. "It can be arranged."

"That's presuming that . . ." Christina's elder sister stopped in mid-sentence. They both knew what she was going to say. Everything depended on whether or not Roger Walden made it to Taiwan alive.

Several hundred miles away in another mansion a Chinese man opened a black leather bag and pulled out a file. Circling a number with his pencil, he picked up the telephone.

A servant brought a cordless phone to Christina. "Wei," she said expectantly, "is it you? Tell me. Is Professor Walden safe?"

"Miss Chang. Good news."

She held the phone slightly away from her ear. Her eyes grew larger. She pressed her forehead as if forcing the news to enter her brain. Then she nodded and said, "Thank God. You're really our true friend. I can't tell you what this means to me."

CHAPTER TWELVE

FAMILY

THE CHINESE DOCTOR EXAMINED

the motionless body; everything pointed to death. The face was gray, the clothes stained with morbid sweat. Officially, Albert Simpson was dead; according to the doctor's report, which was accepted by the Taipei medical examiner, the heart attack had killed an elderly man who ought never to have attempted trans-Pacific travel. Within a few hours, a coffin was flown back to the United States.

The doctor pulled up Roger's eyelids and focused a tiny penlight at his pupils. Roger stirred a little and groaned, raising his hands to his eyes to block the light. The doctor quickly filled a syringe from a small vial. Taking his hands from his eyes, Roger saw the man through the haze. "Oh God, not again, please don't do it again!" he screamed and struck out. The syringe flew through the air and broke against the wall.

The doctor held Roger down and spoke firmly. "Please, I know you're upset. I'm not trying to kill you. I'm Dr. Ren, family physician to the Changs, doctor to Christina's family. I flew with you from Los Angeles to look after your safety. Things got out of hand and I had to sedate you. You were about to reveal yourself."

Roger grabbed the doctor's wrists, his voice hissing like a cornered snake. "I don't know what to believe. All I know is that if you try to jab one more needle in me, I'm going to kill you. I don't have anything to lose."

Dr. Ren shouted. *"Kwai lai, Kwai lai . . . Waiguoren fafengle."* Three burly men rushed in. One held Roger's shoulders down while the other two pried his hands open to free the doctor's wrists.

Roger stopped struggling. "Okay, you bastards, go ahead. Kill me. You won't get the box anyway."

Suddenly the men's eyes snapped in the direction of the door. A small, elderly Chinese man with a wispy beard stood there. He waved his hand with a sweeping motion and the bodyguards immediately relaxed their grips. Roger made a move to get up, but the man pointed a long fingernail toward the bed; Roger fell back before the authoritative gesture. Placing his hands inside the sleeves of his blue gown, the man walked across the room and sat down in a chair next to the bed. He stared at Roger for a long moment, stroking his beard. Then he motioned to Dr. Ren to sit beside him and spoke in a quiet voice, *"Ren Daifu, ching ti wo fanyi."*

Even in his distress, Roger sensed the power emanating from the small figure. Dr. Ren spoke softly. "It is my honor to introduce the Patriarch of the Chang family, Chang Cheng-tai. He is better known as the Elder Uncle Chang or Chang Laobo to all of us. He is Christina's father. He wants me to interpret for him."

Roger, still groggy from the drugs, lifted himself on his elbows. "Why the hell should I believe that? Everyone's trying to kill me. All you want is the lacquer box. Let me out of here and then I'll believe you."

Dr. Ren translated Roger's outburst into Chinese. The old man glowered, obviously shocked by the sharp rejoinder; then he smiled and reached into his sleeve, pulling out a yellowed news clipping. Dr. Ren held up the clipping so that Roger could read it. It was a photograph of Christina displaying a piece of calligraphy with the old man standing at her side. The caption was in English: "Miss Christina Chang, reknowned calligrapher, and her proud father, Chang Cheng-tai. The clipping, Dr. Ren explained, was from Taiwan's English-language daily a year before, when Christina had returned to Taipei and won the annual calligraphy competition.

Roger stared at the photograph and then fell back on the bed and rubbed his head, trying to let reason overcome the pain and fear. Finally he nodded in acceptance. "I'm sorry. I hope you understand. I've been through hell these last few days. I wish we could have met under more pleasant circumstances. Your daughter's a remarkable woman. She's also been through a terrible trauma. How is she? Is she all right?"

Dr. Ren moved between the two languages with a surgeon's precise swiftness. Chang Laobo reassured Roger that Christina was well and staying with her sister in Hong Kong. He also apologized for the failure to inform Roger about Dr. Ren's identity. "The doctor is skilled in medicine, but perhaps he needs to take some postgraduate courses in psychology. Or at least he needs to remember to take his bag with him when he leaves his seat. Except for that little mistake, we thought it was better to keep his identity secret so that you would not seek to contact him and thus compromise your own disguise."

Roger sat up in bed as Dr. Ren put some embroidered pillows behind his back. Dr. Ren, Roger decided, was a true professional, not even reacting as he translated a criticism of himself. "I assume that this is Taiwan. Is this your home? What happens next?"

Favoring him with a fatherly smile, the Patriarch spoke through Dr. Ren, never taking his eyes off Roger. "You're in the hills outside Taipei, at the Chang estate we've occupied since the Communist bandits took over the mainland. As to what happens next, unless you have other plans for dinner, I'd welcome your company. Perhaps you'd like to freshen up a bit. Maybe a bath and a shave would literally take years off your life."

"One more thing, Professor," said Dr. Ren. "For safety's sake, and to keep from confusing the servants, we've decided to give you a Chinese name. I think you'll like it. It's Wang."

"Dream?" Roger wondered.

"No, different character, different tone. It means prince or king."

After his visitors left, Roger examined the room, which was hardly exotic. A crystal chandelier illuminated simple beige-uphol-stered armchairs and faded Oriental rugs. Opening the window, Roger found another disappointment when he scanned the city of Taipei. Instead of romantic temples and soft clouds, it looked like a valley of brick and cement with an acute case of Los Angeles smog. He could hear factory noises and make out the buzz of motor scooters in the distance. Neon lights flashed in the early evening. The hillsides seemed to have sprouted television antennas. Roger inhaled the odd combination of odors: musty old furniture, gritty soft coal dust, acrid garlic, sweetly burning incense.

"Gooda eveninck, Mista Wang."

Roger turned swiftly. The speaker was an attractive young woman in a light-blue cheongsam. She giggled as she took soft, quick steps across the room and stood in front of Roger, tugging at his hand. She looked up at him with a childlike smile. "I you help. Now bath. Okay, Mista Wang?"

Roger laughed nervously. "I may look like an old codger, but I can still take a bath by myself." He waited for the girl to leave, but she stood there smiling. "Okay," Roger said, gently pushing her hand away, "Mista Wang do bath himself. Thanks anyway."

Somehow she seemed to miss his point. "Good, Mista Wang." She opened the door to the bathroom and ran the water, testing it with her hand. "*Aiya*," she exclaimed with coquettish shyness, "too hot." Adjusting the taps, she returned to Roger. "I . . . Miss Sun. I you help."

Lightly pushing Roger into a chair, she knelt beside him, brushing her warm body against his leg as she unbuttoned his shirt. Roger blushed, trying to fend off her tiny hands. She shook her finger as if scolding him and continued to undo the buttons. She stood up to pull the shirt gently from his back. "Don't nervous," she giggled. "You American?"

"Yes," gulped Roger as Miss Sun unbuckled his belt, pulled down his zipper, and tugged his pants from his legs. "Yes, I American."

Roger ran into the bathroom and wrapped a towel around himself. Shutting the door, he took off his undershorts and sank into the steaming tub, groaning with delight at the heat on his aching muscles. He shut his eyes and let the sensation envelop him.

"Mista Wang strong man," said Miss Sun. She had moved silently into the bathroom. Roger knifed forward to cover himself; she knelt down and began to massage his neck and back.

"Mista Wang," she laughed again, "don't nervous . . . strong man . . . don't nervous." She pushed his torso back into the water and Roger grabbed a washcloth to cover himself. Then Miss Sun slowly massaged the tension out of his feet, calves, and thighs.

"God, I wish you were there in my marathon days," Roger exclaimed, glad to think of something to say.

As she continued to rub his forehead and chest, Roger found his anxiety turning into tingling. He opened his eyes and looked at Miss Sun. Her hair was starting to fall out of its neat bun, and her dress had opened just enough to reveal partly her uncovered breast.

159

She caught his glance and lightly slapped his hand as she buttoned her dress higher. "Mista Wang, no look." Then she accidentally brushed aside his washcloth. "Oh, Mr. Wang, you really American!"

Roger gulped, replaced the cloth, and then felt both relief and disappointment as Miss Sun ran out of the bathroom. When he walked into the bedroom, he found a blue silk gown laid out on the bed. Miss Sun returned with underclothing and black cloth slippers. "Mista Wang . . . no more old?!" she said with astonishment, looking at his freshly shaven face. She helped him into his gown. Walking over to the full-length mirror, Roger enjoyed the portrait of a Chinese scholar with a Western face.

"*Ni shi Waiguoren . . . huoshi Zhongguoren?*" asked Miss Sun with a little smile. When Roger looked puzzled, she switched to English. "You foreign? Or Chinese?"

Roger touched her lightly under the chin. "My dear Miss Sun, you already know the answer to that . . . up close and personal. American foreigner, all the way."

She laughed, not because she understood but because he was laughing, and it was her duty to make him feel comfortable.

Miss Sun guided Roger down a long corridor to a palatial staircase that led to the public rooms. Surveying his surroundings, he found Miss Sun's question to him oddly appropriate for the huge house. Was it foreign? Or Chinese? It resembled nothing so much as an English manor house with an Oriental flavor. His feet creaked across heavy oak floors; beamed ceilings hung at least twenty feet above his head. The intricately carved woodwork of the central hall was lit by heavy crystal sconces. Massive Chinese furniture, fashioned in fantastic rococo patterns of the late-Qing dynasty, stood like emissaries from the Middle Kingdom to an alien culture. Even the huge blue-and-white ceramic vases and the exquisite Song landscape on the wall seemed to be chinoiserie decorating the country seat of an English duke.

At the great doorway to the dining room, Miss Sun nodded for Roger to enter; then she vanished into the shadows. Here, Roger decided, China emerged victorious. Four large bronze lanterns distracted the eye from the vastness of the room and provided a crisscross of light. A twelve-panel gold-and-black lacquer screen divided the room. The Patriarch and Dr. Ren were seated in front of the screen.

"Mr. Wang, glad to see you." Dr. Ren shook Roger's hand warmly, gesturing for him to sit down. "My goodness, it looks like you've found the Fountain of Youth."

"My thanks for your attention, Dr. Ren. Would it be impolite to ask why your English is so good? And where did you hear about Ponce de León?"

"It's not so surprising. I studied at Duke and then took my M.D. at Johns Hopkins. A great many Chinese from Taiwan have similar educations. Besides, everyone on Taiwan learns American history in school."

The Patriarch nodded formally to his guest and then gestured to a servant who brought Roger a Scotch on the rocks. "Chang Laobo," Roger exclaimed. "I've heard about Chinese hospitality. But how did you know my favorite drink?"

The old man smiled and put his fingertips together, accentuating the long nail on his left little finger that symbolized the scholar's aversion to manual labor. He began to speak, nodding sharply to Dr. Ren when he wanted a translation to begin. "We know a lot about you, Mr. Wang. A combination of computers and confidants can reveal a lot. Besides, you have shared moments of intimacy with my daughter. Intimacy reveals even more."

Roger choked on his drink and fumbled for a reply. "Not really intimate . . . just good friends . . . brought together under trying circumstances."

Chang Laobo touched his beard and looked into Roger's eyes. "Certainly you must agree that viewing the private areas of my daughter's body constitutes a moment of intimacy. Now I am aware that the relationship has not been fully consummated. That is for the best. It shows that my daughter is too prudent for that to happen."

Roger looked in astonishment. "You don't understand. It wasn't that way at all—"

"That's enough," interrupted Dr. Ren. "Don't contradict Chang Laobo."

"But—"

"I mean it. It's not worth it to question his words."

Chang Laobo pretended that the interchange between Roger and Dr. Ren had not occurred. "Under usual circumstances . . . I mean, in a Chinese society, neither side would have let things develop so far. We would have had a go-between. But I know the West is different. Well, so be it. We shall have to start again."

161

Roger looked puzzled. "Start what again?"

Chang Laobo looked equally puzzled. "Start a relationship with my daughter, of course. The right way. You do want that, don't you?"

Roger didn't know what to say. "Well, I'm not sure. You're right. In the West, we would do it differently. We usually let these matters happen between the parties themselves. Sometimes they ripen into love."

Chang Laobo leaned forward in his chair. "You mean you don't love Christina? Surely you have not shared intimate moments with a woman of quality whom you do not love?"

Roger thought quickly. "I feel very strongly about your daughter, Chang Laobo. It might have developed into love. I would certainly like the relationship to develop. The knives of hate cut into our flesh before our hearts could fully open." Christ, thought Roger as Dr. Ren translated, don't overdo it. You're not going to impress the man by trying to sound like a latter-day Confucius.

Chang Laobo looked steadily at Roger. "I'm satisfied. There will be future opportunities for exploring ties between you and my daughter. Meanwhile, Christina has requested that we treat you like one of the Chang clan, perhaps like a distant relative who has appeared in front of the guardian lions pleading for help. I accept my daughter's suggestion. Let us dine together as family."

Dr. Ren steadied Chang Laobo as he walked around the screen to a large square table, its legs carved with four-clawed dragons. Roger was seated in the place of honor.

Servants brought the first dish of cold sliced lamb, chicken, duck, and vegetables. Chang Laobo noted with pleasure that Roger waited to be served by him. "Mr. Wang, this is but a simple home meal. We Chinese don't have banquets unless several people can join us at the table." Chang Laobo lifted his glass. "To the safe arrival of our newest relative. May he find peace in the Chang *jia*." Roger congratulated himself on swallowing without a grimace.

Chang Laobo ate a little food and set down his chopsticks. "Mr. Wang, we admire your extraordinary career. You have achieved considerable success in scholarship, which we revere, and in athletics, which Americans revere. Now you find yourself in a demanding situation that may require both your talents."

Roger opened his mouth to speak, but Chang Laobo raised his finger to stop him. "Mr. Wang, as we look over your past, we also sense something troubling. So does my beloved daughter. You have lived different lives. But you have also suffered many deaths. Tell me, Mr. Wang, what is it you seek? Life or death?"

Roger carefully put down his chopsticks and collected his thoughts. He reached for his glass. "I'd like to propose a toast. To my new friends and my new family. You have saved me from death. But, Chang Laobo, you've done more. You have looked into my heart. My feelings are naked before your eyes . . . just like my body before the curious glances of Miss Sun."

Chang Laobo laughed and drained his Shaoxing wine. "Ah yes, Miss Sun. Not a woman of quality, but she does appreciate quantity. Don't disappoint her. It will ruin her standing in the household."

Roger laughed. It gave him time to construct an honest and thoughtful response to Chang Laobo's question. "Young men often like to climb mountains," Roger said slowly. "Sometimes one scales what appears to be the highest peak, only to find another mountain range ahead with summits that seem impossible. It's then that one wonders why he is climbing at all. That's when one ponders life and death."

Chang Laobo toyed with the giant prawns on his plate. "I am also such a man. When I was young, I inherited my family's ship-building company, but I also inherited the revolutionary spirit of the times. I succeeded at both. The company became the biggest ship-building firm in China. At the same time, I led China's merchants in support of the Nationalist revolution. We followed Generalissimo Chiang Kaishek. I served in his government as Minister of Commerce. I introduced heavy commercial taxes that cost my own family dearly, but no cost was too great if China could be independent, democratic, and proud. Then came my black void." The old man grinned, concealing his pain. "The Communists brought a reign of terror, forcing true patriots into exile. We left everything behind— our belongings, our company, our hopes."

Roger felt Chang's hurt. Taiwan was supposed to have been a temporary stop to recoup strength after defeat in the 1940s. Over the years the island exile had become permanent; the cry of "Re-conquer the Mainland" had become empty rhetoric. Would Taiwan become his own exile as well? Roger wondered.

Chang Laobo smiled faintly. "So, Mr. Wang, I could have taken my life. The silken cord, that's what we used traditionally. No, I thought to myself, the more heroic route is to climb mountains

163

more slowly, see beauty up close, not viewing flowers from horseback. I still have my hopes for China, but meanwhile I have more time to love art, music, friends, and most of all, my family."

Roger inhaled deeply, fighting back tears. "I have not made it to the top of American scholarship. And, with my wife's death, I lost everything that made the struggle more tolerable."

The Patriarch put his hand on Roger's sleeve. "We know these things, my son. You are young, and you still can reach those summits. But it's crucial to know why you are climbing and how to select your mountains with care. I believe that. So does my daughter. I shall try to help you help yourself."

The three men retired to the baronial living room, where they sat before the fire. Roger accepted a fine French cognac and let a servant snip off the end of a Cuban cigar. He gestured around the room. "Is all of this also part of Chinese tradition?"

Dr. Ren answered for the old man. "Hardly. It was built by a British merchant in the 1880s, when Taiwan was just beginning to develop. It was the residence of a wealthy Japanese merchant during their occupation. Chang Laobo has developed unusual ways of appreciating the best of both East and West." Dr. Ren added his own footnote: "Sorry that the art is so inadequate. Chang Laobo chooses to put his money into other things."

Roger puffed on his cigar and took a sip of cognac. "Ah yes, art. Chang Laobo, surely Christina has told you about the lacquer box."

Chang rang a little bell and a servant appeared with a briefcase. He dismissed the servant, pulled a small key from his gown, and opened the case. To Roger's astonishment, it contained a sheaf of color photographs of the lacquer box. "Don't be so surprised, Mr. Wang. It was really quite easy. The papers you signed allowed us to enter the warehouse and photograph the box."

"But you must have done the whole job yesterday."

"Yes. Dr. Ren brought the film with him."

"Can you figure out its real meaning?" Roger asked hopefully. "Does it tell you where the art collection is hidden?"

The old man put on spectacles, perused each photograph for several minutes, finally looking up somberly. "I understand the symbolism, Mr. Wang. But I cannot tell you. It would be wrong."

Roger felt a surge of anger. "Wrong? What do you mean, wrong? How can you possibly say that? That damned box almost killed your daughter. It almost killed me. Don't we deserve to know its significance?"

Dr. Ren cautioned Roger. "Watch yourself, my friend. I won't translate what you said. No one talks to Chang Laobo that way. I'm going to ask him politely if he might explain his words."

The old man smiled as Dr. Ren translated, but the grim set of his eyes showed he had not missed Roger's cutting tone.

"Mr. Wang, I can understand you are puzzled. Let me explain. Each symbol on the box is like a Chinese character. Each panel is like a line of poetry. Every man must read the poem himself. The act of beholding is but the other end of the act of creating. Artistic messages mean nothing in the abstract. They must be absorbed into one's own experience, one's own aspirations."

Roger held himself in check. "With all respect, sir, I understand what you are saying. But can't you see? I know nothing about the Chinese language or Chinese tradition. I can't begin to unravel the box on my own. Worse yet, I'm trapped in a mystery I didn't create."

Chang Laobo poured himself more cognac and swirled it in his glass. "We are all caught in a mystery we didn't create. It is the mystery of life. And the inevitability of death. And the ultimate mystery: can our lives surmont our own deaths?"

"Please, Chang Laobo. I beg you." Roger's composure was ebbing. The damned box had imprisoned him; his life was threatened and he had no idea when, or if, he would be safe again. "You looked at the box for only a few minutes and you know more about it than I would in a lifetime. Please help me out. If not for me, for Christina?"

The old man hobbled to Roger's chair, looking at him much as a father might, with a mixture of affection and annoyance. "Mr. Wang, believe it or not, I am helping you out. Someday perhaps you'll understand better. You want answers, and you don't even know the right questions. All right, I'll give you a clue." He reached into the briefcase, leafed through the photographs, handing one to Roger. Roger recognized it immediately—second panel, scholar holding up his hand with thumb and finger at right angles.

"What does it look like?" the old man asked gravely.

"I think it's a teacher."

"And what does his hand look like?"

"Well, perhaps like a right angle, maybe a corner of something."

Chang Laobo smiled. "The Master said: I teach only those who are eager to learn. Only those who are excited about learning will I instruct. If I hold up one corner of a square and my student cannot come back with the other three, then the lesson is over."

"Thank you, Chang Laobo."

"Don't thank me, thank yourself. It's getting late, but we'll continue the lesson, one more corner of a square. I do know a little about the Gao family." Chang walked slowly to the fireplace, his small body seeming to enlarge in the shadows.

"Gao Zhenggai was a great official of the late-Qing dynasty. He was also closely linked to my grandfather through something known as the *guandu shangban*, cooperation between officials and merchants. Both were committed to China's modernization and they worked together on the shipbuilding firm." Chang recounted the history of Gao Zhenggai, including the tragic last chapter of his life. "When I was a young man, my grandfather told me how Gao Zhenggai faced death by slicing rather than tell the Boxers about the foreigners in his home, the Ma family. For me it has always been a tale of great courage. It is the Confucian virtue of *xin*—literally it means a man stands by his words."

Roger listened attentively. "Did you say that Gao Zhenggai was protecting a foreign family, the Ma family? Could that possibly be a Chinese name for the MacDonald family—my wife's grandparents?"

The old man nodded.

"Oh my God! I might have sold the box. I could have thrown away the hopes of a man who saved my own relatives."

Chang Laobo removed a framed photograph from the wall. "This is a photograph taken in 1898. There's my grandfather and Gao Zhenggai. See the younger man standing in his robes? That's Gao Zhonglu, son of the great Patriarch, who witnessed his father's execution two years later. He wanted to fulfill his father's dream. After the downfall of the last imperial dynasty in 1912, he became a professor of philosophy. He worked with great thinkers, like Hu Shi and Li Dazhao, trying to find an intellectual formula to guide China's modernization."

The old man began to cough and grabbed the mantelpiece to steady himself. A servant rushed to help him, but Chang dismissed him with a wave of his hand. He cleared his throat. "It's a sad story, Mr. Wang. Gao Zhonglu couldn't find the path."

"Couldn't unify thought and action?" Roger suggested.

Chang Laobo smiled wearily. "You're not a bad student. Yes, that was the problem. His estate fell apart, like Beijing itself, torn by war, first with Japan, then between the Nationalists and Communists. In that awful period, he must have sent the box to Mrs. Ma for safekeeping. He had a stroke and died in 1949. Dr. Ren here was Professor Gao's physician. He followed my request not to leave Beijing until the old man was gone."

Roger stood up and took a last puff on his cigar. "But what's the rest? Is that the end of the Gao family? Their treasure? Their dream?"

Chang Laobo sat down next to Roger. "Young man, I told you you'd be frustrated. I've lost touch with the Gaos these past forty years. As Dr. Ren knows, Jonglu had a son, a rather fervent Communist type, but who knows if he's still alive? As for the treasure, there definitely was one. My grandfather told me about it—several thousand works of art of exceptional quality, sort of a miniature Palace Museum. Given today's prices, it must be worth at least a billion, maybe several times that figure."

Roger's jaw dropped. "You're not serious. We're talking about billions of dollars? In U.S. currency?"

"It *would* be worth that much, *if* it still existed. But, Mr. Wang, who knows if such a fortune could have survived the ravages of China in the past century? Nothing gives any hint about where the treasure was hidden in the first place. I looked carefully, but I could not find it in the symbolism on the outside of the box."

"Then what about me? Am I a permanent fugitive?"

Chang Laobo stood up. "Mr. Wang. You know a lot about the West, but when it comes to China, you are just a beginner. Remember what we have learned tonight. Above all, remember this: the Gao dream is much bigger than the treasure. And it's not just a Gao dream, it's also a Chang dream. It is a dream shared by all the Chinese people—over a billion of us—whether we live on the Chinese mainland, Taiwan, or overseas. Someday China must be modern and unified, but China must also rediscover its own roots."

Folding his arms into his sleeves, Chang Laobo continued. "I have not explained the box to you tonight because Gao Jenggai would not have wanted it that way. You, Mr. Wang, have been drawn to the edges of the dream. You may not see it now, but your predicament may be a great gift. You have a choice. You can waste away at the bottom of the mountain, or you can begin a new climb—one that could bring a new life for you and, just maybe, for others as well."

Chang Laobo touched Roger's shoulder with his long fingernail. "You ask if you are a permanent fugitive? Remember this. The most elusive fugitives are those who become the greatest pursuers."

The old man picked up the briefcase. "I will give you these photographs when I think the time is right. The box could unlock two doors—scholarship and wealth—but you're not ready yet." He nodded formally and moved into the shadows.

Roger looked at Dr. Ren. "What did Chang Laobo mean? How can a fugitive become a pursuer? Why can't I have the photographs?"

Dr. Ren spoke with a physician's gentle firmness. "You're tired. In time, you may come to realize that this night may have been among the most important in your life. Chang Laobo is not the most brilliant man on earth, but he's the wisest I've ever known. Ponder his words, as I always do, and you're likely to find profound truths. Meanwhile, Chang Laobo has set aside a suite for you in the south wing. You're free to move about the mansion and you'll be under twenty-four-hour protection, even though you'll seldom see your guards."

Dr. Ren paused, looking hard at Roger. "Of course, we can't risk anyone discovering you. We must transform you into a Chinese-American scholar coming back to learn his language and seek his roots. I'll perform a little plastic surgery around the cheeks and eyes to help the illusion—reversible at a later date if you wish. Fortunately, you're one of those Caucasians whose bone structure, hair color, and physique make it relatively easily."

"An operation?" Roger gasped. "Why an operation? Can't I just stick around the house? I won't take any chances."

"Don't be so worried," Dr. Ren replied confidently. "It's minor surgery and without it, you're a sitting duck. Right now you look so obvious, anyone could figure out you're in hiding. There's no alternative. We'll do it as soon as possible." Only three bodyguards, Miss Sun, and the chef had seen Roger. Chang Laobo had decided the surgery was essential before Roger could take the chance of meeting relatives and other servants. "The Chang household is powerful," Dr. Ren continued. "We can hold off Lamarche's men on the outside. But we need your help within. You've got to play the role."

"For how long? Will I see Christina? Are you sure I'm safe?"

"Take it easy," Dr. Ren counseled quietly. "You're safe as long as you follow instructions. You could be here a long time. I just don't know. Christina's under guard on Lantau Island in Hong Kong. Maybe she'll come here. I don't know. It all depends on Chang Laobo."

"The operation—you're sure it's reversible? I don't mind playing Roger Wang for a while. But I don't want to lose Roger Walden in the process."

"Of course," the doctor answered firmly. "Sleep well."

Roger stared at the dying embers. Nothing seemed to fit. He stood up and tried to shake off the fatigue, alcohol, and confusion. He heard a rustling outside the door. "Oh, Mista Wang. Don't nervous. Don't nervous. Only Miss Sun. I you help."

Roger caught the scent of her perfume as she supported his sagging body. "Poor Mista Wang. Tired." His head still spinning, Roger lost track of their path as she led him to a suite of rooms, the heavy Victorian furniture relieved by Chinese scrolls and the smell of incense. He didn't resist as she guided him to the bed, pulled down the comforter, undressed him, and helped him into a sleeping gown. She brushed her hand over his thighs as she tied the cord and giggled. "You still American?" Then, singing in a light voice, she tugged at Roger's tie cord. "Oasay, canna you see . . . ?"

Roger laughed and she laughed in response. "Good night, Miss Sun."

Miss Sun promptly climbed into the bed, straddling his chest and massaging his temples. Roger found his will to resist deserting him utterly. Her hands flowed down his arms to his stomach where she traced little patterns on his abdomen. Then, looking into his eyes, her hand slipped under the comforter, bringing him an intense, almost excruciating, pleasure. She rose, stood by the bed, and slowly removed her yellow gown and pantaloons. As she bent over him, Roger encouraged her warm hands, mouth, and body as they enveloped him. She arched her back, her small but full breasts with enlarged brown nipples dancing in the soft light. Her throat emitted tiny high-pitched rhythmic sounds as they made love, like a flirtatious bird in a bamboo cage.

Roger was deeply asleep when Miss Sun silently broke from his embrace. He didn't feel Dr. Ren inject the anesthesia. It was a completely Western operation, but the result was to produce a newly Eastern man. Roger Walden had had his last sleep; Roger Wang would awaken the next day.

CHAPTER THIRTEEN

SINIFICATION

TAIPEI, EARLY 1990s

"DR. REN," ROGER SCREAMED AS HE

stumbled out of bed and crawled across the floor. "DR. REN . . . WHERE THE HELL ARE YOU?"

"Right here," the doctor replied as he guided Roger back to the bed. "Don't worry. The surgery went perfectly. Now you have about ten days of wearing these bandages. Miss Sun will always be here to help."

"Why the hell couldn't you tell me *when* you were going to do the surgery?" Roger asked furiously, shoving Dr. Ren's hand away.

"I *did* tell you when," Dr. Ren responded calmly. "I said we'd do the operation as soon as possible. Besides, what difference does it make to you? Chang Laobo ordered me to do the surgery last night. Once the healing is complete, you're safer. So is everyone else."

"You know," Roger snapped, "I'm getting a little tired of being treated like a child. I haven't been able to make a decision for myself since I left New York."

"Maybe it's better that way," Dr. Ren counseled calmly. "At least you're alive."

Roger stayed angry for days. Unable to see anything around him, he looked inside to memories and sadness, to danger and fear.

172

Time was an accordion, compressed frantically in spasms of anger and then drawn out with a sigh into long periods of blankness and sleep.

Dr. Ren attempted to reason with him. "Please try to understand. Chang Laobo is endangering all of us in order to protect you."

"When can I go back to New York?" Roger snapped back.

"I don't know. We're trying to build a legal case that will convict Lamarche. It's not easy. It could be months. It may be impossible altogether."

"Why don't you just kill the bastard?"

"Professor Walden! I can't believe you're saying that. Chang Laobo believes deeply in Chinese traditional humanism and in modern Western law. Both justify killing only in self-defense. We won't kill unless others attack us."

"Why can't I have the photographs of the box?"

"Frankly, even after you can see again, they won't mean much to you. You're going to have to learn classical Chinese before you can go any further with the box. Chang Laobo is right. First things first."

"Why don't I just walk out of here when I get my eyesight back? Why should I stick around?"

"Go ahead," the doctor replied sternly. "You'll get killed, of course. But it will be a lot easier on the rest of us. Now I'd advise you to cool down. Accept things. You might even enjoy it."

Eventually Roger took the doctor's advice. Fury slowly turned into fascination as he began enjoying the challenge of being a blind man in a foreign country. By the end of a week, it was a new game, with Miss Sun his playmate. One morning she presented his first Chinese breakfast that the Chang servants had left outside his door. Roger cautiously touched and sniffed the dishes, gingerly tasting each item. He found the rice gruel bland until he added milk and sugar, prompting him to teach Miss Sun to sing, "Kinga Wheeta, so gooda to eata." Pickles and sliced cold meats were not his ideal breakfast fare, but he immediately became addicted to long thin crullers with soybean milk.

"What are these wonderful things?" he asked Miss Sun. She didn't answer so he asked again. "This food . . . what is it?" Still no answer. "Please tell, Miss Sun."

Finally, after a long pause, she spoke. "Mista Wang . . . sorry, no more English; Dr. Ren say just Chinese." She walked to his chair. "You want say, 'what this is,' must say, '*jeige shi shemma?*'

Roger thought for a moment and picked up a doughnut. "*Jeige shi shemma?*"

Miss Sun giggled, "*Jeige shi yutiao . . . yutiao.*"

Roger held the doughnut and took a small bite. "*Jeige shi shemma? Jeige shi yutiao.* Oh damn, what's next? How do I say, 'Mr. Wang thinks doughnuts are good to eat'?

Miss Sun giggled again. She took Roger's hand and pressed it to her. "*Wo shi Sun Xiaojie.*" Then she jabbed her finger into his chest. "*Ni shi Wang Xiensheng.*" Finally she put the doughnut back into Roger's hands and said, "*Wang Xiensheng hen xiang chi yutiao,*" and broke into laughter.

Using the doughnut as a pointer, Roger poked her in the ribs. "*Ni shi Sun Xiaojie.*" Banging it on his head, he continued, "*Wo shi Wang Xiensheng.*" And finally stuffing it in his mouth: "*Wang Xiensheng hen xiang shi yutiao.*"

Miss Sun couldn't stop laughing. "Mista Wang . . . you say wrong . . . you say, 'Mista Wang wants be doughnut' . . . not say '*shi yutiao*' . . . *say chi yutiao.*' "

"Oops," Roger chuckled, "*Wang Xiensheng hen xiang chi yutiao.*"

"No 'oops'," laughed Miss Sun. "Chinese say '*aiya . . . Zhongguoren shuo aiya.*' "

"*Aiya,*" Roger exclaimed. "*Wang Xiensheng shuo* oops . . . *Zhongguoren shuo aiya . . . Aiya, Wang Xiensheng hen xiang chi yutiao.*"

Miss Sun hopped on his lap and began stuffing *yutiao* in his mouth. As she fed him, Roger's fingers slipped into her nightclothes and he tickled her underarms and inner thighs. She made a weak attempt to push him away and then relented, still giggling, as he opened her silk top and began to nuzzle her breasts.

"*Wang Xiensheng hen xiang chi yutiao,*" he said, his mouth beginning to circle her nipples and draw them out.

"*Aiya, Wang Xiensheng,*" she replied, still pretending to be shocked as he moved from nipple to nipple. Suddenly her head turned around as she felt another presence in the room. She pushed Roger away and jumped up. "*Aiya, Ren Daifu laile.*"

Roger, still laughing, repeated her expression, "*Aiya, Ren Daifu laile.*" Miss Sun tried to put her hand over Roger's mouth, but she was too late. Roger blurted out, "*Wang Xiensheng hen xiang chi Ren Daifu.*"

Dr. Ren walked over to Roger's chair. "My dear Mr. Wang. I

know you barbarians have strange tastes. But somehow it seems inappropriate to begin your Chinese language lessons by learning the phrase, 'Mr. Wang enjoys eating Dr. Ren.' "

Thereafter making certain the door was well bolted, Miss Sun became his teacher as well as his companion. A cassette recorder captured her rendition of key Chinese phrases and his English translations. Wandering around his three-room suite—bedroom, bathroom, and study—he asked Miss Sun, *"Jeige shi shemma?"* each time he bumped into chances to improve his vocabulary. "Writing brush? . . . *bi.*" "Ink? . . . *mo.*" "Tea? . . . *cha.*" "Door? . . . *men.*" "Clothing? . . . *yifu.*" Under Miss Sun's instruction, proper nouns were linked in short phrases. "I'm hungry . . . *wo hen e.*" "Please come here now . . . *ching xiandzai lai jer.*" "Put on clothes . . . *chwan yifu.*" "Drink tea . . . *he cha.*" "Eat food . . . *chifan.*" "I am . . . *wo shi.*" "You are . . . *ni shi.*" "He is . . . *ta shi.*"

At first the four tones of Mandarin Chinese confused him, but Miss Sun patiently taught him to detect the differences—*"ma, ma, ma, ma,"*—high, rising, low, and falling. Each tone, Roger soon discovered, had a totally different meaning and referred to a unique written character—"mother, hemp, horse, scold." He experimented with the simplest form of Chinese humor, linking together the same sounds with different tones: *ma ma ma*—"the mother scolds the horse."

Without sight, Roger acutely sensed sounds and smells around him. The winter winds and rainfalls played across his ears; his skin detected variations in humidity. He asked the chef to bring standard cooking ingredients in different bowls so he could tell them apart and learn their names. The fungi, totally unfamiliar to a foreigner, intrigued him most—white fungus, cloud ear fungus, staghorn bamboo fungus, black winter mushroom, fresh white mushroom.

A radio introduced him to Chinese music, both the gushy romantic variety and traditional Beijing operas. To Miss Sun's endless delight, he mimicked the arias in a screeching voice. Putting a glass-tasseled lampshade on his head, Roger became the noble prince shrieking his love song to a favorite concubine. *"Wo shi Wang wang. Ni shi xiao Sun. Wo ai, aaaiii, aaaiii ni* . . . I'm Prince Wang. You are little Sun. I love, loooove, loooove you."

"Today we remove your bandages." Roger tried to appear relaxed in front of Chang Laobo, Miss Sun, and the bodyguards. He shuddered as Dr. Ren's cold metal surgical scissors cut through the heavy white gauze and winced as the stitches were removed. Then, to a murmur of excitement, Roger opened his eyes.

At first squinting in the full-length mirror, then opening his eyes a little more, Roger dimly saw a Chinese man looking back at him. His black hair set off high cheekbones; his eyes seemed narrower with the lids pulled into an almond shape. He turned to Chang Laobo and Dr. Ren, carefully folding his hands into the sleeves of his gown to enhance the effect. "*Wo mei xiangdao. Wo jen shi Zhong-guoren. Gungxi, Ren Daifu. Duoxie, Chang Laobo* . . . I don't believe it. I'm a Chinese. Congratulations, Dr. Ren. My deepest thanks, Chang Laobo."

The room was silent as Chang Laobo addressed Roger. Even though the Patriarch spoke slowly, his Chinese was too difficult for Roger to follow. Dr. Ren translated. "Welcome, Mr. Wang. Now you're not Roger Walden, you're Roger Wang. But I've decided that you need a real Chinese given name. You can continue to call yourself Roger for informal conversations, but your given name henceforth will be Jishi . . . Wang Jishi . . . Wang the dedicated scholar."

Patriarch Chang tapped his fan sharply three times; the door opened to reveal a procession of servants, each carrying a burden. Like a director blocking an opera scene, the Patriarch commanded servants with gestures of his fan. A heavy rosewood desk with two matching armchairs were set down in a window-lined alcove overlooking the garden. The desktop was neatly arranged with a Chinese-English dictionary, several Chinese-language textbooks, a *Zihai* (the "Sea of Words") thesaurus, pens, brushes, tablets of paper, an inkstone, and a silk-covered box of pressed ink blocks. Bookcases lined the walls where the alcove merged into the room, shelves filled with Chinese classics of literature and history.

The servants formed a bowing cordon around a chunky man in his fifties, circular bald head and smooth face bobbing on triangular blue gown. The Patriarch nodded deferentially. "This gentleman is named Wen, Scholar Wen. He will teach you Chinese."

With that, the Patriarch retired and everyone followed, leaving Roger and Scholar Wen alone. Roger put out his hand and spoke in English. "Mr. Wen, it's a pleasure to meet you."

Scholar Wen, refusing the handshake and thrusting his hands into his sleeves, replied haughtily in Chinese. "I don't speak English. I don't speak any foreign tongues. This is China. Don't ever forget it. We speak Chinese."

"I'm sorry," Roger responded with as much humility as his limited Chinese vocabulary permitted. "I'm really sorry, Mr. Wen. I eat-eat Chinese."

Wen scowled. "You must call me Scholar Wen, never Mr. Wen. Besides, your Chinese is awful. You must say I'll try to speak Chinese, not eat-eat Chinese."

"I am truly sorry," Roger replied, feeling both put down and put upon.

"All right," Scholar Wen continued coldly. "Now sit down. We shall begin our studies."

Selecting a large red volume and pointing to ten large characters written on the first page, Scholar Wen spoke slowly so that Roger could understand most of what he said: "We will study in the old-fashioned way. You will learn the characters, a few hundred basic ones at the beginning. You will learn to recognize them, and to write them. Then, when you have enough, we will start to read. Simple texts at first, more complicated later. Eventually the Classics."

"But I can only speak a few sentences of Chinese. How can I read and write?"

"Don't ask stupid questions. I am a teacher. I know how to teach. You will learn. Ask me if you don't understand a word and I will explain. We will have four hours of class each day, six days a week. Each lesson will begin with a test, and it will require about six hours of work on your own to prepare for the tests. If you fail, we shall stay with the assignment until you pass."

Casting aside annoyance at Scholar Wen's didactic approach, Roger was initially intrigued by the calligraphic language and its mnemonic challenges. Like all beginning Chinese students, he enjoyed how components of simple characters made fanciful little statements. The word for "house," jia, 家 was a roof ⼧ with a pig 豕 under it. The character for "word," zi, 字 was a roof ⼧ with a boy ⼦ studying under it. The word for "peace," an, 安 was a roof ⼧ with a woman ⼥ sitting under it.

Roger's fascination faded as he struggled nightly with flash cards to memorize the first thousand characters. He often hit plateaus of memory when each new character learned would push another from his mind. The characters no longer made simple sense. Sometimes they were mind-boggling in the numbers of strokes—such as Taiwan 臺灣 two characters involving thirty-nine strokes to put on paper. He wondered how Becky had survived Chinese linguistic torture.

He felt like a chrysalis, enclosed in a luxurious silk cocoon, the ultimate sabbatical from life. The lacquer box, which he hadn't seen for months, seemed a distant dream, the cause but not the cure of his predicament. No one answered his questions about Christina, so he stopped asking. As long as he stayed in the protective embrace of the Chang mansion, he seemed safe from Lamarche; at least that was what he told himself when he had awful nightmares about Becky's murder and the escape from New York. His biggest challenge was simply to keep going as he followed Scholar Wen's lockstep curriculum and tried to preserve his sanity in the process.

Why was he doing this? Roger kept asking himself the question. The most obvious answer was that there wasn't any alternative. He couldn't escape. But why put up with Chinese-style grammar school? His long-term hope was to crack the mystery of the box; it seemed only remotely possible at the moment, but the lure of a fortune in Chinese art was hard to resist. It would be delightful, among other things, to see the look on Dorothy MacDonald's face. In the meantime, it was a pretty comfortable existence, a far cry from a Harlem tenement. Besides, he was enjoying the role of visiting Chinese-American scholar, garnering a level of respect from the Chang household quite different from that accorded an assistant professor in the United States.

"Be the best you can with what God gave you." Roger had rested uneasily with his father's homespun American work ethic, especially since he sensed his father yearned to be more than a master plumber in urban Philadelphia. "I told Mrs. Murdock not to flush." His father recounted the story often, the laughter bringing tears to his eyes, mirth disguising sadness. "Write the goddamn book" was his father's last practical advice before dying of cancer, offered when Roger described his publish-or-perish dilemma. "Don't buck the system." Memories of his father evoked both pride and pathos. Americans who bucked the system—progressives, liberals, reformers— were recurrent subjects of Roger's research. Politicians sometimes bent the system, Roger thought ruefully, but not assistant professors.

"My father was really an American Confucian," Roger explained to Miss Sun, who listened attentively, hiding her bafflement. "Okay, I'll be a filial son, at least for a little while."

Roger knew there was a deeper reason why he tolerated his strange confinement. "Miss Sun, when it comes to women, does one owe loyalty to dead lovers or to live ones?"

Love and loyalty were two things Miss Sun knew well. She had also been warned to expect the question. "One must always respect those who have loved us before," she answered carefully. "But one also must live and love in the present. Others need us. We need ourselves."

Roger stared at Miss Sun. For once, she wasn't giggling. She opened her eyes wide. "Mr. Wang. I have something you might want." She reached into her purse. "It's a photograph of Miss Christina. You can have it if you want. Chang Laobo said it's okay." Roger held the framed formal portrait in his hands: Christina in a lavender gown against a lacquer screen, her smile softening the usual rigidity of Chinese studio photographs. "She had it taken just for you. You can put it on the bed table." Miss Sun laughed a little. "Then, if you want, you can look at Miss Christina when we burst our clouds together."

Roger feigned shock, but he put the portrait where she said, all the time professing affection for Miss Sun. That night she watched carefully, delighted to see his eyes flickering surreptitiously toward Christina's portrait as they made love. Within minutes after Miss Sun retired, the whole Chang household knew the story. The servants were convulsed with laughter; Chang Laobo smiled privately.

By the early summer, Scholar Wen plunged Roger deeper into the Chinese language swamp by introducing reading: first simple texts with vocabulary lists, then more complex passages forcing reliance on a dictionary. The dictionary, Roger's nemesis, was based on 214 radicals, small calligraphic components that appeared, often not obviously, in every written character. After spending several minutes finding a character, he then began the hunt for its precise meaning from among several possibilities. One night, reading a three-hundred-character passage, Roger counted eighty-five times of resorting to the dictionary—the total process took more than eight hours to complete.

Scholar Wen exhorted his student. "Remember what Confucius said. Studying is not enough. He who learns but does not think is lost. Put your heart into your work."

Roger looked up sharply. Unknowingly, Scholar Wen had revealed another allegory from the box—the teacher on panel two, book in one hand, the other pointing toward his heart. Roger's smile soon dissolved into a frown. What could he do with the insight? When would he get the photographs? When would he get out of here?

* * *

Roger's only freedom came on Sunday, beginning with a long morning walk through the Chang gardens, enjoying blossoming fruit trees, brilliantly plumaged birds, miniature forests of tiny pine trees, mysterious clusters of gray rocks. By noontime relatives began to arrive, thirty or forty of them, in black limousines symbolizing Taiwan's affluent merchant class. Roger now understood why the Chinese word for "everyone" literally meant "the entire family." The Chang clan accepted him as something between a foreign guest and a distant relative who harbored a strange unmentionable secret.

Sunday was also Roger's one day of rest. He usually slept until nine, so he was surprised one sunny September Sunday when Miss Sun awakened him at seven o'clock. He had been in Taipei for nearly nine months and this was the first time she had interrupted his Sunday sleep.

"Why?" he asked, groggily eating *yutiao* and sipping tea.

"I can't tell you," she giggled, dressing him in a sharply pressed scholar's gown and putting on his black cotton shoes. "It's a surprise. It will be in the garden at exactly nine o'clock."

At nine, Roger entered the garden, slowing his pace as he reached an arched bridge. Stepping carefully on flat stones across a shallow pond, he arrived at a gazebo suspended above the water on pilings. Sitting down on a gazebo bench, he reached into a bucket and threw a handful of fish food into the pond. The carp were waiting; the water churned as if a typhoon had struck, then subsided to serene greenness a few seconds later.

A woman's voice from across the gazebo interrupted Roger's meditation. "It's Mr. Wang, isn't it?" She spoke exquisite Mandarin, her words sounding like tiny temple bells.

Roger wheeled around. The woman was dressed in a yellow cheongsam, daintily embroidered in red and green. Her black hair was combed carefully into a traditional coiffure with a dark wooden comb and white flowers. She carried a fan, silk on sandalwood, decorated with red birds and green trees, echoing the colors in her dress. Her face, even with pink makeup and blue eyeshadow, was unmistakable.

"Christina!" Roger gasped. "I don't believe it. It's really you!" He moved toward her, clearly intending to take her in his arms.

She held up her fan. "I'm sorry, Mr. Wang. But here we must not be too close. We're not alone. Lots of people are watching." She laughed quietly. "In fact, I think the whole household."

They stood about five feet apart in the center of the gazebo. "All right," he replied. "If you insist, and must we speak Chinese as well?"

"It must be in Chinese."

"Christina, what's your given name in Chinese?"

"Ruxin. But don't call me by it. My father's a real traditionalist."

Roger smiled. "Don't *I* know! All right, Miss Chang. It's a pleasure to meet you." Then he spoke in a whisper. "You're more beautiful than I remembered. I've missed you terribly."

Christina hid her smile behind the fan. "You flatter me." She spoke loudly enough to be heard by the ears on the banks of the pond. Then, matching Roger's whisper; "I didn't know what you'd look like as a Chinese. You look just as good. In some ways better."

Roger stared at Christina; she cast her eyes downward. He could not believe his surge of emotions as he realized he could not touch this fantastically beautiful woman. He could only talk to her, and those words would be overheard by the gallery.

"Mr. Wang," said Christina, her eyes still downcast. "Please, you're embarrassing me." Then back to her whisper, head down, but eyes back on Roger: "Roger, cut it out. They're going to get the wrong idea."

"What wrong idea?"

"Don't you see? We're being allowed to meet directly, without a go-between. That's because we've met before and because you have no family. This is a very advanced stage of courtship, but don't get carried away."

"I am getting carried away. You're fantastic."

"Hush. I really mean it." She stifled a laugh.

"What's so funny?" It dawned on him that she must know about Miss Sun—this whole thing seemed a step back into Chinese history when there were lots of Miss Suns around.

"It's your Chinese. It's pretty good. But your accent is definitely Overseas Chinese." Roger did look sexy, she thought, perhaps partly because she was the architect of his remodeling. Her sister had reported her father's comment: "Professor Wang is becoming less of a barbarian."

"I'm working on it. Scholar Wen is a pain. When does all this end?"

"What?"

"When do I get out of this elegant prison? When can I see you—perhaps on a more informal basis?"

"The answer to the first question is—I don't know. And to the second—this is as informal as we shall get. Until . . ."

"Until what?"

She held her breath. "Until Father gives permission for marriage."

"But I haven't asked you to marry me yet. And you haven't said yes. We've barely even had a chance to talk."

Christina laughed again. "Don't worry. We'll have a little time for that."

"When?"

"Once a month. Sunday mornings. Nine o'clock." With that, she turned quickly and walked gracefully over the stones to the bank. She looked back over her shoulder, her long neck arched, and gave a fleeting smile. Was it a Chinese version of hard-to-get? Perhaps her own sense of longing? Roger couldn't tell; she had vanished into the garden.

After the delightful surprise at Christina's reappearance, Roger fretted about courtship aimed at an arranged marriage. Maybe, he rationalized, it wasn't exactly an arranged marriage because he had been strongly attracted to Christina well before they arrived in Taiwan. Or perhaps there was something to arranged marriages after all? Formality certainly enhanced desire, a veil lifted only by imagination. Forced distance gave him new perspectives on Christina's beauty and array of talents, sensing creative energy ready to be released. It was like two potent magnets close together, never touching but always testing, a force field enveloping both of them. Gradually, as he stared at her photograph night after night, growing obsession eclipsed nagging doubts. No, it wasn't a marriage arranged by the Changs; it was blissful fate, serenity after a terrible typhoon. But should he marry Christina, then what? Certainly he didn't want to live in the Chang house forever. Maybe he could get out? Maybe no one would recognize him? Maybe he could come back for Christina? Couldn't they hide someplace outside Asia and the States? Perhaps they could decipher the box together and discover the Gao Collection?

Scholar Wen's daytime instruction frequently filtered through

Roger's nighttime imagination, fragmented into kaleidoscopic colors and sounds. One chilly December day, Scholar Wen related the famous Taoist tale of Zhuangzi and the butterfly, secretly relishing its relevance to Roger's predicament:

One time Zhuangzi went to sleep.
He dreamed that he was a butterfly.
When he woke, he was not certain:
Whether he was Zhuangzi who had dreamed he was a butterfly.
Or whether he was a butterfly who had dreamed he was Zhuangzi.

That night Roger dreamed that Roger Wang and Roger Walden fought over the right to occupy his body.

"I've won!" Roger Wang shouted in gleeful Mandarin. "I own you. You've become Chinese."

Roger Walden yelled back in English. "Bullshit! You're just a disguise. I'm Roger Walden, an American. I'll always be an American. The surgery is reversible. I can always go back once it's safe again."

"Look at yourself. You look Chinese. You think Chinese. You even dream Chinese. You've lost."

"Like hell. You can have my eyes and face, but you'll never get my soul."

"EAT YOUR MOTHER'S BEAN CURD."

"You Chinese can't even swear without sounding affected. The appropriate phrase is UP YOURS, MOTHERFUCKER."

Chang Laobo entered the dream, his voice frail but with awesome authority. "You are the two biggest fools who ever lived. Two people cannot live in the same body. One will die. Mark my words. ONE OF YOU WILL DIE BY THE END OF THE FIRST DAY OF THE NEW YEAR!"

Roger woke at four in the morning sweating from the nightmare. He stumbled half-awake out of bed and walked to the closet, where he put on Western clothes. He crept stealthily out of his room, down the stairs, and out through the front door of the house. Looking around to make certain he wasn't followed, he moved quietly down the driveway. He pushed the button inside the fence so that the main gate opened and walked onto the street.

Only after the gate locked automatically did Roger come fully awake. Now the decision was irrevocable—he couldn't reenter the

Chang estate, and he couldn't just stand in the middle of the road. Straightening up, Roger inhaled deeply, free for the first time in almost a year. He felt exhilarated, assuming everyone exaggerated the dangers; he would be okay if he kept calm. He walked cautiously down the darkened road, hugging a long wall, letting his feet test the ground so he wouldn't stumble. Each step increased confidence. It wasn't far to the main road that he'd seen every day from his window. There it was, just ahead, a level thoroughfare, and then maybe a mile walk into Taipei. And then—

"Don't move or your neck's broken." Roger's throat was caught in a viselike grip. The voice spoke sharply in Chinese-accented English.

Roger did as he was told. His body fell limply against the wall.

"If you want to live, tell me where the box is."

The grip tightened, making it hard for Roger to breathe. "I don't know what you're talking about . . ." He gasped for breath.

Suddenly the whole scene was flooded with brilliant light. Roger heard scuffling behind him. The grip on his neck vanished. He fell to the ground, coughing convulsively. He looked up and tried to shield his eyes against the lights. He could just make out the silhouette of Dr. Ren.

"Mr. Wang? Are you all right, Mr. Wang?"

"Yes," Roger coughed. "Barely. You came just in time."

"You're a damned fool!" Dr. Ren shouted. "You were almost killed. Do you know that?"

"Yes," Roger responded weakly.

"Where were you going?" asked Dr. Ren.

"I don't know. I was leaving. It was just too much."

"I hope you learned your lesson. We're not holding you in, we're keeping others out. It's for your own protection. You'll die if you leave without our security. Do you understand?"

"Now I do."

"You must promise me you'll never try to escape again. It endangers not only you, it endangers the entire Chang family. Do you promise?"

Roger promised.

Scholar Wen never found Roger an easy student, but now it was worse than ever. Just a few weeks earlier, Wen had been so impressed by his pupil's progress he had introduced him to the difficult classical Chinese of the Confucian Four Books. Now he spoke sternly. "You must concentrate. These works are precious. You must read them, absorb them, dissect them, know every character. You're only going through the motions." Scholar Wen was frustrated—his student was on the brink of handling philosophy and literature, comprehending allusions and allegories, just as Chang Laobo had desired. A few more months, with the right attitude, and the student could handle classical Chinese on his own, without instruction but with a lot of help from the dictionary.

"I'm sorry," Roger said, appreciating his teacher's irritation. "I'm just distracted. I'll try harder. But next Wednesday is an important day. January first, New Year's. Could I take it off? As a special favor?"

"So that's it. Can't forget your own traditions? All right. Take the day off. But we'll have to make it up. You'll have class this Sunday."

On New Year's Day, Roger pulled out a dusty suitcase filled with clothing taken by George Chang from his New York apartment. He dressed in a red cashmere sweater, gray wool slacks, and dark-brown loafers. Astonishing the servants by boldly pushing his way into the kitchen, he ordered a special meal for the day.

Chef Ting, a master of mandarin cuisine, could not hide his disgust. "Mr. Wang. You can't mean it. One big piece of red beef? Just fried a little on each side? Not cut up? And a whole potato with butter and salt in the middle? Four scoops of ice cream, on a banana, with melted chocolate and a cherry? Six cold beers still in the bottle? Mr. Wang, this could kill you."

"Chef Ting, if I survive, maybe I'll live forever."

When the chef ran to Dr. Ren, the doctor began to laugh. "Follow his instructions to the letter. It's a barbarian custom. I'll take full responsibility."

For the next twelve hours, Roger loafed on the living room sofa, watching football bowl games taped earlier to allow for the time difference. Servants looked on with amazement as he consumed the appalling food, washing it down with cold beer. The Orange Bowl had Penn State against Alabama. Roger watched the game intently, consuming a second six-pack of beer and munching on Chef Ting's version of potato chips. All the while, he kept an eye on the Victorian marble clock above the mantel. Just before midnight, Penn State broke a 24–24 tie with a last-second field goal; Roger flipped off the pandemonium on the television set and watched the clock tick the last seconds toward midnight. As its chime began to strike, he held his breath, counting each little bell as it rang: "Nine . . . ten . . . eleven . . . twelve."

Roger leapt from the sofa, throwing pillows around the room. "I've won . . . I've won . . . Roger Walden lives!" He danced up to his bedroom, gave Miss Sun a big hug, spun her around the room, and fell fast asleep with a grin on his face.

Sunday, January 20, was an enchanted day; shafts of early-morning sunlight raised a soft mist from the cold ground in the garden. Just before nine o'clock, Roger walked into a wooden teahouse. Two kerosene stoves, concealed in large blue-and-white ceramic containers, drove away the drafts; there was just enough space for two chairs and a small table, fashioned from rustic dark roots. Each glassless window in the teahouse displayed a different geometric pattern. Looking through a star-shaped window, Roger glimpsed a frost-dusted pine forest on the edge of the pond. He also caught flashes of clothing and heard titters of laughter. Christina was coming; the voyeurs were settling into place.

"Good morning, Mr. Wang." Christina walked gracefully into the teahouse and took the seat opposite Roger. Under her white fur coat was a red cheongsam, giving heat to the season and suggesting marriage might not be far away. Her words came in tiny clouds of warm breath that lingered by her face and hair. Her hands were hidden in a white fur muff resting demurely on her lap.

"Good morning, Miss Chang," replied Roger, nodding formally and straightening his black topcoat and the blue scholar's robe underneath. He sensed Christina had not been informed of his escape attempt. They looked impassively at each other as two servants giggled and poured tea. Warmed by the tea, Roger removed his topcoat and Christina pulled her arms out of her coat, revealing her dress.

"Mr. Wang, the weather is uncommonly cold, isn't it?" Christina looked up at Roger, her eyes sparkling.

"Yes, Miss Chang," he replied, caressing her face with his eyes. "It has been cold. But you certainly warm the morning." He looked at her black hair and let his eyes linger on her white jadeite earrings. Then his eyes stroked her high cheekbones and roamed around her oval face to her chin.

"Mr. Wang, my father tells me that you have been very busy with your studies." Christina titled her head back so that Roger could see her long neck as it entered the stiff collar of the red cheongsam. Around her neck was a disk of white jade on a gold chain.

"Your noble father. Is he well?" Roger poured another cup of tea for both of them. After taking a sip, he rolled the cup in his hands, enjoying the warmth. His eyes returned to Christina's lips.

She opened her mouth slightly. "Yes, as well as he can be at his age. He expresses great respect for you."

"I'm honored. He's an esteemed figure. And I'm just a beginning scholar."

Roger fixed his eyes on Christina's mouth. Her tiny tongue flirted across her teeth and wet her upper lip. "My father has considered the matter of my future carefully. And he has made a decision."

"Yes?" replied Roger. "And what is his decision?"

"He has decided that I should be married." Christina kept her face properly cast downward but let her eyes flit across Roger's hands and arms.

"That is proper."

Her breath was a little heavier now; the air around her face was misty. His eyes moved from her slightly opened mouth down her neck to the red collar. He fixed his gaze on the first fastening as if opening it with his eyes. Then he stared at the second one, at the base of the collar.

"Yes it is," she responded, her breath coming more quickly. His eyes penetrated deeper into her dress. "He wishes that I be married to you. But there are unusual circumstances."

"What unusual circumstances?" Roger's eyes were now beneath her collar, moving slowly down the slanted opening of her dress, resting for a moment on each embroidered button as if to free it from its clasp.

Christina drew in her breath. "You have no family. And no resources. So my father has agreed to waive the bride price. The dowry will be substantial. He will decide that later."

"But, of course, I can do very little in terms of the actual arrangements for a wedding. Especially given the limitations of my present circumstances . . ." Roger's eyes returned to the opening in her dress and he undid the last button.

"Perhaps I can provide some assistance," said Christina. She pulled the fur coat farther away from her shoulders and twisted slightly in the chair so that the top of her dress was fully visible. "The Chang family will take care of everything."

"That causes me great satisfaction," Roger replied, his eyes continuing to move down her dress as he imagined it totally open all the way to her waist.

"It's the least we can do. Especially given the difficulties you have experienced." Christina's breath began to come in little spasms as Roger's eyes returned to her shoulder as if slowly pulling the dress forward. Her legs trembled a bit as she arched her feet and pushed her thighs apart against the silk enclosure.

"When will the engagement be announced?" Roger felt a surge of desire as Christina looked at him, her neck pulsing with a rush of blood. Her eyes moved from his face down his scholar's gown and rested where the creases showed the divide between his torso and his legs.

"On the Chinese New Year. An astrologer has already confirmed it. It's a good omen. We are born in very compatible years. You're a horse. And I'm a rabbit." Christina put her hands back in the white muff and dropped them to her lap.

"I'll bet you are." Roger smiled.

"And perhaps horse is appropriate for you as well?" She kept her body as still as possible. But Roger could see the tremors in her thighs and arms. Her mouth opened in a tiny "o" and her breath came in little puffs.

A smile came to Roger's lips as he watched Christina's face and body relax slightly. "Very auspicious indeed," he replied.

"Yes," she said, drawing her fur coat back around her. She stood up, put her hands in the muff, and began to walk out of the teahouse. Turning back, she spoke with a satisfied smile. "Wouldn't you like to join me? It's permitted, you know. As long as there's a chaperone."

"No, Miss Chang, I think I'll remain here." Roger smiled back and pulled his overcoat around him.

"Oh, I understand, Mr. Wang." She stifled a grin. "Out of modesty. Not yet ready for us to be seen in public."

"No, Miss Chang." He buttoned his overcoat. "Out of necessity."

CHAPTER FOURTEEN

EXILE

ROGER WALDEN WAS REALLY SMILING

for the first time since coming to Taiwan. Even Scholar Wen was affected by his mood; he actually complimented his student on reading a difficult passage in Mencius. Roger reveled in preparations for the Year of the Monkey—watching Chef Ting prepare spring rolls and silky long-life noodles, helping write good-luck phrases on red rice paper, observing workmen as they repainted the house and made small repairs.

He knew it would be his year—his and Christina's—a chance to start a completely new life. After all that had happened, it had to be a fresh chapter. The danger on the outside was real, but Roger suppressed his anxieties. Instead he turned his attention elsewhere. He felt ready to tackle the lacquer box, seeking to unlock its code and reveal the treasure, but he had to wait until Chang Laobo gave permission. In the meantime, Christina filled his thoughts.

Finally, in early February, the great night arrived. For the first time since arriving in Taipei, he was at the same table with both Chang Laobo and his daughter; smaller tables were set around the dining room. It was a night for rice wine and mooncakes; nothing could possibly dampen such a magnificent occasion.

As the toasts flowed, Roger surprised the company by standing up and rapping his chopsticks against a glass. "My friends, I know my Chinese is still very weak, but somehow the wine makes me bolder. Or perhaps it will make you forget my mistakes." Laughter fluttered around the room. "This really is the year for Scholar Wen. He is a venerable old monkey. Long-lived. Full of wisdom. He also jumps around and screeches a lot." Scholar Wen, face flushed with embarrassment and too much drink, tipped his glass in Roger's direction and joined the laughter.

Roger walked to the dais where the musicians sat and took a two-stringed *erhu* from one of the players. Positioning the instrument on his lap, he drew the bow and produced a slow, lyrical melody, marred by an occasional squeak. He sang lyrics that Scholar Wen had helped him write for the occasion:

On the banks of the Keelung River, flowing through Taipei
A blinded stranger walks with slow, uncertain steps.
Down below, the god of the river reaches out to pull him in,
Up above, the heavenly deities do not know how to save
    him.
The cold winter winds cut through his body and his heart,
Is there no warmth to cradle him?
His sobbing tears form icicles on his face,
Until the *jia* becomes his protecting father and tender mother.

Chang Laobo stood up with tears in his eyes. Putting his arms around Roger and Christina, his face radiated satisfaction. "My dear family and friends. Tonight has an even deeper significance. I have determined that my daughter shall be married. And I have looked long for the appropriate husband. She is an extraordinary woman, and so I had to find an extraordinary man. He had to be a scholar. He had to show courage and commitment. And he had to have the true affection of my daughter. I have found such a man. Wang Jishi will be my son in every respect. Let me propose a toast to the engaged couple. I announce their engagement tonight—the first night of the Year of the Dragon."

After several rounds of toasts, Chang Laobo leaned over to Roger. "Would you mind coming with me for a moment?" He nodded to Dr. Ren, and the three men walked to a small room that served as the Chang ancestral shrine. Chang Laobo stood quietly in front of the candlelit altar, his head bowed.

After a moment, he turned around and spoke slowly. "You, my

son, have brought new joy to our lives. I was not certain at first, but you have devoted yourself to your studies. Even more, your heart seems at peace. Yet I know that some part of you must still be with your former self. I do not know that former self, but I feel deeply for you. I have some sad news for you. I hope you will take it in the right spirit."

Roger tried to sober himself. "Chang Laobo, what sad news? What could it be on the New Year?"

The old man stared at the floor for a moment, then raised his head to look at Roger. "It grieves me to tell you . . . how to put it? There is no other way to say it . . . Roger Walden is dead."

Roger froze. Dr. Ren walked over to him and steadied Roger by holding his shoulders. "My friend, what Chang Laobo says is true." He handed Roger a clipping from *The New York Times*. Roger read slowly, his eyes unaccustomed to the English prose, a cold sweat coming over him:

WALDEN, COLUMBIA HISTORIAN, DEAD AT 34

Roger Walden, assistant professor of History at Columbia University, was killed in a bizarre and still unclear episode in Taiwan. His body, which washed ashore south of Taipei on February 4, was positively identified by local police using dental records. Mr. Walden had been shot through the chest with a single bullet. No explanation for the shooting was available from local police nor from the American authorities on Taiwan. Another body, tentatively identified as Sampson Ng, a Chinese-American resident of New York City, also washed ashore at a nearby location.

Mr. Walden was author of several articles on American intellectual history. Several colleagues cited the importance of his article, "Pastors for Hire," a study of nineteenth-century Protestant clergymen in the pay of wealthy industrialists. He was honored by Phi Beta Kappa as one of the finest teachers in the United States. He was also well known as a world-class marathon runner and almost won the New York Marathon before collapsing just yards from the finish.

Mr. Walden was predeceased by his wife, Diane MacDonald Walden, who was killed in an automobile accident. He disappeared mysteriously over a year ago during his sabbatical. Efforts of Columbia University authorities to locate his whereabouts, prior to the shooting, proved fruitless. New York Police, collaborating with the Federal Bureau of Investigation, had also failed to find Professor Walden. No one in authority seems to have known why he traveled to Taiwan, although there are reports that he was reading about Chinese art during his sabbatical year. He was also an associate of Rebecca Aspen, a New York attorney specializing on China, who was brutally murdered. No suspects or motives have been discovered in the Aspen slaying, nor is there any evidence connecting Mr. Walden to her death.

Mr. Walden leaves no survivors. A memorial service will be held at the Columbia University Chapel on February 22.

Roger reread the article slowly and examined the picture of himself. He turned to Dr. Ren and spoke sharply in English. "I suppose there's an explanation for this little joke."

"There is an explanation," Dr. Ren answered sadly. "And it's no joke. In December, remember your escape attempt?"

"Of course. But I promised not to try it again."

"That's not the point. The man who almost strangled you was Sampson Ng, one of Lamarche's men. He had already told Lamarche that he thought you were the 'barbarian Chinese' he'd heard was staying at the Chang household. We killed Ng after we got that information, but we knew his death would confirm that you were in Taipei. We knew others would follow. We had no choice. We had to put them off the track. We consulted the Patriarch and he told us there was only one alternative: Roger Walden had to die. A local mortician helped us. He redesigned the teeth of a recent corpse so that they were similar to yours and then fired a bullet into the body to make it look like a murder. Now at least you're less likely to be tracked down in Taiwan. I know it must seem awful to you, but it was the only solution."

Roger paused, then replied slowly in Chinese. "Both of you are dear friends. Twice you saved my life. You gave me a new family when my own disappeared. You have drawn me together with your daughter. But you must understand my anger tonight. You thought you were doing the right thing. Your motives were noble. But you took a life—my life—without informing me. I'm treated like a prince in your household. But you still seem to look upon me as a barbarian. This I cannot forgive. You have great wisdom about China. But you are ignorant about humanity."

Chang Laobo, holding on to the arms of his chair, rose shakily. "I can feel your anger, but I cannot understand your impertinence. How can you speak like that to me? We provided you refuge. We brought you into the family. We gave you a new identity. The danger was not just a danger to you, it was a danger to the Chang family as a whole. When the family is endangered, only one person can

193

make the decisions. I did what was best for the family. It was also what was best for you."

Roger spit out his words without thinking. "Who are you to decide what is best for me? You may be Patriarch, but you are not God!"

Chang Laobo's eyes flashed angrily. He hobbled out of the room, aided by Dr. Ren. When the doctor returned, his face was drawn. "You have made the worst mistake imaginable. No one insults Chang Laobo. He wanted to dismiss you from the household altogether, but I implored him not to do so for his daughter's sake. He had compromised. You will leave Taipei tomorrow and travel to the family's mountain cottage in Alishan. You will be provided with an amah for the housekeeping and whatever books and other materials you wish. Miss Sun will remain behind. And, of course, all marriage plans are suspended."

Roger gritted his teeth and spoke in English. "You son of a bitch. For Christ's sake, can't you understand? You wiped out my life tonight—at least my American life. You concocted some crazy plot to eliminate Roger Walden without even asking me. Now instead of sympathy, you give me exile. Damn it, don't I have a say in anything?"

"No, you don't," Dr. Ren said sharply.

A frigid wind cut through the windows and cracks in the Chang cottage, cantilevered on a steep mountain in Alishan, in the high country in central Taiwan. Left in natural cypress wood inside and out, the cottage hovered like an exhausted little bird above the craggy gorge below. Chang Laobo had selected the remote location—at an altitude of several thousand feet and over five miles from the nearest village—as an escape from Taipei's summer crowds and stifling heat. Even in August the family gathered around the natural-rock fireplace in the evenings and enjoyed the small Swedish stoves in the mornings. In February, the place was bitterly cold.

The wind seeped into his thin mattress, mocking the down comforter Roger had bundled around him. A shaft of sunlight pierced the latticed window above him, forcing his eyelids open slightly. "Miss Sun," he groaned, trying to avoid the light. "Please come here."

Instead of the usual light footsteps, he heard the heavier flopping of padded shoes. Looking up, he met the gaze of an old woman dressed in black quilted clothing who stood over him and spoke in guttural native Taiwanese dialect. "There's no Miss Sun here. I'm Mrs. Yang, just your amah. Time to get up. Your clothes are over there."

Donning a down mountain parka, Roger walked onto the balcony, and beheld a panorama evoking both reverence and fear. Blue-white snow shrouded the peaks of a rugged mountain range. Below the tree line, steeply angled mountainsides were carpeted with velvet-green cypress forests and knifed by outcroppings of dark gray and black granite. The night winds had subsided; only the soft rumble of cascading water several thousand feet below interrupted the silence. Roger rocked back and forth, teetering like the cottage at the edge of nothingness. He pushed himself back from the railing, inhaling frosty air and looking at the razorback ridges rising from the wintry mists, feeling like a tiny figure in a monumental landscape painting.

Back inside, he felt an overwhelming need to vent fury, to assert that he was in fact alive. "The Patriarch is dog shit," he yelled out loud. "Son of a dog. Pig dick. Chang Laobo, eat your mother's bean curd." Amah Yang stood rigid with shock. "Don't worry," he said more quietly. "I feel better now. Besides, those are all the Chinese swear words I know. Now give me a hand. I'm going to show the old bean-curd eater that he can't beat me."

Amah Yang helped Roger move a large desk to a window overlooking the mountains. Clicking open a briefcase given to him by Dr. Ren, he withdrew photographs of his lacquer box, perusing them for the first time in a year. "Chang Laobo wants you to use your time to advantage," the doctor had explained, pointing to the briefcase and several cartons containing Chinese reference books and dictionaries.

Outside, towering mountains formed a massive circle of stone and ice, a prison constructed by divine forces. Inside, the books began to pile up, a castle of concentration. Roger remembered his moments with Becky, recalling how they had begun to learn the meaning of the box. He scrutinized a scene on panel one—boxes within boxes, like looking at a double mirror with images telescoping into infinity. Could one ever hope to find the end? Why, he wondered, was he shaking so much? Was it anger at Chang Laobo? Fear of Lamarche? Hopes for the Gao art collection?

He flipped to a photograph of panel two. What about the scholar pointing back to panel one, the Confucian panel, while the other hand held a writing brush? What could that possibly mean? Roger pressed his fingers to his forehead to drive his brain into deeper thought.

"I've got it!" he shouted, throwing his arms in the air in a victory signal. When Amah Yang ran in, he astonished the old woman by hugging her. "You're the most beautiful woman in the world. You've inspired me. We're back in business." He flipped through a Confucian concordance until he found the right passage. "It's Neo-Confucianism! Don't you see it, you lovely lady? It's Zhu Xi, twelfth century—there can be no thought without action, and no action without thought. You see, the teacher is holding the brush—it represents thought, all that one learns from books. The other hand points back toward good Confucian action in panel one. Fantastic! I figured one out. All by myself."

Roger beamed, his laborious studies in Taipei finally had a purpose. The angry fugitive faded as the scholar in him reemerged, a scholar with old instincts and new skills. Not since a year and a half before, buried in the stacks at Columbia, had he entertained the romantic possibility that he alone could cut through the mysteries of the box. He laughed at his naïvité—imagine trying serious research on Renaissance art without any ability in French or Italian? Now he had the ability to struggle through any passage in classical Chinese, and he surely had the time. At the least, he would be examining a strange strand of intellectual history—the "dream" of a prominent late-Qing statesman. If he ever returned to Columbia, it might just make for a book that could get him tenure. At the most, he allowed himself his own dream: uncovering the mother lode of Asian art.

Easing back into his studies, Roger's mind worked at a different tempo. His watch, broken during the first week at Alishan, no longer had any relevance. Instead his pace was set by other forces. The mountains encircling him like a gigantic Stonehenge, and the sun warming him only a few hours a day, enforced a rhythm of cold-warm-cold, dark-light-dark, fear-ease-fear. Three meals, brought by the silent Amah Yang, boxed the days neatly. Pre-breakfast was reserved for exercise; post-breakfast and post-lunch were devoted to the box and to Chinese classical literature and philosophy. Post-dinner was for lighter reading and reflection. At first Roger swung between two extremes: extreme hope in the morning as he first gazed at the photographs, and then extreme frustration in the afternoon as his work yielded few answers. He felt angry whenever he thought of Chang Laobo, benevolent father turned ruthless warden. He stared at the figure Chang Laobo had explained—the great student who supplies the other three corners of a square. Damn it—he clenched his fists—how can you see the other three corners when you are in the box yourself?

Gradually, as the early spring began to melt the ice and lengthen the days, Roger's moods began to moderate. In the early afternoons, when it was warm enough, he explored the mountain trails, watching more life unfold each day. Little purple flowers forced their way through the granular corn snow. Red and yellow mountain birds cautiously came near as he scattered seeds on the edge of a meadow. Immersing himself in Alishan's annual renewal, the vicious cycles of Roger's heart, cycles of hate and hope, softened into a more consistent feeling of acceptance. For the first time in his adult life, he began living each day as it came, not demanding too much, not despairing too much. As the high-altitude paths became dry, Roger started a new regimen of jogging a few miles each day. Week by week, his body hardened, and, conversely, his mind gentled. Little things started to matter: a silver fox spotted on the trail, a snowy-white owl hooted awake by his steps, a waterfall discovered down a craggy ravine, a baby forest of dwarf blue spruce seen on the edge of a cracked-ice pond. Even Amah Yang, pleased by Roger's change of mood, began to chat with him about her childhood in Taichung.

After jogging and before cooling down in a spring-fed pond, he devoted a half hour to *taiji*, shadowboxing, using exercises from a book. He stood silently to empty his mind, then slowly raised his hands and settled into the position of "eagle resting." Pausing briefly, he moved through the sweeping motion of "stroking the tiger's tail" and the remaining movements. The ancient art improved his body tone and enhanced mental concentration.

Each day as he pondered photographs and reviewed classical Chinese texts, a quiet energy infused Roger's work. Taoism, the toughest tracts of all, became easier to translate when he relaxed and let the characters flow through his mind. He frequently focused on panel three: the joyful turtle, the accomplished butcher, the sad Baoyu of the *Dream of the Red Chamber*. Only one symbol from the Taoist panel remained beyond his grasp, an old man holding a cinnabar bird in a golden cage, the smallest carving on the entire box.

197

One day, he stared at the lacquer bird for a moment and then listened
to live birds chirping outside his window. Without thinking, he leafed
through a Chinese poetry anthology, stopping at a work by the famous
Bo Juyi of the Tang dynasty, titled "The Red Cockatoo." Within
an hour, he finished his translation:

A gift was sent from Annam,
A red cockatoo,
With the color of the peach-tree blossoms,
And speaking with the sounds of men.
They treated it as they usually do,
When dealing with those who are educated and thoughtful.
They took a cage with thick bars,
And locked it up inside.

Something welled up in Roger—not the ecstasy of insight, but
the sorrow of metaphor. Spreading out a sheet of rice paper, selecting
a fine brush, and mixing jet-black ink, he wrote in painstaking
calligraphy:

To the Patriarch, Chang Cheng-tai, Master of the Chang Family:

*Your humble servant, Wang Jishi, cannot hide his shame. He has
insulted the Great Patriarch. The Patriarch has shown his boundless
kindness by sending the foolish Wang into exile. Here for the past many
months your humble servant has repented. He has lived with his shame
and stupidity. He has tried to apply his limited skills to study of the
Great Classics. He has found the wisdom in the Analects of Confucius.
He now knows the proper relationship of the Superior and the Inferior.*

*Your humble servant, Wang Jishi, dares to write this letter. He begs the
Patriarch to overlook his lack of scholarship and his crude calligraphy.
He begs the Patriarch to grant him an audience. As he writes, the silly
servant's tears fall like the spring rain. He lies prostrate before the power
and mercy of the Great Patriarch of the Chang Clan.*

*May the Patriarch show mercy and grant this humble request. May the
Patriarch live a long life.*

After sealing the letter with red wax and jade chop bearing his
Chinese name, Roger implored Amah Yang to deliver it to the Chang
residence when she visited Taipei. The typhoons came and went and
still Roger had no response. He queried Amah Yang, sometimes on
the brink of anger, "Are you sure you delivered the letter? To Dr.

Ren himself?" In spite of Amah Yang's assurances, Roger grew more doubtful that the Patriarch had read his communication. Finding it difficult to concentrate on books, he devoted himself to excercise, the jogging turning into running, sometimes more than twenty mountain miles a day. At night he drank rice wine and wrote poems in calligraphy. More often than not, he awakened in a cold sweat, head pounding from drink, preparing for another day of purging himself with exercise.

One late September day, Roger heard a Land Rover whining up the mountain, bringing Amah Yang back from Taipei. She waddled out of the vehicle and shook an envelope in the air. "Here it is! Here it is! A letter from Taipei!" Roger grabbed the envelope and tore it open.

Dear Roger:

Chang Laobo wishes me to convey his satisfaction that you wrote to him. The letter, despite its less than perfect style, expressed proper humility. Until you see him in person, he feels it is not yet appropriate for him to write directly. He feels it would be better for me to write as an interested person outside the family.

I believe that Chang Laobo feels your punishment should come to an end. It sorrowed him greatly to send you to Alishan. Ironically, it may have been for the best. We have since learned that Lamarche himself has recently come to Taipei. It appears he's still suspicious. He's been seen at several locations around town, always inquiring about a Professor Walden. He once mentioned the name Albert Simpson. We've kept him under surveillance.

At some point, Chang Laobo will send instructions for your return. In the meantime, he consulted me about a symbolic gesture to indicate his forgiveness. He asked me about American customs and seemed amused when I told him that Americans believe that "good things come in threes." He laughed about that and said, "Maybe we can arrange it."

I can't say what to expect. In the meantime, I'm sorry that I had to be part of the sad drama that led to your departure. Please understand, I do feel for your plight. But my life is linked to the Chang family. I will live and die in the service of Chang Laobo and his heirs. He did do the right thing. And you did do the wrong thing. I think you know that now.

With affection,

Dr. Ren Chih-tung.

Roger sat on the balcony overlooking the mountains, pondering the letter. Good things in threes? Maybe Dr. Ren was just toying with him. Lamarche in Taiwan? How long would it take him to find Alishan? And wouldn't—

"Mista Wang. Mista Wang. Do you still like to eat *yutiao?*"

Roger hugged Miss Sun, whirling her around with delight. For the next week, they played like children. Instead of solitary afternoon runs, he took her on mountain picnics in the autumn sun. At night, she bathed him and fed him, and when they slipped under the down comforter, their passion was almost without limit.

One day, Roger gathered the courage to ask her a question. "When we sleep together, do you find it really satisfying? Or are you just acting?"

Miss Sun was startled. "Sometimes in the past, I had to act with other men. But not with you. I wouldn't fool you. You always make my cloud burst."

A week later, Miss Sun woke Roger early, poking him in the side and tickling his legs. "Why so early?" Roger chided her. "Still hungry for more? One more cloud to burst?"

He reached out for her, but she twisted quickly out of bed, pulling the comforter with her. "I know something. But I won't tell."

After breakfast, she handed Roger a package wrapped in heavy corrugated paper. He cut it open, pulled apart the drawstrings of a red velvet bag and, his heart pounding, lifted out the Gao lacquer box. It glistened in the mountain sun. Shutting his eyes, he ran his fingers around its carvings, his head spinning with memories of Becky and Christina. Then he stared at the box as if looking in a mirror. He was not the same man who had touched it two years before, nor did the box itself seem the same as it had in New York. He was farther from home and the box was closer. Both of them were still exiles, both forgeries of different sorts; both still searched for their identities, and each needed the other to find it.

Roger took Miss Sun's hand. "You can't know what this means to me. I thought I'd never see it again. But how did it get here? Who brought it? Was there a letter? Have you heard from Miss Christina?"

Miss Sun looked into his eyes, feeling his deep need for answers. She could only shake her head sadly.

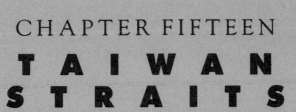

CHAPTER FIFTEEN
TAIWAN STRAITS

THAT NIGHT, MISS SUN PAMPERED

Roger, rubbing his neck and massaging his body in a steaming bath. After pouring him a cup of warm rice wine, she teased him. "How about one more present?" She opened a parcel and held up a new robe, dark-green silk embroidered with red dragons, accompanied by white silk pajamas and green slippers. Miss Sun helped him dress, carefully smoothing out a few wrinkles in the robe and tying the white sash with special care. "Tonight," she said, smiling, "you really look like a Chinese prince."

Roger warmed his hands over the Swedish stove, pleased she had lit lanterns rather than using the electric lights. In the soft glow, the wooden walls and beams of the Chang cottage mysteriously embraced them. He inhaled a flowery jasmine incense and saw Miss Sun standing by the door in a fresh yellow evening robe, her hair in a tight bun laced with tiny flowers. He started to embrace her, but she raised her hand to stop him, her finger to her lips so he would not speak. She beckoned him, smiling a little but staying well out of his grasp.

Walking into the living room, he laughed. "Miss Sun, what's come over you? After a hundred nights, you suddenly become shy? Do you want me to . . ."

His voice faded as he sensed someone else in the shadows of the room. It was a woman dressed entirely in red—a formal tradi-

202

tional costume with a long inner gown and an intricately embroidered shorter outer gown. An elaborate crown of jade, pearls, and rubies was on her head. He remembered seeing that costume before, at the wedding reception for Chang Laobo's grandniece. It was the costume of the Chinese bride.

He stood transfixed as the woman turned to face him. "Christina! Is that you, Christina? My God, is it really you?"

Christina held up both hands to indicate that Roger should not approach her. Then she raised a small candle that illuminated her face. She spoke quietly in archaic, formal Chinese reserved for occasions of great moment. "You are Wang Jishi. I am Chang Ruxin. I have received instructions from my father, Chang Cheng-tai. He wishes that we be joined in marriage. The ceremony has already been conducted this morning before the Chang Ancestral Shrine in Taipei. The ancestors were consulted to find the most auspicious date. They blessed our marriage and this date. A dowry of five million dollars in U.S. currency has been put aside in the name of Wang Jishi at our family bank. My father has graciously waived the bride price. Only one ceremony remains. We must kneel and drink rice wine together."

Christina lifted two translucent jadeite domes from a table serving as makeshift altar; she lit the candles and replaced the domes, the soft green glow barely lighting their faces. Both knelt on red cushions before the altar; Christina raised a ceramic cup of rice wine, gesturing for him to do the same.

"Christina," he said softly, "before we drink I must know if this is your wish as well."

She did not speak for a moment. Then she said in formal Chinese, "It is my father's wish. I could not disobey." She paused and whispered in colloquial Chinese, "It is also my deepest wish and greatest dream. I love you, Roger." She drank her wine and waited motionless, staring at the wedding lamps.

Roger held his cup and looked at Christina's face in the dancing light. "If the Patriarch of the Chang family commands it," he said, trying to remember the formal patterns, "then I, Wang Jishi, must obey. The Chang family has been my protector. I owe the Patriarch my loyalty and my life." Then he touched her hand and spoke colloquially. "Christina, I adore you. I love you to eternity." He drank the wine.

* * *

In the three weeks of honeymoon that followed the wedding, the Alishan cottage became a bower. Christina guided Roger to crystal mountain waterfalls and secret places she had known since childhood. He discovered his new bride had a remarkable array of talents. She not only taught him the proper movements for *taiji*, but she also introduced him to the basic elements of *wushu*. He was stunned one afternoon when she donned a black tunic and loose pants, then stood in an orchard, jumping at least four feet in the air and knocking fruit off branches using her feet and elbows. She concluded her demonstration by dodging a stick that Roger swung at her while she was blindfolded.

"Where did you learn all of that?"

"Actually you wouldn't have been so surprised if I'd been a Chinese man with those skills, would you?" she answered with a grin.

"No, I guess not."

"You don't know about the tradition of the woman warrior in China? Women were thought to be inferior, so some of them fought back, quite literally."

"I just can't believe that someone as tiny as you can make all those moves."

"Actually," Christina responded with a smile, "small size helps agility. Even more, my calligraphy has been the key."

"Calligraphy and martial arts?"

"Of course. They're both from the same roots. They require balance, agility, and above all, concentration. Emptying the mind and then focusing it." To make her point, Christina picked up a small stone, shut her eyes, snapped her wrist and hurled the stone. It hit an apple on the end of a branch. The apple hung for a moment, then fell with a thud.

In the evenings, the harvest moon above Alishan cast a pumpkin-orange glow around the cottage and cool blue shadows behind it. As the warmth of the fire mingled with the fragrance of incense, two once-frightened strangers probed each other's secrets. In interludes between passion, they sat facing one another on the moonlit bed, fingers interlaced and eyes locked together. The Western cliché "it's better to give than to receive" misses the point, Roger thought. The two acts are inseparable: giving *is* receiving. The ultimate gift, unqualified love, is the ultimate self-realization.

The eyes, Roger and Christina discovered, were windows to their souls. Staring deeply at her, Roger softly stroked her long hair back over her ears and ran his fingers gently down her neck. A smile flickered on her lips when he found the spot at the top of her spine; Christina sighed audibly as his fingertips gently massaged her neck. She reciprocated by squeezing the muscles in his shoulders, biceps, forearms, and fingers, then running her tongue around his chest, teasing his nipples. He slowly drew his hands to her breasts, barely touching their tips, then pulling them tenderly, each in turn. Their eyes caught each other in unblinking exploration, rendering both more naked than their unclothed bodies, revealing knowledge and vulnerability, offering and accepting love. Deeply satisfied smiles passed across their faces, acknowledging that together they were infinitely more than the joining of two lonely souls. Sex surpassed the satisfaction of separate desires; it was a symbol of a an enormously promising union, a religious as well as a physical expression. They let an unconscious rhythm guide them, changing tempo and key, until successive orgasms brought them to blissful stillness.

"Am I really worth five million dollars?" Roger asked Christina one night in bed.

"At least," Christina laughed.

"No, not that," he laughed back. "You know what I mean." Although Dr. Ren had explained about large dowries, Roger had never expected anything like that amount.

"Actually it made Father enormously happy to give it. He desperately wanted my marriage. And he hoped to make amends to you. He wanted you to be without financial worries."

"Why?"

"So you would devote yourself to the lacquer box for the right reason—seeking the Gao dream."

Christina had revealed only part of the truth. "Tenure?" her father had asked. "What's tenure?" When she explained, the old man laughed. "Mr. Wang is brilliant. American professors must be idiots not to see that. Academic freedom? I'll give him freedom from academics!"

As the moon fell behind the horizon, the radiant white light of the Milky Way cast a quiet spell over Alishan. Outside the cottage, a guard patrolled silently, looking toward the mountain and away from the cliff because he knew that another guard was protecting the road at the bottom.

Far below, another light began an ominous journey up Alishan.

A powerful flashlight cut a path up the rugged mountain slopes, darting back and forth across rocks and trees, slowly coming closer to the cottage. Still farther below, at the top of a waterfall, a stream of blood from the throat of a Chang bodyguard seeped into the river. Only the frightened deer heard the occasional rumble of dislodged stones and broken branches as the light moved relentlessly upward. The great horned owl, its eyes shining like reflecting saucers, gave a deep hoot of warning and flew off into the cold darkness. Four hours later the light slowly explored the timbers and boulders supporting the wooden building where Roger and Christina slept. Then the light snapped off.

Roger stirred in his sleep as he heard a loud crack and a groan outside the cottage. Just another mountain noise, he thought sleepily. He pulled Christina closer to him and fell back on the pillow, unaware that piano wire had circled the neck of the guard outside, severing his spinal column.

The door to the cottage opened. Ever so slowly, to keep the floor from creaking, the intruder made his way into the building. The light scanned the bedrooms. The hand reached into the pocket of a dark leather jacket, slowly removing the piano wire, glistening with blood. In the outer bedroom next to the kitchen a small body stirred on the bed; her glossy hair glowed in the moonlight. She yawned slightly and turned in her sleep, cuddling the comforter with a trace of a smile. The wire flashed in the darkness, twanged a whining discordant note, and snapped through the tender neck. Miss Sun's eyes opened wide. She clutched desperately at her throat. Then her body was still.

The intruder entered the master bedroom and hovered over Roger and Christina. He pulled a heavy handgun with a silencer from his pocket. Then he aimed the flashlight at the bed, fixing its beam on the eyes of the sleeping couple.

Both of them sat up with a start, shielding their eyes with their hands. Roger screamed out, "*Aiya. Dzemma le. Ni shi shei? Sun Xiaojie! Kwai lai!*"

Lucky Liu shoved the flashlight against Roger's face and snarled back in English. "For Christ's sake, that's really cute. He even speaks Mandarin to match his little operation. You asshole, speak Cantonese or speak English. None of that faggy talk."

Liu played the light over Christina's naked body, moving it across her skin as she tried to cover herself with the sheet. Roger struck out at the flashlight. Liu brought the barrel of his gun against Roger's forehead, opening a gash.

"That's just for starters"—Liu grinned—"a little repayment for yours in New York. You almost had us fooled for a while—the same dental records, that was a good trick. But we kept an eye on Christina, she made it easy. Now get up and walk into the living room real slow. If one of you makes a move, I'll kill the other."

He tied them securely to two chairs, then he tore open the velvet bag and pulled out the box. "All you had to do was hand this over. It would have saved a lot of grief. Just a crummy little box. Is it really worth your lives? You jerks, you didn't even open it. Even Lamarche is an idiot. 'Don't open it,' he said, 'there's a bigger treasure someplace else.' Bullshit. Watch this!"

Shining his light on the front panel of the box, Liu pulled a knife and a screwdriver from his jacket. He scraped some lacquer from a corner of the box with the knife; as a tiny crevice opened, he pushed in the screwdriver and began to twist it. The box made a creaking sound. Liu pushed the screwdriver harder, trying to pry the top from the box.

Roger heard a sharp cracking noise, just as when he'd dropped the box in Becky's apartment, then Liu cried out. One hand still holding the box, he reached for his gun and pointed it at Christina's head. Suddenly his eyes opened wide and blood spurted from his mouth. He pulled the trigger as his body began to convulse, then fell to the floor with the box still clutched in his hand. After a last gush of blood from his mouth, Liu lay still.

"Christina, are you all right!?"

"Yes! Thank God!" she cried out.

After wriggling free, Christina sliced the ropes from Roger. She pulled the box from Liu's puffy blue hand. A long thin needle at the corner was coated with blood. They watched in horror as it slowly retracted into the box.

Christina turned over the box and read out loud the final Taoist passage on the bottom. They both understood its terrible message:

Those who try to control the mortal world by manipulating,
They do not succeed.
The mortal world is like a holy container,
It is very dangerous to tamper with it.
If you try to manipulate it,

You will destroy it.
If you try to grab it,
You will lose it.

By two o'clock in the afternoon, scarcely eight hours after the massacre, Roger and Christina sat together stiffly on a couch in the Lantau Island mansion of Christina's elder sister. Chang Laobo faced them, his black silk gown creaseless and his face without expression.

"My children," he said, "we are disturbed that misfortune has occurred. But we are pleased by the union between you. Although the union will not further the Chang clan, that's the sadness of having a daughter, it promises much in perpetuating our intellectual traditions. Calligrapher and scholar. Hand and mind. Surely your children will have abundant talent."

"Father." Christina spoke quietly, her hands folded demurely in her lap. "I am not the usual Chinese bride. The doctors in America have determined that I cannot bear children. I apologize for my failures."

The old man smiled gently, hiding his disappointment. "Our bodies sometimes fail us. I should know. So the challenge facing you is different. It is that of accomplishing all you want in a single lifetime. In my experience, the answer is adoption. Unfulfilled unions must adopt something. If not children, perhaps a cause. Wang Jishi, what are your thoughts?"

Roger measured his words, knowing a lot depended on the right answer. "Two years ago, I would have found your question intrusive. I would have thought that matters of adoption, of whatever sort, were for the couple to decide, not the father. That's right for those in the West. But this is China, so we must behave in a Chinese way."

"So you will adopt?"

"Yes. If it is your wish. Either children, or a cause. But, if it pleases the Patriarch, in our own time and our own way."

"Your response pleases me. So does your demeanor. You have studied well. What else have you learned?"

"In the West, we have two words for mind and heart. In China, there is but one—xin. There can be no gap between learning and thinking. None between knowledge and action. None between self and society. Values cannot stand as abstractions. Individuals cannot operate by different standards. There must be an unbroken chain that links the individual to family, to broader society, to the culture and the nation. That's the meaning of the interlocking boxes on the first panel of the lacquer box."

"And what are the values that hold it all together?"

"A commitment to the precious five relationships—between master and subject, father and child, older brother and younger brother, husband and wife, and between friends. A lifelong, unchanging commitment. Motivated by key forces—loyalty, sincerity, discipline, humanity."

"And how do you gain these values?"

"By education. The Classics. Constant reading and constant practice. Talented people must take the lead, serving as moral exemplars. The less talented must be taught to accept their place. Everyone has an equal chance to show his talent. Everyone must accept the inequality of talent."

As Roger completed the catechism, Chang Laobo folded his hands and rocked them three times, the traditional Chinese gesture of congratulation. "You have done very well. I knew I had made the right decisions. First, protection. Then, isolation. Now, marriage. But there's one thing missing. Tell me, my new son-in-law, what is it?"

Roger searched for the right answer. "I'm sorry, Chang Laobo. I don't know what it is."

The Patriarch smiled. "That doesn't surprise me. It's not something you can learn in a book. It is what you discover along the way. You either find it or you don't. It's motivation."

"Motivation?" Roger asked, barely concealing his hurt. "Have I failed to show you that? Almost two years of constant study. Under conditions that were, let us say, trying. If that isn't motivation, what is?"

"Don't be so quick to take offense. You have worked very diligently. But why have you worked? Partly because I forced you to do so. Partly because of your own fascination with our language and culture. Probably because of your hopes for finding the Gao art collection. Certainly out of growing affection for my beloved daughter. But the very best students go one step further. They develop their own positive, even passionate, motivations. They no longer come back with the three remaining corners of an old square. Instead they hold up the first corner of a new square. I think you have boundless talent. You still lack this essential ingredient."

"I'm sorry if I've failed you, Chang Laobo." A year ago, Roger thought fleetingly, I would have been irate at the old man's audacity. Now I'll show him something else I've learned—patience.

"You haven't failed me. It's just that you have not fully realized yourself. If you find your own dream, you may find the Gao dream at the same time."

The old man struggled to his feet, wheezing from the exertion, placing each of his gnarled white hands on one of theirs. "My dear children, I wish I knew how to keep you safe in the dangerous times ahead. Shortly your pursuers will find out precisely what happened on the mountain. I don't know how to protect you."

Roger slowly stood up, putting his hands on Chang Laobo's shoulders. "Chang Laobo, do you remember the parable of the mature man who wanted to show his filiality?"

"Why yes, of course," Chang Laobo responded, startled by Roger's unexpected commanding presence. "He dressed up like a child and played with toys to amuse his parents."

"Then, Chang Laobo, let me be a silly child. Let me tell you a crazy idea."

"Yes?"

"Why don't you arrange for both Christina and me to go to Mainland China?"

"Mainland China?"

"Yes! You told me you have contacts at the highest levels in Beijing. Dr. Ren could arrange everything. We could be what they call foreign experts. Perhaps I could teach American history and maybe Christina could teach calligraphy. Wouldn't Beijing be relatively safe if we had official sponsorship?"

The old man's shock faded into a huge grin. "My son, that's brilliant! Chinese security is among the best in the world. As long as the moderates are coming back, I feel very comfortable with you in Beijing."

"And there's more," Roger interrupted. "Once in China, we could try to make contact with the Gao family, if any of them are still alive. We might just find the secret to the Gao box."

"Oh, my son." Chang Laobo's eyes were watering. "You really *are* filial. What you just said—that's what I meant by motivation. I'm blessed—I lived to see it."

The old man coughed again; he paused to let the spasm pass. "Now I must leave you . . . with two final thoughts. First, the box will be safest if it remains in Taipei, in Dr. Ren's care. In the past, it has brought pain to you. Ask for it whenever you want it, but make certain that the next time it will bring the joy you deserve, and it deserves." Chang Laobo hesitated, staring at both Roger and Christina. "Finally, I must tell you that we shall never meet again, at least not in the mortal world. Dr. Ren is always candid. A few weeks, maybe a few months. So be it. My life has had its share of rewards, perhaps made richer by contrast to tragedies around me. The fact that I know there is more for you means I know there is more for me."

CHAPTER SIXTEEN
MIDDLE
KINGDOM

EARLY 1990s

THE SMALL TRAIN, PULLED BY A MAGNIFICENT

green steam engine with two red flags flying above the cowcatcher, hissed impatiently on a siding outside the Guangzhou Station. Inside the ash-paneled rear passenger car, the Premier sat in a crimson armchair reading the newspaper that circulated only among high officials. He enjoyed his private train, a perquisite that came with his newly acquired post. It was his favorite form of transportation around China.

"Mr. Premier," a uniformed attendant announced, "your guests have arrived."

The couple stood at the door, blinking for a moment after the transition from brilliant autumn sunshine to the darkened interior of the railway carriage. Christina was dressed inconspicuously in a blue sweater and skirt. Roger looked like an overseas Chinese professor—tweed sports jacket, gray slacks, wire-rimmed glasses.

"Professor Walden. Miss Chang. How nice to see you again."

Roger's head snapped toward the speaker, shocked to hear English and his former name. Squinting, he saw a distinguished-looking silver-haired man in his early sixties.

"Minister Chen?"

"That's right. Golden Pavilion Restaurant. Almost two years ago. I'm back home now with a recent change in status, from Finance Minister to Premier. Not bad for an old reformer."

"Congratulations," Christina intervened. "My brother always said you were destined for great things."

"Thanks, but don't overdo it. I'm just a member of the Politburo. There are some who don't relish my appointment." The Premier was not being modest. Although he headed China's government, ultimate power rested with the twenty or so members of the Political Bureau of the Chinese Communist Party, better known as the Politburo. Premier Chen was at the fulcrum of a precarious balance between moderates and conservatives, the perennial seesaw of Chinese politics. Adroit factionalism had won Chen the Premiership; vicious factionalism could also bring him down.

The Premier smiled at his guests. "And congratulations to both of you." He had been well briefed; he didn't react at all to Roger's Chinese face. "Let's speak Chinese now. It's a long ride ahead and I'm not sure my English is up to it. I thought the train would give us time to chat while giving you a chance to see more of China."

He noticed Roger's raised eyebrow.

"Don't worry. This train is protected by my private security forces. I would never talk that way to you under other circumstances. In fact, you'll probably never hear the name Professor Walden again in China, and you'll almost never hear English."

The Premier checked his gleaming gold-and-stainless Rolex. "We've got to get going."

"Notice anything unusual?" Premier Chen replaced his crystal wineglass on the formally set table.

Roger and Christina shook their heads. "Forgive us, Mr. Premier," Roger responded, "but everything's unusual. Riding through China. Eating prime ribs and Yorkshire pudding. With a head of government. And—"

"No"—the Premier smiled—"something more specific. Look at my glass."

"Oh, I see," Christina said. "It's staying level and not bumping around."

"Ever ride on American railroads?" The Premier beamed. "Amtrak will knock out your fillings. I've just had the Guangzhou-Beijing trunkline roadbed rebuilt. It shows what we Chinese can do when we use our two greatest assets—labor and organization."

"But why waste so much effort on an antique form of transportation?" Roger wondered.

"Because China is an antique society. Look out there." The Premier raised the window shade to reveal rural China in the early evening. Bicycles wobbled along unpaved roads, carrying improbable burdens: a rider and three children, a tower of wicker baskets ten feet tall, cages of chickens, a squealing pig hung from a crossbar. A smoke-spewing tractor pulled a rickety wagon; smaller hand-tractors pushed bundles of rice stalks along narrow paths in the paddies.

"We're way behind the West in economic development," the Premier continued. "We don't need superhighways, supersonic aircraft, super anythings. We just need efficiency. That's the best thing I can bring to my people."

"The West could learn something from this train," Christina said, "a little slower, but in style."

The Premier lifted his glass in appreciation. "I'm going to let you in on a little secret. China's on the brink of a new wave of modernization. We need new middle-level technology—transportation, communications, mineral extraction, construction, energy. It's not cheap. I figure it will cost about a hundred billion dollars. And guess where we're going to get that?" The Premier smiled. "It's not an obvious source for money."

Roger's fists tightened involuntarily. "Not you too?" He caught Christina's sharp look and stopped himself. "You're not, ah, planning to sell cultural treasures?"

Premier Chen shook his head. "Of course not. I've been able to weed out most of the ideologues who crushed the student demonstrations in 1989. But there still are some lunatics who would sell our great art to buy a few weapons, and we can close China's doors to the outside world. Just like the Empress Dowager and the Boxers. Just like Mao's Cultural Revolution. Power and purity, that's all they talk about, never thinking about people and progress. Privately they still call foreigners barbarians. I'm not kidding."

"Who are 'they'?" Christina asked.

"I can't really be specific. Take my word, there are a few idiots in very high positions. Some of them have connections with our friend Lamarche."

Roger and Christina stared at the Premier.

"Oh, I don't think you have to worry about Lamarche here. Our private agents control all entry into the country and we have all of Lamarche's known agents on our list. Besides, Beijing University has its own security guarding the campus, especially the residences of foreigners. Most of all, as you'll soon discover, China is held together by a tight network of mutual surveillance."

"You mean everyone is spying on everyone else?"

"Yes, Professor Wang, but not the way you mean. It's not a Communist plot, it's in our tradition. Look out the window and maybe you'll understand."

A tiny village absorbed hundreds of farmers returning from checkerboard paddy fields, somehow squeezing into narrow streets and cramped houses. The Premier stabbed his finger at the scene. "Imagine that happening over all of China. In east China alone, we have over eight hundred million people. That's like fitting four times the entire American population into an area east of the Mississippi River. Privacy is a luxury we can't afford, so everyone watches out for everyone else. It's the ultimate security system."

"I see your point." Roger was impressed but unconvinced. "But isn't there still a chance that the killers can get through?"

The Premier stared out the window for a moment. "Yes," he said. "I suppose there's one way. But it would require someone in very high government authority undermining the security and letting the thugs through. I think that's very unlikely . . ." The Premier patted his lips with his napkin. "You're safe as long as I'm safe. Besides, I'm going to assign a guard to each of you at all times. Don't worry, you'll be all right."

Roger looked at the Premier and then out the window, shadows of doubt on his face. He wanted to believe the Premier. After all, it had been his idea to come to China in the first place. He was tasting his first freedom in almost two years, away from confinement in Taipei and Alishan. But why couldn't the security spring a leak? Didn't personalized armies and security forces crush an unarmed demonstration in the Spring of 1989? He wanted to get down to serious research on the box, but did he have to keep looking over his shoulder? Did the Premier know about the box? Probably the Chang family had conveyed as little as possible. It would be better to say nothing.

"Why are you doing this?" Christina asked. "Why such efforts to protect us? Just a deathbed request from my father?"

"No, Miss Chang. I deeply respect your family and your father. But it's much more than that. I'm surprised. You really don't know?"

"No."

"Remember the hundred billion dollars I told you about? Where do you think I'm going to get it?"

"You've got me," Christina replied.

"From the West, of course, from private banking sources. From friends of China, particularly wealthy overseas Chinese. Long-term loans at low interest."

"But where do we fit in?"

"Miss Chang, about one third of the loan depends on your brother."

"My brother?"

"Of course. George Chang is a good businessman. He knows that Asian trade depends on China's growth. When China is stable, Asia is also stable. The United States, Europe, and Japan are all banking on China's continued economic growth and stability. It's a crucial investment, more important than political differences. So your brother has brought together seven key American banks and that, along with some of his private capital, is the largest part of the loan."

"And so we . . . ?"

"And so you, Professor Wang, along with your lovely wife, are collateral for the biggest consortium loan in history. If anything happens to you, the loan is off. Your brother-in-law is an *excellent* businessman."

A day and a half later, the Premier's train chugged the last leg of its journey through Shandong and southern Hebei provinces, providing dawn vistas of the golden wheat stretching endlessly across the North China Plain. China's north, Roger could see, lived a harsh existence, subject to harsher Siberian weather from Mongolia and Manchuria. The Yellow River, slowly carrying silt to the shallow sea between China and Korea, flowed above the ground, precariously cradled by dikes and levees from its habitual tendency to flood. Roger and Christina shared tense excitement as they rumbled into Beijing, the capital for all Chinese wherever they lived. Christina wished her father could have been with them. Roger sadly thought about Miss Sun: "Mista Wang. Mainland China bad. People no food. Very sad. Beijing only place pretty."

Premier Chen watched with quiet satisfaction as Roger and Christina, hands interlaced and shoulders gently touching, seemed to communicate without talking. Two bright people in love and not afraid to show it, the Premier thought to himself, now that's something I can believe in. Maybe that's the fifth modernization, he chuckled; luckily it doesn't need Politburo approval.

"I'm not going to see you very often," the Premier said as they parted. He handed Roger a card. "Here's my private number. Use it whenever you want to contact me."

He watched as Roger and Christina entered the black Mercedes limousine for the half-hour trip to Beida. When the automobile had pulled away, the Premier removed his glasses and rubbed his forehead. He knew the pain would be there for a long time. Damn the tradition of *guanxi*, he thought. A network of obligations that may get all of us killed.

The limousine's curtains were supposed to make the occupants look more important. Roger and Christina destroyed the impression by pushing them back and staring out the window. Their disappointment was immediate.

"Where are the walls?" Roger asked the driver. "The gates?"

The driver, a cheerful fellow who enjoyed his task of dodging pedestrians and bicyclists, replied brightly. "You mean the old walls and gates? They're all gone, torn down in the fifties. To make more space for buildings and to speed up traffic."

Roger and Christina stared at each other. Why hadn't someone warned them about Beijing? All they saw was run-down buildings, dust-covered streets, blue and gray clothing. Even the air was gray —filled with the heavy fumes of industrial plants and the soot of soft coal.

"It reminds me of Taipei," Christina mused, "but it doesn't have modern lights and motor scooters."

Roger rolled down the window and sniffed. "It sure smells like Taipei. But it looks more like Harlem, only without wild clothes and ghetto blasters."

"You want to see old Beijing?" the driver broke in. "We can take a little detour."

In a moment, they saw a huge gate, lavishly painted in red and green, clearly a relic of dynastic China, standing nakedly without the walls attached to it. "That's the old Qianmen," explained the driver. "Front Gate to the Imperial City." The driver pointed ahead.

Roger and Christina looked beyond the Qianmen to an expanse of concrete, a mile long and a half-mile wide, surrounded by elongated tawny-gray buildings with the unmistakable imprint of Russian architecture. "That's Tiananmen Square—History Museum, Great Hall of the People, Chairman Mao's Mausoleum. That's where no one was killed in June, 1989." The driver winked, then shook his head—everybody knew the official "no deaths" accounts were a cruel joke.

"It looks like the whole area was destroyed by an atomic bomb," Roger exclaimed.

"And then rebuilt by some idiot using a giant Lego set," Christina completed the thought.

"I can see you're not impressed," the driver interjected. "Frankly, I don't like it much either. I've got to admit that it used to be a nice place for parades. Now it's filled with memories. Democracy martyrs of 1989."

The driver stopped the car in front of a vermilion wall, almost a quarter mile long, with a dark wooden gate in the middle, surmounted by balconies beneath a deep-yellow tiled roof. "Now that's what's left of the real old Beijing. It's the Tiananmen, the Gate of Heavenly Peace, entrance to the Gu Gong, the Forbidden City. In olden times, commoners would be executed if they tried to enter. Up there, that's where Mao announced the People's Republic. The Chinese people have finally stood up. That's what he said. Now it's open to the public. Want to go inside?"

Roger looked at Christina. She shook her head. "No, thanks. Not now."

The driver, from the Beida motor pool, had no desire to return quickly just to start another job. "You can get a glimpse of it from Coal Hill. You can see the whole Gu Gong from there." The limousine stopped smoothly in a parking lot behind the Forbidden City. The driver jumped out, opened the door for his passengers, and locked his vehicle. He led them up the steep path snaking to old Ming dynasty pavilions preserved near its summit.

As they absorbed the dramatic landscape of red and yellow buildings, the driver lectured. "That's the Gu Gong itself. Hundreds of palaces, for emperors and empresses and their servants, concubines, and eunuchs. Over there is Jongnanhai, the Central-Southern Lake, just west of the Gu Gong, where the highest Communist Party officials live. I guess it's still a sort of Forbidden City. And there's

Beihai, the Northern Lake; now it's a public park. People like to rent boats in the summer and skate in the winter. Nice hideout for lovers, too."

The splendor of the Forbidden City struck Roger as a gorgeous jewel in a bed of ashes. As he surveyed the architectural relics, an American "Friendship Tour" group arrived at the peak of Coal Hill, the enthusiastic guide wearing a pin of crossed American and Chinese flags. "I told you Beijing was great. All this devotion to tradition in the midst of so much modernization. We can do it all in three days. Today the Forbidden City and the Temple of Heaven. Tomorrow the Summer Palace. The next day the Great Wall and the Ming Tombs. You'll be staying in China's most luxurious Great Wall Hotel." Roger and Christina shared a look of disgust.

As the limousine sped to Beida, Roger leaned toward the driver. "Do you think you could take someone to all of Old Beijing in a day?"

"Oh, sure. You'd need a good driver. Of course, you'd also have to get an early start if you wanted the Great Wall too. If you want to do it, I'm free the day after tomorrow."

"No, thanks," Christina said quickly.

"Oh, I understand," replied the driver, smiling as he wove through traffic. "You're Overseas Chinese. You're probably here actually to see people, not like the other foreigners. They just want to see old buildings and snap photographs. They think they're learning about China from their official guides. See that over there? It's the Beijing Zoo. If you want to know how the animals feel, you don't ask the zookeeper."

CHAPTER SEVENTEEN

EDUCATION

"WHO SAYS CHINA IS SEXLESS?"

Christina exclaimed, jumping out of bed into the cold room. The only heat came from an undersized radiator and the morning sun. She covered her skimpy white panties with her new blue parka, pulled on a woolen worker's cap, and paraded around the little bedroom. Then she jumped back onto the bed and threw open her coat. "You call this sexless?"

"Christina! For God's sake!" Roger chided. "Haven't you ever heard about bugging?"

"Bugging!" she sang out gaily. "A new way to do it? Sounds kinky. Show me how."

"I mean it, Christina," he scolded her. "They could be listening to us right now."

"Oh, Roger," she pouted. "Of course they *could* be listening, but you don't know anything about bugging, and certainly not about bugging in China. First off, it's expensive. Somebody has to listen and then make a transcript. Second, it assumes the technology actually works, and that's one big assumption in China."

Roger gestured around the bedroom. "Well, bugged or not, it's not exactly a palace for my bride."

Christina had to agree with him. The cramped white cubicle held a double bed, a night table, and a closet too small for even a minimal wardrobe. Indeed, the entire fifth-floor walk-up apartment left a lot to be desired. Paint was peeling in the cold-water-only bathroom; the living room contained only two lounge chairs, a wall of bookshelves, and a metal-and-Formica desk.

Pulling on woolen underwear, blue cotton suits, parkas, and hats and making sure they had the mandatory red plastic-covered identity cards ("status: foreign expert; unit: Beijing University"), they walked to the dining hall for a breakfast of bacon, eggs, and toast. It annoyed them that they had to eat in a dining area reserved for foreign faculty and students, just one manifestation of the practice of separating Chinese and foreigners whenever possible. The Great Wall between the Middle Kingdom and the barbarians applied even to Overseas Chinese, who were viewed suspiciously since they often imported expensive gifts for relatives.

Nudging Christina with his knee to get her attention, Roger tipped his head toward two burly, gray-suited men at a nearby table. "Puppy dogs," she whispered, "always on our heels." Roger hoped their bodyguards would become German shepherds if the occasion demanded it; but thus far, after several months in Beijing, there had been no sign of Lamarche or his henchmen.

"Our biggest danger isn't physical violence," Christina mused between bites of bacon. "It's a new form of Chinese torture—death by boredom. They don't seem to want a foreign expert in art education. They're just reprinting old textbooks to replace those burned by Red Guards." Christina laughed a little. "The books from before liberation have all the nudes cut out. It's like *Penthouse* in Japan and Hong Kong. You know, magic marker to wipe out the pubic hair. Maybe next semester things will be better. They've promised to let me teach some calligraphy courses."

"Good luck trying to change anything in China," Roger chimed in cynically. "There's another torture—death by obstinacy." Roger had been utterly frustrated trying to track down possible Gao family survivors. "The Beijing University phone directory?" a university secretary had smirked. "There isn't one. Most faculty don't have private phones. And a faculty address book? If you want to know where someone lives, just ask him and write down the address yourself." Undaunted, Roger managed to convince an associate dean to open rickety, irregularly shaped filing cabinets labeled "Beijing University Faculty, 1949–present." "Professor Gao Zhonglu, Philosophy, deceased 1949" was the sole information in one file. "Professor Gao

Jinru, History, removed from service, 1966" was the only other information. And when he asked older faculty about a former Professor Gao in the History Department, Roger uniformly encountered blank stares.

"Teaching going any better?" Christina asked, putting her hand gently on his.

Roger sighed and shook his head. Initially he had been excited about teaching Western Intellectual History to thirty advanced students, third-year history majors who had come from "advanced-track" high schools. But Roger's enthusiasm cooled when he discovered the required textbook dryly summarized Western philosophers from Plato to Hegel to Dewey, no links to the political and social context, each chapter concluding with a list of "dates and people to remember." His department chairman told him not to worry, to "teach from any materials you like," but he found Beijing University Library almost devoid of contemporary Western history. The Cultural Revolution had systematically destroyed foreign ideas for ten years; China would require decades to recover from its worst intellectual storm in modern history.

"I've got an idea," Christina said brightly. "It just might turn things around a little. Why don't you assign a special exercise? Why not force the students to make their own interpretations, using your own materials?"

Later that day, Roger borrowed a collection of interpretive essays about the American revolution from a fellow foreign faculty member, eventually selecting two different interpretations of the Founding Fathers: one arguing their commitment to democracy and freedom, another claiming their manipulation of an already grossly unequal political and economic system. Roger laboriously replicated the articles on an ancient typewriter and then cranked them out in purple ink on a Chinese-made mimeograph machine whose key parts were held together with paperclips. He gave each student a mimeographed copy with instructions to come to class ready to give his own interpretation.

A week later, Professor Roger Wang sat at his raised desk in front of the cold and drafty classroom, illuminated more by sunlight than by the three low-wattage bulbs overhead. The students filed in, took assigned seats, opened notebooks and waited respectfully.

Like the students, Roger wore a sweater and long underwear under his dark-blue cotton jacket.

Clearing his throat from the morning pollution, Roger turned to the blackboard and drew a vertical line. He printed a heading above each column: "Founding Fathers: Heroes" and "Founding Fathers: Villains." Stepping back off the dais, he smiled formally. "I think we're ready to begin. Good morning to all of you."

"Good morning, Professor," they replied in unison.

"Okay, you've been given two interpretations. Let's begin by understanding these different points of view." Turning to a ruddy-cheeked woman in the third row, he asked, "Miss Zhou, can you give us the arguments for the Founding Fathers as heroes? What were their positive characteristics?"

The woman stood up, closing her eyes to help her memory, and began to recite. "The article said that there were six basic reasons why the Founding Fathers were good men. The first reason is that they were genuine revolutionaries, trying to create a government that emphasized freedom of choice, democratic institutions, and equality of opportunity. The second reason is that they had all been fighters themselves, fighting against the tyranny of outside power. . . ." Roger followed her recitation with his chalk, summarizing each point and placing a number next to it.

"That's a good start. Now who can tell us about the Founding Fathers as villains?" Several hands shot up. Roger selected a vigorous hand-waver in the front row whose drawn face showed the effects of all-night preparation.

"Thank you, Professor. If you read the article closely, there were eight main reasons why the author said that the Founding Fathers did not have the interests of the people at heart. First and foremost, they all came from the rich classes and wanted to preserve their wealth and power. Second, if you compare the Declaration of Independence and the Constitution, you will find great gaps between the revolutionary ideology and the conservative system of government. . . ." Again Roger dutifully copied the points in the second column.

"That's a very solid job, Mr. Zhu. Between the two of you, we have a pretty good outline on both sides, and now we come to the big challenge. Which of these two interpretations do you think is correct?"

The classroom remained silent, students fidgeting nervously.

He waited, then began to scan the room, looking for eyes reflecting an answer, any answer. The students avoided his stare, their eyes fixed on the two columns on the blackboard.

Roger walked to the dais, sat down in his chair, and spoke encouragingly. "You're the best students in China. You've made it to the top. You've studied the American Revolution for years. For goodness' sake, you've had your own revolution, just forty years ago. You must have some thoughts about it. How about you, Mr. Ling."

The small man at the back of the room quivered, shuffling the articles and notes in front of him, finally standing up. "I . . . I just don't know. They're both good arguments. Both smart historians. I can't guess. Which one is the right one, Professor?"

"That just won't do," Roger said coldly. "It's not for me to give you an answer. It's not a simple case of right and wrong. Miss Du, give it a try. Come on, it won't count toward your grade. I promise."

Miss Du, an attractive woman with short hair, struggled to her feet. Trying to extrapolate from what the professor had just said, she blurted out, "I think . . . well. I think maybe both interpretations are correct."

"Why?"

"Because some revolutionaries were good people. And others were bad people."

"Well, at least it's an answer. But it's too simple. All people, including revolutionaries, are more complicated than that." Finally spotting Mr. Zhu with a tentative hand raised in the front row, he said, "Good. At least someone is willing to volunteer."

Mr. Zhu disentangled his bony frame from his chair and stood up, taking a deep breath as he faced the awful fate of possibly being wrong. "I think that the number-two interpretation is correct, Professor Wang."

"Yes? Why is that?"

"You see, the number-one interpretation only has six main points. The number-two interpretation has eight points. Doesn't that make number two the winner?"

Roger slumped forward in the chair and cradled his head in his hands. The class watched him silently, dumbfounded by his behavior. Then he stood up and glowered at them, unable to find the words to express his dismay.

"Professor Wang. Perhaps I might have a try?" He looked at the speaker, a slight, plain-looking young woman with glasses, who sat slightly apart from the rest of the students in the very back of the room. She was an auditor and he had never noticed her before; auditor's names were not on his class list.

"Yes, miss, anything would be better than this."

Everyone watched her as she stood and began to speak in precise, uninflected sentences. "The question is not which interpretation is correct. They are both partly correct and partly wrong. They stand as extreme characterizations, almost caricatures, of the motivations behind the Founding Fathers. Thomas Jefferson, for instance, might be motivated by some of the so-called heroic principles at times. At other times, he was probably thinking more like the so-called villains. The interpretations are like tools for the historian. They are only useful when you look at real people, confronting real events."

Roger stared at her for a moment. Then his face broke into a relieved grin. "Finally! Someone here is thinking. That's what I want all of you to do. Don't just memorize. Think!" He dismissed the class and erased the blackboard. When he turned to speak to the young woman, she had disappeared.

Picking up his papers, he walked briskly out of the building, inhaling crisp December air. He sat on a bench by a pond, trying to regain perspective. The big difference between Beida and Columbia, he thought, was that Columbia students were pushed to analyze; they couldn't get away with rote memorization. Chinese students were the most brilliant memorizers in the world, but they weren't challenged to think. That would have appalled Confucius. Perhaps intellectual rigidity was the true tragedy of modern China: the reason millions babbled slogans from Mao's little red book; the source of dogmatism in decent men like Scholar Wen. Roger remembered the euphoria he had seen on the faces of Chinese student demonstrators in May, 1989—utter joy after years of suffocating in lockstep Chinese classrooms.

"Professor Wang?" Roger looked up at the woman who had spoken in class. "Could I join you for a moment?"

Roger smiled warmly, shifting on the marble bench to make room. She seemed so inconsequential; her parka hung limply over her scrawny body like a rug thrown over a stray cat. Her glasses hid a face that was throughly unmemorable.

"That was quite a performance," Roger said sincerely, trying to make contact with the eyes behind the heavy optic glass. "I was almost ready to explode. You saved the day."

He looked in vain for even the glimmer of a smile. "It wasn't anything much. I just felt that I had to say something. You deserved more than silly answers."

"Tell me," he asked, leaning forward so that she couldn't dodge his eyes, "are you the only one who's really thinking in the class? Are there others secretly thinking on their own but not willing to speak out?"

She shifted her sparrow like body to face him. "I don't know. Maybe one or two in every class. Perhaps more. But you'll never know. You see, there's no advantage in it."

"No advantage to thinking?"

"No. None at all. You surprise me by asking, Professor Wang. You're Chinese. At least you're Overseas Chinese. You should know. The whole system works on *guanxi*, connections. Lots of the students come here through the back door, connections through the party or government. Powerful fathers make for promising children."

"Are you saying that they're not really very smart?"

"Not at all. Most are very smart, many are brilliant. You can't get in without talent. But they know that they can't rock the boat. Their careers, and the reputation of their families, depend on conformity. They've been trained in school and at home to do what they're told, not ask questions, not show their talent except in accepted ways. And now, after the democracy movement, it's even worse. You can be sure that one of your fellow students is a spy."

"That's awful."

"Not awful. That's China."

"But what about you? How come you dare to be different? Aren't you worried?"

She smiled at last, wryly. "Would you have dinner at my home tonight, you and your wife? With me and my father? It's not far from campus, close enough so that the authorities won't see it as anything irregular. I've written down the address for you."

Roger took the paper and smiled warmly at her. "We'd be delighted."

"Good. At six o'clock."

She rose and began to walk away. Then she stopped and turned around. "I haven't properly introduced myself. My name is Gao. Gao Rushi. You can call me Xiao Gao."

"Mrs. Chang, I assume? And Professor Wang. Glad you found your way," she said warmly. "Now be careful. These old hallways are badly lit. Just follow me."

The smells were an especially pungent version of the familiar formula of garlic, sooty coal, and human excrement. Feeling his way through a corridor, Roger just missed stepping on a live chicken. Dozens of families lived in makeshift wooden apartments clumsily fashioned on either side of the main corridor. He watched an old woman open her ramshackle door and throw out a pail of dishwater that quickly seeped through cracks in the wooden floor. Xiao Gao pulled aside a dingy quilt of burlap sacks covering the main doorway at the end of the corridor, a flimsy effort to preserve a bit of heat.

"Don't worry. We're almost there."

Roger and Christina looked around at a courtyard paved with cracked, moss-covered stones. On one side were several small apartments constructed of cinder blocks with corrugated tin roofs and small metal chimneys belching heavy black smoke. On the other side were stacks of the same cinder blocks, enough to make another five or six more drafty apartments. Ahead was a large building with red columns and a tile roof; a procession of carved animals marched along the edges of the roof, clearly silhouetted against the moonlit sky. Xiao Gao opened the heavy door, revealing a spacious cavity divided into apartments by massive faded-red pillars supporting oak cross beams. Murmuring conversations, punctuated by an occasional crescendo of arguing shouts, filtered through the darkness; Beijing Opera music blared over radios.

"Here it is," Xiao Gao shouted over the din. "Third door on the right."

Roger ducked to permit his six-foot frame through the low opening; inside the cramped box that served as kitchen, bedroom, and living room, he had to assume a permanently bent posture. A two-burner coal stove supported a wok and a steamer, both bubbling away. The room was dominated by the *kang*, a six-by-six-foot raised brick platform, heated by coal. The *kang*, couch during the day and bed at night, was neatly covered with a white-and-yellow quilt and pillows of various colors. Bookcases, stuffed with Chinese history and literature paperbacks and tattered tao binders, surrounded a small wooden desk. Wall space was covered with yellowing photographs; the floor sported a ragged geometric-patterned rug, probably quite a treasure in its prime. The room had been carefully swept and tidied, like a haggard old woman back from the beauty parlor.

"Father, please come in now. Our guests have arrived."

As Xiao Gao held aside a red blanket covering a doorway next to the *kang*, an ancient wooden wheelchair creaked into the room. Its occupant's legs hung down limply, thin and immobile, one foot badly deformed. His upper body, clothed in sweaters and a padded jacket, supported feeble arms struggling with the wheels.

"Good evening, Professor Wang, Mrs. Chang. Welcome to our little home. My daughter has told me much about you." The voice was startling, so much more vigorous than the body. His face conveyed inner power: sharp features, lively, thoughtful eyes, well-combed silver hair, eyebrows still a youthful bushy black. He must have been an extremely handsome man once; a proud mandarin in a mutilated frame.

"Professor Wang, I'm pleased to present my father, Professor Gao. Actually you have something in common. My father was a professor of Chinese history here at Beida. Until his accident, he taught full-time. Now he's no longer on the faculty list. But he still does research. And—"

Professor Gao raised his hand, gently stopping his daughter. "You'll have to forgive her, Professor Wang. You see, she's like my mother, especially since her own mother died many years ago. She's always trying to convince strangers that I'm her little prodigy." Lifting a trembling hand, he caressed his daughter's arm. "She's covering up the fact that she's got the brains in the family. She knows the system like a clock, she's always got the keys to Beijing's back doors. Brilliant student, too—"

Roger gestured admiringly at Xiao Gao. "I've seen it. Today in class, a remarkable display. I was going crazy listening to the quacking of ducks. Then she said something extraordinary."

Xiao Gao, usual shyness intensified by praise, broke in to announce dinner. They ate steamed dumplings, and then finely sliced chicken, served with bokchoi, a dark-green cabbage. When Professor Gao asked their reactions to China, Roger glanced around the room, thinking, surely they've got to hate this, especially if they are who

I think they are. "Frankly, it's a disappointment. A dreadfully poor society. A terribly boring country."

Christina nodded her head sadly. "It's not much of a home-coming for me. China has lost its traditions. There's little hope for the future. I feel for you."

Professor Gao's jaw stiffened. He put down his chopsticks and rested his feeble arms on the table. "At least you're not like the tourists who believe the line about comprehensive modernization by the year two thousand. Just like they swallowed the garbage about the wonders of Chairman Mao and the Cultural Revolution. But please, give us a little credit. We're on the right track."

Professor Gao pushed himself to a small table, removed a thin red blanket, unveiling a Japanese cassette stereo and color television set, sitting like temple gods on an altar. "My friends, perhaps some music?" he asked proudly. A Mozart violin concerto filled the room. Turning down the volume, he smiled smugly. "Twenty years ago, this would have been unthinkable. Nobody had these little miracles to brighten their lives. To play Western music was to risk arrest. Now we're becoming modern, slowly but surely. There's a rural rev-olution, with private plots and thriving markets. And an urban revolution—increased wages, better jobs, consumer goods. Finally, the *real* Chinese revolution. Just think, twenty years ago—"

"Father, stop it!" Xiao Gao broke in angrily. "I remember twenty years ago—when Mother wasn't dead yet of tuberculosis after being sent down to the countryside, when the Red Guards hadn't torn apart Beida and paralyzed you from the waist down! Every generation has its terror. I lost at least five close friends when the tanks came to Tiananmen."

Professor Gao tensed. "Professor Wang. Mrs. Chang. I apolo-gize. I thought I was giving you Mozart. Instead you got the Gao Family Beijing Opera. We play it every night—"

Xiao Gao cut him off. "And we'll continue to play it. Every night, if need be, until you come to your senses. We've got to get out of here. Out of this madhouse. Out of China."

The professor pulled himself up as firmly as he could. "Never. A hundred times never! China has had a great past. It will have a great future. I know it. It requires good minds—like yours. You can't give up. Even after I'm gone, you have to stay, and realize the Gao dream."

"Realize the Gao dream, Father? What has that dream gotten

this family except a century of nightmares? Will you never wake up?"

*　*　*

No one spoke for a long time. What Roger had suspected from the moment Xiao Gao uttered her name, he now knew for certain.

Professor Gao spoke quietly, his voice barely carrying above the music. "Without a dream, a Gao cannot exist." Pausing for a second, he continued, "You've heard of the Gao dream, haven't you, Professor Wang?"

Roger nodded his head.

"And you know who we are? And where you are?"

"Yes. At least I think I can guess. You're the descendants of the famous Gaos. And this is what's left of the old Gao mansion?"

"Yes. Forgive us for our little argument a moment ago. I guess we felt you knew us well enough that . . . well, at least you should feel complimented that we don't consider you strangers."

"But how did you know about me?"

Professor Gao inched his chair forward. "Dr. Ren wrote me on behalf of old Chang. After all, our families share a long history, and I remember Dr. Ren took care of my own father. China now has a rather efficient underground postal service. He was just hoping I was still alive."

"Didn't you know I've been desperately trying to find you, hunting through the Beida records? There's nothing there."

"I know," Professor Gao grimaced. "The Cultural Revolution used its most vicious weapon—obliterating people's identities. My records, my books, my teaching materials—all were destroyed. When the madness stopped in the mid-1970s, I was almost at retirement age. So no one bothered to change anything."

"But why didn't you contact us earlier?"

"Even though Dr. Ren vouched for you, we had to know for sure your motives were genuine, that you weren't just some more fortune hunters. For years the authorities have been trying to get their hands on the art collection. They're always spying on us. This apartment is probably bugged right now."

"But how do you dare meet with us?" Christina wondered. "Aren't you afraid?"

"It makes very little difference what we say and do," Professor

Gao answered calmly. "If those in power are sympathetic to intellectuals, then we're all right. If not, we suffer. Right now, we think it's getting better. And of course . . ." The professor winked and turned up the stereo. "Of course, when it comes to delicate conversations, I always let Japanese technology override Chinese technology. It's the only form of Japanese imperialism we tolerate in this family."

"How do you know we're not treasure hunters?" Roger asked.

"We didn't know for sure until this morning's class. Then Xiao Gao sensed you were the right couple." The old professor beckoned his daughter to stand beside him. "You see, we don't see eye to eye about China's future. She's more cynical, but we both believe education is the only answer." He nodded to Xiao Gao, who disappeared into the other room and returned with a manila envelope.

"It's something else Dr. Ren sent along," the professor said. "He said not to look inside until you were with us."

Xiao Gao slit open the envelope; Roger and Christina watched as the two Gaos scrutinized each photograph of the lacquer box. It was as if two brilliant students, having prepared for a test over a lifetime, were finally given a chance to collaborate in giving the answers. The professor took the lead, pointing to each allegory in turn; Xiao Gao pondered for a moment and then gave a precise quotation or interpretation. Each time Professor Gao nodded sharply, indicating that his daughter had passed the test.

"It isn't often," Professor Gao said as his daughter wiped away the old man's tears, "that the past speaks so clearly to the present. What Gao Zhenggai wanted is right here on this box. It's what China still needs today. I thought I'd never live to see this day."

"You mean you can understand it all?" Roger said. "Does it tell you where the art collection is hidden?"

Professor Gao put the photographs back in the envelope and placed the packet next to the television set. Selecting another tape and raising the volume, he leaned his neck pensively against the chairback. "It's the dream in perfect miniature. It tells everything about the thought and philosophy. But it doesn't come out and say 'Here's where the art is.' "

"You understand the box, and yet you can't find the collection?"

"That's the way Gao Zhenggai wanted it. It's his way of saying 'I've given you my most important treasure—my philosophy, my dream for China.' I think he's also saying 'You must first seek to realize my dream, then I'll show you the way to the art.' Above all he's saying 'This art must be used only for a noble purpose, therefore it won't be easy to find.' "

"So what do we do?"

"My guess is that there's a code on the box. But Gao Zhenggai probably designed it so that only a Gao, or someone very close to a Gao, could find it. We have to do what he would want us to do. And I'll need your help to do it."

"How can we help?"

"Liberal education. You know in your bones what we know only in theory. Help us implement educational reform. It's critical to our future. Advise me so I can pass along the ideas to those in authority. Will you do it?"

"Of course," Roger replied. "Christina and I will be glad to try, but I'm not sure we can do much." Roger desperately hoped they were finally on the right track. It seemed such an indirect way to conduct a search. Was the old man a little senile? Had torture cracked his mind?

"Whatever ideas you have are important," the professor said. "I'm certain we're doing Gao Zhenggai's bidding. It's the only way to the art collection." The old professor held back on just one detail: he knew they were embarking on the riskiest part of uncovering his family legacy. Almost a century of waiting, punctuated by pain and death, was coming to an end. He shivered at the dangers that might lie ahead. Worse yet, they might discover that the Gao Collection had already been plundered. The risks might lead nowhere.

"Where do we start?" Roger tried to sound confident.

"Follow me," Professor Gao replied, his eyes dancing beneath his bushy eyebrows. Xiao Gao wrapped the old man in blankets, forcing the creaking chair through the doorway and into the murky hallway.

Professor Gao whispered as he pointed to a barely visible pillar. "Here's where it happened. Almost a century ago. That's where the Boxers cut him apart. Tonight, a hundred years later, maybe he has a chance to live again." The professor looked up at the darkened beams overhead. "Here. In the Gao Ancestral Temple."

Xiao Gao pushed the chair into the moonlit wintry evening, past the temple and over a rocky bridge covering a stream littered with garbage. The chair grumbled through several rocky portals, bumping as the wheels struggled over broken stones.

Then the chair stopped. Professor Gao and his daughter both lifted their heads. Rising above them was a towering cluster of oddly shaped boulders, silhouetted against the moon, a Chinese landscape painting in black and white.

"It's the Pinnacle," Xiao Gao whispered to Roger. "Father refused to let them tear it down to build more apartments. He said he would commit suicide if they tried."

CHAPTER EIGHTEEN

LAYERS OF LACQUER

MAO'S DEATH IN 1976 PAVED THE
way for a new era in Chinese history, an era in which modernizers,
led by the feisty Deng Xiaoping, dominated the stage. Deng inau-
gurated an unprecedented array of reforms causing rapid industrial
growth, much larger harvests, and substantial increases in income.
"To Be Rich Is Glorious" was the slogan of a new generation of small
shopkeepers and private plot owners. Deng's objective was to bring
China's standard of living closer to that of the dynamic Pacific
region—particularly the flourishing economies he saw in Hong Kong
and Taiwan. Foreign trade and foreign capital were essential to his
scheme; he lured thousands of Japanese, American, and European
entrepreneurs to his "special economic zones" and "open cities."
Deng's China would merge naturally with Asia, a far cry from Mao's
China, which had withdrawn ominously from Asia and the rest of
the world.

By the mid-1980s, however, Deng's revolution was prompting
more frustration than enthusiasm. Citydwellers complained of ramp-
ant inflation and low quality consumer products. Farmers laughed at
the notion that they could all become rich like the model "ten
thousand yuan peasants." Students and intellectuals were openly
cynical about a Communist Party that repressed most efforts for
greater academic, political, or press freedom, while spawning corruption on a massive scale.

Hidden to the outside world, politicians were taking sides in what would become one of the greatest cataclysms in modern Chinese history. As Deng's star faded, figures such as Hu Yaobang and Zhao Ziyang were on the rise, openly siding with student demands for a more liberal society. Against such moderates stood Li Peng and Yang Shangkun, advocating more centralized economic planning, stronger roles for security forces, and repression of intellectual dissent.

After serious political tremors in 1987, massive popular earthquakes shook China in the spring of 1989. Several factors sustained the massive demonstrations—Hu Yaobang's death in April, total inflexibility on the part of government authorities who described demonstrators as "counterrevolutionaries," the Deng-Gorbachev summit meeting that brought media attention from throughout the world, the tough-worded declaration of martial law followed by a weak show of force. More deeply, the demonstrators hoped they were leading China to a new era of greater openness, a sort of democracy Chinese-style, symbolized by a Chinese version of a statue of liberty.

Tragically, the waves of joyful, peaceful demonstrations in May were met by tanks and automatic weapons on June 3–4, 1989. The world watched aghast as Deng and Li sanctioned the massacre of hundreds, perhaps thousands, of Chinese citizens. China was now governed by purge, repression, terror, and execution. On the surface, China's voices of dissent were silenced, urban life returned to an eerie normalcy, foreign television cameras focused elsewhere, foreign businessmen returned to pursue China trade. Under the surface, millions of Chinese seethed with fury as they watched Beijing use Stalinist techniques.

The new China of Deng and Li bore some uncanny resemblances to the old China a hundred years earlier. A conservative government sought to break the spirit of more moderate reformers. Dissident intellectuals confronted prison bars and public executions. Foreigners watched in disbelief as China devoured its most talented minds. Everyone wondered about political succession for a geriatric leadership.

In the 1990s, as in the 1890s, the questions were remarkably similar. Where was the Middle Kingdom headed? Could conservatives stay in power through the use of terror and force? Would conservatives live up to their promises of promoting China's modernization or would they foster corruption and thus drain away precious resources? Could moderates stage a comeback, prompting both economic growth and political liberalization? Or would more

241

extremist elements—ideologues like the Taipings, the Boxers, the Red Guards—seek another hour on China's stage?

A security guard snored at his station just inside the locked gates of the Party's Propaganda Department. The building was hidden behind the walls of Jongnanhai, the brain trust of Communist China, right on the western edge of the Forbidden City. The Propaganda Department was supposed to be a secular priesthood, providing ideological guidance to the forty million Party members. Deep in the Propaganda Department's cavernous basement, near the wire cages that housed archives marked "Top Secret," eight men, all wearing the tailored gray suits of top-level officials, sat around a table in a locked, windowless room.

The clandestine meeting was chaired by Cai Dongshi, recently elevated to Director of the Propaganda Department and membership in the Politburo. A stout, bald man in his seventies, Cai was among the few ideologues still holding office after the purges following Mao's death. Sticking out of his cadre suit jacket pocket was his trademark, a well-thumbed paperback of Marxist quotations, which he wore like a handgun, often drawing it out quickly and disarming opponents with bulletlike recitations.

"The date is now certain," Cai announced. "The Premier and the Modernization Faction will hold their special celebration on May fourth, the anniversary of the famous Nationalist uprising."

An angry murmur went around the table, like bees confronting an intruder. "Damn the Modernization Faction!" a voice shouted. "Damn the May Fourth Movement! It's the great sellout."

Cai's voice rose above the din. "That's not all. Guess where the celebration's being held? In the Forbidden City itself. For the first time since the Qing dynasty. Bourgeois modernizers worshiping feudal traitors! And the main guests are Western capitalists." He sneered. "There'll be a banquet, fireworks, and dancing, all to celebrate a huge loan to finance Premier Chen's schemes."

Cai's ashtray slammed on the table. "China is selling its soul," he intoned, "all in the name of modernization. We must purify the country. Do we want to become another Japan?"

"No!" came the shout in unison.

"Another Western Europe?"

"No!"

"Another United States?"

"No! Never!"

The ashtray crashed down again. "That's right, comrades. We agree. But we can't do anything sitting here and shouting. We must take dramatic action. Otherwise we'll watch our power ebb away. At our future meetings, I'll give you the detailed plans."

Taking a sheet of white paper and a long needle, Cai lanced his finger so a drop of blood fell to the center of the sheet. Then he passed the needle and paper around the table, each man repeating the ritual. When it returned to him, he folded it so all drops of blood ran together. He unfolded the paper and held it up to show the single smear.

"This blood is our strength. It is Chinese strength. Down with the foreigners! Down with the modernizing compradores! Long live the Celestial Roots Movement!"

Zhou Rong remained behind after the others left, smiling with satisfaction. "We deserve this moment." Zhou was now Minister of Public Security, chief of police for the world's most populous country.

"We've been screwed for over a decade," Cai sighed, "but it's not going to happen again."

"China was once the greatest country in the world," Zhou fretted. "Now everyone laughs at us—the Japanese, the Americans, the Russians. Make a yen, a dollar, a ruble, and laugh at the dirty, backward Chinese. Well, fuck them all."

"Are you sure the explosions will work?"

"Don't worry. It's a simple job. Some plastique, a nice detonator, and it'll all be over."

"Anything more on the Gao art collection?"

"Maybe we're on to something. Remember Lamarche?"

"You mean that French sissy?"

"That French sissy has gone big-time. Finally he's learned your lesson—nice capitalists are poor capitalists. A little pressure and he's finally put us on the trail. Some professor in New York found the lacquer box. The professor not only married a Chinese, but he's also become Chinese himself, had an operation on his face. Now they're foreign experts at Beida and they're in touch with old Professor Gao and his daughter."

"Let's pick them up, force them to talk."

"We can't do that. They're all under Premier Chen's direct protection. Besides, it wouldn't help to arrest them now."

"It wouldn't?"

"No. They don't know much more than we do. They're working off photographs; the box itself is hidden someplace in Taiwan. If they figure it out, fine—we'll just follow them. If not, after May fourth, it's a much easier job. We'll simply round them all up. With no one to protect them, a little persuasion might prompt them to give us the box directly."

"And then?"

"And then, when we find the art, we have Lamarche to sell it. He says the price tag has soared since the sixties. Now it's several billion. Enough to buy a lot of weapons. Enough to go it on our own without the fucking imperialists."

Roger had started running again—a way to get in shape, a way to see Beijing. Running offered him freedom, although he found comfort in being followed by the limousine with the Premier's security men. He liked to wear his sloppy blue sweatshirt with the white characters for "Beijing"; his running shoes were China's best, heavy but functional, the red color with white stripes looked sporty.

Beijing's smaller streets, lined with grimy buildings unrepaired for decades, threw constant obstacles in his path. Roger had to dodge unyielding bicycles, clusters of jump-roping girls, boys playing badminton without nets, piles of bricks and rubble, stacks of rotting vegetable stalks, slippery pools of soapy laundry water tossed onto potholed pavement. But Roger's slower, erratic pace also gave him a chance to look beneath Beijing's grayness. He chatted with children on their way to school, waved to adults in queues outside vegetable markets. He ran around Beijing's small parks, occasionally stopping to listen to a young flutist practicing in the only privacy available. He became a familiar figure on the streets; sometimes young runners would catch up to him and ask how they could leave the country. Did he know of anyone who wanted to sponsor a foreign student? Each morning he cooled down at the Double Happiness Tea Shop, where he bought two *yutiao* for three cents and engaged in endless conversations about marriages, schools, and relatives. As an Overseas Chinese, Roger's advice was sought constantly about the best stereos, cameras, and television sets.

To Roger, China no longer fit into neat stereotypes. It was not the land of mechanized happiness portrayed in the foreign-language propaganda periodicals. China's own internal newspapers were much more honest, featuring stories about street crime, broken marriages, and official corruption. The Chinese people were remarkably adept at keeping a safe gap between themselves and the authorities. Despite occasional ragged beggars, hunger wasn't a problem except in some remote rural areas. Housing was a mess; the monumentally incompetent construction industry couldn't begin to keep pace with the demand. The great tradition of entrepreneurship was alive in the black market that handled everything from currency and food to refrigerators and holiday travel. For the proper price, one enterprising marketeer told Roger, he could purchase the "right career" complete with university degree, military service, and work record, and identity papers to match.

Roger began to see that there was a system, a web of practices, enveloping everybody. It wasn't managed by a dictator, but rather operated like a rickety old steam engine, no one wanting to be the one part that broke down. You accommodated the system. You never, but never, tried to change it radically.

Christina most definitely did not like running. Too much sweat, and zero on the scale of mental cultivation. She would stick to calligraphy and wushu. As for seeing the sights of Beijing, her Phoenix Brand bicycle was the right way to travel. And as the spring rains washed away the ice and snow, cycling in Beijing became fun again.

One April morning she parked her bike at a rack on Liulichang. The entire street had been recently repaved and the shops had new fronts designed to impress foreigners; to Christina it looked like a run-down shopping mall in the United States. All of the signs were in English: "Calligraphy Shop." "Painting Store." "Rubbings and Sculptures." "Book Store." "Musical Instruments."

Christina walked into the Calligraphy Shop. She looked through a few albums of calligraphy and glanced at several rubbings. The old woman at the counter, thinking Christina might buy something, also showed her the collection of inkstones and brushes. It didn't take an expert to realize that everything ranged from very low quality to outright junk. Christina, usually superb at controlling her emotions, had reached her limit. She began screaming in Chinese.

"This is absolutely pathetic! How can you call yourself Chinese and sell this trash?"

The woman flinched. Many Overseas Chinese had left the shop

quickly, but no one had become so vocal. "But madam, we try to sell the best Chinese calligraphy. Perhaps you would like to see some other brushes? Or paperweights?"

"In the United States I had first-year calligraphy students who produced better work than anything in this shop. Your brushes aren't good enough to use on teeth. Your paperweights and inkstones are jokes."

"But many foreigners buy our goods. They say that the works are of high quality."

"My dear woman, many foreigners also think that Beijing's hotel food represents the great tradition of Chinese cuisine. You should be ashamed."

"We are ashamed." Christina spun around toward a man, roughly sixty years old, wearing an old sport jacket covered by a dark-green smock and sleevelets to protect his forearms.

"You are? You're ashamed?" she asked, surprised by his honesty.

"Of course, madam," he replied, gesturing around the room. "You're quite right. This is junk. Everything in these stores is worthless. The amazing thing is that people buy the stuff."

"I can understand their lack of taste," Christina replied tersely. "They don't know any better. But you?"

"Madam, would you be kind enough to share a cup of tea with me?"

He pulled aside a curtain concealing the back of the store.

Christina walked through the doorway, beginning to regret her outburst. In the center of the room was a plain wooden table holding a stretched piece of paper, a stone with wet ink, and a brush.

Christina admired the calligraphy on the paper. "Now that's pretty good. Poem by Du Fu. Calligraphy in the style of Dong Qichang. Who did this?"

"Madam," replied the man with a little smile, "I did. And you do know your calligraphy."

"Of course, it could stand some improvement," Christina said. "You might practice for a little more fluidity. You're thinking too much about each character, too little about the overall impact."

"Madam, I beg your pardon," the man responded, his pride wounded. "Do you think you could do better?"

"Oh, sir," she bantered in the traditional way. "How could I dare instruct a master? Besides, you're an older man. And I'm only a woman."

"With all due respect, madam," he interjected, "if you can, show me."

Christina took off her jacket, sat down at the table, placing his calligraphy on the floor. Then she stretched out a new piece of paper, weighted it, and wet the brush. Glancing at the passage, she steadied herself and began quickly. In two minutes, the page was filled with delicate traceries of writing, punctuated by an occasional bold character. She set down the brush and put on her jacket, never looking at the man.

"Madam, I extend you my sincere apologies," he said, staring in wonderment. That's the finest calligraphy I've seen in the past forty years. Who are you?"

"Just an Overseas Chinese from America. My name is Chang Ruxin."

"Not the daughter of Chang Cheng-tai?"

"The very same."

"Oh, my sincerest apologies. Your family used to frequent the humble shop of my family many years ago. Our little lacquer store."

"Lacquer?" Christina asked with surprise.

"Yes, Mrs. Chang. But let me make another apology."

"For what? You've apologized enough."

"You've got to understand Liulichang—it deserves a huge apology. Right after liberation the government took over this entire section. The good works were either hidden or sold to foreigners, mainly Japanese. Since the seventies, our job has been to sell off cheap reproductions or low-quality originals at incredibly high prices. The state wants volume, not quality. Recently, I tried to go into business for myself, but the state wouldn't permit it. They don't want private competition that might undermine their businesses." The man paused. "You see, madam, I really am ashamed."

"Mr . . . er . . . ?"

"It's Mr. Zhao. Zhao Dingmu."

"Mr. Zhao, what was it you said about lacquer?"

The man paused for a moment and poured tea for Christina and himself. He picked up Christina's calligraphy. "Do you mind if I keep it?"

"I would be honored."

"Now about lacquer," he continued, his face brightening as he spoke. "The Zhao family was in the lacquer business for six generations. My grandfather was one of the greatest masters of all time.

247

He continued to produce fine lacquer even in the late Qing, when both carvers and clients were satisfied with cheap works."

"And what happened to the lacquer tradition in your family?"

"My grandfather died in his prime. At the turn of the century. My father continued the tradition. He was almost as good. Let me show you something."

Zhao walked to the curtain, making sure no shoppers were in the store, then moved to a padlocked door. Concealing the lock with his body, he spun the dial a few times and opened the door. A moment later he returned with a red velvet bag, opening it carefully on the table. Christina looked in astonishment at a three-color polychrome plate—black, yellow, and cinnabar, a mountain landscape with minutely detailed pavilions, bridges, waterfalls, clouds, and people. It was late Ming in style, about three-quarters finished, the rest sketched in ink on the red surface.

"I don't believe it," she said reverently.

"I know what you mean," Zhao replied. "It's magnificent, isn't it?"

"It's more than that," she answered, her eyes still riveted on the plate. "It's identical."

"Identical to what?" he asked tensely.

Christina caught herself. "Uh . . . Identical to . . . well, almost identical to a piece I once saw in the British Museum."

"I know the piece," Zhao responded. "This one's better. And I think you know that as well. You're too fine a traditional artist not to know that. Let me ask again. Identical to what?"

Christina tried to evade the question. "Tell me, what happened to your father? Have you continued his tradition?"

"My father died in 1949, before finishing this masterpiece. Me? I was trained in lacquer, but after liberation, I was only allowed to teach apprentices to make trinkets for foreigners. Eventually I gave up and asked to be transferred back to Liulichang. Actually this was the old lacquer shop—"

"Really?" Christina asked, surprised by the information and relieved that the man wasn't pushing her. "Is there anything left of the lacquer works?"

"Nothing at all. Stripped clean. The Red Guards smashed the few good remaining works."

"That's awful."

"Yes, it was," Mr. Zhao acknowledged. He hesitated and then

looked hard at Christina. "Now I've told you everything I know. But you're holding back something."

"I don't know what you mean."

"Yes, you do," Zhao retorted. "Even more than that, you need my help, but you don't even know it. Now tell me truthfully. You've already seen a piece of lacquer in this style and quality, haven't you?"

Christina bit her lip, then nodded.

"You know it was made by my grandfather, don't you?"

Christina nodded again.

"You know it contains an important secret, don't you? And yet you can't yet find the crucial clue?"

Christina nodded yet again.

"I sense, Mrs. Chang, you're desperate for answers. Please realize I don't know the actual clue. Only three people did: Gao Zhonglu, who decided where to move the collection in the 1940s; his servant Lao Wu, who probably supervised the relocation of the art; and my own father, who changed the information on the box."

"But they're all dead."

"That's the tragedy. Gao Zhenggai never anticipated that his son would disinherit his only grandson, nor that the Wu line of servants would come to such an awful end."

"But you, Mr. Zhao, must know where to find the clue on the box itself."

"Yes, Mrs. Chang." He paused, shaking his head. "But I'm bound by oath never to tell anyone. Our duty was to change the code on the box. It was the duty of the Gao family to know the name."

"But they don't know it! Doesn't that change your duty?"

"No, Mrs. Chang, I'm sorry. But maybe there's one thing I can suggest. Lacquer is still made in China. It's bad export lacquer, sloppy craftsmanship and no artistry. It's made outside Changsha, a place called the All-China Traditional Arts and Crafts Factory. Nice proletarian ring, yes? I'm told they have a small library, including some of my father's old books. Perhaps they would help."

"Sounds a little farfetched. Have you been there? Have the Gaos gone there?"

"Are you kidding? This is China. No one is permitted to travel without permission. Only foreigners and Overseas Chinese travel. Besides, you need permission from the Cultural Relics Bureau to visit such places."

"Thank you, Mr. Zhao. For your courtesy and your candor." Christina left the shop and rode off on her bicycle.

Christina wanted to tell Professor Gao immediately, but Roger disagreed. "It's something, but hardly conclusive. Let's give it time. We must not get him too excited. I worry about the old man's health." Actually Roger was less worried about Gao's health than about safety for himself and Christina. What would old Gao do with the information? Would he act too quickly? Would Premier Chen's opponents make a move? Would Lamarche come back into the picture?

Christina reluctantly accepted Roger's logic, but the slowness of everything, the constant waiting, was becoming intolerable. Roger, she worried, was becoming too adept at the Chinese art of patience. She found herself yearning for a bit of the old New York Roger—a man who forced things to happen quickly, a man who assumed he was always in control. Their relationship was deep and satisfying, but somehow it too had slowed down. They still shared intimacy, but no longer many secrets. Maybe, she reflected, it was the nature of good marriages to mellow into mutual respect, losing some of the early fire. Maybe, she hoped, it's just China itself, wearing everybody down; perhaps rekindling would occur when they left.

In one positive respect, Christina felt as if she had never left New York. The Beijing Art Institute had agreed, now, in her second semester, to let her teach calligraphy courses six days a week. Dedicated Chinese students flocked to her, learning so that they could teach others, practicing to touch deep cultural roots. Those in Christina's master classes were quite exceptional, showing evidence of clandestine practice during the Cultural Revolution. As with Roger, Christina struggled to unlock her superior students' creative potential. Unlike Roger, she was successful, employing such radical techniques as pre-class calisthenics, blind-folded calligraphy, and loud Chinese classical music in the background. She fought back successfully when the Institute administration, pressured by traditionally minded instructors, ordered her to conform or depart. Her ultimate victory was the annual Institute art exhibition in May—eight of the ten calligraphy winners came from her classes (the other two prizes, obviously inferior work, were given as a sop to morale).

"I'm proud of you," Roger said, admiring Christina's framed citation, "Beijing Art Institute, Teacher of the Year." He suppressed a twinge of jealousy, comparing his current frustrations at Beida to his previous teaching successes at Columbia. Then his face wrinkled in an impish grin.

"That's your devilish I've-got-an-idea look," Christina said hopefully.

"You bet it is," Roger replied. "I'm going to take a little trip while you're teaching summer school. To Changsha. To the lacquer factory. I'm not going to tell Professor Gao, but I'll bet Xiao Gao can arrange things with the Cultural Relics Bureau."

Less than a week later, Roger was bouncing along in a 1940s vintage school bus, which jerked and coughed its way along a pot-holed rural road outside Changsha, in China's interior province of Hunan. Two hours out of Changsha, the bus bumped by Mao's birthplace in the village of Shaoshan; the cluster of Mao family rich-peasant farmhouses, once a national shrine attracting millions of tourists during the Cultural Revolution, was now almost deserted. Four hours later, the bus stopped abruptly at an unmarked intersec-tion. Roger gazed perplexed at a dirt path separating an endless sea of recently harvested paddies and remnants of rice stalks in brown dried soil. The scene reminded him of an unshaven, sunburned peasant face.

"It's there," said the bus driver in a thick Hunanese accent, pointing to the horizon, "a short walk, only three miles, then you'll find the village."

"All-China Traditional Arts and Crafts Factory"—Roger, sweat drenching his newly purchased brown cadre suit, could barely read the faded characters on the peeling signboard above a crumbling stone gate. "Don't believe the sign," laughed a middle-aged man, dressed in an unpressed white short-sleeved shirt, amused by Roger's relatively more formal attire. "It's not all-China—we only work for Hunan Province now that local authorities control their own exports. It's not arts and crafts—only lacquer now that other areas specialize in pottery, cloisonné, and woodworking. And it's not a factory—it's really a village that just happens to make lacquer."

Roger walked uncertainly into a chaotic assortment of dank tin-roofed brick buildings. Each building served multiple purposes: as a dwelling for a dozen or more families, a communal cooking and dining area, and a tiny shop for one specific aspect of the lacquer-

251

making process. Roger peeked inside a few buildings, always exiting quickly, choking after inhaling the awful smell. "Cigarettes, shit, and lacquer," the man laughed, coughing up and spitting out a load of blood-streaked, brown phlegm, "we get used to it."

"The lacquer library? Is that what the Cultural Relics Bureau calls it?" The man was convulsed with laughter. "Here it is. Feel free to browse in the stacks." A few moments later the man whispered to Roger: "Don't worry, I'm not only your guide, I'm also your bodyguard today, working part-time for Beijing."

Roger was deposited in a brick building at the edge of the village, illuminated by a single bare bulb, filled with giant wooden barrels covered by heavy stone disks. "Don't touch the lac," the man warned, "it's poisonous." Propped on a pile of lumber in a dusty corner were several boxes of moldy books, obviously untouched for years. Holding his breath to escape noxious fumes, Roger carried the boxes outside, where he sat on the ground with his back to the building, curious children and stray chickens scampering around him as he perused the collection. Box after box contained the same disappointing materials: all lacquer brochures from the 1930s and 1940s, no pictures, just lists of lacquer products and prices from various shops in eastern China. The books documented inflation but little more. Roger fretted, noting how the price in Chinese dollars for a simple cinnabar dish had risen from $2 in 1946 to $11,340 in 1948.

"Want something special, mister?" Roger looked up. A dirt-streaked, barefoot boy stared earnestly, his hand clutching a tattered book. Roger glimpsed at the title on the brittle, brown cover—*Lacquer Masterpieces*—along with a handwritten name: "Zhao, Liulichang Lacquer Shop, 1947." Astonished, Roger nodded quickly.

"It will cost you."

"How much?"

"How much you got?"

Roger pulled out his wallet, hiding it so that the boy couldn't see all the contents, offering him what he thought was an excessive price—fifty yuan, more than a month's salary in the city.

The boy grinned; clearly this man was rich and he wanted the book badly. "Not enough. The price is five hundred yuan. In foreign script. Not *renminbi*."

Roger tried to look shocked, but he found himself laughing. Good God, Gresham's law worked even in rural Hunan! The Chinese authorities had issued special currency for use in Friendship Stores and other commercial establishments not open to ordinary Chinese.

252

Within weeks, the experiment backfired; the black market became a boomtown in foreign script, its value skyrocketed, Overseas Chinese made the purchases in the elite stores, usually for a handsome percentage.

Roger handed over five crisp notes, the boy gave him the book, vanishing behind the corner of a building where he joined his friends, all whooping in delight. As soon as he opened the cover, Roger knew he had been duped. It was just another catalogue, higher quality goods from Liulichang, to be sure, but still listing only products and prices. He was angrily thrusting the book in his brown canvas bag when something caught his eye, a handwritten notation on the last page in the late Mr. Zhao's precise script: "The best source on my profession is the *Qi Shi*, The History of Lacquer. It tells the inner secrets of lacquer. All the secrets."

After returning from Changsha, Roger arranged a meeting with Christina and Xiao Gao in the recently constructed Beijing University Library. The stacks were sparse, but they hoped the card files might indicate where the old books had been moved. "Sorry," Xiao Gao lamented, "no *Qi Shi* listed here. Just like the other libraries I checked—museums, institutes, government cultural offices—absolutely nothing. I'll keep trying, but don't get your hopes up. Don't tell my father. He couldn't stand the stress."

The flurry of excitement, now turned to frustration, made their foreign-expert routine even less tolerable, especially for Christina. Biweekly dinners with the Gaos, while pleasant and mildly informative, were beginning to grate on Christina, especially since they had deteriorated into an intellectual chess game between two male history professors. In good Chinese fashion, the women were left to cook and chat among themselves in the corner.

"Remember what we hope to do," Professor Gao said after supper. "We're trying to understand Gao Jenggai's dream for China. Unless we think in his terms, we'll never find the collection. Now let's have a little background music." Professor Gao selected Tchaikovsky's *1812 Overture*; he didn't like the piece particularly, but the crescendos and cannon fire would blow the ears off anyone bugging the room. Holding the arms of his wheelchair, the Professor smiled. Time for his seminar to begin.

"I've got a theory —" Roger began confidently.

"But I've got something else—" Xiao Gao interrupted.

"This is China," Professor Gao said. "Men first."

"I've been fascinated by the fact that everybody seems wrapped up in a system. It's an elaborate game, but if you weren't born here, they don't tell you the rules."

"You're right," Professor Gao nodded. "It's always been true. Chinese people come in three categories. Almost everyone is category one—the accommodators. That's why Chinese history seems to move so slowly. Most great minds only tinkered with the giant machine."

"Father, can't we talk about something else," Xiao Gao interjected. "I think you'll find it interesting. You see—"

"Of course, my dear. In good time. These youngsters are so impatient," he reprimanded, smiling knowingly at Roger. "Now let me resume my analysis of Professor Wang's observation." Xiao Gao sulked in her chair. "In addition to the accommodators, there's a second category—the radicals, the tiny minority who really changed our history, those who led revolutions and toppled dynasties. Category two is filled with crackpots and geniuses. They scare me because they always argue that one must burn before he can build. Then there's category three—the reformers, the most frustrated group of all. They want massive change, but not total destruction. They're always vulnerable, usually crushed by the other two categories."

"And you're category number three?"

"I'm a classic category three. It's a family disease." Professor Gao feebly pulled the photographs from the envelope on his lap. "Look here at the lacquer box. The last panel is a chronic case of reformism."

Christina peered over their shoulders as Professor Gao and Roger sifted through the photographs. Xiao Gao remained apart, still smarting from her father's reprimand. Selecting a blow-up of panel four, Professor Gao tapped it with his finger. "Here it is. Look at that!" Roger examined the scholar holding a brush and a microscope. "Now, Professor Wang, can you figure that one out?"

"No. Becky Aspen and I tried it for hours. We only concluded that the microscope was Western and the brush was Chinese. Not very brilliant."

"Not brilliant. But correct. You just don't know your Chinese history well enough yet. It's the symbol for *ti-yong* modernization."

"What's that?"

"An expression used by my grandfather and his colleagues. *Jong xue wei ti, xi xue wei yong.* 'Chinese learning as the essence. Western learning for its practical use.' That's what we still need. Let's import

Western education while keeping Chinese values like family, loyalty, and discipline."

Roger nodded vigorously. "That's precisely what you need. Are these other symbols on the same theme?"

Professor Gao grinned. "Once you've got the *ti-yong* theme you have it all. Look at this one. Two ministers in an audience before the emperor. What's special about it?"

Roger stared at the photograph for a long time. "One's kneeling and the other one is standing up?"

"True. But no significance. The key point is that one is dressed in long flowing robes—a Ming-dynasty court costume. The other is in a skirt and a tunic with sleeves shaped like a horse's hoof—Qing-dynasty robes. Just like my ancestors wore at the end of the last century."

"What does that mean?"

"There's an old Confucian saying that the rituals and customs must change to suit the times. Here it's symbolized by the change in court dress between the Ming and Qing dynasties. This notion was always a favorite of the reformers."

Roger smiled admiringly at Professor Gao. Over two years of research was coming to fruition. "And how about this one. Ming robes, right? But standing up, same level as the emperor, and pointing above his head?"

Professor Gao laughed. "That's a tough one. You've really got to be a Gao to understand it. That's Hai Rui, a famous late-Ming scholar. He criticized the emperor, told him everything was corrupt, told him he had to reform. He points to a higher authority than the emperor. He points to the Confucian tradition."

"And what happened to him?"

"He was booted out of office. He died powerless, but he was famous for standing up for principles. He's our family hero."

Xiao Gao, who had been sitting quietly on the kang, straightened up and spoke sharply. "Father, don't you see it? The whole Gao family consists of Hai Ruis. Well intentioned, but impotent. Destined to failure."

Roger recognized her frustration, but he also saw Professor Gao's hurt. He sat down on the kang next to Xiao Gao. "You're very bright. But you expect everything too quickly. You and your father represent something great. Greatness doesn't happen suddenly."

Professor Gao fastened his eyes on Roger.

Roger put his arm around Xiao Gao, gently smiling at her, and

255

then looking back at the professor. "I think China is regaining its health and muscle, but it's still searching for its heart. And in Taiwan they have the modernization, but they spout the old ideology. Category three—real reform—remains elusive. And Xiao Gao, with all respect, you're category four. It's all too much for you. You want to throw it away."

Professor Gao laughed and pounded his fist feebly to show his approval. "I've finally met a true reformer. For the first time in decades. Right in the Gao tradition."

Xiao Gao stood up abruptly. "Category four?!" she shouted. "So you're the great reformers and I'm just a quitter? It sure hasn't done you a lot of good. Are you any closer to real reforms? Any closer to finding the art collection? Are you closer to anything?"

Xiao Gao's small body was infused with new energy; she crossed her arms and lectured her elders. "If you want to reform China, you've got to start outside. You've got to find neutral ground, someplace where the system won't suffocate you, someplace where bright minds can feel comfortable in their talent. If you want to know the secret of the box, you can't do it in a stuffy little apartment. You've got to play the system. You've got to make the system talk to you."

Professor Gao looked at his daughter as if she had lost her mind. "My dear, you're just not making sense. Inside the system, to get outside the system, to reform China. That sounds like Taoist gibberish."

Xiao Gao knelt before the wheelchair and held her father's hands. "You've taught me everything I know. I cherish that. But please recognize something. I grew up a long time ago. I was forced to become a mother before I had really been a daughter. Professor Wang calls me category four. Well, maybe so. But that's only because I've become the best at category one. I'm accommodator first class."

Professor Gao looked at his daughter. "My little cricket, I didn't mean to insult you. It's just that while I've needed you as a mother, I also wanted you to remain a daughter. I know you've learned an enormous amount."

Xiao Gao stood back up and smiled confidently. "Then you won't be surprised to hear that I know how to find the treasure."

Everyone stared at the small woman. Xiao Gao savored her moment of triumph. "Father, we haven't told you, but Professor Gao uncovered the possible existence of a key book, the *Qi Shi*. Unfortunately, we couldn't find it in any library. So I did a little unconventional research—in the Cultural Relics Bureau."

"The Cultural Relics Bureau?" her father asked astonished. "That's directly under the State Council."

"Yes." Xiao Gao grinned. "Not easy to get in, but what a card catalog they have! And guess what? There's only one copy of the *Qi Shi*. It's a rare book, handwritten, produced at the turn of the century."

"Where is it?" Roger asked expectantly.

"It used to be in the Library of the Imperial College, then in the Beida Library. In the early fifties, it was moved to the secret vaults of the Propaganda Department of the Chinese Communist Party."

"Why there?"

"Because in the madness after Liberation, someone was given the task of labeling books 'top secret.' It was a great job, so good he kept at it for ten years. I'll bet there are a million mislabeled books at the Propaganda Department. It could only happen in China."

"Can you get to it?"

"I have my ways."

CHAPTER NINETEEN
CELESTIAL ROOTS

THE TRICK TO DOING ANYTHING

unusual in China, particularly if difficult or dangerous, is to do it as inconspicuously as possible. No one was better suited than Xiao Gao. Ever since she could remember, she had worked Beijing's back doors. Her assignment until now had been to keep herself and her father alive. Radicals like Boxers and Red Guards always hated the *zhishifenzi*, the intellectuals. She felt it unlikely that China might experience another Cultural Revolution, the product of a special era of ferocious romanticism; but there was still danger from ideologues who wanted one more scene on center stage.

Although Xiao Gao lamented what she saw in the mirror, she also knew her plainness was a valuable asset; no one looked twice at a woman with a short spindly body and a featureless face. In a country where minuscule gestures were noticed, Xiao Gao wore nothing but ordinary faded blue cotton suits, avoiding even a hint of color in her blouse.

On a late Wednesday afternoon in April, she stood motionless at the reception desk inside the Propaganda Department. For the longest time, the three matronly attendants missed her, concentrating instead on a stubborn black telephone that, like so many in Beijing, had decided not to work. Finally, as Xiao Gao sidled closer to the desk, one heavy-faced woman looked up. "Yes?" she asked gruffly. "What do you want?"

260

"I'm sorry to bother you," Xiao Gao replied meekly, "but I have instructions from the Party Secretariat to pick up some papers from the vaults." She handed over a form with the Secretariat's seal and letterhead; since the Secretariat supervised the Propaganda Department, her orders were bound to elicit a response. Xiao Gao struggled to keep composure as the woman examined the document. Could she spot a forgery? Was there something missing? A new code?

"This looks in order," the woman said sharply. "But what about your papers? Where are you from?"

Xiao Gao was ready for the inevitable question; it was asked at every official location in China. "Here they are," she said, pulling her red plastic identity booklet from her breast pocket.

The woman scrutinized the card, looking back and forth from Xiao Gao to the photograph and data. "Mind if I check this?"

Xiao Gao nodded as if it were routine, desperately hoping she had done her homework adequately. She knew the name she was using, Wu Ruxia, was accurate; she had taken it from a recently mimeographed list of Secretariat clerical staff showing Wu Ruxia on messenger duty that week to the Propaganda Department. What she didn't know was whether Wu Ruxia would be on assignment or, heaven forbid, back in the office at the time of the call. Xiao Gao held her breath as the woman scanned the tattered government directory and began to dial.

"Shit." The woman slammed down the receiver. "The phone's broken again. All right, dammit. You can go ahead. Downstairs to the C-level basement. Show this slip to the attendant."

Xiao Gao walked at a businesslike pace, suppressing a smile at the wonderful inefficiency of Chinese engineering. She reached a door marked "Top Secret Vaults," guarded by a matron dumpy enough to be the older sister of the one upstairs.

"Just sign in here."

Xiao Gao complied. Opening the book listing "name, purpose, time in, time out," she selected a fresh page for her entry and scribbled in the required information. "Oh, before I go in, is there a ladies' room nearby?"

The matron pointed down the hall. Xiao Gao waited just inside the slightly open door and watched the matron absentmindedly picking her teeth. After a moment, the matron looked around, locked the door to the vaults, and walked toward the ladies' room. Xiao Gao stood by the door, preparing to walk out as the matron walked in.

"You still here?" asked the matron, surprised that the girl had been in the ladies' room for over ten minutes.

"It's that time of the month," Xiao Gao mumbled.

"Used to be awful for me, too." The matron laughed. "I found out why they called them Red Flag Brand Sanitary Napkins. Sorry, you're going to have to wait for me now. Just a couple of minutes. No longer your problem. Not since they cut out my goodies."

Xiao Gao smiled shyly and waited until she heard the door of the stall shut. Moving quickly to the attendant's desk and looking around to make sure no one was watching, she pulled open the big log book and, using a small safety razor blade, swiftly slit out the page with her entry. She had just closed the book when the matron returned, unlocking the door and gesturing for Xiao Gao to enter. She sighed with relief; the first part was over. There was no record of someone named Wu Ruxia entering the vaults. Xiao Gao was prying the system apart at the edges.

Making her way slowly through the hundreds of rows of gray metal stacks, Xiao Gao smiled to herself. We Chinese, she mused, are the world's greatest labelers. Ah, they're using the archaic four-corner labeling system, she observed, recalling her childhood when Professor Gao had taught her the several ways for listing Chinese books. Conjuring up the image of the character *qi* for lacquer, she dissected its four corners in her mind, each shape giving her a number for a four-digit code. Within ten minutes, she was deep in the stacks next to two shelves of books beginning with *qi*. At the bottom corner, covered in a lavish yellow silk tao binder, was the *Qi Shi*, the title written in black calligraphy on the spine.

She'd found her quarry; now the waiting began. Forcing her birdlike body into a crevice in the stacks, she waited as people came and went, waited until a loud bell rang and everyone filed out. A light switch snapped, throwing the cavernous vaults into blackness. Still she waited. She remained motionless as a guard's flashlight played up and down each of the rows. Pressing her tiny frame deeply into the crevice, she watched the light move up and down the *qi* row, hesitating right next to her as the guard lit a cigarette. Finally, the footsteps receded, the light switched off, and the door slammed closed. It was eight o'clock and she was alone. The waiting was over.

Xiao Gao, cross-legged on the floor with a penlight in her teeth, scanned the *Qi Shi* page by page. But what to look for? The Gao box was not described in the book, nor were there references to codes on lacquer or to boxes that did not open. After an hour's reading she finally discovered something unusual—a stroke missing from a complicated character; then another, thirty pages later. Her father, who had once counseled, "The greatest historians spot the littlest details," was going to be very proud. Four hours later, she had written six irregular characters on a small pad, *qi xia jong xi zhi jian*—"under the lacquer, between China and the West." She smiled, knowing precisely where to look on the lacquer box.

Her work completed, Xiao Gao replaced the *Qi Shi* and embarked on her escape plan. After leaving the vault, which fortunately was locked only from the outside, she would wait in the ladies' room until morning, where she could melt into crowds of government workers. She had just moved to the end of the *qi* stack when the overhead lights blazed on; she jumped back into her crevice, heart racing in terror, as a group of men walked down the corridor. Another light clicked on, illuminating a table clearly visible from her hiding place, where the men waited silently until a burly figure entered from another direction. I recognize him, thought Xiao Gao, her heart thumping with fright as she recalled Politburo and Central Committee meeting photographs in the newspapers. That's Director Cai. And, over there, that's Minister Zhou.

She jumped involuntarily as Cai began the proceedings by smashing an ashtray on the table; her arm struck the stack, making a dull ringing sound. "What was that?" Cai asked, looking in her direction.

"I didn't hear anything," Zhou said.

"Maybe it was just my imagination." Cai's eyes returned to the group. "We can't be too careful, not now when we're so close. This will be our last meeting until our victory celebration."

A hawk-faced man spoke. "You're right, Mr. Director. The longer we wait, the greater the danger of exposure. What are the details?" The deputy commander of the Beijing Garrison was worried about a screw-up, especially since civilians in the Party and Government were in charge. Why couldn't they leave the tough stuff to the Army?

Cai handed out sealed envelopes. "Everything's in here. Follow instructions to the letter. It tells you what to do after the bomb explodes—at precisely nine-thirty on the evening of May fourth."

"Are you sure the bomb will kill the Premier?"

Cai smiled. "Trust me. It's a neat surgical strike. A single bomb

263

will obliterate the Premier's table. The Party General Secretary will be arrested at the same moment, and his confession will be given to the press. Our military supporters will take over the key Party organizations and the major ministries."

Director Cai paused and smiled. "I shall be forced to respond to the call of duty. I'll be named General Secretary. All of you will get key posts. We'll purge the intellectuals, modernizers, and compradores. Once we've got our new weapons, we'll kick out the barbarians. China will be ours."

Cai nodded appreciation as the others applauded. "Any questions? Remember, this is our last meeting."

"Mr. Director, why not assassinate the Premier with a rifle? Why risk using a bomb?"

Cai nodded to Minister Zhou to answer for him. "Recent American history shows assassinations with firearms are very unpredictable," Zhou said confidently. "The bomb can be detonated from a distance. I'll personally handle the detonator, setting the charges so that only the Premier and those right next to him will die. The Japanese are doing nice things these days with focused explosives."

"Besides," Cai intervened, patting Zhou on the back, "a rifle suggests a single assassin, a bomb indicates a broader plot. We want it to look like broad popular disapproval of the event. Officially, we'll deplore it, of course, but privately we must be like surgeons, using scalpels to cut out China's cancer. The blood of a few will purify the blood of a billion people. The Celestial Roots Movement cannot be stopped."

The needle punctured his finger and the fingers of the others. Waving the dripping paper in the air, Cai slammed down the ashtray again. Everyone filed into the corridor and out the door. The light switched off. There was silence again, except for the pounding of Xiao Gao's heart.

After fifteen minutes, Xiao Gao summoned the courage to grope her way down the corridor. The penlight battery was dying and she could just make out the outline of the door. She opened the door just wide enough to squeeze her little body through, gently releasing the handle so that there would be no click. Flipping off the penlight, she tiptoed toward the ladies' room, hands in front of her to make sure that she did not hit anything.

Beams suddenly blinded her. Powerful hands grabbed her arms, almost breaking them. Her glasses fell to the floor, but she clearly recognized Director Cai's voice. "Just as I said. You can't be too careful. I knew I heard something. Take her away."

A blue-black paddy wagon rolled through northwestern Beijing at dawn. Pressed against a small wire-mesh window was a sparrowlike face whose almost sightless eyes desperately tried to pierce through the lightly falling rain. As the paddy wagon sped by Beijing University, a folded piece of paper fluttered down from the van, sticking to the damp pavement. A young girl saw it fall, reached down and picked it up. Pushing back her pigtails and brushing the mist off her glasses, she read the scrawled message: "To Professor Gao. Urgent." She put it in her pocket and trudged onward.

"I'm sorry, Professor Wang." The old woman kept sweeping soggy debris off the broken steps of the Gao mansion. "Professor Gao's had a stroke. I think he's in the Capital Hospital. And no one knows where Xiao Gao is."

Roger raced his bicycle across Beijing, dropping it on the steps of Capital Hospital. The nurse warned him to be brief. "He's had a terrible stroke. We don't think he has much time."

Roger stood at the side of the iron bed. All the color had drained from Professor Gao's face. His mouth hung open, sucking in air and then coughing it back out.

The old man stirred and focused vaguely on Roger. "Professor Wang," he whispered. "Xiao Gao. She's gone."

"Gone?"

Roger could barely hear the response. He leaned closer. "A note came this morning. A plot. She heard about it. Party Propaganda Department. The Director. A plot. Celestial Roots Movement." His breath came in faint heaves interspersed with coughing. Roger wiped the bloody phlegm from the Professor's mouth. "Plot to kill. The Premier. Overthrow modernization. Repel foreigners. Purge intellectuals. Must stop it."

Roger watched as Professor Gao tried to say more. "Don't talk," Roger said, "you can tell me more later."

"Must talk. There is no . . . later. Xiao Gao's gone. Arrested. Found secret to box."

The old man heaved, his breathing stopped, then he struggled

265

to life for a moment longer. Forcing his eyes half open, he looked at Roger. "Only a Gao can find it. Must become Gao. Must promise. I . . . adopt you. You . . . accept?"

Roger, watching the man fade before his eyes, spoke quickly. "Yes. I accept. I'm honored."

"Last symbol. Read *Analects* Volume Four. Chapter Five."

Professor Gao's chest heaved and his face contorted. "And the clue. It's . . . under the lacquer, in between China . . . and the West."

"I understand. And the plot? When will it occur?"

"An important day . . ." Professor Gao stopped breathing. Roger waited for a moment and then ran out into the hall for the nurse, but he knew the professor was gone.

Roger stood in front of the crumbling Gao mansion, his mind reeling with grief and confusion. The news of Professor Gao's death and the disappearance of Xiao Gao had already spread through the mansion as quickly as it might have a century earlier. By the time Roger reached the Ancestral Hall, the door to the Gao apartment was already draped in white crepe. A ring of weeping women stood outside; curious children peeked around. The circle opened to let Roger pass by. It was appropriate for a close friend to pay his last respects at the house of the deceased.

Roger accepted a mournful hug from a little girl with pigtails and glasses. In the middle of the small room was the empty wheel-chair; on its seat was a manila envelope containing the color photographs of the box. Roger picked them up and then, looking around the walls, selected a few yellowed snapshots: one of Professor Gao and Xiao Gao, one of each of the previous generations of the Gao family back to Gao Jenggai, one of the Gao mansion in its prime. He realized there was no one left who would miss the photographs; he was now an adopted member of the Gao family, the only male descendant, perhaps the only descendant.

Roger glanced directly above Professor Gao's desk to a worn copy of the Confucian *Analects*. He thumbed to Volume IV, Chapter 5. The classical Chinese, once such a monumental obstacle, came easily:

When a son follows his father's instructions during his lifetime, one can say that he has a strong sense of duty. But when a son follows his father's way after his father's death, for the full three years of mourning, only then can one say that he is truly filial.

Opening the envelope of photographs, Roger examined the blow-up of the first panel. There it was, the last scene: an old man on his deathbed, his son kneeling at his father's side. Filiality was the ultimate commandment of the Confucian tradition, the only hope for the Gao family dream. Filiality had almost killed Professor Gao in earlier years; now it was his final request to Roger.

Returning to their apartment, Roger quickly told Christina everything that had happened. Dialing Premier Chen's private telephone number, he requested the Premier to choose a place where they could meet without being overheard.

Above multi-leveled marble steps, the Temple of Heaven's vermilion walls formed a perfect circle, capped by a brilliant yellow tile dome. Twelve round columns supporting the roof symbolized the hours, the twelve years in the traditional cycle, and the animals of the Chinese zodiac. The dome's interior was a masterpiece of carved wood—intricate patterns of octagons that became smaller and smaller as they reached the top—painted in brilliant colors of red, yellow, and green. At the apex was a large circular disk with five-clawed dragons racing around it.

"Magnificent, isn't it," Premier Chen said softly.

"Truly magnificent," replied Roger. "It symbolizes so much of what China has been."

"And what it could be again," continued Premier Chen, "if only we have time for splendor in our lives. Time for creativity, time to reach back while we seek to rush ahead."

"I wish we had such time," said Christina, her eyes moving from the dome to look at the Premier. "But not today. We must tell you some awful news. First—"

"Not here. These walls have ears," the Premier said as he fastened the buttons on his trimly tailored gray raincoat, beckoning Roger and Christina to follow him into the Temple of Heaven Park. Premier Chen knew well that the Temple of Heaven, constructed by Ming emperors in a time of devious court intrigues, had a built-in echo chamber, amplifying whispered conversations hundreds of feet away.

"We need help desperately," Christina blurted once they

267

reached a quiet spot. "Professor Gao died this morning of a stroke. It was caused by the news that his daughter had been arrested. We think she was arrested for breaking into the Propaganda Department at night."

"I'm sorry to hear about Professor Gao," Premier Chen said reflectively. "He was a brilliant man. With a life of such pain, he deserved a better end. But why would his daughter break into the Propaganda Department?"

"She was on a mission for her father," Roger said. "Looking for a book. Not an important book, just one that had been improperly designated 'top secret.' "

"Her arrest is most unfortunate, but there's really nothing I can do. She committed a crime. Unless she's unjustly accused and you have evidence to prove it, I cannot help you."

"Where will she be taken?"

"If it's a straightforward crime, probably to Beijing Prison to await trial. If it's more than that, then she'll go to a maximum-security penitentiary."

Roger tried to decide how much it was safe to tell. "Please try to find out. She's like family. Almost like my own daughter."

"Please," Christina reinforced the plea.

"I'll try, but I can't promise anything." There were, after all, limits to his power. Using his influence to override the Party bureaucracy, particularly to help out an intellectual who had committed a crime, was sure to create a flap at the highest levels. He had promised to protect Roger and Christina, not their Chinese friends.

"Now is there more to your story? Is there—" The Premier stopped abruptly and looked back toward the Temple. Four black limousines disgorged a dozen men in gray cadre suits. The Premier drew in his breath sharply.

"Something to worry about?" asked Roger.

"You never know," replied the Premier, looking relieved as the men moved toward the Temple. "They're not my own guards. I guess they're some kind of security police, probably looking for a petty thief. Just for safety's sake, let's walk a bit farther into these trees. Now tell me, is there more?"

Roger hesitated. "Yes . . . yes, there's more. But . . ."

"But what?"

"You'll find it hard to believe."

"Try me."

"Xiao Gao sent her father a message. In a note after her arrest. She said that there was a plot to kill you."

"What?"

"That's what Professor Gao said. A plot from an organization called the . . . uh . . . Celestial Roots Movement. Involving the Director of the Party's Propaganda Department."

Premier Chen laughed. "That's crazy. Everyone knows Director Cai is old-fashioned, that he hates foreigners. But the old codger wouldn't try a stunt like that."

Roger shrugged. "I'm only telling you what I heard. I have no way to check its validity. Xiao Gao is a pretty balanced woman, and Professor Gao was hardly given to extremes."

"Well, I'll check it out. But don't worry. Our security won't let anything disastrous happen."

Premier Chen didn't speak for a moment; then he put his hand on Christina's shoulder. "Now I'm afraid that I have some more bad news. I wasn't going to tell you, but I don't think it's right to hold back. Dr. Ren just called me. Your father is dead. He died quietly and painlessly."

Christina collapsed into Roger's arms. "Christina," Roger tried to get through. "Your father was a fine man. A great man. But we knew he was dying. He told us."

"Knowing he was dying is not the same as hearing he's dead," she sobbed.

"I know," replied Roger, stroking her head. "But it's for the best. You know that in your heart. He was very ill. Our marriage gave him happiness."

Christina and Roger watched Premier Chen's limousine move around the Temple of Heaven and into the streets of Beijing. They started to walk their bicycles out of the park. Suddenly they were surrounded by gray-suited men. One of them spoke firmly. "We're the Premier's secret service. He has given strict orders. You are not to contact him again."

"That's crazy," Roger retorted. "We just talked to him. He said nothing of the sort. In fact, he said you were not his own security. Who are you?"

The man's eyes sharpened; he stared at Roger, then at Christina. "If you want Miss Gao to live, don't contact the Premier again. If

269

you want to live, don't contact anyone outside China. We will be watching you."

They vanished as swiftly as they had appeared.

"We've got to talk before we get home," Christina said as they pedaled slowly along dark streets. "Now our apartment is surely bugged. We've got to figure out what to do. There's a lot at stake, our lives at a minimum."

"But what can we do?" Roger asked. "We're completely alone. No protection. No friends." Roger glanced back fearfully, frightened because he *wasn't* being followed. There was no limousine, none of Premier Chen's guards.

"There's an old wushu theory," Christina said as calmly as she could. "Do the opposite of what your opponent expects. When he expects passivity, that's when to go into action." Christina put her hand on Roger's handlebar, bringing them closer. "For me, I know what I *must* do. I must go to the old family home near Suzhou. I've got to pay respects to my ancestors and prepare them to welcome my father."

"Christina." Roger took his eyes off the road and stared at her. "That's plain crazy. You'll be much more vulnerable alone. That's lunacy."

"No, it's not," she snapped back. "It's essential. It's what I must do."

Roger looked across at Christina incredulously. "So my little job is to figure out whether there really is a plot against the government. And if so, to stop it. Is that it?"

"Exactly. I'll be back as soon as I can. Please *do* something. Try. I'll be trying, too."

CHAPTER TWENTY

ANCESTORS

CHRISTINA, KNEELING BEFORE A

mound of earth spiked with several small character-inscribed posts, bowed her head in prayer. Then she filled an envelope with paper money and included a teardrop pendant of light green jade, a high school graduation gift from Chang Laobo. Using a trowel, she buried the envelope at the base of the mound. She felt at peace; it was not a moment for tears but rather for reaffirmation. Her father had never made it back here alive, but she had brought him back in death. She surveyed the other graves on the family mound; all were swept clean and identified with fresh markers and flowers. Christina knew her father would be pleased his relatives still observed the grave-sweeping festival. Chang Laobo was now an ancestor; she had done her part to support the family lineage. Now her father could do his part; Christina needed his help as never before.

A circle of Chang relatives gathered around as she stepped back from the mound, sharing hugs and words of condolence. Waiting for them at the roadside was a large wagon attached to an unmuffled two-cylinder hand tractor. It wasn't the most luxurious funeral limousine, but in rural China it represented quite a sacrifice to remove a wagon and tractor from the fields, especially during the spring planting season. The tractor deposited the mourners in front of the village meeting hall. Over a hundred people had congregated to express sorrow in the traditional way, the way they also expressed joy. A banquet reaffirmed the family, gave people something to talk about, and emphatically confirmed that life must go on.

After the banquet, Christina received private condolences from close family members. Last in line was the oldest member of the Chang clan—Chang Laobo's brother, now well into his eighties. The old man's senility was famous: he wore strange patchwork-quilt clothing and puttered around the garden, talking to vegetables, occasionally reprimanding a bird with his spiral cane. The family took good care of the old man, scolding children when they called his head an empty rice bowl. Today, he had stuck a white flower in his quilt jacket in memory of his brother.

"You're the little Chang girl, aren't you?" he asked Christina.

"Yes, esteemed Elder Uncle," she replied with sincerity. "I'm the second daughter of your deceased brother."

"Such a pity. Such a pity. What a pity. A pity indeed." His rhyme tried to show respect, but it came out wrong.

Christina motioned the old man to a chair, sitting down next to him and taking his gnarled hands in hers. "Elder Uncle, my father told me many wonderful things about you."

"Wonderful things? Wonderful things, that's what he said. He said some wonderful things. Isn't it wonderful?"

Christina looked at him sternly. "Now, Elder Uncle, my father told me he respected you most in the entire family. I want you to listen to what I'm saying. Do you hear me?"

The old man looked around, startled by her loud tone, his eyes slowly focusing on her face. "You're not a little girl, are you?"

"No, I'm not, Elder Uncle," she replied, keeping her voice firm. "And you're not a senile old man either. I need your help and I must have you thinking clearly."

A glimmer of a smile lit the old man's face. "No one ever talks to me like that anymore. Everybody gave up on me years ago."

"And so, Elder Uncle, you also gave up on yourself?"

He folded his hands on top of his cane and nodded his head. "I suppose that's what I did. You see, the Communists undercut my position in the village. Then the Red Guards mocked me because I represented old ideas. No one really cared what I thought anymore."

Christina leaned over and touched the old man's face. He looked into her eyes, tears flowing down his cheeks. "Elder Uncle, I'm not like the others. I truly need your help. In fact, without it I may be lost."

"What is it, my child, that I can possibly do for you?"

"Esteemed Elder Uncle, I need two favors. First, can you find a private way to communicate with our family back in Taiwan? I have a message of the utmost importance."

The old man spoke clearly and precisely. "Of course. We communicate frequently by mail, through a go-between in Hong Kong. It's not very complicated. But you do run a risk of the authorities seeing the message. However, we could use the code—"

"Code?"

"Yes. I invented it many years ago. Your father and I used to use it in our correspondence. Often through a man named Dr. Ren, I believe."

"That's right, Dr. Ren. He's the man I want you to communicate with. Use the code by all means."

"And the message?"

Christina spoke slowly, trying to make sure that the message was clear without being explicit, trying to make sure that the old man heard every word. "The message is this: 'The dream has new value. Try to get it to safety. And please send help here. Both of us need it. As soon as possible. Contact Premier if you can.' "

The elder Chang listened carefully. "Okay, I have it."

"You do?" Christina asked with wonder. "Don't you want to write it down?"

"No, that's too dangerous. Believe me, I have it in my memory. I owe it to you and to my brother not to forget. And, my dear girl, what's the other favor?"

Christina shook her head in amazement. "Esteemed Elder Uncle, the other favor may be even more difficult to grant."

"Yes?"

"Father once told me that you were the real pioneer in modernization among the Chang clan. Is that right?"

"Quite right. I read all the Western literature and scientific writings. It was I who modernized the management of the shipping company."

"Then, Elder Uncle, you might just know. Can you think of a date—a day of the year—that best characterizes the devotion to modernization and nationalism? A date that would make modernizers celebrate, and that would infuriate radicals?"

The old man tapped his cane on the floor. "Stop, my little niece, please stop. The date is absolutely obvious."

"It is?"

"Of course. The date is May fourth. The famous May Fourth Movement of Nineteen-nineteen. Still an inspiration for reformers."

"Oh, Elder Uncle, you're brilliant! How did you possibly think of that?"

"Not brilliant, my niece. I organized the demonstrations in Shanghai after May Fourth. Those were the days!"

Christina hugged the old man. The *jia* had worked its miracles again. No one could possibly know what had transpired. As he walked down the path, her uncle's senility returned. "Funerals are fun," he mumbled loudly. "It's fun to be in a funeral. It's fun for everyone. Unless you're the one." The children all laughed and the old man laughed with them.

It was late afternoon on May 2. Heavy traffic on Changanjie forced Roger to pause in his long run. He jogged in place, keeping muscles loose and blood flowing, waiting for the policeman in an elevated kiosk to halt the ceaseless river of bicycles, trucks, and automobiles. Roger looked up at the massive Tiananmen, one of the few places that still displayed a portrait of Chairman Mao, along with the inevitable slogans: "Long Live the People's Republic of China" and "Long Live the Unity of the Peoples of the World." Down below, workmen were constructing bleachers that cascaded down from the red gate to the sidewalk of Changanjie.

"What are the bleachers for?" he asked a man pushing a rosy-cheeked infant on a bicycle.

"For the Beijing Marathon. It's tomorrow. The top ten finishers get to meet the Premier. Up there." The man pointed to an elevated reviewing stand on top of the bleachers.

Roger nodded his thanks. The Beijing Marathon—the word conjured up powerful images. Maybe he could watch it. Then he stopped himself. He couldn't watch a marathon. He was supposed to be uncovering a plot to overthrow the Chinese government. He was supposed to be finding out the date, time, and place. "Do something"—he heard Christina's voice echoing in his mind. Roger shivered as he saw a gray-suited official on a motorcycle eyeing him. He kept jogging east along Changanjie, near the old Foreign Legation Quarter, encountering preparations for the coming celebration everywhere. Huge red banners hung across the boulevard: "China Warmly Welcomes the Great Linking of Past, Present, and Future," "The

Chinese People Enthusiastically Support the Great Linking of Chinese Nationalism and Foreign Friendship."

Roger decided to take a break from his jogging in a location where a sweaty runner wouldn't feel out of place in Beijing. Besides, there might be a message from Christina. Knowing they were under surveillance, they had agreed to use the Beijing Hotel as a message center. The Beijing Hotel bar was a strange place attracting strange people. Located just across from the gift shop, which sold everything from carved sandalwood fans to stuffed pandas, the bar was open to everyone in China except the native Chinese. Roger sat alone sipping a Heineken and watching the other tables—a scruffy group of Communists from the Eastern bloc, two well-dressed American businessmen debating how to sell computer software to the Chinese, a cluster of tall African blacks chanting drunkenly, and a woman, perhaps English or Australian, intently sorting her collection of tourist pins from various sites around China.

A large-screen television blared the last scene of a Beijing opera and faded into the six-o'clock news, featuring a primly dressed woman reading a script on an undecorated set. "Tomorrow is the beginning of a two-day Great Linking celebration. It starts with the Beijing Marathon in the morning. On May fourth, there will be a huge parade in Tiananmen Square. And in the evening, for the first time in over fifty years, there will be a banquet in the Forbidden City, hosted by the Premier. China's leaders and distinguished foreign guests will hear a speech and enjoy a fireworks display."

For once, Roger was interested in the government-controlled news. Celebrations on Tiananmen Square meant that Premier Chen's Modernization Faction was making a play for public support. Mass celebrations had been rare since the early 1970s; the worry was that they would turn into uncontrollable demonstrations just as they had in 1989. The use of the Forbidden City for a banquet was remarkable. The Communists had treated the Forbidden City as a shrine to show the grandeur of China's past and the horrors of the imperial system. A banquet would bring the Forbidden City back to life, indicating that this government was not afraid of Chinese traditions.

Roger shuddered, a thought beginning to form. *If there was to be a bomb, then wouldn't it*—He grabbed the table, accidentally knocking over his beer, which soaked his jogging suit. Roger mopped up the beer with napkins as best he could, then walked quickly to the message board in the hotel lobby. There was the coded name—

Professor Gao Zhangwang. He tore open the envelope the hotel clerk handed to him:

Roger. Definite information. May 4. Public gathering. Danger. Am returning.

How could he stop it? Whom should he tell? His confusion would have turned to terror if he had looked up. Four men, all dressed in gray suits, were walking slowly toward him. The chief officer, wearing a small ear monitor, whispered instructions through a microphone concealed in his sleeve. As Roger moved to the lobby telephones, one of the men started to grab him, but his superior cautioned him to wait. The phone call might implicate others.

Pulling a small black book from his pocket, Roger dialed the number for the United States Embassy and asked to speak to the Ambassador. The Embassy receptionist hesitated, asking his name. "I'm Professor Wang. American citizen. Foreign expert at Beijing University." There was a pause. "What do you mean, I'm not listed among Americans resident in Beijing?" Roger listened for a second. "Okay. If the Ambassador's not there, then how about the DCM? Oh, not there either?" Another pause. "Yes, ma'am," Roger raised his voice over the static. "I'll tell you why I'm calling. There's a serious threat against the life of the Premier." Roger ignored the crowd growing around him. "No, ma'am. I am not . . . I'm not drunk. I'm deadly serious. Don't hang up . . ."

The crowd snickered at the fellow reeking of beer and claiming sobriety. One of the gray-suited men, smiling to the crowd as if dealing with just another inebriated foreigner, took Roger's arm and began to lead him toward the elevator. Remembering Christina's wushu lessons, Roger shot his arms out and broke free of his grasp. The man reeled back and crashed into the glass counter of a Chinese medicine shop, shattering it as he fell into plastic-wrapped packages of deer antlers and ginseng. Roger spotted the three other gray-suited men running in his direction, one of them carrying a nightstick. He whirled around and ran through the long lobby linking the old and the new wings of the Beijing Hotel. Pushing through groups of tourists and businessmen, he thrust aside a waiter, sending his tray to the carpet, and ran out the revolving door.

As he sprinted through the gates, Roger heard police whistles behind him. He started to turn west, toward Tiananmen, but then

277

realized all of the roads were blockaded for the coming celebrations. Spinning in the other direction, he ran at full tilt along Changanjie. There they were, three security officers, standing in front of him and blocking his way. Without breaking stride, Roger ran directly into the middle one, knocking him down and ducking to avoid the nightstick that whirred over his skull. He turned left, up the crowded sidewalk of Wangfujing, plowing through a mass of Chinese shoppers. The police whistles were just a few yards behind him. He jumped to the edge of the street, making better progress by pushing down bicyclists instead of pedestrians. The whistles began to fade.

Now, he thought. Now's the only chance. He bolted into a small tea shop on a darkened side street. The patrons stared at the red-faced stranger who smelled like a brewery. Roger stumbled to an empty seat in the corner. The shocked workers remained still; a younger man instinctively put his arms around the child in his lap. Roger collapsed on the table, his chest and shoulders heaving.

"What the hell's going on?" the man with the child demanded.

Roger looked up in fright, still openmouthed and sucking in air. "I'm sorry," he gasped, "really sorry. It's the police. They're after me." Everyone looked appalled. If the police were after you, you had to be guilty. Roger knew he had made a mistake.

"What did you do?"

"Stole some coal," Roger lied, trying for sympathy. "Just to heat the *kang*. My mother's dying of consumption. I just wanted her to die in peace. With a little warmth."

The door to the tea shop swung open and three security officers entered. They scanned the smoky room, examining every face except for one, a blue-capped worker facing the wall trying to comfort a screaming baby. They were looking for a criminal, not a devoted father.

Roger rode a packed bus across the city. Thank God, he thought, the Chinese love soap operas almost as much as they hate the authorities. And thank God, knowing he couldn't return to the Beida apartment, Roger remembered the proprietor of the Double Happiness Tea House had offered him a room if he ever needed it.

Wednesday morning was crisp and clear, the temperature in the mid-forties. Five thousand runners huddled in warm-up suits on Tiananmen Square; hundreds of dignitaries sat in the bleachers above them. Higher still, the Premier watched from his private box.

Wearing shabby sweatclothes, Roger looked up at the reviewing stand a quarter mile away. He could just make out the Premier. Roger had to warn him, there was only one way he had left. He looked around him—no one in a gray suit, no one on a motorcycle. Of course you couldn't enter the Beijing Marathon at the last minute. You had to get official approval because of the security surrounding the race. But there was always the back door. All it took was knowing the proprietor of the Double Happiness Tea House, who had a patron with a soldier as a son who was planning to run in the marathon, and who was willing to take twenty yuan instead of a remote chance for glory. He had provided Roger with the necessary papers and the Number 3694, which was now pinned under his sweatclothes.

The loudspeaker blared. "TAKE YOUR POSITIONS."

Roger jostled his way into the middle of the throng, over three thousand runners in front of him.

"REMEMBER IT'S TWICE AROUND THE FORBIDDEN CITY. GET READY."

Like everyone else, Roger dropped his sweatclothes onto the pavement of Tiananmen Square. For once, Roger thought, the weather seemed perfect, refreshingly cool with mixed clouds and sunshine. Maybe the runners in China prayed to more potent gods than the marathoners in the West.

"HERE WE GO. FIVE. FOUR. THREE. TWO. ONE. BANG!"

A full two minutes passed before anyone around Roger moved. Finally, the throng around him started the slow jog that would be their pace throughout the race. Knowing the leaders were already at least half a mile ahead, Roger sprinted outside the ponderous wave of slower-moving runners. A couple of miles into the race, the solid wall of runners began to thin, and he ran more easily. *Just like the old days. Body's warming up. Nice and smooth. Fast but not too fast.* Glancing down, he grinned at his bright-red nylon jersey with raised yellow characters for the People's Liberation Army. *Xiao Gao would love this. Right through the back door into the Forbidden City.*

The miles continued to roll by; the line of runners seemed endless. Unlike the New York Marathon, Roger had no way to measure his position against the front runners. He did notice that the runners he was passing were more fit and that the numbers pinned to their jerseys were decreasing. *Number 949. Number 897. Not bad. Probably less than a thousand ahead. Oh damn, there's Number 1342.*

At the rear of the pack no one surged, they just plodded behind the back gate of the Forbidden City, under Coal Hill, west of Beihai, alongside Jongnanhai. Finally back on Changanjie, nearing the end of the first lap, Roger could see hundreds of runners still in front of him, a long thin strand of multi-colored nylon.

Oh my God. That's too far. I'm not in shape for this. The wall. Already. Not even halfway through.

He struggled down Changanjie, trying desperately to keep his pace. His mouth was wide open, gasping for oxygen. Pains grabbed his sides and shoulders. He forced himself ahead, his hand grasping his stomach, trying to knead out a cramp. Roger lurched onto Tiananmen Square. His running had become a stumbling jog. He had to stop, just to catch his breath. He walked a couple of steps, hands on his hips to open his lungs. Then he sat down, head between his knees.

"Come on," someone in the crowd yelled. "You can make it. Don't quit. *Jiayu.* Throw on the oil." Roger looked up, tried to smile, but shook his head.

A gentle hand touched his shoulder and started to knead the pain out of his neck. *Who could possibly know where the pain was most intense?* He spun around. Christina! She was kneeling beside him, tears running down her face. She rested his head on her shoulder and kept rubbing his neck. Roger reached out and put his exhausted arms around her, letting her take the full weight of his body.

"You crazy fool," she said. "You wonderful crazy fool."

"It's all I could think of," Roger gasped.

"I know," she said. "It was a brilliant idea. It's just not meant to be. Maybe we can think of something else."

A voice shouted from the crowd. "Take him home, lady. He shouldn't go any farther. He did well for an old guy. Take him home. It's not a matter of life and death."

Christina turned around in anger, trying to find the person who was insulting her husband. Roger had a different reaction. *Not a matter of life and death?* He slowly pushed himself back up to his feet, using Christina's shoulders to brace himself. He took a sip of water from a hand that reached out to him.

"Roger! What are you doing?"

Roger didn't reply. He just stood as straight as he could and inhaled deeply. He took another swig of water, finishing the cupful.

"Roger! Don't do it, Roger. It's not worth it."

"Christina, it is worth it. Lives are at stake. The future of China could be at stake."

"But Roger—"

"No time to argue. Tell me, Christina, how long since I stopped?"

"Maybe a minute. Maybe a little more."

"Okay. That means I've only lost a quarter mile. Probably puts me about a mile or so behind the leaders."

Roger ran forward, slowly at first, his legs still knotted. Christina tried to follow along the sidewalk, but the crowds were too thick. Roger tried to pick up the pace. The cramps were not nearly so bad now, the faster he ran the more they eased. He could breathe again and hear the swelling screams of the crowd.

You can do it. You've run through the wall. There's no pain anymore. You've reversed the order. The wall first. Then the high.

He ran faster. There was no clock; he could only guess. Maybe 5:15 or 5:20 for the mile. Not good enough for even the top hundred in New York. But in Beijing, who knew? He kept pushing around the gigantic box that was the Forbidden City. North Gate again. Coal Hill. Roger looked ahead. Maybe a hundred runners in front of him. Perhaps a half mile to the leaders. About four miles to go. It could be done. All he needed was tenth place. A young runner in great condition could do it. But a thirty-five-year-old in marginal shape?

Run. Run, you bastard. Run for all you're worth.

Around the northwest corner of Beihai, Roger saw the line ahead of him had thinned to fifty or sixty. Still five or six hundred yards to the leaders, but seeing them was a powerful shot of adrenaline. The leaders, no longer unseen fleeting fantasies, were now mortals like himself. He focused on their jerseys, bouncing specks of color.

Now's the time. Don't wait until the end. Don't wait for them to surge. Begin your own surge. From behind.

Roger heard a giant shout off to one side. A detachment of soldiers from the People's Liberation Army had seen him sprint ahead. Roger waved feebly, wondering what must be going through their minds, probably that some major had lost his marbles. But their cheers gave him life.

As he neared Changanjie, he watched the leaders peel off to the east. He could count them as they turned. *Forty runners still ahead. I've got to finish in the top ten. They're going to see a sprint to beat all sprints. A little over a mile to go. Start now. And don't quit.*

Roger dug deep within himself. A 4:45 mile at the end was what it would take. His red jersey and red-and-white shoes flashed around the corner of Changanjie, cutting it as close as possible to trim the distance. And then he ran flat out down the longest and widest boulevard in the world, riding a wave of screams that grew to a roar as the crowds realized what was happening. In a country where age is revered, one of the older marathoners was teaching a lesson to younger runners ahead.

The great Square lay in front of him. Three hundred yards to go. Fifteen runners between him and the finish. The first broke the tape to the screams of the crowd. Two or three more finished just behind. Roger pushed even harder and passed two more. Another began to fade and stumbled to the side of the road. Just two now. First the yellow shirt. Roger's legs became elastic bands, stretching to their limit and then snapping across for the next stride. He ran on the balls of his feet, hoping that the running shoes would continue to grab at the smooth stone. The yellow shirt made a fatal mistake. He looked back. Roger was by in an instant.

One to go, blue shirt of the Chinese People's Navy, just five or six yards ahead. A hundred-yard dash to the line. A perfect finish for the crowds. Army versus Navy. Age versus Youth. The winner would take the final medal.

Roger's legs spun under him, eyes fixed on the blue shirt ahead. Now he was on his shoulder. The blue shirt sensed another presence and hurled himself toward the white line. Roger's head rocked back in agonized effort, veins bulging from his neck. With one huge scream—"*Aiya!*"—he made the push of his life. His neck and head thrust forward, inches ahead of the blue shirt to his left.

Roger collapsed into the arms of a man beyond the finish line. He gasped for breath as a blanket was put around his shoulders. Finally, he was able to stand on his own. Only then did he look at the man who had held him. The man, wearing a gray uniform, grinned savagely as Roger fainted onto the pavement.

CHAPTER TWENTY-ONE
FORBIDDEN CITY

FOUR SECURITY OFFICERS HUSTLED

Roger to a black van waiting at the edge of Tiananmen Square. Christina finally broke through the throng around the finish line. She saw Roger struggling, but there was no way to get to him. "Don't take him!" Christina screamed. "He's no criminal. He's trying to prevent a crime. He's a hero! Don't take him!"

The men walked faster. One of them doubled back in Christina's direction. She shouted again, her piercing voice cutting through the noise of the crowd:

"SOLDIERS! SOLDIERS OF THE PEOPLE'S LIBERATION ARMY! DON'T YOU SEE WHAT'S HAPPENING? THAT SOLDIER IS A HERO. HE WON TENTH PLACE. HE WANTS TO RECEIVE HIS MEDAL. DON'T LET THEM TAKE HIM TO THE HOSPITAL. HE RAN A GREAT RACE FOR YOU. NOW SHOW HIM YOU CARE."

The men carrying Roger looked around apprehensively. Suddenly a soldier ran up and pulled at Roger's arm, ignoring sharp kicks from the guards. Other soldiers yelled as they ran toward the black van. A cry cascaded from soldier to soldier. "JIE-FANG-JUN." "PEOPLE'S LIBERATION ARMY." The response was immediate and dramatic; hundreds of soldiers wrenched Roger from the security officers and onto their shoulders. Riding a human wave to the Gate of Heavenly Peace, Roger called out. "My wife? Where's my wife?" His words were repeated and rippled across the square. "HIS WIFE? WHERE'S HIS

284

WIFE?" Within seconds, Christina was found and hoisted above the crowd. Slowly the soldiers managed to bring Roger and Christina together, their joined arms aloft in triumph.

Roger and Christina were escorted to the bleachers beneath the Gate of Heavenly Peace. Like the other nine winners before him, Roger climbed the carpeted staircase leading to the reviewing stand where the Premier was waiting. As he climbed, a cheer rang through the Square: "JIE-FANG-JUN." Halfway up, Roger stopped briefly to pull on the bright-red warm-up suit given to all the winners and to accept a bouquet of red roses. Another chant started: "WHERE'S HIS WIFE?" Roger, pulling Christina up the bleachers, gave her his flowers and they both waved to the crowd; then they turned and walked hand in hand up the final steps of the staircase.

As they reached the Premier's box, an announcer's voice reverberated through the square: "AND THE FINAL WINNER. IN TENTH PLACE. ZHANG WEILAI. REPRESENTING THE PEOPLE'S LIBERATION ARMY."

The Premier, holding a large gold medal, turned toward Roger and prepared to place it around his neck. Then he stopped. "This isn't Zhang Weilai," he exclaimed, his words echoing over the loudspeakers. "These are criminals. Guards! Arrest them!"

The secret service surrounded Roger and Christina. They were handcuffed and pushed back down the staircase through a cordon of security men. A black Mercedes sped them down Changanjie to the west. The crowds emptied Tiananmen Square in stunned silence.

"I'm sorry," Premier Chen said, sitting with Roger and Christina on a park bench in Jongnanhai. "I realized something was wrong when I saw the commotion down on the Square. But it wasn't until I was about to present the medal that I knew it was the two of you. You were obviously trying something extraordinary to see me privately. Your arrest was the only way to make sure that you came under my protection immediately. I sensed something was wrong anyway. Both of the guards who had been assigned to you suddenly disappeared. And then, just an hour ago, I got a strange message from your friend, Dr. Ren, something about your needing help."

"We've been desperately trying to get through to you," Christina explained. "We think the assassination attempt will occur tomorrow night in the Forbidden City. Everything points to it."

The Premier looked out over the two great lakes of Jongnanhai, one shaped like a dagger and the other like a drop of blood. "So that's when they're planning to do it. I never thought they'd dare try an assassination at such a public event. We've overhead some of the interrogations of young Miss Gao. She's directly implicated the Director of the Propaganda Department and the Minister of Public Security. They're the ones who arrested her."

"Is she all right?" Christina asked fearfully. "Can't you get her released?"

"She's tough. I think she'll be okay. Apparently there's something about a lacquer box that keeps them from treating her too harshly. I'd like to release her now, but that would show my hand. We need dramatic proof of this plot. I want to put an end to this stupidity once and for all. It won't be much longer."

"What are you going to do about tomorrow night?" Christina asked bluntly.

"I guess we'll have to cancel the celebration," Premier Chen replied mournfully. "I can't risk the lives of hundreds of dignataries from around the world."

"I respectfully disagree," Roger intervened. "I think you should have the celebration at the Forbidden City just as planned."

"What?!"

"With just two minor changes. Why not invite your dear friend, Director Cai, to sit at the head table? I know it violates protocol, but he'd be an elite hostage. If a bomb explodes, he'd be killed as well. And second, I'd be happy to assist your security in undermining the plot. It's my guess that whoever plans to detonate the bomb will seek a vantage point where he can watch the entire proceedings. I've got a hunch where that might be."

"Not a bad idea, Professor," the Premier replied, admiring Roger's ingenuity. "But if I sense there's serious danger, I'll clear the Forbidden City. And, my enterprising friend, please keep yourself out of harm. You've had enough trouble for a lifetime."

At precisely six-thirty on the evening of May 4, the massive Gate of Heavenly Peace swung open. The Premier and the other top Chinese leaders stood together to greet their guests—ambassadors, chief executive officers of major foreign corporations, editors of key foreign papers and their Beijing bureau chiefs, leaders of the Overseas Chinese communities in Asia, Europe, and the United States.

George and Angela Chang were at the front of the crowd; his red bow tie and cummerbund matched her satin evening gown. "This is the right way to return to China," George beamed.

Five hundred guests walked slowly through the Tiananmen and into the first large courtyard just to the south of the Forbidden City itself. Chinese and foreigners moving together along the traditional axis would have been shocking a century earlier, but that was precisely the Premier's point. Young men and women in Qing court robes lined the route. Buddhist monks led the procession, hitting gongs and bells.

Twenty minutes later, at nightfall, as the procession moved through Meridian Gate, where emperors had once announced the calendar of the new year, cymbals and drums sounded thunderous crashes. The guests entered the Forbidden City's grandest courtyard, a spacious rectangle gracefully bisected by a moat known as the Golden River, spanned by five marble bridges outlined with glowing lanterns. The evening was mild, the moonless sky scattered with jewel-like stars. As they entered the Gate of Supreme Harmony, two large orchestras played on either side of the courtyard; zithers and drums keeping a quiet rhythm, erhu viols evoking the joy of a springtime evening. The hornpipes sounded a contrast—frogs croaking and crickets chirping; while wooden flutes played the whole range —birds singing, wind whispering through the trees, water trickling into a pool.

As the procession approached the elevated Three Great Halls, lights suddenly bathed the great vermilion buildings and their yellow roofs. The white marble platform seemed to glow, making it appear as Ming architects had intended—the meeting point of Heaven and Earth. Several hundred gaily dressed children escorted guests to their seats in each of the Three Great Halls, all of which had been decorated with colorful pennants. In the Hall of Supreme Harmony, golden bells sounded for the first time since the Qing dynasty. In the smaller Hall of Perfect Harmony, virtuoso soloists strolled, serenading the guests.

The Hall of the Preservation of Harmony had been the throne room of the Ming and Qing dynasties. The Premier selected this Hall as his stage for the evening; banquet tables for ten were placed throughout the room, spilling onto the elevated terrace outside. George and Angela Chang were delighted to be only a table away from the Premier. Actually they originally had been slated for the head table, but a last-minute change brought the honor instead to

Cai Dongshi and his wife. Cai sweated profusely, even though he was sure he could leave the table before nine-thirty, when Zhou Rong was scheduled to detonate the charges.

The Three Great Halls formed the apex of a pyramid, with everything around them lower, an architectural kowtow to the power of the emperor. But sometimes security was more important than symbolism. For that reason, one could actually look down on the Three Great Halls from the covered walkway at the top of the Meridian Gate. The Gate had not been used since the 1910s, when the child emperor Puyi, who had abdicated the throne of the Qing dynasty, departed the Forbidden City as the last Son of Heaven. Revolutionaries had locked the gates and guard towers once protecting China from rebels like themselves. The Communists left the locks in place. Why reopen guard towers to protect palaces where no one lived?

Tonight, however, the central tower was occupied by one man who sat in a semicircle cut into a black beam, worn smooth by the backsides of five centuries of Ming and Qing guard commanders. He watched through a wide slit providing an excellent view of the Golden River courtyard and the Three Great Halls. The wind blowing from the northwest filled the Meridian Gate with music.

Zhou Rong had dreamed of this night for decades. Tonight would be more than revenge. One massive explosion—and history would be set right. Modernization, and the modernizers, would be obliterated. Ideology, the true faith, would once again infuse Chinese communism.

A giant gong vibrated through the courtyards below. Zhou focused his binoculars on the Three Great Halls.

The sumptuous banquet had concluded, twenty courses in all, and the Forbidden City fell silent—no music, no conversation, not even the clinking of ivory chopsticks against yellow dishes and bowls. The only sound came from the breeze flapping the long pennants and tinkling the chimes hanging from upswept roof tips.

"Foreign Friends. Chinese Friends," the Premier's voice filled the walls. "There's an old Chinese custom I want to perpetuate tonight. It requires that I apologize to all of you for this modest dwelling. I know it's not up to your standards." The Chinese in the audience laughed immediately. It took another few seconds for the Premier's comment to be translated into a dozen languages and for the foreigners to join in.

"Actually, I'm taking a great risk tonight. Indeed we're all in real danger." Cai Dongshi's eyes opened wide. "Don't worry. It's not a physical danger, but rather a spiritual one. We risk worshiping the past. As you can see, much of our past was splendid. But let us not forget the poor who built it, the artisans and workers who were never allowed to enjoy these splendors. So I wish to dedicate this night, in part, to the unsung heroes of Chinese history.

The Premier paused, then spoke more firmly. "Tonight is May Fourth. Twice on this date—in nineteen-nineteen and in nineteen-eighty-nine—brave Chinese have demonstrated for democracy, reform, and modernization. I dedicate this evening to the martyrs of both May Fourth Movements."

The applause was immediate and sustained.

The Premier waved, then raised his arms to still the applause. "They did not die in vain. We will fulfill their hope. But we cannot do it alone. We openly acknowledge our need for foreign trade and technology. We need the help and understanding of our foreign guests here tonight—and the hundreds of millions of people you represent. We will not build our country in precisely the same way you have done it in the developed world. But modernize we will. And our modernization will bring both profit and pride to you as well. This we pledge. This is what we mean by the Great Linking." The cheers made him pause; after a smiling acknowledgment, he raised his hands again.

"Tonight I can announce our future has been given a special guarantee. We have just confirmed a consortium loan for the modernization of China. It's a pretty good deal. Fifty years at five percent. For one hundred billion dollars!"

The sound of the standing ovation, contained as it was within the great walls of the Forbidden City, was almost deafening.

"The prick is selling out the country," Minister Zhou murmured to himself. "A Great Linking between foreign dicks and his behind."

Zhou knelt on the creaking floor and snapped on a flashlight.

He pulled out a shiny black object about the size of a cigar box with several knobs on top and an aerial that Zhou extended to its full three-foot length. In the middle of the box was a raised metal rectangle housing two buttons, one red and one black. He switched on the instrument, tuning a knob until a red light glowed brightly.

Zhou smiled confidently. The detonator was activated. All he had to do was to press the two buttons at the same time. He knew the explosive plastique would not be detected; it was concealed in a column next to the Premier's table. He had bribed an artisan, one of a team of restorers constantly repairing and repainting the Forbidden City. Of course, when the work was done, he had not forgotten to kill the artisan.

The applause was still roaring throughout the Three Great Halls. "Could I . . ." The Premier waited a bit longer for quiet. "Could I have your attention for one last moment?" The crowd slowly quieted.

"This evening will conclude with a fireworks display. Let me remind my barbarian friends that it was we Chinese who invented gunpowder. As always, we turned it into an art form. It was you who used our invention for other purposes, including some rather nasty purposes here in China. But tonight we'll overlook that little bit of history.

"Before the fireworks, I must ask two things of everyone. First, for security reasons, no one may leave his seat during the fireworks display. And second, please join me in a toast. To my foreign friends and Chinese friends. To our joint efforts. And to the Great Linking of China's present with its past for an ever better future. Ganbei."

The Halls were silent except for the clinking of hundreds of *maotai* glasses. Cai Dongshi drained his glass and started to walk away from the table. Two security officers politely escorted him back to his seat. He checked his watch, shuddered momentarily, and then grabbed the arms of his chair so firmly his knuckles went white.

Zhou Rong anxiously watched the staging of the spectacle. The first rockets exploded in unison, showering multi-colored flowers into the sky, finishing with five thunderous resounds over the Three Great Halls.

Zhou was momentarily shaken by the Premier's announcement; the bomb would surely kill Cai Dongshi. Then Zhou Rong grinned. If Cai was dead, then Zhou himself would be the most powerful man in China. After all, he held the reins of the dreaded Internal Security forces. "Premier Zhou"—it had a wonderfully familiar ring to it—what an ironic posthumous slap in the face of Premier Zhou Enlai, once the most forceful advocate of modernization.

The fireworks exploded about five seconds apart, each sending out a spray of shimmering colored ribbons. Four rockets sailed aloft at precisely the same instant, lighting the four corners of the innermost rectangle of the Forbidden City. The percussions produced a powerful rhythm, four smaller explosions concluding with a louder bang.

Any performing artist knows that his finest moments should be preceded by a pause, a caesura, adding to the drama. Tonight Premier Chen and the fireworks experts had collaborated on the score. At precisely nine twenty-nine by the ornate Victorian clock in the Hall of the Preservation of Harmony, the fireworks ceased abruptly, but in such a way that the pause caused the entire audience to listen for the real finale. Colored spotlights played around the Three Great Halls.

Suddenly a voice shouted out: "No! Don't let them do it!" A spotlight focused on Cai Dongshi, who was yelling from the head table. "Watch out! There's a bomb coming!" Security officers grabbed Cai and held him squirming in his seat. They put their hands over his mouth to silence him.

Someone in the audience thought it was all an act to heighten the suspense and began to laugh. The laughter spread through the Three Great Halls. The Chinese were not only tops in hospitality, they also won first prize in melodrama.

Zhou Rong focused the flashlight on his watch. With a minute to go, he positioned the light so that he could see both the watch and the two buttons on the black box.

"Thirty seconds," Zhou said to himself. His hands moved to the edge of the box.

"Fifteen seconds." Index finger on the red button and middle finger on the black.

"Ten seconds . . . five, four . . ."

At precisely that moment, Roger, who was hidden in the Meridian Gate only thirty feet from Zhou Rong, put his hand firmly on the shoulder of the Chinese marksman kneeling next to him. The marksman aimed carefully through an infrared sighting scope and squeezed the trigger of a high-caliber target rifle equipped with a silencer. The rifle emitted a muffled *pop* as a hollow-nosed bullet made a small hole in the back of Zhou's head, the explosion of shrapnel totally blowing apart his face. Zhou's body snapped backward, his fingers flying up and away from the buttons. Within seconds, the Premier's security forces had defused the detonators. For the first time since the Qing dynasty, the Meridian Gate had served its proper function, protecting the leader of the world's most populous county.

As the clock chimed, Premier Chen raised his hand. A single rocket rose vertically into the black night. From a height of a thousand feet, a waterfall of white began to flow downward, each wave becoming larger than the last, until the entire Forbidden City glowed.

Dozens of parachutes dropped from a small plane. The first suspended a gigantic red-and-yellow Chinese flag fashioned of flares. The next two parachutes unveiled vertical strings of characters that read: "Long Live the Great Linking" and "Long Live the Friendship between the Chinese People and the People of the World." The remainder of the parachutes carried a flag for each of the countries represented in the Three Great Halls—over fifty flags in all. Each flag brought the national delegation to its feet cheering as the familiar emblem floated from the sky.

CHAPTER TWENTY-TWO
BEYOND THE WALL

IT WAS AN ODD PLACE FOR A REUNION.

George and Angela, Roger and Christina, Premier Chen and Xiao Gao confronted a massive beige-clad army, horses prancing in the front ranks, foot soldiers bearing spears and swords, officers deciding tactics, sergeants ordering the troops. The soldiers' faces remained calm and determined, each a different personality, each devoted to a sacred collective task: protecting leaders, unifying China, killing intruders.

"It's awesome," Christina gasped. "They're alive. After two thousand years, they're alive."

"Awesome indeed," the Premier concurred. He was always moved by the tomb of Qin Shihuang, China's first emperor. He'd been delighted to grant Christina's special request for her last day in China—"Couldn't we go to Xian?"—transporting the small group by military jet. Qin Shihuang, Mao Zedong's hero, had realized China's historic dream: one country, militarily powerful, profound pride. But Premier Chen, like Premier Zhou Enlai before him, knew China needed more: revitalized humanism, liberal education, foreign expertise.

"Yes, they *seem* alive," Roger agreed with Christina. "But we *are* alive. We have the Premier to thank for that."

"On the contrary." The Premier put his hands gently around

the shoulders of Roger and Christina, smiling as he and his friends assembled for a group portrait in front of the tomb. "It's you who saved me. And quite possibly the hopes for China's future."

"You meant what you said about Xiao Gao?" Christina asked, hugging the slight woman whose oversized glasses were foggy with emotion.

The Premier nodded. "She can leave China whenever she wishes, but for now she's decided to stay as an intern in my office. I'll take good care of her."

"I think it will be the other way around." Christina grinned, squeezing Xiao Gao's hand.

The good-byes were quick, as they should be when emotion is deep; four hours later three Changs and one Wang were riding first-class in a CAAC Boeing 747SP back to New York. Christina, unable to sleep, chatted endlessly with George and Angela. Roger sat alone, not certain whether he was leaving home or returning home, wondering whether he would need protection on the scale of Qin Shi-huang's army.

The idea for transporting the box to the United States—while keeping it out of the hands of Lamarche's agents—occurred to Dr. Ren while he was watching an American television program about nuclear warfare. "MIRV," droned the narrator, "stands for Multiple Independently targeted Re-entry Vehicles. A single warhead can carry a large number. Most of them are decoys, designed to disguise the real nuclear bombs."

The next morning Dr. Ren took his set of color photographs of the lacquer box to a local craftsman. Making fakes was Taiwan's greatest specialty. "Of course," the fellow said, smiling, in reply to Dr. Ren's question. "How many would you like?"

"Two or three. Whatever you can manage in a short time."

"It's cheaper if you buy six. We can have them all ready in a week."

A week later, Dr. Ren put his plan into action. Each morning for five days, he shipped off a package containing one of the fake boxes. The first box went via special delivery air freight at Chiang Kaishek Airport. The second traveled in a locked vault inside the cargo hold of a Liberian freighter. The third morning, the box was escorted by a high-priced courier service featuring a guard who was handcuffed to the package. On the fourth day, Dr. Ren took his limousine all the way to the southern port of Kaohsiung, where he personally gave the cargo to the captain of an ocean liner.

On the fifth day, Dr. Ren felt inspired as he drove to a Buddhist temple. Walking slowly to allow Lamarche's agent to follow easily, he looked at the giant golden Buddha surrounded by large red pillars, smaller Bodhisattva statues along the walls. Old women knelt by burning pots of incense and chanted ritual prayers. Dr. Ren clapped his hands in front of the Buddha, then bowed to a figure in a long brown robe, the chief abbot of the monastery. He handed the man a package along with an envelope filled with money. Dr. Ren pointed to the Buddha, then both the abbot and the doctor looked at the sky.

He didn't begin to laugh until he was safely inside his limousine. If only he could have watched the abbot tell Lamarche's man the package was being delivered by a heavenly emissary of the Buddha himself. He trusted the abbot would add that for the right price, human beings could also be sent by the same heaven express.

On the sixth day, Dr. Ren headed toward Chiang Kaishek Airport again. He ordered his driver to slow down a bit; it was raining and he didn't want the tail to lose them. When they arrived at the terminal, Dr. Ren put on his raincoat and hat. Cradling the package in his arms, he walked to the Pacific Northwest counter and glared at a female agent. "I'm booked on one of your private planes," he said loudly. "Boeing 727, tail number N32683RC, to the U.S."

"Your name, sir."

"Ren. Dr. Ren."

"Passport? And special visa?"

Dr. Ren reached into his pocket, grasping the package securely in his other arm, and handed her the documents.

"I'm sorry, sir," the agent said after looking at the passport and then at her computer. "You're not on the passenger list. And your visa isn't correctly validated. I can't let you board."

"Madam," Dr. Ren's voice verged on a shout, "this is a matter of the utmost importance. I can't deal with your trivial concerns. Let me see your supervisor."

The woman's eyes flashed, but she led Dr. Ren through a door behind the counter. Another man in a raincoat ran up to the counter and fidgeted, afraid he might have lost his quarry. A few moments later, the doctor was escorted back through the door by a man whose golden tag read "Chief Supervisor."

"I don't give a damn *who* you are," yelled the Supervisor. "You're not getting on an aircraft without the proper papers. You're not on the passenger manifest, and you don't have the right entry documents for the U.S. I suggest you go through the proper procedures. And perhaps also take a course in courtesy."

The doctor pulled down his hat and walked off angrily, clutching the package close to his chest. The car drove back to the Chang mansion, followed closely by another car.

Dr. Ren took off his hat and coat and loosened the strap that fastened the package to his waist. He leaned back in the overstuffed seat of the Boeing 727, gratefully accepting a cup of tea from the stewardess. You could fake anything in Taiwan, he thought with satisfaction. You could even hire a drama company to stage any play you liked, including a ticket agent, a chief supervisor, and a perfect replica of Dr. Ren. Bravo! he thought, and praise be to Buddha.

Roger and Christina spent most of their week at Padanarum trying to relax. Even in their cloistered setting, culture shock was intense: strange television programs, packaged foods with curious brand names, vast open spaces without people. At night the silence woke them—no trucks without mufflers, no water pipes banging, no one in the bathroom coughing up phlegm.

They were just learning to sleep without background noise when they were startled awake at dawn by a loud whine. A security guard put his head into their bedroom.

"Don't worry," he shouted above the din. "It's not Lamarche. It's only a jet-driven helicopter. Dr. Ren's here from Taipei."

After dinner, Dr. Ren joined Roger and Christina on the porch, watching the water of Buzzards Bay turn from blue to purple and then to black.

"Are you happy to be here?" Dr. Ren asked.

"Oh yes," Christina exclaimed, snuggling closer to Roger on the glider. "Until now, we were always escaping from something."

"And you, Roger. Are you happy to be here?"

"Christina and I are happier than we've ever been," Roger answered. "And I guess I'm happy to be out of China."

"You don't sound so sure," responded Dr. Ren.

"It's just that we haven't completed our mission," Roger said. "The mystery remains unsolved."

"Maybe I can help," Dr. Ren replied.

They could see the slight chip on the lacquer box where Liu's screwdriver had tried to pry it open. "I can't believe how many people have died for this box," Dr. Ren said, "and how many would still kill for it." He looked at Roger and Christina. "You know, there's nothing inside it."

Roger looked at him in surprise. "How do you know?"

"We had it X-rayed in Taiwan. The only thing that showed up was a spring mechanism linked to needles at all eight corners. We also used a laser scan that can pick up objects down to a ten-thousandth of an inch. We thought there might be something like a piece of paper inside. Absolute zero."

"So," Christina said, "there's only one clue. From the *Qi Shi*. 'Beneath the lacquer, between China and the West.'" Christina delicately turned the box to the fourth panel. "There's where I'd look." She pointed to the scholar who held up the writing brush and the microscope, her fingernail directly between the two instruments.

"That's got to be it!" Roger exclaimed, his hand resting on top of Christina's. "And 'beneath the lacquer' must mean underneath the finish."

"The word *xia*," Dr. Ren spoke reflectively, "can mean under or beneath or below. I'd start by checking out the section just below the microscope and the brush." He took a magnifying glass from his black bag, examined the box for several minutes, then shook his head.

"So Roger's probably right," Christina said. "In which case, there's only one way to get at it. You've got to scrape off some lacquer, with a knife or something sharp. No chemical will do it."

Dr. Ren removed a scalpel from his bag. He put a high-intensity lamp around his head.

"Be careful," Christina warned. "Do it one layer at a time. And keep your hands away from the corners."

Dr. Ren stood and placed the fingers of his left hand directly on top of the character *wang*, his wrist and arm held as vertical as possible to avoid the needles if they sprang out. He touched the knife to the surface of the cinnabar and slowly began scraping in smooth short movements, blowing away the lacquer dust as it accumulated. For half an hour he worked painstakingly, a layer at a time. As he began to scrape away the sixth layer, he saw something. He scraped even more lightly.

"What is it?" Christina asked, sensing the change in rhythm.

"I don't know," he replied, squinting. Without shifting his posture, he reached into his bag and pulled out a tissue. Wetting it with his tongue, he dabbed at the box. Then he looked through the magnifying glass.

"Can you see it?" Roger asked impatiently.

"I see something," the doctor grunted, his body aching. "Yes. It's clearer now. Two characters. The first is *zheng*. And the second is . . . *tian*."

"Which *zheng*? Which *tian*?" replied Christina, frustrated she wasn't looking through the glass herself.

"It's the *zheng* meaning straight, even, fair, balanced. And the *tian* that means field. Do you know of any *Zhengtian*? Anywhere? In any part of China?"

Christina shut her eyes to help her think. "No. I can't think of one. But I certainly don't know every little town."

"Dammit," Roger exclaimed. "Would your brother know?"

"Wait a minute! Upstairs my brother's got a pretty complete Chinese library. See if you can find an atlas. Also any historical guide to place names."

Within minutes, Roger was back, carrying five books. He opened the modern atlas and began scanning the index. "Nothing," he exclaimed, slamming it shut. Then he moved on to three older atlases. "Still nothing," he groaned. Finally, he turned to the classic historical work in English—Playfair's *The Cities and Towns of China*, published at the turn of the century.

"No *Zhengtian* anywhere," he sighed. "Three years to find out that the clue to the box leads nowhere. An absolute dead end." Roger looked at the box as though he wanted to throw it against the wall.

Christina took Roger's hands in hers and spoke quietly. "I think I know what it means."

"What?" he asked, grabbing her hands.

"It's not a place name. In fact, it isn't any place at all."

"What is it then?"

"It's the final admonition. The final instruction. *Zhengtian*. It literally means "Keep the fields level." More colloquially, it could read, "always maintain balance." It's the psychological state Gao Zhenggai wanted to convey. The state of mind for realizing the Gao dream."

"You mean there's no treasure?"

Christina paused for a moment, tenderly closing her hands around Roger's. "I think we've already found it."

Dr. Ren remained in Padanarum for a few days, making certain Roger and Christina were all right. The discovery that there was no *Zhengtian* was a profound shock to a couple who had just returned from three traumatic years in Taiwan and China. Still, he concluded, they were handling it well enough. There was no more that Dr. Ren could do. He had returned the box and examined his patients.

"Always retain balance," Dr. Ren reminded them warmly as he left the house and walked toward his helicopter.

The night Dr. Ren left, Roger and Christina sipped a brandy on the living room sofa before the fireplace. "Remember the last time we sat here?" Christina mused.

"I never thought I'd be able to laugh about it," Roger chuckled under his breath. "I'm sure George still thinks we made love."

"God, that seems so long ago."

"A lifetime ago." Roger cradled Christina in his arms, looking at the lacquer box on the coffee table. "I suppose you're right about the box. Good Confucian advice, that's the final clue."

"WHAT CLUE, MES CHERES AMIS?"

Roger and Christina jumped to their feet, staring at the ominously familiar voice coming from the shadows. Daniel Lamarche strutted across the room like a little Napoleon. In his red silk shirt and white cravat, he looked the perfect clown, except for the .45-caliber automatic in his pudgy hand. "Ah, my dear friends, what a pity you rejected my hospitality back in New York. I hate to impose. But what choice do you give me?" Lamarche poured himself a snifter of brandy as he grinned at the couple. "Professor Walden, what a remarkable transformation! Why didn't I think of becoming Chinese to get into dear Christina's sweet panties?"

"How the hell did you get in here?"

"No great intellectual feat, dear Professor. When your doctor friend abandoned you, it was only a matter of two security guards.

Chinese sweet talk put them off guard. Ooh, I'm so clever with words. Poor puppies, I just hate violence, but you nasty folks gave me no choice."

"What do you want?"

"Christina, my sweet, I've always wanted you, but I've had to live with your rejection. So I'll take second best. I thought I might take that little bit of fake Ming lacquer." Lamarche waved his gun at the coffee table.

"Take it, you idiot," Roger replied. "It's absolutely worthless. Just a philosophy lesson. Maybe it would do you good. Take it."

Lamarche, puzzlement on his face, snatched up the lacquer box. "Worthless? What do you mean, worthless? You said there was a crucial clue. Tell me!" Lamarche pushed the cold gun barrel against Christina's forehead.

Roger watched Christina tense slightly, preparing for wushu, then slump back as she decided it was too dangerous. "I'll tell you," she said defiantly. "The clue is two characters. *Zhengtian.* 'Keep the fields level.' Can you figure it out?"

Lamarche sat down in an easy chair, snapped on the floor lamp, the lacquer box in his lap, casually waving the automatic in their direction. "I'm not going to figure it out. You're going to do that for me. Where is Zhengtian?"

"There isn't any Zhengtian," Roger replied. "That's the irony. It just means being balanced, level-headed. We're guessing old Professor Gao Jonglu, knowing the art collection had been stolen, decided to turn the clue into some homespun wisdom."

"You're lying," Lamarche shouted, holding the gun in both hands, pointing it first at Christina, then at Roger. "You've got five minutes. Then I'll kill one of you."

"But we don't know any more," Christina protested.

"Sure," Lamarche snarled. "Just as you didn't know about the box back in the blizzard. Four minutes."

"Just take the box," Roger urged. "If you're right, the art is yours."

"Shut up. I've followed your every step for three years. Colombia, Chinatown, Taipei, Alishan, Guangzhou, Padanaram. The Gao Oriental Express. You're going to tell me! Three minutes."

Lamarche rapped his knuckles on the box. "You could have been killed anytime. Especially in China. My friend, the late lamented Director Cai, just adored torturing barbarians. I saved you!

'Wait,' I said, 'wait until they find out the secret.' Now you know it. Two minutes."

Lamarche held the box to the light, examining the scraped area. "One minute. Let's see. Zhengtian? Zhengtian . . ." A gleam of recognition flashed across his face. "Zhengtian! Of course, I know where it is! It's—"

Lamarche never finished the sentence. His hands suddenly grasped his neck, the automatic dropping to the floor, his eyes bulging in shocked pain. He jumped to his feet, body quivering involuntarily. Thrusting one hand behind his neck, he pulled hard, screaming as he withdrew a scalpel from his spinal column, its shiny blade dripping with blood. Lamarche stared at the scalpel in disbelief, then collapsed over the box on the coffee table.

Dr. Ren walked across the room, touched Lamarche's neck to make sure there was no pulse, and wiped the scalpel with a handkerchief. "I thought he might try something. So I decided to let the helicopter go without me. I must say it's a unique way to use a scalpel. Thank God, you're both safe."

Before leaving the next day, Dr. Ren assigned two new guards to the Chang estate, just as a precaution. Lamarche's death had a curious effect on Roger and Christina: enhancing security while increasing frustration. Had Lamarche really discovered a secret meaning for Zhengtian? Was there something they were missing?

Summer's end brought troubling transitions to Padanarum. The water lost its sparkling interplay of deep blue and white; waves became black streaks through gray mountains. Biting October gales drove out memories of softer September breezes. One stormy day, the lights went out at the Chang estate.

"Dammit," Roger exclaimed, stumbling around to find a candle. "I've had enough. A few months ago, you were accusing me of inaction. Now it's you! We've got to do something. We've got to get out of here."

"Do what?" Christina snapped. "Go where?"

"There's a world outside Padanaram, you know."

"Like where?"

"Maybe we could take some long drives. Up to Boston. Into New Hampshire or Vermont. Oh, I know. There's a great restaurant in Darien. La Vitesse. Terrific French food. Have you ever been in Fairfield County?

Christina paused, thinking for a second, then jumped to her feet. "That's it," she exclaimed, "that's it!"

"Obviously you know the restaurant. We could try another one."

"Not the restaurant. That's it! Don't you see . . . Fairfield County. That's it!"

"That's what?"

"*Zhengtian*. Fairfield. FAIR . . . FIELD."

A chill ran through Roger. "Oh, my God. That *is* it! We were thinking of China, and it's here in America. And I know where."

CHAPTER TWENTY-THREE

ZHENGTIAN

DOROTHY MACDONALD WAS WAITING
in the driveway of her large Greenwich house, standing next to her red Mercedes 300SL. "Still the same Snotty Dotty," Roger whispered to Christina, "just a little fatter and with a more expensive dress."

"Oh, Roger," Mrs. MacDonald cooed. "My goodness, you *have* changed. But I can still see the old Roger. In fact, your face aside, you look so much better than you used to."

"Thanks, Mother," Roger replied, giving her a peck on the cheek, as if it had been three days rather than three years since their last meeting. The two guards parked the car; one remaining inside, the other stationing himself at the front gate.

"And this must be Christina," she continued, trying for something appropriate to say. "Congratulations, Roger. You've married a beautiful woman. Almost an Oriental duplicate of Diane."

Christina spoke before Roger could flare up. "Why, thank you, Mrs. MacDonald. Roger always told me you had marvelous taste."

Mrs. MacDonald looked unsure about whether she had been complimented or insulted. She pushed it aside. "Welcome to Soundview," she said, opening her arms wide.

"Soundview?" Roger asked.

"Yes, don't you like it? Estates need names. George would have liked it. You can see Long Island Sound from up here."

She led them into the living room. It wasn't the same house

at all; it conjured up no memories for Roger. The Greenwich interior decorating firm, Make It Yours, must have been working nonstop since she inherited the place. The style seemed to be Late Archaic Funereal with dark-blue and maroon hand-blocked wallpaper, heavy brocade draperies, and dark velvet upholstery. Not a shaft of sunlight penetrated the room. Instead, red and blue crystal lamps, each with matching glass shades and tassles, gave off little pools of light.

"Like it?" she asked expectantly.

"Oh, yes," Christina said. "How innovative."

Mrs. MacDonald rang a little bell and a black butler appeared dressed in tails. "Yes, madam?"

"Jonah, we'll have our tea now. Perhaps in the Octagon."

Mrs. MacDonald led them down a marble-floored corridor lined with Greek statues, through a billiard room too pristine to have been used, and finally to an eight-sided greenhouse filled with flowers and pungent-smelling fruit trees. A white wrought-iron table and chairs were at the far end.

"I've revived the formal garden," Mrs. MacDonald informed Roger, proudly pointing to the meticulously trimmed maze of shrubbery extending from the house to the huge lawn beyond.

"It's nice to retain something of the past," Roger said, sipping his tea. He had always thought the formal garden pretentious; but after Mrs. MacDonald's redecorating, it fit right in. "Frankly, Mother, we don't have too much time. Thanks for the tea. But we came for a different reason."

"Oh yes. You said it over the phone. You wanted to visit the mausoleum."

"Yes. It's something I've wanted to do for a long time."

"Of course. I understand. Maybe finish the tour of the house later?"

"We'll see. If there's time."

"Of course. I suppose you'd like to be alone down there. I don't visit it myself. Dreary place. Here's the key."

Roger led Christina down the wide stone steps and across the slate terrace to a sweeping grass incline. To the left, a small forest of firs stood in a semicircle around a marble structure aping the Parthenon with Ionic columns, a triangular roof, and a frieze of muscular mourning figures.

The door opened easily. Roger's nose was ready for the dank

smell. He guided Christina inside. He reached along the cold marble wall until he found the light switch. It was a much smaller structure than it appeared from the outside, primarily because the ten-foot central aisle was lined on both sides by coffin chambers.

Roger walked to Diane's slab and looked at the black marble with her name chiseled into it. Christina waited motionless by the door.

"Are you all right, Roger?"

"Yes . . . yes, I am. I really am." Diane's death seemed so long ago, a lifetime away.

He walked with Christina slowly down the corridor, staring at the black marble markers. All but three of the thirty slabs on the right were engraved. On the left, all the stones still waited for other MacDonalds.

Each slab was held in place by four heavy bronze hexagonal nuts, now covered with a light-green patina. Roger removed a flashlight and a crescent wrench from his pocket. He began investigating each nut, looking for some sign that another wrench had turned it since the mausoleum had been constructed seventy-five years before.

Several minutes passed. Then he paused. "I think I've found something."

"What?"

"These four nuts on this bottom slab aren't quite as green as those on the other side of the aisle. Oh, my God."

"What?"

"These are the same. Just the same. So are these. And these." He swept the flashlight along the rows.

"What do you mean?"

"Somebody has tampered with the nuts on all thirty slabs on this side."

"Do you think you've found it?"

"There's only one way to know."

Roger adjusted the wrench around one of the nuts and turned. The nut slowly gave up its purchase. After a full turn, the nut responded easily to the wrench; a dozen spins and the six-inch nut was out. It took two minutes more to loosen the other three nuts. Christina pushed a small crowbar into the thin slot above the end stone; Roger groaned as he lowered the stone to the floor. His hands shaking, Roger shone the flashlight into the blackness. The color revealed wasn't the white of marble that he had feared, nor the black or brown of a coffin, which he had thought possible. Instead it was cinnabar red with touches of yellow and black.

"Christina! We've done it! We've found it! It's a lacquer box. The size of a coffin. I'll bet there are thirty more just like it."

Together they reached in, took hold of the box, and slid it toward them. Rocking it back and forth, they moved the lacquer coffin halfway out of the tomb, set one end on the floor, and eased it the rest of the way.

Christina knelt down. "Roger! It's a giant version of your box. Only the carving isn't as good. Probably the master let the apprentices do it."

"And it also doesn't have a lid. This time, I really want to get inside."

"I'll bet we already know how to do it."

"How?"

"The secret's probably the same as the Gao box," Roger said, kneeling by the coffin and using a jackknife to scrape the area between the Western microscope and the Chinese writing brush. "Look here, Christina. There's a little button under the lacquer. Stand back. I don't know what's going to happen."

He pressed it and stepped back quickly. After a hissing sound, like the puncturing of a vacuum-packed can, one edge of the coffin lid lifted slightly. Roger moved closer and listened; no more sounds. Edging behind the coffin, he slowly pulled the lid, uncovering a giant spring mechanism holding silver spears ready to fly at anyone trying to break open the coffin. Keeping his hands away from the spears, Roger cautiously removed a charcoal-impregnated liner designed to keep the contents dry. As he shone his flashlight into the coffin, his eyes opened wide.

"AH, MY DEAR FRIENDS, HAVE WE FOUND SOMETHING VALUA-BLE?" Dr. Ren's voice echoed in the stone chamber, his silhouette clearly visible against the sunlit marble door, a double-barreled shotgun in his hands. At his side was Mrs. MacDonald, smiling with satisfaction.

"Dr. Ren? Mother?" Roger quivered with shock. "What are you doing here?"

Dr. Ren spoke for both of them. "Dear Roger, your mother and I have formed a little alliance. If the collection was ever found, we agreed to split it fifty-fifty. It appears that lucky day has arrived."

"But, Dr. Ren," Christina objected, staring in disbelief. "How could you possibly do this? We've treated you like family. You've made a very good income. Whatever you needed, we've always provided."

"Sure. I'm a high-priced servant. Servant to the Changs. Whatever you want, Dr. Ren will get. Just give him a nice salary, add a new year's bonus, and he'll come running. I know what you thought of me—a eunuch, a eunuch in the Chang inner court."

"Dr. Ren, we trusted you totally," Roger intervened. "You've been involved almost since I inherited the box. Why didn't you kill us earlier and take the box?"

"I wasn't after the box," Dr. Ren smiled, enjoying his moment of revenge. "I was after the art. Why do you think I took care of silly old Professor Gao? Why do you think I spent so much time protecting you in Taiwan? Why do you think I worked so hard to keep you alive in China?"

"You mean you controlled it all?" Roger gasped. "You knew only a Gao could find the treasure. So . . . you helped me become a Gao?"

"Of course. An incredible challenge. Dr. Ren, the trusted little eunuch, pulled it off brilliantly. Now I won't be anybody's servant. I want my own estate. The art belongs to me. Not to the Communists. And certainly not to a barbarian whom I made into a Chinese."

"And so," Christina interjected solemnly, "you'll kill us for the art?"

"I'm afraid I must. I don't really like killing, you know. It's against my nature, to say nothing of the Hippocratic Oath. Maybe I'll clear my conscience by setting up a Ren Research Hospital—it does have a nice ring."

Mrs. MacDonald was becoming impatient with the chatter. "Please, Dr. Ren, you promised. I get half the art. Right? Can't I see it?"

"Of course, Mrs. MacDonald. You can see it right now. It's going to make you rich and famous. Can you imagine reactions at the Metropolitan Museum? You'll be the talk of the New York art scene."

"Christina, tell me what it's all worth," Mrs. MacDonald ordered.

Christina stood by the coffin and stared for a moment. Then she knelt down and pulled out a narrow yellow box about five feet long and read the Chinese characters inscribed on it. "Ju Ran. *Egrets on a Snowy Mountain*," she said with awe.

"What does that mean?" snapped Mrs. MacDonald.

"One of the most famous landscape artists in Chinese history. Tenth century. If it's genuine."

"Well, open it. Let's see it."

Christina delicately removed the top of the box and pulled out the large scroll. Her arms barely reached the two ivory knobs at either end. She held the knobs while Roger pulled the scroll open. Christina stood there and shook her head.

"What's the matter?" Mrs. MacDonald asked fearfully. "It's a fake, isn't it?"

Christina still shook her head. "No. It's not a fake. It's a genuine Ju Ran. An incredible painting. Perfectly preserved—"

"Oh, shut up, Christina," Mrs. MacDonald shouted. "I didn't come here for a lecture on Chinese art. What's the damn thing worth?"

"I don't know. It's priceless."

"Nothing's priceless. Give me a round number. Make a guess. A conservative one."

Christina thought for a moment as she rolled up the scroll. "I suppose . . . at an auction perhaps . . ."

"Yes? How much?"

"At least half a million, maybe a million."

"Perhaps even more than that." Dr. Ren grinned.

"That's marvelous." Mrs. MacDonald's face lit up. "Is that the only one? Are there more in that coffin?"

"Yes, Mother," Roger said. "Yes, there are more."

"How many more?"

"In this coffin alone, let's see." Roger moved his flashlight around the inside. "I would guess perhaps eighty more scrolls. Maybe a hundred. And also several smaller cases that—let's see the labels —contain ceramics, bronzes, jades, and lacquers."

"Christina," Mrs. MacDonald said imperiously, "pick another one. Try a bronze this time. Just pick one at random."

Christina followed Roger's flashlight beam, selecting a tall rectangular box, removing the wooden lid, and pulling out a vaselike object about ten inches tall, wide at both ends and gracefully pinched in the middle. As Roger's flashlight illuminated the bronze, Mrs. MacDonald could see it was tinged with green.

"Oh, too bad," said Mrs. MacDonald.

"What do you mean?" asked Christina.

"The moisture's wrecked it. It's all green and moldy."

311

"That's called patina, Mrs. MacDonald. It's supposed to be that way. It's from the Shang dynasty. I would guess that it's about thirty-five hundred years old. Unbelievably good condition."

"Okay. Okay."

"Yes, I know, Mrs. MacDonald. How much? Bronzes have gone up enormously in the past twenty years. Conservatively, at least a hundred and fifty thousand dollars. Maybe twice that."

"That's lovely. Just lovely. Now, Roger dear, just you take a little guess. How much would you guess the whole coffin is worth? Everything inside it?"

Roger shrugged. "It's amazing how much Chinese art you can fit into a small space. Maybe there are two hundred objects in this one coffin alone. If they're all this quality, then perhaps they're worth . . . Let's see, I'd guess a hundred to two hundred million dollars."

"And the whole collection?"

"Four or five billion. Perhaps even twice that."

"I'm a billionaire!" Mrs. MacDonald exulted.

"Okay, Mrs. MacDonald, you've had your fun," Dr. Ren said forcefully. "Now, dear Roger and Christina, you have a little job. You're going to remove all the coffins. No silly business. Don't forget I've got this nice shotgun Mrs. MacDonald loaned me."

Dr. Ren held the gun at his side, finger poised on the trigger. Mrs. MacDonald smirked as Roger and Christina struggled with the nuts and slabs, stacking the coffins in threes along the mausoleum floor. Two hours later, sweating in the closed space, Roger and Christina finished their job.

"Just one last task," Dr. Ren announced. "I'm sure Mrs. MacDonald doesn't want Chinese art all over the floor. She'll probably want to keep most of it packed away. So perhaps you could show her how to open it. You know, the way Lucky Liu did it in Alishan."

Roger and Christina stared blankly at Dr. Ren, who stood unflinchingly with the shotgun.

"Like Alishan?" Roger asked in wonderment.

"Of course," Dr. Ren said in Chinese. "Let her open it herself so she'll know how. Now! If you say a single word, other than telling her how to open it, I'll kill both of you on the spot."

"Well, it's tricky," Roger said shakily, looking incredulously at Dr. Ren, then turning to Mrs. MacDonald. "You've got to use a crowbar. Right beneath the lid."

Mrs. MacDonald grabbed the crowbar Roger and Christina had used previously. "Where do I insert it?"

Roger pointed to the top corner between the first and second panels.

"I thought so!" Mrs. MacDonald slammed the sharp edge of the crowbar into the corner of the coffin, sending chunks of lacquer falling to the marble floor. After exposing bare wood, she looked for the joint and tried to wedge the crowbar into the seam. She rocked the crowbar back and forth, beads of sweat forming on her forehead.

"Now!" she exclaimed, a look of conquest in her eyes. She heaved her body against the crowbar. The box creaked and groaned. Slowly the seam split open. She pushed harder, trying to make the side of the box break apart. "Damn," she screamed, the box still resisting her efforts. One last push shoved the crowbar six inches into the box. She barely heard the crack of the coffin. Other sounds drowned it out—a metallic whir, an explosive snap, a whining *zing*.

Mrs. MacDonald's eyes opened to the sockets, blood vessels popping across her forehead. A river of red gushed out of her mouth; her arms rose in a quivering gesture of terror. She gripped the silver spear impaling her, white poison leeching through holes in its side. Her body shook like a child's clown on a stick.

Christina and Roger, pale with horror, stared at Mrs. MacDonald's body, her blood dripping on the cinnabar coffin.

"You bastard! You killer!" Christina screamed at Dr. Ren.

"Not really. She killed herself. And Roger showed her how. Now unfortunately, the killing isn't quite over. Stand against the wall. Both of you."

Roger and Christina looked at each other, interlaced their hands, and walked the few feet to the far end of the mausoleum. They squeezed hands to offer strength to each other. When they reached the wall, they turned around and looked at Dr. Ren.

"Face the wall," he ordered.

"No, Dr. Ren," Roger said, "you're going to have to remember our faces as we die.

"As you wish," Dr. Ren replied angrily.

"Dr. Ren, could I have one last look at the Ju Ran?" Christina asked, pointing toward the long scroll on a coffin lid.

"No," he replied firmly, glancing toward the object.

As Dr. Ren looked down, Roger sensed a ripple of energy flow through Christina's body. She uncoiled like a spring, leaping eight feet across the room, slamming her foot against Dr. Ren's head, and knocking the shotgun from his hands. He sprawled backward over the coffin where Mrs. MacDonald was impaled. As he fell, one leg grazed the point of the silver spear, making a small tear in his trousers.

Christina grabbed the shotgun. "Now, Dr. Ren. Get on your feet."

Dr. Ren looked puzzled. He pulled himself to his knees and tried to rise, but his right leg collapsed under him. He gazed perplexedly at the cut in his trousers; beneath it was a trickle of blood and tiny flecks of white powder. He stared wide-eyed at Christina, then slowly moved his head toward Mrs. MacDonald's corpse and saw the spear still clutched in her hands. His lips mouthed the words "help me" in Chinese, but the sounds never emerged. He grabbed his ankle above the wound as a tourniquet; it was too late. A tremor started in his legs, moved to his torso and arms, crept up his neck to his face. His head quivered as the poison injected white death into his brain. Dr. Ren slumped forward and collapsed at the feet of Mrs. MacDonald.

Christina and Roger stumbled outside and sat down on the steps, staring vacantly at the lawn, afraid to confront the reality behind them.

"I can't believe it," Roger said mournfully. "My mother-in-law. And your doctor."

"Incredible," Christina said softly. "The Gao family dream realized. What can we do with the greatest Chinese art discovery in history? We're stuck in Connecticut with two corpses and a treasure. Can you imagine the reaction of the police? The press?"

In shocked stupor, they plodded to the front of the property. The Chang bodyguards were stunned to learn what had happened; who might have suspected a daffy Greenwich matron and a trusted Chinese physician?

"We have the *jia*," Roger said quietly.

Christina watched Roger handle the crisis, as he had observed her three years earlier. He dispatched one bodyguard to protect the art; the other stayed by the limousine. Using the cellular telephone, Roger called George Chang in New York City and Premier Chen in

Beijing. The two bodies were declared a double suicide and cremated before autopsies could be performed. Meticulous documentation gave Christina and Roger clear rights to the art collection. International transportation was handled by the government of the People's Republic of China.

CHAPTER TWENTY-FOUR

DREAM

HONG KONG, MID-1990s

THE LANTAU INSTITUTE WAS CONSTRUCTED

on the spectacular Chang family property overlooking Hong Kong. Its Taiwanese architect had fashioned buildings that blended Western and Chinese design; for once, the result was not hodgepodge but serene splendor. The Institute encompassed a hundred acres, rising up from guardian lions at the mountain base to three buff-colored, green-roofed buildings at the top: the Center, with auditorium and classrooms; the Commons, with dining room, reading rooms, and music rooms; and the dramatic Art Museum at the very summit. The three buildings, like the Forbidden City's Three Great Halls, were linked by a path running south to north, surrounded by dormitories and faculty residences. The landscape architect had sculpted pitches and plateaus, graceful rock gardens, steeply arched bridges over streams, pools with small pavilions.

It was twilight in the early fall. The Institute sparkled with lights—floodlights bathing the central structures, traditional stone lanterns marking entryways, footlights twinkling up winding paths. A tiny Chinese woman in her mid-thirties looked out the classroom window framing the fluorescent pyramid of Hong Kong Island in the distance. She was dressed simply in a blue skirt and a white cotton blouse. Her fragile hand rested against the white-ash-paneled walls of the Institute Center. She turned, adjusted her glasses, and sat down at the round rosewood table in the small seminar room.

"Welcome to the Advanced Philosophy Seminar. It's the pinnacle of your four years. It's the chance for each of you to put together a personal philosophy, a blueprint for your lives."

"But Professor Gao," asked an earnest young man, looking perplexed as he twisted a pencil in his fingers. "Isn't that just a sort of academic hedonism? A kind of game? Sort of like Western individualism in the classroom?"

"It could be," responded a well-built man in his early forties sitting across from Professor Gao, his fingers running through his peppered hair. "But don't forget. We're not the only ones who comment on your honors papers. You're responsible to the entire group. Everyone else will comment and then you rewrite and resubmit. In the end, it's your personal philosophy fashioned in a collective environment."

"So Professor Wang, it's really communal education," said a pretty woman, a sneer on her pale-red lips. "Self-criticism, collective judgment, and then confession."

"You don't need to remind me about the Cultural Revolution," Professor Gao interjected in a brittle voice. "Besides, Taiwan is hardly famous for its open, liberal educational system. Intellectual lockjaw is a Chinese disease."

When the laughter subsided, the two professors explained the seminar was the curricular keystone for the thousand students attending the Institute. The first two years centered on a fixed reading list, both Chinese and Western works, with Western-style term papers. Tutorials and small seminars characterized the final two years, leading to this penultimate course. Rigorous admissions standards meant that only one of every sixty applicants was admitted to the Institute. All had full scholarships, but every student had to return to his own country afterward, whether mainland China, Taiwan, Hong Kong, or an overseas Chinese location.

Professor Gao, hands neatly folded, looked around the table. "Remember, though there are only a few hundred of you, there will be several thousand graduates in the next couple of decades. The most brilliant Chinese in the world. Whatever professions you pick, you will be teachers. Models of thought and action."

"Isn't that pretty elitist, Professor Gao?"

"Of course it's elitist. China's elitist. Taiwan's elitist. Hong Kong's elitist. But it's elitism with a purpose. Opening Chinese minds, focusing them on the riches of our past, absorbing the achievements of the outside world. All to serve the needs of the future."

"Will the Institute remain free from outside control? After the Chinese take over Hong Kong in 1997?

Professor Wang closed his books, his characteristic gesture dismissing the class. But he looked uncharacteristically worried. "That's the question I prayed we were escaping when we came to Lantau. I desperately hope so. Without such freedom, there's no Chinese dream."

The two professors climbed the steep path to the summit, pausing to look down to the mountain base. Circling the Lantau Institute were twenty guard stations, but both professors knew that the ultimate security was out of their control; it rested in the hands of a few men in Beijing. The night sky was clouding over; flashes of lightning illuminated the magnificent Art Museum. As the professors walked inside, their eyes were drawn to a brilliantly varnished, natural wood dome, supported by twelve wooden columns.

They joined a group of students standing in a large semicircle. A lyrical woman's voice was speaking. "This is one of Zhao Mengfu's horse paintings. Yuan dynasty. It's the first time we've displayed it here. As you know, we change the entire exhibit once a month, bringing out a new object for each of the twelve display areas. Given the size of the collection, that means that a full rotation will occur every sixty years."

"Just two horses? On that huge scroll?" wondered a young woman enrolled in "Classics of Chinese Art," the most popular course at Lantau Institute.

"Not just two horses. There's a lot more. Look closely. What do you see?"

The student peered at the painting. "One of the horses is resting, just beside that vertical line. Is that supposed to be a cliff?"

"It's what you want to make of it. And?"

A male student offered his thoughts. "The other horse is totally different. He's jumping from left to right. As if trying to get over the cliff. Right?"

"So we have two totally different states. Repose and action."

"Oh, I've got it!" said an energetic woman, eyes lighting up behind her horn-rimmed glasses. "It's yin and yang."

"Or?"

"Or Taoism and Confucianism."

"But you're all missing one important clue. There's something else in the painting."

"Oh I see it!" exclaimed the woman. "It's a little butterfly. It seems to have been startled by the jumping horse."

"Butterfly? What does that tell us?"

A gawky male student raised his voice. "I think it's Zhuangzi. Not sure whether dreaming or awake. Is that right, Professor Chang?"

"Quite right. Think about it now. One simple painting. Just two horses and a butterfly. But a powerful array of emotions, an existential statement about life. All done in perhaps thirty strokes of ink on silk. The final work probably was painted in less than five minutes. A masterpiece."

By the time the students filed out, the storm was about to break. The three professors remained behind in the museum. The lights had been dimmed in the center of the rotunda, leaving the art objects around the walls in almost total darkness. High-intensity spotlights from the dome focused on a small case containing a vibrant lacquer box. Up close, its miniature figures were clearly visible in their world of red, yellow, and black: strict fathers, Confucian teachers, a turtle, a butcher, a bird, a child, and a procession of courtiers before their emperor. The figures shimmered, almost moved, around the top of the box, where a four-clawed dragon and a phoenix chased one another in an endless circle around a single stationary character.

It was just as Gao Zhenggai had planned it. The box unlocked the largest discovery of Chinese art in modern history. The objects helped realize the dream—five percent had been sold to build the campus and to establish an endowment. The auction had brought the entire art world together, bidding ferociously for less than half the contents of one coffin. An even greater competition occurred every year as brilliant Chinese by the thousands vied for admission to Lantau Institute.

"Tonight I'm so glad to be Chinese," Christina mused. "We're the most compulsive collectors in the world."

"I'm content to be both American and Chinese," Roger mused. "Both cultures are obsessed with principles, but willing to bend the rules when necessary."

"And I'm proud to be the great-granddaughter of Gao Zhenggai," Xiao Gao added. "He so desperately wanted to revive China's soul by opening its mind. It will work. Won't it?"

The question hung unanswered in the stillness. The three of them stared hopefully at the box for one last moment. Then they walked outside, stepping quickly down the path as the rain began to fall.

Behind them spotlights remained fixed on the small lacquer rectangle. A simple label was affixed to its Plexiglas case. Like all the other labels in the museum, it left students with the challenge of probing further:

Lacquer Box.
Three-Color Polychrome.
Purpose: Uncertain.
Date: Ming Dynasty, Wanli Reign (engraved on box).
Probable Forgery.